VOSTOK

Other titles by Steve Alten

MEG SERIES

MEG: A Novel of Deep Terror/MEG: Origins (Rebel Press)
The TRENCH (Kensington/Pinnacle)
MEG: Primal Waters (Tor/Forge)
MEG: Hell's Aquarium (Tor/Forge)
MEG: Night Stalkers (Rebel Press... coming in Summer 2015)

MAYAN DOOMSDAY SERIES

DOMAIN (Tor/Forge)
RESURRECTION (Tor/Forge)
PHOBOS: Mayan Fear (Tor/Forge)

GOLIATH (Tor/Forge)

The LOCH (Tor/Forge)

THE SHELL GAME (Tor/Forge)

GRIM REAPER: End of Days (Tor/Forge).

THE OMEGA PROJECT (Tor/Forge)

SHARKMAN (Taylor Trade)

DOG TRAINING THE AMERICAN MALE (Taylor Trade)
A comedy, written under the pen name L.A. KNIGHT)

STEVE ALTEN

NEXT CENTURY
PUBLISHING

VOSTOK

ISBN: 978-1-68102-000-6
Library of Congress Control Number: 2014956795

Published by Rebel Press, an imprint of Next Century Publishing
Las Vegas, NV 81948

Printed in the United States of America

ACKNOWLEDGMENTS

It is with great pride and appreciation that I acknowledge those who contributed to the completion of *VOSTOK.*

First and foremost, many thanks to Ken Dunn and the great staff at Next Century Publishing/Rebel Press, with special thanks to editors Shane Thomson and Simon Presland. My heartfelt appreciation to my agent, Melissa McComas, CEO at Tsunami Worldwide Media Productions.

Very special thanks to Bill Stone, explorer, inventor, and CEO of Stone Aerospace, for providing me with invaluable information regarding his Valkyrie laser robots, which will one day penetrate Vostok as well as the frozen ocean on Europa. Thanks also go to Dr. Steven Greer, the world's foremost authority on extraterrestrials, as well as his wonderful wife, Emily. As always, forensic artist William McDonald contributed with his brilliant artwork and submarine designs.

Thanks as always to the tireless Barbara Becker, to whom this book is dedicated, for her editing and her work in the Adopt-An-Author program. And to my webmaster, Doug McEntyre, at Millenium Technology Resources for his excellence in preparing my monthly newsletters.

Last, to my wife and soulmate, Kim, our children, and most of all to my readers: Thank you for your correspondence and contributions. Your comments are always a welcome treat, your input means so much, and you remain this author's greatest asset.

Steve Alten, Ed.D.

To personally contact the author or learn more about his novels, go to www.SteveAlten.com

VOSTOK is part of ADOPT-AN-AUTHOR, a free nationwide program for secondary school students and teachers.

For more information, click on
www.AdoptAnAuthor.com

For my friend,

Barbara Becker,

whose tireless work in the
Adopt-An-Author Program
has helped so many.

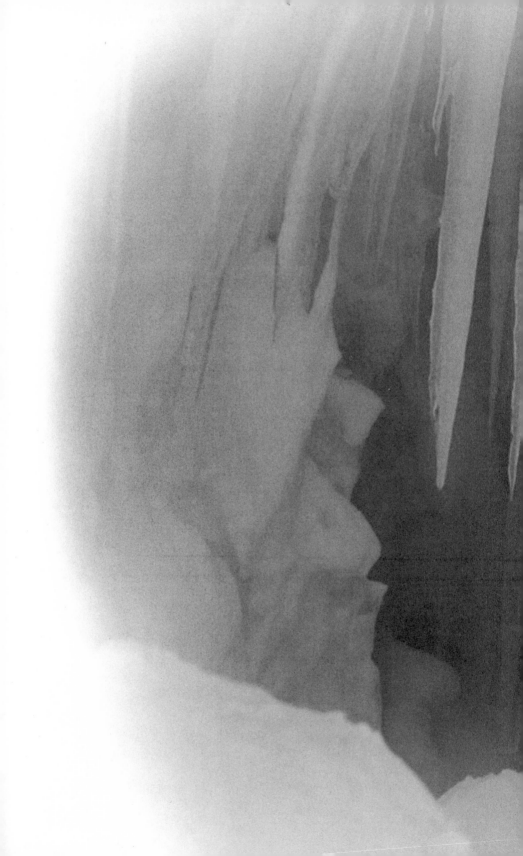

VOSTOK

STEVE ALTEN

VOSTOK

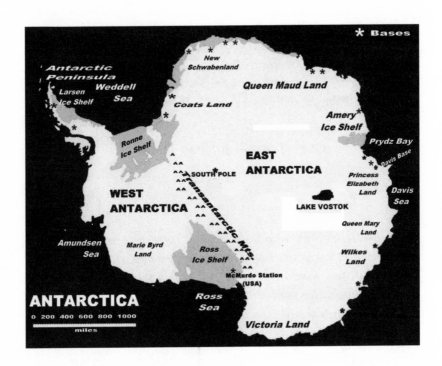

"There is a place, like no place on Earth. A land full of wonder, mystery, and danger. Some say, to survive it, you need to be as mad as a hatter. Which, luckily, I am."

—Lewis Carroll, *Alice in Wonderland*

"I fully believe we're not alone and have not been for many years even though at the time I went to the moon it was the conventional wisdom both in science and theology that we were alone in the universe. We're just barely out of the trees even though we like to think we're fairly sophisticated."

—Dr. Edgar Mitchell, former NASA astronaut

PROLOGUE

2 March

Thomas Nilsson definitely had his "monk-on."

"Monk-on" was Antarctic slang for being in a foul mood, and the fifty-one-year-old marine biologist's temperament fit the bill. His day—if you could call four hours of sunlight a day—had begun twenty hours and eighteen hundred miles ago back at McMurdo Station with a "Dear John" e-mail from his wife, Keira. She had begun the transmission with, *"You know how I've been telling you how unhappy I've been,"* and ended with, *"I sold the house. Your belongings are in storage. I left the dog with your mother."*

Twenty-two years of marriage... deleted in an e-mail.

In Antarctica, they called it being "chinged." It happened a lot among the scientists and support staff stationed at McMurdo and the other thirty-seven international bases located around the continent. It wasn't enough to work in the coldest, driest, windiest, and most isolated environment on the planet. Accepting a research grant to go there, if you were crazy enough to winter on the ice, meant leaving your loved ones for a minimum of six months.

Like most of the four thousand visitors (there are no indigenous people in Antarctica), Nilsson's six months had begun at the start of summer, which ran from late September through February. In Antarctica, the difference between winter and summer was literally night and day. When the vernal equinox arrived on March 20 the sun would disappear, casting the continent into six

17

months of frigid darkness, with temperatures plunging as low as minus seventy degrees Fahrenheit. Nilsson was scheduled to fly out on one of the last C-130 transports and had been counting the hours until he would see his nineteen-year-old daughter again, could take his first hot shower of the New Year, and could make love to his wife.

He would have to settle for two out of three.

For twenty minutes he had stared at the laptop monitor, contemplating a response. For inspiration, he rolled up his left sleeve and glanced at the tattoo on his forearm. *Contemptus mortis, pulchra vulnera amor laudis.* "Contempt for death, beautiful wounds, joy for victory."

Keira had just stabbed him in the heart; his only response was to find a way to make the wound beautiful.

His base commander knocked and entered moments later. "Hey, Tom. Heard you're the newest member of the Ching Club. Been there twice myself. My condolences."

"You tell Shaffer the next time he hacks into my e-mail, he'll wake up bound and gagged in his long johns out on the ice."

"It's a rough gig. The strong relationships survive; the weak crumble. I remember my first winter—"

"Paul... another time, okay?"

"Right. I actually came by with an assignment. Got a transmission this morning from the Aussies. They're in desperate need of a marine biologist out at Davis. You're one of the few remaining eggheads still left on the ice. There's a cargo transport leaving in twenty minutes if you want the gig."

"Davis? On Prydz Bay? That's clear across the continent. And why the hell do the Aussies need a marine biologist? Aren't they studying the Amery Ice Shelf?"

"A Tasmanian team apparently discovered a fossil or something frozen in a fissure, and they need help."

"Field work? In this weather? It's gotta be fifty below outside.

You know me, Paul, I'm a city mouse. Ask the Russians stationed at Progress or Vostok to send one of their "beakers." Those guys have anti-freeze in their veins."

"The Aussies don't want to involve the Russians on this one. You'd score me serious points with Scripps if you manned up and took the job. Won't cost you any time on your homeward bound. I'll have the Chalet director fly you out of Davis as soon as you're through."

* * *

Nilsson's trip had been a rough one, strapped in the cargo hold of a C-130 buffeted by head winds. Their flight plan had taken them east over the Trans-Antarctic mountains, then northeast over the East Antarctic circle—the coldest, most desolate region on the planet. Four-and-a-half hours later, the plane had mercifully set down on an ice field along the coastline of Princess Elizabeth Land.

Davis Station was located on Vestfold Hills, an ice-free stretch of geology facing Prydz Bay, located just south of the Amery Ice Field. Two other stations shared this gravel-covered rise: Progress Base, operated by the Russians, and Zhongshan Station, which was run by the Chinese. The Australian base functioned as both a scientific research center and a staging area, its primary focus to study the effects of global warming on the Amery Ice Field.

Nilsson disembarked from the rear of the massive aircraft on wobbly legs, stepping from the relative warmth of the cargo hold into an ice box, the predawn temperature—a snot-freezing minus forty-nine. The scientist was bundled in multiple layers of loose-fitting clothing that covered every inch of his flesh, from his battery-heated thermal long johns to his fleece trousers, sweater, jumpsuit, and parka. Two pairs of socks, two pairs of boots, a pair of skin-tight gloves covered in elbow-high mittens, scarves, head gear, and tinted goggles—and still Nilsson felt the icy wind penetrating his bones.

It was just after seven in the morning, the night sky conceding a sliver of gray light on the cloud-dense eastern horizon.

To the north, Prydz Bay remained frozen as far as the eye could see, its surface reflecting the emerald-green Aurora Australis as it danced across the charged heavens like a slithering ethereal serpent.

The lights of Davis Station beckoned to the west.

Nilsson slung his duffle bag over his right shoulder and double-timed it across the runway, targeting the nearest building. Like other Antarctic bases, Davis was a community of rectangular metal buildings linked by generator lines, antiquated sewage systems, and roads crushed into the snow by four-wheel-drive vehicles, the difference here being the snow had receded to a brown gravel-covered earth.

A relentless gale whipped across Prydz Bay, pelting the marine biologist with "crawlies"—powdery snow particles. Snow blew across Antarctica far more than it fell from the sky, the frigid temperatures keeping it dry and loose, and the wind moving it back and forth like a neurotic decorator. By the time Nilsson reached the drab olive building, every nook and cranny of his clothing was packed with the stuff, forcing him to "degomble"—a term defined as the act of rigorously brushing off before entering a building, thus preventing a future meltdown and sorry mess inside.

Nilsson tugged open the door and passed through an anteroom that helped prevent the loss of heat, then entered the facility. After stripping off his headgear, goggles, gloves, and parka, he set out to locate his contact—a Dr. Liao.

The research center appeared empty. With winter nearly upon them, Davis's population had dropped from a hundred scientists and support personnel to about a dozen. Nilsson was about to give up his search and move on to the next building when he heard music coming from behind closed double doors at the end of a corridor.

A sign read: COLD LAB. KEEP DOORS CLOSED.

Nilsson entered a heavily air-conditioned chamber connected to a freezer vault. There were four stations set up with long tables to accommodate ice cores, a cutting tool to shave samples, and a microscope. The lab was deserted save for a female scientist in a white lab coat and gloves who was reloading an ice core into a tubular plastic zip-lock bag.

When Nilsson saw the woman, his first thought was that he had mistakenly crossed the wrong airfield and wandered over to Zhongshan Station. She was Chinese and quite stunning. A ten—not an *Antarctic* ten, which was really a five anywhere else in the world—but a legitimate ten. She was in her late twenties, perhaps her early thirties, her long hair brown and wavy, her skin more tan than pale from having spent the summer months "bronzing" out on the ice.

"Dr. Liao?"

"Ming Liao, yes. Are you the marine biologist?"

"Yes. Thomas Nilsson. What's the emergency? You find the Abominable Snowman or something?"

"Sorry. What is Abominable... ?"

"The Yeti. It was a joke... Never mind."

"Ah, very funny. No, not the Yeti. Tell me, Dr. Nilsson, what do you study in Antarctica?"

"Emperor penguins."

"I see. No big predators?"

"You mean like killer whales? Sorry. Just the penguins."

"What about Loose Tooth? Are you familiar with it?"

"Your killer whale has a loose tooth?"

Her expression soured. "What?" She shook her head as if to erase the conversation from her brain. "Loose Tooth is an ice rift. We have a chopper waiting. I will explain on the way."

* * *

Thomas Nilsson held on to the seat in front of him as the AS-350BA Squirrel flew with its nose down against the wind, the single-engine five-passenger helicopter soaring over Prydz Bay en route to the Amery Ice Shelf.

21

Seated in back next to Nilsson, Liao had to use her headset to be heard over the thunderous rotors. "For the record, doctor, I am a geophysicist assigned to Zhongshan Station. China is working with Australia and the United States on this discovery."

"But not the Russians?"

"The Russians control Vostok. There may be a conflict of interest."

"What does Vostok have to do with the Amery Ice Shelf? The lake's a good eight hundred miles away."

"True, but beneath the ice are interconnecting rivers and lakes. You did not know this?"

"Sorry. I'm not well-versed on the geology of the freezer, just the penguins. Where are we headed?"

She removed a folder from a mesh pocket behind the pilot's seat in front of her and opened it, handing him a satellite photo.

"This is the Amery Ice Shelf. It is over four hundred kilometers long, or about two hundred and fifty miles. We've been studying this highlighted area—a twenty-nine-kilometer-long rift nicknamed 'Loose Tooth' that first appeared seventeen years ago. It consists of two longitudinal-to-flow crevasses. Two transverse-to-flow rifts formed years later. The fissures had been opening at a rate of three to four meters a day, but the rift has recently accelerated. We anticipate Loose Tooth will calve into Prydz Bay within the next five to seven years."

"I'll alert the Tooth Fairy. Again, why am I—"

Nilsson hugged the seat in front of him as the helicopter suddenly climbed to a higher altitude. Stealing a glimpse out of the cockpit window, he saw the sheer white cliffs of the Amery Ice Shelf rising a thousand feet above the frozen bay.

Moments later they were flying over the top of the ice shelf—a flat white plateau of packed snow violated by an immense, jagged crevasse. The fissure was as wide as an eight-lane highway, its sunken crack filled with loose blocks of collapsed snow and blue ice originating from below. The rift seemed to run endlessly to the southern horizon, splitting open the ice desert like the San Andreas Fault.

"It's huge. How deep is it?"

"It drops four hundred meters to the sea—about a quarter of a mile down—but it will thicken to four times that depth as we move away from the bay. Our destination is up on the left."

The chopper slowed to hover, the pilot attempting to stabilize the aircraft for a landing. Below was a hastily assembled base camp. Nilsson counted three four-wheel-drive vehicles, each

23

possessing skis for front tires and traction belts rigged to their rear axles. There were also six Ski-Doos—small transports that resembled motorbikes on skis.

Dominating the scene was a crane that towered three stories over the eastern edge of the rift, its cable attached to something hidden beneath a white tent large enough to conceal two eighteen-wheel trucks.

The pilot targeted his landing area, adjusted his pitch, and dropped the helicopter. Nilsson's teeth rattled when the strut hit the ice.

Liao dressed, speaking quickly. "You are here, Dr. Nilsson, because we found something in the crevasse that is beyond explanation. We need you to identify the species."

Suddenly more curious than irritated, Nilsson followed her out of the swaying cabin onto the ice sheet. By now the sun was up, the wind maintaining temperatures of minus thirty. Steam rose from beneath the hoods of the running vehicles, their built-in electric heaters preventing the engine blocks from cracking.

Liao led him to the tent. She unzipped a door flap and he ducked inside.

The air was heavy with musk and exhaust from the gasoline generators that powered the lights and hot-air blowers. Perhaps a dozen men—Asians and Aussies and a few members of the Scripps Institute—were busy snapping photos. One researcher hacked at the melting ice with a bog chisel, impatient to reach the coveted tissue samples.

Thomas Nilsson staggered toward the object, wide-eyed as he stripped goggles and gear from his head. "My God. You say you found this in the crevasse?"

"Yes. The water pressure pushed it up from the bottom. One of the Tasmanian researchers spotted it three days ago while en route to a GPS station."

The object was the remains of not one species, but two, a

prehistoric battle preserved in a block of ice. The creature that had been doing the eating was serpent-like and immense. Nilsson estimated its length at perhaps sixty feet. Flaky mouse-gray patches of skin were visible over its exposed skeleton, its girth impossible to gauge accurately as it was coiled around the crushed, unconsumed remains of the second monster—its meal. The tail of this second creature extended out of the terminally open fangs of the first along with part of its left rear leg, which was a skeletal mess, the exposed bones having been damaged long ago by the relentlessly shifting ice. The rest of the second animal's body was concealed within the serpent's belly, the cartilage of which had expanded to the size of a sperm whale to accommodate its undigested, life-choking supper, which had caused the attacker's demise.

"Can you identify either of these two species, Dr. Nilsson?"

"No. But I know someone who can."

Part One
The Beginning…

1

"Who in the world am I? Ah, that's the great puzzle."
—Lewis Carroll

Drumnadrochit, Scottish Highlands, Scotland

The village of Drumnadrochit lies on the west bank of Loch Ness, a sleepy Highland hamlet of nine hundred nestled between Urquhart Bay, the Caledonian Forest, and two thousand years of history. I was born in Drumnadrochit. In fact, I died here and was resurrected—*twice*. I suppose that last rebirth was more of a metaphor, but when your existence is haunted by demons and you exorcize them by staring death in the face, that's what we Templars call a resurrection.

More about that later.

Drumnadrochit achieved its modern-day fame by proclaiming itself the Loch Ness Monster capital of the world. Two hokey museums, a few smiling plesiosaur statues, hourly tours by boat, and enough souvenir shops to shake a stick at was all it took—that and Castle Urquhart.

No doubt you've seen photos of Urquhart, its ruins perched high on a rocky promontory like a medieval memory, the loch's tea-colored swells roiling against its steep cliff face, the surrounding mountains drifting in and out of fog. Perhaps the photographer caught an unexpected wake or a mysterious ripple, or better still something that resembled humps violating the surface. Such are the sightings that once enticed a quarter of a million tourists to Drumnadrochit each spring and summer, everyone hoping to catch a glimpse of the legendary monster.

My name is Zachary Wallace, and I'm the marine biologist who resolved the legend. Using science, I brought light to seventy years of darkness, separating a contrived myth from the presence of a very real, very large amphibious fish that had become a serious threat to locals and tourists alike. In the end, I not only identified the predator, I baited it, stared into its eyes, and vanquished the miserable beast from its man-imposed purgatory.

In doing so, I turned a thriving cottage industry into a bunch of vacant bed-and-breakfasts, rendered two local museums obsolete, and brought ruin to a brand-new family-owned five-star resort. If you're curious, the whole story is there in my tell-all biographical thriller, aptly titled *The Loch*.

This is the story of what followed, a tale I had intended to leave by audio diary to my wife, Brandy, and our young son, William. As usual, it began when I was manipulated into accepting a mission by the most diabolical creature ever known to inhabit the Great Glen—my father.

In his youth, Angus Wallace was a brute of a man who possessed the piercing blue eyes of the Gael, the wile of a Scot, the temperament of a Viking, and the drinking habits of the Irish. Now in his seventies, he's less temperamental but just as wily, and abuses Viagra and women along with his whiskey.

In his younger days, it was yours truly that he abused, mentally, not physically.

Angus met my mother, the former Andrea McKnown, when she was on holiday. It didn't take long for the older, dark-haired rogue to sweep the naive American beauty off her feet. I was born a year later, heir to the Wallace heritage. I was small compared to my big-boned Highlander peers, leaving my father to right his namesake's "bad genes" the only way he knew how—by intimidating the runt out of me.

I won't bore you with the details, other than to mention one pivotal event that transpired on my ninth birthday. Angus had promised to take me fishing on Loch Ness so I could try out an acoustic fishing lure, my new invention. Those plans changed, however, when I caught my inebriated sperm donor naked in a tent with a local waitress.

Allowing a childhood's worth of anger to get the better of me, I returned to the loch and launched the boat myself. As fog and night rolled in, my reverberating acoustic device attracted a school of fish and with it a very real creature that rarely left its bottom dwelling. Without warning my boat flipped over, and I found myself treading in forty-two degree water. Then something closed around my lower body and dragged me with it into the depths.

Terrifying darkness surrounded me; the growling gurgles of the creature accompanied me into the abyss, my lower body held within its jaws. I saw a flash of white light, which caused the demon to release me, and then those tea-colored waters quenched the fire in my aching lungs... and I drowned.

When next I opened my eyes it was to hellish pain, a veterinarian's needle, and the frightening face of my rescuer and best friend's father, Alban MacDonald. At the time Alban served as water bailiff, and it was lucky for me that the man I disrespectfully called "the Crabbit" had happened upon the scene to rescue my sorry, pulseless arse.

When my mother learned what had happened (the Crabbit and the vet claimed I had become entangled in barbed wire and thus the bloody markings), she saw to my recovery, divorced my no-good father, and moved us to the good ole U.S. of A.

America: land of the free, home of the brave—only I was neither free nor brave. In an attempt to escape the mental abuse associated with my drowning, my traumatized brain had compartmentalized and isolated the incident. Buried in denial, the unfiltered memory remained dormant, waiting for just the right moment to return.

That moment occurred fourteen years later.

By the age of twenty-five, I had earned bachelor's and master's degrees from Princeton and a doctorate from Scripps, and my research into deep-sea acoustic lures had been featured in several prominent journals. As a budding "Jacques Cousteau," I had been asked to lead a *National Geographic*-sponsored expedition to the Sargasso Sea, in search of the elusive giant squid. To attract the legendary colossus, our three-man submersible was armed with a lure I had designed, that emulated the sounds and vibrations of salmon.

We descended into the blackness of the depths and waited, our patience rewarded with what would be the first visual documentation of *Architeuthis dux*—the giant squid. Unfortunately, the lure summoned not only a hungry squid but a swarm of unexpected and unknown predatory fish. The squid panicked and tore loose our ballast tank, sending us spiraling into oblivion. The acrylic cockpit cracked and threatened to implode as we waited desperately for a drone to secure a towline. The underwater robot finally reached us in four thousand feet of water.

It seemed we had been spared a horrible death, but as the surface ship drew us out of the depths, the crack in the bubble cockpit continued to spiderweb until the sea burst in on us—233 feet below the surface. The sea rushed in and killed the pilot. Dragging the cameraman from the sinking sub, I kicked for the surface... and drowned again.

This time when I came to, I was in a hospital bed. My colleague, David Caldwell, conveniently blamed me for the pilot's death and for the loss of the submersible. Fired from my teaching position at Florida Atlantic University, I left the hospital intent on finding a new job.

My brain had other plans.

Unbeknownst to me, this second near-death experience had released long-dormant childhood memories from the first. Sleep became my enemy, as I constantly woke up screaming from night terrors. Worse, I found myself deathly afraid of the water, the anxiety threatening my future as a marine biologist.

In the span of a few months, I had lost everything—my job, my career, my fiancée, and my quickly fading sanity.

I began drinking heavily. Being inebriated kept me from entering the deepest stages of sleep where the night terrors lay in wait. Days were devoted to recovering from hangovers, nights reserved for binging on expensive booze and cheap women, both of which I found in abundance in South Beach, my new haunt.

That's where Maxie Rael found me. My half-brother, whom I never knew existed, had come to bring me back to Scotland.

The aforementioned five-star resort, known today as Nessie's Retreat, had been Angus Wallace's idea, and my father rarely met an idea (or a woman, for that matter) that he didn't fall in-love with. The Wallace clan had left him title to a prime stretch of waterside real estate just south of Urquhart Bay, and once the zoning laws had been manipulated in his favor, Angus wasted no time in leasing the land to Mr. John Cialino of Cialino Ventures. As partners, my father and the well-connected "Johnny C." intended on bringing luxury accommodations to the Scottish Highlands.

Then one fateful afternoon during the construction phase, my father and John engaged in a heated argument on Urquhart Bluff, and before you could say, "Yer bum's oot the windae!" Angus struck his younger partner with a right cross, sending Johnny's arse (and the rest of him) into Loch Ness, "ne'er tae be seen alive again."

While I was struggling to survive my own post-traumatic symptoms in Miami Beach, Angus was locked away in a Highland prison cell awaiting his murder trial. He had sent Maxie to bring me to Scotland so that my estranged father would have both of his sons by his side in his fight to stave off the gallows and prove his innocence.

Seventeen years away from the old man, and I fell for his lies hook, line, and sinker.

It was all part of a well-orchestrated plan intended to save my father's neck, jumpstart his new venture, and force me to face the demons of my past—all by placing *my* head in *his* noose.

That noose unexpectedly tightened when the creature's temperament suddenly changed.

* * *

Two years have passed. With my demons exorcized, I felt free to marry my childhood sweetheart, Brandy MacDonald, a dark-haired beauty with sultry blue eyes and a body that could have landed her in any swimsuit catalog on the planet. Our son, William Wallace, named after our legendary ancestor, was born fifteen months ago. Last summer Nessie's Retreat, bankrolled by Angus's lover Theresa (Johnny C.'s widow), opened to great fanfare.

Ten months later the resort and Drumnadrochit were both on the verge of bankruptcy.

Don't get me wrong, the hotel is first-class. Every one of its 336 rooms features a balcony view of Loch Ness, and each of its third-floor luxury suites is equipped with a fireplace, sauna, and Jacuzzi.

The problem: no monster.

Loch Ness, without its legendary creature, was just a peat-infested twenty-three-mile-long deepwater trough filled with water far too cold in which to swim. It wasn't just Angus's hotel that was hurting. Without Nessie, all of the Highland villages had become destitute, the vacation equivalent of Orlando without Disneyworld and its other local theme parks. Of course, Orlando is a modern city located in sunny Florida. The Scottish Highlands are an isolated cold-weather region with seasons more akin to Alaska's. Centuries ago, our Highland ancestors worked the land to feed and clothe themselves; these days the villagers were committed to tourism. It was the feast of summer that got them through the famine of a long winter, and the sudden downturn to the

Highlanders' livelihood threatened an economic and cultural collapse.

Concerned over the state of its villages and the economic toll they were taking on the capital city of Inverness, the Highland Council had been holding monthly brainstorming sessions to figure out how to bolster tourism for the coming season. My father attended these meetings with Brandy's father, Alban, and her big brother, Finlay "True" MacDonald, my boyhood friend. The imposing Highlander with the auburn ponytail and Viking aura served as master of arms. Although the meetings were open to the public, True's *Do Not Allow to Enter* list had one name on it—mine.

In the span of two years, I had gone from local hero to *persona non grata*. With tourism down, hundreds of villagers faced the prospect of being unable to feed their families without government subsidies, and I soon felt their wrath. *Why couldn't Wallace have subdued the creature without vanquishing it in the public eye? Had he no respect for the legend?*

As they say, no good deed goes unpunished.

By December, I had become a hated man and was forced to move my wife and son from our once-rent-free cottage into the near-vacant resort. I no longer visited Sniddles or Drumnadrochit's other watering holes, preferring the hermit-like quiet of Nessie's Lair, the resort's closed restaurant and pub.

To be honest, I never wanted to return to Drumnadrochit in the first place, let alone live here. I was a U.S. citizen, and the American lifestyle was what I coveted. Moreover, I was a marine biologist and an inventor, and most of the serious job offers were coming from the States. But Angus had given me twenty-five percent ownership of the resort and had asked me to be around as a celebrity in our inaugural tourist season, plus my old man was bonding with our newborn. So we stayed.

Then the disaster of summer struck, and my father-in-law Alban was diagnosed with ALS. Suddenly relocating was put on the backburner. By Christmas I felt like a caged tiger.

To make matters worse, Brandy and I argued on a daily basis, most of our spats having to do with money. For nearly a year, I had earned a good living traveling the world, signing books at sold-out appearances where I'd tell enraptured audiences how I had battled a sixty-foot barbed-toothed species the Navy had nicknamed the *bloop* and our Highland ancestors had called *guivres*. But fame is fleeting, and my fifteen minutes in the limelight faded quickly, thanks to a myriad of YouTube videos overexposing my tale.

Having gone through most of our savings, we soon found ourselves financially underwater, like the rest of the Highlanders. Unlike the villagers, however, I had options—lucrative teaching and research offers from private facilities and major universities. But my loving wife made it quite clear that until her father passed she would not leave Drumnadrochit.

Brandy MacDonald-Wallace was the yang to my yin, a fiery-tempered Scot who believed in God and faith and that her husband suffered from an addiction to logic. I believed in cause and effect, science and the laws of physics, and that petitioning the Lord with prayer every Sunday was the equivalent of tossing quarters in a wishing well. We had been childhood pals but she was clearly the alpha dog, the one person who could get me to climb a tree to its canopy, jump in a half-frozen pond as part of an initiation into her "club," or pursue my dreams as a marine biologist. I was Brandy's emotional ballast, the person she sought when things went bad, like when her father was feeling ogreish—a common occurrence after her mother died. Had we remained together during our adolescent years we'd have married ten years sooner, but my mother had moved me to the States long before our hormones took over, and that was probably a good thing.

While my early years of puberty were chastised by long hours devoted to study and a physical regimen designed to give me a fighting chance on the football field, Brandy's teen years were spent rudderless and rebellious. Pregnant at sixteen, she found herself abandoned by both her boyfriend and her overbearing father, whose response to his daughter's loss of innocence was to cast her

36

adrift. Brandy moved into a women's shelter, miscarried in her fourth month, and spent her remaining years of adolescence in a boarding house run by nuns. Ten years would pass before she spoke to her father again.

When she was nineteen, Brandy met an American stockbroker and accepted his marriage proposal as a passport out of the Highlands. Seven months after the couple had moved to California, Brandy was riding her ten-speed bike on a mountain highway when she was struck from behind by a car. Her injuries were severe and she spent several weeks in intensive care—during which time her husband had an affair. A year later she returned to the Highlands divorced and lonely, with just enough money to purchase a second-hand passenger houseboat from which she eked out a living giving tours of Loch Ness during the warmer months.

Her life changed when she worked winters as a volunteer at the hospital in Inverness.

"Negative energy, Zach. I brought about my own darkness as a wayward teen and attracted negative people to my aura. T'was God's will that sent me to the hospital on the brink of death, but really I was dyin' spiritually in a bad marriage, having cast myself from His Light. Volunteering at the hospital in Inverness changed my energy and summoned ye to Drumnadrochit to marry me. It takes a selfless act tae bring one back into God's heavenly Light."

Brandy had already gotten into two fistfights with locals who had the bollocks to criticize her husband and his work. Yet as the days of winter grew shorter and the villagers' desperate hours grew longer, she began to sound more and more like my father.

"Been o'er to the neebs, Zach. There's bairns bein' put tae bed hungry. Instead o' grabbin' yer daily nips and starin' at the loch every day, why dinnae ye use that big ol' brain o' yers and figure oot a way tae lure another monster into the Ness."

"We've been over this, Brandy. The creature only grew big because she was trapped in Loch Ness and couldn't return to the Sargasso Sea to spawn. It was a freak situation, one in a million.

There's none like her out there anymore. And even if there was, the tourists flocked to Loch Ness to see a plesiosaur, not a predatory fish that went insane due to hydrocarbon poisoning."

"Zach, don't git yer panties in a ball. Ye dinnae have tae lure a *real* monster; ye could jist claim tae find clues. A few white lies and ye could jumpstart tourism again. Ye could save Drumnadrochit and the other hamlets. Ye'd be a real hero tae yer people."

"Brandy, I'm a scientist, a respected marine biologist, not a cryptozoologist or some headline seeker feeding fake monster stories to the weekly tabloids. Do you want me to destroy everything that I worked for?"

"There's wee uns goin' hungry, Zach. What if it were yer son... yer kin? They're starving because o' ye bein' such a great and respected marine biologist."

"You're blaming me? Brandy, the damn thing killed three people!"

"Aye. And far more will go hungry this winter because of yer bravery and brains. But ye can still make things right again."

"You've been talking to Angus."

"Aye, and he has a plan. But he needs yer help. All ye have tae do is authenticate a monster kill, and the press will do the rest."

Months of pent-up frustration set my blood to boil. "I won't do it, Brandy. I can't do it. It goes against everything I've dedicated my life to. My father, on the other hand, has no morals. He'd gamble his own sons' souls in a poker game with the devil if it meant filling his resort to capacity."

"And tae whit devil have ye sold yer soul, Zachary Wallace? The one who feeds yer own massive ego?"

That conversation took place in late January. Best friends and lovers, we allowed our desire to be right to overrule our marital vows. Days passed in silence. With each passing week our love grew colder, and the noose of debt around my neck grew tighter, making me resent her even more. My thoughts turning to the previously unthinkable, that maybe Brandy and I were not meant to be together after all.

Without discussing it with my wife, I began contacting private companies and major universities, letting them know I was now fielding offers. By March I had narrowed my choices down to a faculty position at Cambridge University, a research position at Scripps Institute, and an interesting offer from Masao Tanaka at the Tanaka Oceanographic Institute.

Tanaka and I shared a common love for cetaceans. One of the most respected marine biologists in the world, he had constructed a man-made whale lagoon some twenty years ago on the coast of Monterey, California. The idea had been to offer pregnant gray whales migrating south from the Bering Sea a shallow harbor to birth their calves before reaching Baja. Instead, the facility had been sealed off to hold a newborn megalodon pup captured off the coast. Believed to be extinct, megalodon was a sixty-foot prehistoric cousin of the great white. The shark's pregnant parent had escaped the deep waters of the Mariana Trench after Jonas Taylor, a deep-sea submersible pilot, had dived the abyss with Masao's son to retrieve an earthquake sensor. The pregnant female had given birth to the pup before being captured and eventually killed (in self-defense) by Jonas. The offspring, an albino named Angel, had grown to monstrous proportions, and for the next four years, the Tanaka Institute had been the most popular tourist destination in the world—until the creature broke free and returned to the trench. That was fifteen years ago, but the megalodon's scent trail persisted, keeping whales out of the vacated pen. Masao Tanaka was offering me three hundred dollars a week, with free room and board, plus a twenty-thousand-dollar bonus *if* I could figure out a way to lure whales into his empty lagoon.

Cambridge University's salary offer wasn't much higher, but it was guaranteed. And its proximity to the Great Glen would allow me to visit my family on weekends.

But it was the work at Scripps that enticed me the most. I would be set up in my own lab with a staff of my choosing. In

39

addition to a decent salary and benefits package, I would receive thirty percent of any profits generated by my inventions, sharing the patents.

Scripps it was. I would accept their offer and then reach out to Brandy to join me. I would apologize and tell her how much I wanted her in my life, but I would refuse to remain a victim of my circumstances or languish in a loveless marriage. If my happiness and self-worth resided outside the Great Glen, then I needed to follow that road and see where it took me—even if it meant leaving my family.

Then one dreary afternoon in March, I received another offer—one that would change my life and the future of the Highlands forever.

2

Nessie's Lair was located on the third floor of my father's resort. I entered the restaurant at half past one in the afternoon, seeking solitude and a private place to call Professor John Rudman, the director at Scripps who had been recruiting me. The chamber was dark, the only light coming from the floor-to-ceiling windows, which offered a breathtaking view of Loch Ness and the snow-covered peaks of the Monadhliath Mountains rising along the far eastern bank.

It was only eight-thirty in the morning at Scripps. Knowing Professor Rudman usually didn't get into his office until nine, I flipped open my laptop to check today's *Science Journal.*

Life on Earth—Death on Mars: New Evidence

Scientists agree that life on Earth began approximately 3.8 billion years ago, but exactly *how* it began has long remained an unanswered question. Biologists theorize asteroids, which are space rocks containing water molecules that created the precipitation that filled the oceans, bombarded our still-evolving planet. But Dr. Sankar Chatterjee, a professor of geosciences at Texas Tech University, believes that in addition to bringing water, these asteroids contained the chemical constituents of life that ultimately gave rise to living cells.

"Earth was once a bizarre, hostile world that would seem like a vision of hell, reeking with the foul smells of hydrogen sulfide, methane, nitric oxide, and steam that provided life-sustaining energy," Chatterjee says. "Meteorites punched giant craters into the planet's surface and deposited organic materials in them. Then icy comets crashed into Earth and melted, filling these basins with water. Additional meteorite strikes created volcanically driven geothermal vents in the planet's crust that heated and stirred the water. The resulting 'primordial soup' mixed the chemicals together, leading to the formation of molecules of ever-increasing complexity and, eventually, life."

About the same time as Earth's primordial soup was spawning life, death was occurring on Mars with the eruption of Olympus Mons. The largest volcano in the solar system, it towers sixteen miles above the surface of the Red Planet—three times higher than Mount Everest—and is roughly the size of the state of Arizona. Olympus Mons contains six collapsed craters known as calderas. These magma chambers are stacked atop one another to form a depression that is fifty-three miles wide at the summit. The worst of the lot are resurgent calderas—geological timebombs responsible for massive eruptions and

```
extinction events.
```

```
     There are three resurgent calderas
in the United States that are less than
1.5 million years old—the Long Valley
Caldera   in   California,   the   Valles
Caldera   in   New   Mexico,   and   the
Yellowstone Caldera in Wyoming. The last
caldera   eruption   on   Earth   occurred
74,000   years   ago   on   the   Indonesian
Island   of   Sumatra.   The   Toba   caldera
generated   nearly   three   thousand   times
more pyroclastic material than Mount St.
Helens  and  unleashed  an  ash  cloud  that
encompassed  Earth's  atmosphere,  which
led  to  a  decade  of  volcanic  winter  that
wiped   out   nearly   every   hominid   on   the
planet.
```

I set the laptop aside, my eyes gazing out of the bay windows at Loch Ness. It was hard to fathom that every drop of water on the planet could have been delivered by meteors, comets, and asteroids, each impact blasting moisture into the atmosphere until a seemingly endless rain had fallen to cool the molten-hot world and fill its lowlands.

I glanced at my watch. It was nearly two o'clock.

I was about to dial John Rudman's office number when Brandy entered the restaurant, accompanied by four strangers—three men and an exotic Asian woman dressed in a tight-fitting black silk dress and carrying a briefcase.

Women remain a foreign species to me. For two months my wife had barely shown me an ounce of interest. Yet in the presence of this Chinese beauty I could sense the acidic jealousy churning in her belly as she escorted the woman and her three male companions to my table.

43

"Zachary, this woman is here tae speak with you. Are ye sober?"

I stood, my temper flaring. "Of course I'm sober. Hi, I'm Zachary Wallace."

"Dr. Wallace, this is a great honor. My name is Dr. Ming Liao. I am a geologist working in East Antarctica. These are two of my colleagues: Dr. Rehan Ahmed from Karachi, Pakistan, and George McFarland, a marine engineer working at Stone Aerospace. Mr. McFarland was recruited for this mission by NASA."

"NASA? Now you've got me curious." I motioned for my guests to sit. I was about to ask the third gentleman his name when I noticed Dr. Ahmed shivering. "Would you like something warm to drink? Coffee? Tea?"

"Tea would be most appreciated."

"For me also," added Dr. Liao, with a smile.

"Coke," said Mr. McFarland.

I turned to the stranger to whom I had not yet been introduced. He was a rugged man in his forties, with a taut physique, dark brown hair, and a scruffy, short beard. He wore a sullen expression, like he had seen death.

A kindred soul?

He looked up at Brandy through bloodshot gray-blue eyes. "Coke, only put a shot of rum in mine."

I turned to my wife, foolishly hoping she'd volunteer to bring my guests their beverages on her way out. Instead, she plopped down in the remaining chair. "Whit? Do I look like the barmaid, then?"

Red-faced, I strode around behind the bar and filled two cups with bottled water. I placed them in the microwave and fished out a few tea bags, then grabbed a can of cola from a stack of sodas and filled two glasses with ice, adding a splash of rum to the second. Loading everything onto a tray, I returned to the table.

"Zachary, did ye ken yer new scientist friends here are all single? And here ye are, aboot the same age but married wit a bairn."

I handed out the beverages, refusing to be baited by her remark. "Guess that makes me a lucky man. Brandy, would you mind giving me a few minutes alone with Dr. Liao and her colleagues so we can talk?"

"These gentle folk are here tae recruit ye for something. Bein' as I'm still yer wife and the mother of yer child, I think I'll give a listen. Is that a problem, Ms. Liao?"

Dr. Liao smiled. "No problem, Mrs. Wallace, provided you abide by a non-disclosure agreement like the one your husband will be asked to sign."

Brandy smiled back. "Sure, I'll sign. Whit 've I got tae lose? Willy's crib?"

Her response did not please Liao. "Dr. Wallace, we've come a long way at great expense to speak with you. While I can assure you the subject matter will both interest and astound you, it is not something we want exposed to the general public."

Seeking unfiltered answers, I turned to the fourth stranger, the man who had not bothered to introduce himself. "You were recruited for this mission?"

"Something like that."

"What's your role?"

"Submersible pilot."

"What's mine?"

"Money. Your association with the expedition will bring the sponsors that pay the bills."

I stared hard at the man's face. "I've seen your photo before. You said you're a submersible pilot?"

"Not by trade. Benjamin Hintzmann. Ben to my friends. I'm a fighter pilot—at least I was until the United States Air Force discharged me after an incident nearly triggered a war."

45

"Hintzmann, you're the F-18 pilot who had the Pakistani air force shooting at him. Why'd you cross into their airspace?"

"It's classified. Anyway, that was a long time ago. Since then, I've traded in my wings for flippers and been working with Graham Hawkes, piloting his deep-sea submersibles. Amazing machines. They fly through the water just like a jet. I was training in San Diego when Ming and the ding-a-ling boys here made me an offer I couldn't refuse—contingent, of course, on your participation. After what happened to you in the Sargasso Sea, I'm guessing they figured you'd feel safer with someone like me piloting our three-man sub."

"Who's the third man?"

"I am." Ming Liao removed a document from her leather briefcase and handed it to me. "This non-disclosure agreement allows me to share classified information about an amazing find my team made recently. By signing this agreement, you are forbidden from sharing this information with anyone, whether you join our mission or not."

"You mean, at least until the television special airs."

"While every aspect of this mission will be documented, there will be no television crews. Nor will there be any published reports, at least for quite some time."

"I don't understand. What good is a new discovery if you can't share it with the world?"

"The discovery will be shared once we have garnered the vast treasures this exploratory mission has to offer. Because the location of the discovery is in Antarctica we cannot prevent other nations and their scientific teams from accessing, exploiting, and contaminating the resource; therefore, we must protect its secrets as long as possible.

"Dr. Wallace, please sign the agreement so that we may speak freely. And if your wife insists upon participating in our discussion, she must also sign. Nothing personal," she added as she met Brandy's glare.

I glanced at Brandy. As she liked to say, it was a "shyte or get off the bowl" moment, only it had nothing to do with Liao's pitch. If Brandy signed the non-disclosure now, it meant she cared enough about our marriage to be concerned where this journey might take me, assuming I was even interested. If, however, she walked out, then our marriage was as good as over.

"Give me the bloody paper." Using Liao's pen, she signed the document without reading it and slid it over to me. "It's your life. Do as ye will."

I reviewed the agreement and then signed it above Brandy's signature. "Okay, Dr. Liao, both Wallaces have anted up. Make your pitch."

"Please, call me Ming. As I said, the discovery is located in Antarctica. What do you know about the continent, other than it's the coldest, most desolate place on Earth?"

"I know it wasn't always that way."

"Correct. Before it was covered by ice, Antarctica was fertile land with lush forests and fresh-water lakes and streams. That was during the Miocene, a period of time that began about twenty-five million years ago. The climate abruptly changed about fifteen million years ago, leaving most of the continent covered with a dome-shaped glacier two-and-a-half miles thick. Gravity is actually pulling the ice into the ocean by way of the continent's ice shelves. As these ice shelves reach the coastline, their bottom sections hit seawater and melt faster, causing sections of the flow to crack—a natural process known as rifting.

"Global warming has accelerated the process. Last year alone, Antarctic ice sheets lost a combined mass of 355 gigatonnes, which is enough to raise global sea levels by 1.3 millimeters. That may not seem like a lot, but combine that with Greenland's melting ice sheet, diminishing mountain glaciers, and the polar caps—all multiplied by the present rate of acceleration—and your winter home in sunny Florida may be underwater by the time you are ready to retire."

"Actually, my wife and I winter here in Drumnadrochit." I smiled at Brandy, who rolled her eyes.

Liao returned to her briefcase and removed a thick accordion file sealed with a combination lock. "The photos I am about to show you were taken eleven days ago by scientists from Beijing University. The preserved remains of these two creatures were found frozen within a twenty-nine-kilometer-long rift nicknamed Loose Tooth. The fissure is part of the Amery Ice Shelf in East Antarctica." She quickly maneuvered the lock's numbers to the correct three-digit sequence and opened the file, removing several glossy color photos, which she laid out before me.

I stared at the objects in the images, particularly at the excavated block of ice flanked by two humans to add the perspective of size.

The flesh on the back of my neck prickled.

"The marine biologist on loan to us could not identify either species, though he believed the animals may have lived during—"

"—the Miocene," I finished. "This creature here—the one that's being eaten—I'm reasonably certain it was a giant species of caiman called a *Purussaurus*."

Brandy looked perplexed. "Caiman? Ye mean, like a crocodile?"

"Yes, only this one was fifty feet long. *Purussaurus* remains have been found in the Peruvian Amazon in South America. Two distinct species of Crocodylia were discovered—*brasiliensis* and *mirandai*. *Purussaurus mirandai* had a wider, far more elongated skull that was extremely flat. Its nostrils were unusually large, the openings three feet long. No one seems to know what they were used for."

Ben glanced at Dr. Ahmed. "Looks like you found your brainiac. Hey, Zach, what do you call the big python that choked trying to eat the pussy-saurus?"

"*Pu-rus-sau-rus.* And I have no idea. The biggest snake fossil ever found belonged to *Titanoboa*, which grew to forty-five feet. But it lived sixty million years ago, and even that monster was too small to go after an adult *Purussaurus.* Dr. Liao, you say your team found these remains on the Amery Ice Shelf?"

"Yes, but that's not where this epic battle took place. Dr. Ahmed, please show Dr. Wallace the I.P.R. image."

Reaching into the file, the Pakistani scientist removed a black-and-white satellite image taken of the Antarctic continent, only without its two-mile-thick ice cap.

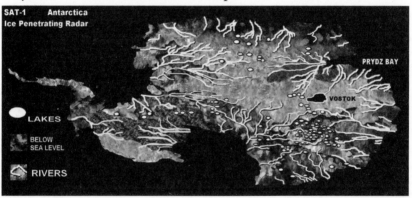

"Thanks to the development of radio echo-sounding, reflection seismology, and ice-penetrating radar, we now know what Antarctica's geology looks like beneath the ice sheet and how the terrain would have appeared millions of years ago. As you can see, Dr. Wallace, the Antarctic landmass possesses more than a hundred and fifty lakes. Think of them as subglacial reservoirs of meltwater. As the ice sheet moves, its flow rate is affected by the level of these lakes, which rise and fall like the locks on the Panama Canal. The meltwater drains into a network of subglacial streams and rivers, which in turn keep the glacier moving out to sea. As the ice sheet passes over a lake, it causes some of its surface water to freeze. Anything caught in this accretion ice becomes part of the ice sheet."

"Which is how these monsters' remains came to be discovered in the Loose Tooth rift."

49

"Precisely. As the ice sheet moves, its weight compresses gases like oxygen and carbon dioxide downward while raising sediment and other objects caught in its wake. The frozen remains of these two behemoths were squeezed topside as the ice became part of the Amery Ice Shelf. By analyzing the ice attached to the creatures' remains, we were able to determine the location of their habitat while they were alive."

"Which is...?"

"Lake Vostok—the largest and deepest body of water on the continent."

I looked more closely at the satellite image. At one hundred and sixty miles long and fifty miles wide, Vostok was roughly the size of Lake Ontario, only its eleven-hundred-foot depths easily dwarfed those of the Great Lake. My eyes traced a river that appeared to run from Vostok's northern border to the Amery Ice Shelf. "Dr. Ahmed, how far would these creatures' remains have had to travel down this river to reach that rift?"

He was ready with the answer. "We calculated the journey to be between eight and nine hundred miles, depending upon what section of Vostok they were in when they engaged in battle. The lake also possesses two islands, so they might have fought on land. We are bringing in a team of paleontologists to inspect the fossils for traces of soil."

Brandy inspected the satellite image. "Ye say this lake is buried beneath the snow?"

Dr. Ahmed nodded. "Beneath an ice sheet thirteen thousand feet thick. The lake was sealed off approximately fifteen million years ago."

"But its waters are frozen..."

"No, Mrs. Wallace," Liao replied. "Lake Vostok's waters are actually quite liquid."

"That makes no sense. How can a lake remain unfrozen beneath, what... four thousand meters of ice?"

Dr. Liao seemed slightly annoyed at Brandy's distraction. "The water remains liquid because of two factors: the tremendous pressure generated by the weight of the ice sheet from above and the presence of geothermal vents pumping superheated waters into the bottom of the lake, which may actually be a tectonically active rift."

Dr. Ahmed pushed back from the table. "Dr. Wallace, Lake Vostok represents a precious, unspoiled time capsule into our past, a fossil-rich water reserve that may still harbor life. This recent discovery has accelerated everyone's interest in both the government and private sector. The United States has joined China and Australia in a joint effort to develop the means to explore this lost world, while taking every measure to protect its microbial life from contaminants—something the Russians have not taken to heart. With a new budget in excess of a billion dollars, the conversation has changed from developing cleaner methods of deep ice-core drilling to actually sending drones into the lake itself."

"You didn't recruit a deep-sea submersible pilot to operate a drone." I glanced at the shaggy-haired American, who looked more like a graduate student than an engineer. "Mr. McFarland, why don't you cut through Dr. Ahmed's politics and tell us how Bill Stone and his team at Stone Aerospace intend on delivering a manned vessel into a lake buried under two-and-a-half miles of ice."

George McFarland grinned. "As I'm sure you know, Dr. Stone has been developing robotic explorers to access hard-to-reach exotic environments for years. Our focus of late has been the frozen ocean on Jupiter's moon, Europa, which has an ice sheet twenty times as thick as Antarctica's. Europa and Vostok present similar technical challenges. First and foremost, we need a far more efficient way to descend through miles of ice while maintaining the integrity of the borehole. The Russians have been pouring kerosene and Freon down their ice shaft, a move that has pissed off the entire international community. Vostok has remained preserved for fifteen million years; the last thing we want to do is introduce toxic chemicals into the habitat.

"Then there's the issue of hydrostatic pressure created by the sheer weight of the ice sheet sitting on top of these subglacial bodies of water. Vostok is essentially a massive topographic hollow filled with water that is being squeezed beneath trillions of tons of ice. Think of it as a giant water-filled balloon. Puncture Vostok and water explodes out the exit at five thousand pounds per square inch of pressure. The Russians learned this the hard way when they retracted their last ice core and water blasted up through the borehole, flooding their drill cab with a hundred cubic meters of kerosene."

McFarland powered on his laptop and turned the monitor to face Brandy and me. On screen was a six-foot-long cylindrical device. "This is Valkyrie, the cryobot we designed for Europa. The vehicle is an autonomous ice-penetrating machine. It is linked by fiber-optic cable to a power source that remains on the surface and is equipped with a high-powered laser that quickly melts the ice ahead of it. The hole then re-freezes behind the cryobot, preventing the pressure from forcing water out of the shaft. To return topside you simply invert the unit and blow ballast, and the capsule melts its way back to the surface, rising up on its own bubble with the hole re-freezing behind it.

"The three-man submersible we've designed will be flanked by two Valkyrie lasers. Once the lake is reached, the sub will run autonomously. When it's time to ascend, the Valkyries will burn a borehole through the ice, raising the sub on a geyser of water created by Lake Vostok's own internal pressure. Cool, huh?"

I shook my head in amazement. "It's an incredible feat of engineering, but why a submersible? Why not simply let the Valkyrie unit do its job?"

Dr. Liao appeared irritated by the question. "Why put an astronaut in orbit when a chimpanzee will do? Why put a man on the moon? Lake Vostok is the equivalent of journeying to another world. A robot can collect a few fossils, but it cannot experience the wonderment of exploring an ice sheet from below, nor observe Vostok's underworld through a scientist's eyes. Are there dangers? Of course. But we've minimized the risks, and I dare say exploring a subglacial lake is far less taxing than rocketing into space. There are no less than a dozen scientific organizations participating in this venture, with volunteers vying to be among the chosen few to visit this lost world."

"If that's the case, why choose me?"

"You have been blessed with the unique ability to see what others have seen and think what nobody has thought. While we'll have teams of paleobiologists at the camp, none have your field experience or reputation. Who better to resolve what will no doubt be a Rubick's Cube of fossils and processes—"

"And perhaps a life-form or two," interjected Dr. Ahmed. "It is my belief that your team will come across bacteria and biologicals that have survived in that isolated environment for millions of years. As Captain Hintzmann mentioned, your participation also helps us procure the necessary funds to expedite this mission—funds from which you shall be well compensated."

Dr. Liao handed me an envelope. Inside was an offer for a research stipend covering September through February of the coming year. I passed the sheet of paper to Brandy, whose eyes widened at the mid-six-figure salary. "Who do ye have tae murder, then? The Queen, I hope."

"I'd be gone six months. The way things have been lately, maybe that's a good thing... ."

Brandy's eyes teared up. "Go, then. I ken ye want tae. It's in yer blood as sure as the plaid's in mine." She straightened in her seat. "Besides, we need the money."

For months we had poisoned our arguments with the threat of divorce. Threats are threats until they force you to make a decision. At that moment we both sensed that this was it—we'd either commit to staying together or officially end our marriage with my acceptance of Dr. Soto's lucrative offer.

Put to the test, neither of us wanted to be without the other.

"Here's another alternative, Brandy. I was just offered a teaching position at Cambridge University. It's not nearly as much money, but at least I'd see you and William on weekends."

She reached for my hand beneath the table. "Or we could stay wit' ye during the week and see my father on weekends. True could handle things while I'm away."

It was as if a vise had been removed from my heart. I squeezed my wife's hand, suddenly anxious to end the meeting. "Dr. Liao, gentlemen, while I appreciate the offer, I'm afraid I'll have to pass."

3

Brandy had felt certain I would abandon my family, accept Dr. Liao's offer, and end up in her arms. In turning the offer down, I had placed the needs of my loved ones ahead of my own. Or as my wife put it, "I had changed the energy in our marriage from negative back to positive." In turn, Brandy could now leave Drumnadrochit in good conscience to join me in Cambridge.

Maybe she was right. Having rendered my decision I felt uplifted, as if my life had meaning again.

Dr. Ahmed looked shocked. "Perhaps you need a few days to think this through?"

I assured him my mind was made up, sending Dr. Liao into a ten-minute diatribe about my obligation to the scientific community and how this expedition could affect everything from our knowledge of how life began to climate change and its threat to the planet. When I still refused her call to duty, she argued that some major investors had threatened to withdraw their support if I passed on the mission and that if it was simply a matter of money, perhaps she could manage to up the offer another ten to fifteen percent. When I assured her my objection had nothing to do with money, she interpreted my response as one of fear. Challenging my manhood, she again assured me that there'd be no risk, certainly nothing on par with what had happened to me two years ago at the bottom of Loch Ness.

"Trust me, Dr. Wallace, I wouldn't be making the descent if I had any doubts as to our safety. As for water creatures, I sincerely doubt we'll find anything larger than a salmon. There is no food supply."

She was baiting me to oppose her statement, which dismissed an entire chemosynthetic food chain. The bizarre thing was Brandy's reaction; the more I held my ground against Liao, the more turned on she became. At one point she interrupted the conversation to remind me that Willy's nanny was due to leave soon and that we really needed to get back to our room.

And then she winked!

That was all the prompting I needed.

Ending the meeting, I shook my guests' hands and said goodbye—unaware that Liao had one final card to play.

"It's late, Zachary. Rather than drive back to Inverness for our return flights in the morning, may we stay in the resort for the night? I'm sure there are vacancies."

Perhaps it was Ming's addressing me informally; perhaps it was the implications of her wanting to sleep under the same roof. But the Asian beauty's request clearly set Brandy off, her mood swing threatening my anticipated bout of make-up sex.

I scrambled to neutralize the brewing storm. "I think the north wing has a few rooms open, but we're not serving food. Are you sure you wouldn't be more comfortable in the village?"

"And miss out on this view? No, we'll stay here. Besides, I'm sure Ben would love to speak with you about his undersea work. You two have so much in common. Ben?"

Ben finished the last of his drink. "Maybe later. Right now I think Dr. Wallace would rather be with his wife."

Like I said, a kindred soul.

"Go downstairs to the check-in desk. True will meet you there."

* * *

My brother-in-law and best friend, Finlay "True" MacDonald, was a gentle giant, carrying two hundred and sixty pounds on his six-foot-five-inch frame. He kept his beard short and his auburn hair long and in a ponytail. You could kid him about it unless he was drunk, which he was a lot these days. My father had hired the big fella as his hotel manager, but the lack of business had added handyman, electrician, plumber, lord of the laundry, and groundskeeper to his job description. True didn't mind, he lived rent-free and always had a clean room in which to bed his women, most of whom he met "interviewing" for summer housekeeping jobs.

Entering the lobby, he greeted Liao like a hungry tiger. "So, Zachary tells me ye'll be spending the night. Don't get many visitors this time o' year, and none that look as good as you. The name's Finlay, but my friends call me True. How many rooms then, Miss… ?"

"Liao. Four rooms, non-smoking. I assume you accept credit cards?"

"Aye, but ye'll be needing tae eat, and most of the places in the village only take cash. It's a fair walk intae town, but I can drive ye."

"That would be nice."

"My pleasure. Fiddler's serves the best haggis and tatties this side o' the Ness. Your friends can drink in the café while you and me sit in the backroom and get tae ken one another."

Liao ignored True's attempt at romance. "Fiddler's sounds fine. Make the reservations for four. Oh, and could you arrange for Angus Wallace to meet us there?"

"Angus? Whit do ye want with that old buzzard?"

"Please tell him I have a business proposition to discuss."

* * *

Fiddler's was located on the other side of the A82 highway across the road from the Oakdale Bed and Breakfast. The two-story white stucco structure housed a pub and restaurant downstairs along with a café extension that was strictly for drinking. The rooms upstairs were for rent. During tourist season the restaurant was always crowded, with seating overflowing outside onto the patio. The frigid March weather kept its local patrons indoors, most stopping by to partake of a Fiddler's homemade malt whisky chosen from over five hundred selections.

My father was seated alone at a table in the back room behind the bar, feasting on venison steak and black pudding with a bottle of cider. Angus Wallace's mane of silver-gray hair was tucked under a green Nessie's Lair golf cap, and his matching beard and mustache sported remnants from his meal. His piercing gray-blue eyes glanced up as Liao entered the hideaway. "Dr. Liao, I presume? My-my, aren't ye a dazzling Chinese dish. Enough tae set my daughter-in-law off, I'll wager."

"May I sit?"

"Sit, piss, shyte, do whitever ye want. Ye came a long way tae get rejected. Antarctica, huh? Imagin' it gets quite Baltic in that ice box."

"Baltic? Ah, you mean cold. Yes, very cold. But how did you—"

"Lass, I've connections all aboot the Great Glen, including immigration, and I like tae ken who's stayin' under my roof. Three eggheads an' a sub pilot, all here tae recruit my Zachary. All that way ye traveled and the lad turned ye down."

"He would have signed on if—"

"Brandy? Ye think so, do ye? Ye ken nothing aboot my son."

"We offered him the chance of a lifetime, and he passed it up for a faculty position at Cambridge."

"What was yer offer?"

"I'm afraid that's confidential, but it amounts to quite a figure for the summer season."

"Summer in Antarctica… is that anything like winter in Hell?"

"It's cold, but we will assemble an environmental dome to protect our team from the elements."

"Aye. And ye'll be accompanying him on this chance-of-a-lifetime mission?"

"Correct. My role is to analyze the geology of Lake Vostok. As for the mission itself, the risk is minimal. I think he's more afraid of upsetting his wife."

58

"Lass, yer bum's hangin' way oot the windae. Yer talkin' rubbish. This ain't aboot money or pleasin' his auld lady. It's aboot fear. Ye think yer the only one who's come calling on my son since his latest resurrection? The lad's passed on every underwater expedition offered, and better paying ones than yers. Ye forget, Zachary near died aboard one of them submersibles three years back. If it means going underwater, the answer is always no."

"What if he didn't have to make the dive? Right now, I just need him on the expedition to secure a few private investors."

"And so ye've come tae me for help because ye heard the lad listens tae his auld man like I was Jesus climbed down from the cross."

"Well, no. But if that is true—"

"Lassy, butts are fer crappin'. Ye came here tae bribe me, so start yer bribing."

She reached into her bag and removed an envelope. "This is a letter of commitment. When your son signs it and arrives at our new station in East Antarctica you will receive a sum equaling five thousand U.S. dollars."

Angus snorted a laugh. "Lass, who do ye think yer dealing wit'? A Highland pig farmer? The plane fare to Antarctica for you and the other eggheads alone costs more than five thou. No, ye'll pay me that sum tonight jist for acceptin' the job. Then you'll pay me another fifty thousand when he signs. That fee will be wired intae my bank account before Zachary leaves Inverness."

"Out of the question. I can go as high as ten, provided the contract is signed within the next twenty-four hours."

"Tells ye whit, I'll accept five tonight and twenty when the signed contract is faxed. Go on and discuss it at the bar with yer friends, but be quick; there's been another kill and I'm needed—*ach*, there I go, blabbin' again like a schoolgirl. Dinnae listen tae me, lass, it's those three haufs of whiskey talkin'."

"Has there been... a murder?"

59

"Shh!" Angus grabbed her by the arm while his eyes took inventory of the room. "Can I trust ye with a secret, lassy?"

"Of course."

He leaned in close enough for Liao to catch the scent of booze on his breath. "We have another creature loose in Loch Ness—a big one. Killed three deer in the past two weeks. Last night an elk. She dinnae come ashore like her mama; she's water-bound. Feeds on 'em as they cross the loch at night, and we collect the remains in the morning."

Liao's eyes lit up as she swallowed the bait. "You said like her *mother?* Are you saying the Loch Ness Monster gave birth to an offspring before your son—"

"Aye, but let's be clear; it's not the same species. Nessie must've bred with somethin' else. Dinnae ask me whit."

"But how do you know this?"

"Bite radius on the dead deer, an occasional sighting... Plus there's the tooth."

"You found a tooth?"

"Not me. Back in February a coupla' college students from the States were taking photos by boat along a stretch known tae us locals as the Kill Zone. They saw the half-eaten remains of a deer and went ashore. One of the American lads spotted something protruding from the dead deer's rib cage. Bloody thing turned oot tae be a tooth—four inches long and barbed. Fortunately, the water bailiff took it from them, or we'd have been invaded by scientists and Nessie hunters. I thought word had leaked when yer team showed up unannounced."

"And have you seen the tooth?"

"Aye. And missin' one dinnae stop it from killing tha' elk last night. Sheriff called me not ten minutes before ye arrived. The remains washed ashore in Invermoriston, jist down the road. Wannae take a peek wit' me before they dispose of the evidence?"

* * *

It was half past six at night. While my father was enticing Dr. Liao and her entourage into his web of deceit, Brandy, Willy, and I were getting ready to eat dinner in our humble resort abode.

Suites 300 and 302 were connecting rooms that provided us with the living space of a three-bedroom apartment. There was a kitchen and double balcony overlooking Loch Ness, and a living room filled with baby toys.

I was feeding Willy in his highchair, and Brandy was reheating day-old Scotch pie when my cell phone rang. It was a California area code.

Jonas Taylor...

"Jonas, I was waiting until later to call you. I really appreciate Masao's offer, but I've decided to accept a faculty position at Cambridge."

"I understand. The money was dogshit. Unfortunately times have been tough. We may end up selling the facility to a developer who wants to build waterfront condos."

"J.T., while I have your ear, have you ever heard of a submersible diver by the name of Ben Hintzmann? He says he trained under Graham Hawkes."

"It's possible. I don't get up to Hawkes's facility much these days; we've become competitors. My son, David, and I have been designing a new submersible we call the Manta. If things work out, I hope to sell them as the ultimate rich man's toy."

A knock on our other front door hastened the end of the call. "Well, good luck with that. And send my best to Masao."

Brandy chided me with a scowl. "Are ye expectin' anyone, Zach?"

"No, but I'm secretly hoping it's the pizza delivery boy. The smell of that re-heated mutton concoction is making me ill."

"When ye get yer first paycheck from Cambridge we'll feast on take-out. Until then I'm making do." Opening the door to Suite 300, she turned to the man knocking on Suite 302. "Can I help ye?

Oh, it's you."

Ben Hintzmann stepped into view. "Evening. Hope I'm not interrupting anything."

Brandy blocked him from entering. "We were jist aboot tae eat supper."

"Are you hungry, Ben?"

Brandy turned to face me, her eyes daggers.

"No, I ate earlier. The others went to the village with the big fella. I stayed behind hoping we could talk. I can come by later—"

"It's all right, come in."

Brandy allowed him to squeeze past her before returning to the kitchen. "Something tae drink, then?"

"No, I'm good. Who's this little guy?"

I smiled proudly. "This is our son, William. Willy, say hello to Mr. Hintzmann."

Willy smiled bashfully, then swatted his dish of applesauce and strained spinach off the highchair's tray, turning Ben's jeans into something that resembled a Jackson Pollock painting.

"Willy! Ben, I'm sorry."

"It's okay."

Brandy wetted a dishtowel and handed it to Ben. "Perhaps one day ye'll have bairn of yer own?"

"Bairn?"

"Baby."

"Sure. Maybe. My girlfriend's more focused on her career."

"But ye want a wee un, I can tell. Perhaps this girlfriend of yers is not the marryin' type?"

"Brandy!"

Ben finished wiping down his pants. "Amanda's still adjusting to me no longer being in the Air Force. And with all the changes, I'm not exactly ready to be anyone's father. What's that smell?"

I inhaled, catching a whiff of the baby's soiled diaper. Releasing Willy from his chair, I handed him over to his mother. "Brandy, would you mind?"

"Time for his bath anyway. Serve yerself the mutton pie before it gets cold."

"It's okay, I'll eat later."

Brandy shrugged and carried the baby into the connecting suite, closing the door behind her.

Ben smiled. "Mutton?"

"Sheep meat," I said. "It's like lamb, only tougher and drier. Want to try some?"

"God, no. I'd rather eat Willy's leftovers."

"Let's talk out here." I led him to the terrace door and outside to the enclosed balcony. The glass walls blunted the cold to near-tolerable levels, the night concealing Loch Ness from view. Ben made himself comfortable in one of our padded rocking chairs while I ignited a portable heater.

"Must be nice out here during the summer."

"It's peaceful," I agreed, flopping down on a lounge chair. "So what's on your mind? This isn't a last-ditch effort to recruit me for Vostok, is it?"

"Just an opportunity to get to know someone I admire. For the record, I wasn't interested in the Vostok mission until I heard they were recruiting you." His eyes settled heavily on mine. "When I read *The Loch* last year, I remember thinking how hard it must have been for you, as a reputable professional in your field, to have been ridiculed by your peers for believing in the water equivalent of Bigfoot or the Abominable Snowman."

"I had a close encounter. It didn't matter what my peers believed, I knew the truth."

"A close encounter, exactly! The truth can't be coerced, can it? I mean, it can. People falsify evidence whenever the truth conflicts with their own agenda. They make you sign things and

63

threaten you, but the truth is still the truth no matter how crazy it sounds, right?"

"Right, uh, what are we talking about?"

"We're talking about finding the truth by thinking outside the box. For instance, that giant croc—what if it's still alive?"

"*Purussaurus*? Not likely. It was a saltwater species. Vostok's fresh water. Besides, the pressure would have crushed its lungs long ago."

"What about those fossils Ming's crew dragged out of the crevasse?"

"There was no epic battle in Vostok millions of years ago; a python that size could never kill a *Purussaurus*. I'd wager good money the Crocodylia was already dead when that giant snake found it lying on an Antarctic shoreline and choked attempting to eat it before another predator could claim its prize."

"Ming said they traced the ice that held those two creatures back to Vostok."

"Translated: the ice sheet dragged it into Vostok and probably across a dozen other subglacial lakes en route to the Amery Ice Shelf. It doesn't mean the lake was populated with giant crocs and pythons."

"Then you think this whole expedition is a waste of time and money?"

"Not at all. Vostok presents scientists with an incredible opportunity to study what our planet was like during the Miocene. I think there's a good chance some sort of microbial life has survived. I'm sure the paleo guys will be studying water samples for years."

"Be honest, Doc. Why did you *really* turn down Dr. Liao's offer?"

"I thought I made that clear. I don't want to be away from my family for six months, especially in minus-forty-degree temperatures."

"It's all about that Sargasso Sea incident, isn't it? In your memoir you wrote about nearly drowning to save your cameraman."

"*Did* drown."

"My point is you'd think they'd honor that kind of sacrifice. Instead they blamed you for the crewman you didn't save. What kills me is the same thing is happening to you again, here in Drumnadrochit. The creature was killing people; she was a serious threat to every villager around Loch Ness, not to mention the tourists. You resolved the problem and risked your life doing it and this is how they repay you—by turning you into a recluse?"

I felt my blood pressure rise, as if Hintzmann's words had flipped a switch on an internal furnace. "Where's this going, *Ben?*"

"You and I have a lot in common, Doc. We've both made sacrifices. We both answered the call of duty, and now we're both on the outs. And don't tell me you always wanted to teach. The man who solved the mystery of the Loch Ness Monster isn't going to feel satisfied grading papers. Will those challenges fulfill you for the rest of your days, or will you wake up one morning old and gray, wondering what might have been? See, I get what you're going through—it sucks being the ugly girl at the dance. But that's no reason to skip the prom, no reason to settle for a life of mediocrity. For a marine biologist, Vostok is the moon landing. Don't pass it up. The world remembers Neil Armstrong; no one gives a damn about the back-up astronauts who stayed behind."

"Are you done, Hintzmann? Or are there a few more metaphors you'd like to recite? No? Well here's one to mull over as you leave my home: don't blame the dog after you step in shit."

"What's that supposed to mean?"

"Give it time. I suspect it'll come to you."

4

"Fools look to tomorrow. Wise men use tonight."
—Scottish proverb

The hamlet of Invermoriston lies ten miles south of Drumnadrochit on the A82 roadway at the junction of the A887, which cuts west through some of the lushest woodlands in the Great Glen. Snaking its way east through the forest's rocky ravines is the mighty River Moriston. Approaching Invermoriston, the waterway churns into rapids and flows over a series of falls before it passes under the two-hundred-year-old Telford Bridge to empty into Loch Ness.

It was after eight o'clock at night when a Nessie's Lair mini-van driven by True MacDonald pulled into a scenic lay-by off the A82. In the front passenger seat was my father. In the back seats were Dr. Liao, Dr. Ahmed, and George McFarland, the engineer from Stone Aerospace.

Red-and-blue strobe lights from a police vehicle cut across a campground nestled between the highway and shoreline as Deputy Sheriff Mark Plumley made his way up a steep trail to greet Angus.

"Ye heard, then? This new monster is a hungry one."

"Aye. Who found the remains?"

"Esther Jacobs. She was walking by the water at sunset when it washed ashore. My brother Chris is takin' photos of whit's left. Who's all this, then?"

"Scientists. They arrived yesterday on business wit' Zachary. Mind if they 'ave a look?"

"Jist watch yer step on the rocks. Lots of blood."

Plumley shone his flashlight on the trail that cut through the campsite, leading Angus and his entourage to the shoreline.

Twenty-two months earlier, an American tourist named Tiani Brueggert had arrived at this very destination with her husband, Joel, and their two teenage daughters. Having spent the day hiking the forest trails, Tiani left her tent late that night to soak her swollen feet in the loch's frigid waters. While returning to the campsite, she was attacked by an amphibious creature more than forty feet in length. It spread her remains across the clearing like an exploded melon. My father made sure he relayed these gruesome details to his guests on their way down to the water.

The shoreline was covered in smooth rounded stones. Dark waves lapped beneath a barren pier that extended thirty feet into the loch, the boats stored indoors for the winter.

Chris Plumley, the assistant fire chief and EMS supervisor in Inverness, was busy positioning battery-powered lanterns around the remains of a European red stag. The buck's four-foot-long antlers were wedged sideways into the ground, the deer's head propped at an awkward angle facing the heavens. The animal's hind quarters were missing, its stomach eviscerated.

The deputy sheriff shone his light on the wound. "Took it in one bite from below as it crossed the loch. This was a big buck, too. Had to weigh forty to fifty stone."

Liao covered her mouth as she stared wide-eyed at the half-eaten elk's spilled innards. "What could have done this? Surely it had to be the same species as the one discovered by your son?"

"Ye mean a guivre?" Angus shook his head. "The guivre was amphibious. This creature stays in the water. Ain't that right, Sheriff Plumley?"

"Aye. This wasn't a guivre. Big like a guivre, but no' a guivre, right, Chris?"

"Absolutely. If this was a guivre like ol' Nessie, she would have come ashore tae finish her meal."

"Good point," Angus chimed back. "Whitever this one is, she's big but stays tae the water. She's not a threat tae the locals."

"Agreed," the Plumley brothers said.

Dr. Ahmed attempted to interrupt the mental circle jerk. "Excuse me, gentlemen, but how can you possibly surmise all this without having performed a necropsy?"

"Performed a whit?"

"A necropsy. An examination of the elk's remains in order to determine the cause of death."

Angus eyeballed the Pakistani as if he had just cursed the Wallace clan. "Are ye daft? Do ye need a bloody examination tae see that the poor animal got his arse bitten off by a water monster?"

Before Dr. Ahmed could reply, the scene was invaded by three reporters and two photographers, all of whom seemed to appear out of a fog bank.

"Another feeding, Deputy Sheriff?"

"Aye, lad, but I'm no expert. Whit dae ye think, Miss... ?"

"Liao. Dr. Liao. And, yes, it would appear something large killed this elk."

The locals swarmed upon her like bees to honey.

"Dan Porter, *Inverness Courier*. Assuming a water creature killed this stag, how large would it have tae be to inflict a bite wound this size?"

"Honestly, I couldn't say."

"Go on, Dr. Liao," Angus pressed. "Bein' a proper scientist, I'll bet ye can provide a proper estimate of this beastie."

"I don't wish to be quoted, Mr. Wallace."

"Who's quoting ye? By the way, my son estimated the guivre at more than twelve meters. Would ye agree this completely different species is probably bigger?"

"I wouldn't know."

"Whit aboot ye, Dr. Ahmed? Yer a lake specialist."

"Yes. But like I said—"

Two photographers snapped the visitors' photos.

"Issac Pringle, nice tae meet ye, Dr. Ahmed. I understand you and Dr. Liao traveled all the way from Antarctica tae be in Loch Ness. That's quite a journey. When did you find out we had a second monster?"

"I didn't know— no comment. Dr. Liao, perhaps we'd better—"

"Mr. McFarland, is it?"

"How did you know that?"

"You're a guest at the Lair. Records show ye work for Stone Aerospace. With all the drones yer company builds, how would ye go about locating a second monster trapped in Loch Ness?"

"That depends. How big is Loch Ness?"

"Twenty-four miles long, a mile wide, and six hundred feet deep. Deeper still in Nessie's grotto where Zachary Wallace confronted the last monster."

"I'm not sure. Underwater drones perhaps."

"Dr. Ahmed, I understand your field of expertise involves extinct species. Is there a chance this new species could be a plesiosaur?"

"None at all. Again, there's no need for conjecture once your experts perform a proper necropsy on this animal."

Angus interjected. "Then a necropsy could help determine the new monster's species?"

"Absolutely."

"Then you agree Loch Ness has a second monster?"

"Yes. I mean, no. I mean no comment!"

* * *

Fifteen hours later, an exhausted Ming Liao and her three male associates found themselves in line at the airport in Inverness, waiting to pass through customs. Having barely slept, Liao had spent the better part of the morning arranging for her office in Beijing to wire five thousand U.S. dollars into a Bank of Scotland account belonging to one Angus Wallace. The inebriated Scot had kept her up until dawn, reassuring her that his son would sign commitment papers before the weekend was out, but that his power of persuasion needed persuading. They finally agreed that Angus would receive an additional ten thousand dollars once Liao had received a notarized signed agreement, which was a far cry from the fifty thousand the Scot had demanded at dinner.

The finder's fees were not unexpected. Had she been dealing with the Saudis, Russians, or her own people, the price would have been triple. Dr. Zachary Wallace's name carried a lot of weight among investors in both the private sector and the Chinese government, and if bribing the marine biologist's father secured his six-month commitment to the project, then so be it. While negotiations were Liao's forte, it was her ability to source private and state funding for the Vostok expedition while working with scientists and engineers in both the United States and Australia that ensured she would not be usurped as project director—that and the fact that her biggest donor insisted she make the descent. Dealing with an unsophisticated kilt-wearing buffoon like Angus Wallace was nothing compared to appeasing the heads of private family-run corporations whose combined investment in the Vostok expedition exceeded a billion dollars.

Stepping up to the immigration officer, she handed the man her passport and airline ticket.

"Quick in and oot, eh, Dr. Liao?"

"Excuse me?"

"Won't ask ye if ye have anything tae declare. I think ye said enough already."

"I'm sorry, but what are you referring to?"

The Scot stamped her passport and handed it back with a wry smile. "No worries, lass. A nod's as guid as a wink tae a blind horse. Pleasant flight."

Perplexed, she continued on to her gate, where her companions had their noses buried in the morning paper. George

McFarland was shaking his head. Dr. Ahmed's eyes were wide, filled with outrage. Only Ben Hintzmann seemed amused by what he was reading.

"What is it?"

Dr. Ahmed handed her his newspaper. "Wallace's father set us up."

Liao glanced at the front page of the *Inverness Courier*. Below the emboldened headlines was a color photo taken of Dr. Ahmed hovering over the bloodied carcass of the mutilated elk.

INTERNATIONAL TEAM OF SCIENTISTS CONFIRM A NEW MONSTER LURKS IN LOCH NESS

Inverness, Scotland (Associated Press)

Nessie may be gone, but the legendary monster that once inhabited Loch Ness appears to have left behind a hungry relative. According to eyewitnesses, a large water creature has been spotted stalking deer as they cross the waterway at night.

The monster's latest kill occurred sometime Thursday evening. Invermoriston resident Esther Jacobs said she was walking along the shoreline of Loch Ness around sunset when she saw a disturbance in the water some twenty meters away. She later discovered the remains of a 290kg male elk washed ashore on the western bank, its hindquarters devoured in what appeared to be a single bite. "It was gruesome," said Jacobs. "Thankfully this particular monster

prefers to stay in the water, or my life
might have been in danger."

Dr. Rehan Ahmed, a marine biologist
specializing in ancient sea creatures,
was on hand to examine the kill. He agreed
that this particular species probably
measured more than twelve meters, but
preferred not to speculate on whether it
could be a plesiosaur. Ahmed and his
colleague, Dr. Ming Liao, had arrived in
the Highlands Tuesday evening from
Antarctica for a special conference at
Loch Ness's new five-star resort,
Nessie's Lair. They were joined by
George McFarland, an engineer out of
Texas who works for Stone Aerospace.
McFarland suggested underwater drones
might be the best way to identify the
species of this new Loch Ness Monster,
though Esther Jacobs and other
eyewitnesses claim the creature is not
shy about surfacing by day. Said Ms.
Jacobs, "With the tourist season
approaching, it's just a matter of time
before someone videotapes the beastie."

Liao gritted her teeth. "Bastard even managed to get in the
name of his hotel."

"This isn't just a local story," George said. "Those reporters
last night spoon-fed this to the Associated Press. Our names are all
over this."

"Once I get the signed agreement from Dr. Wallace, it won't
matter. His presence at Vostok will quash this story."

Ben chuckled. "Wake up, Ming. Zachary Wallace lost his nerve years ago. He has no intention of signing on to Vostok or any other underwater expedition, and his old man knows it. Angus Wallace played you; he planned this whole Loch Ness Monster story the moment we landed."

"I don't understand."

"Tourism died with the monster, and last night the three of you helped bring it back to life. While you thought you were wooing Angus, the old man was baiting you, distracting you with false promises to get you to Invermoriston to see that carcass. Your presence last night served to validate the hoax and give his story legs—no pun intended. And the beautiful part is you paid him five thousand dollars to do it."

5

Hell hath no fury like a woman scorned.
—Male proverb.

There is a saying among Highlanders that translates to "a tale never loses in the telling." Angus must have repeated his tale a hundred times that first week, relishing how he had conned the "Asian harlot" out of five thousand U.S. dollars while priming the pump of tourism in the Great Glen.

To keep the momentum going, the Highland Council voted to use an infusion of grant money coming from British Parliament to install thirty visitor perches around Loch Ness. Each ten-foot-high covered platform would house three high-powered mounted telescopic cameras that ould allow tourists to snap downloadable photos of anything that crossed the lens of their viewport. Meanwhile, Alexander MacDonald, the Council's new provost (and second cousin to Brandy and True) held a press conference to announce an international symposium, scheduled to convene at my father's resort April 15 through April 22 to determine what this aggressive new species was. The Council extended invitations to marine biologists, cryptozoologists, and amateur monster hunters from around the world, with all resort guests receiving free passage aboard nocturnal voyages that would attempt to film the creature feeding on deer as the herds crossed the loch.

Reports of new sightings and photos purportedly taken by locals drove the story like a social media tsunami. Within weeks every hotel and bed-and-breakfast in the Great Glen was sold out for the season, led by Nessie's Lair.

It was all great theater, except that now the public demanded to hear from the marine biologist who had not only identified the

74

real Nessie two years earlier but had tracked it down and killed it. I was hounded twenty-four/seven, which made my life miserable and drew mixed reactions from the normally conservative administrators at Cambridge University.

Brandy, William, and I had been at Cambridge barely a week, living in a two-bedroom rented flat. Having arrived mid-semester, I was relegated to guest-speaking spots, rotating between undergraduate and graduate courses in oceanography and the marine sciences. The experience allowed me to re-acclimate to the academic environment, but the attention coming from my father's escapades was affecting the student body's perception of my role at the university—*was Dr. Zachary Wallace a teacher or an entertainer?*

And then a week before the Nessie's Lair event, a serious-looking fellow entered my lecture hall, marched up to my lectern, and ceremoniously presented me with an envelope. Baffled, I opened it, my students bearing witness to the publicly staged event.

It was a subpoena.

* * *

"State your name for the record."

"Angus William Wallace."

The preliminary hearing was being held behind closed doors at the Sherrifs' Court in Inverness. Present in the chamber was the judge, a court stenographer, my family, and a school of circling sharks in three-piece suits hailing from a law firm rated by England's *Legal Business* magazine as the fifth most successful in all the United Kingdom. Judging from their number, it appeared as if they had summoned every attorney from their offices in Glasgow and Edinburgh.

If my father was intimidated by their full court press, he wasn't showing it, but his barrister, my stepbrother, Maxie Rael, would need to change his underwear before the morning was through.

The lead litigator representing Dr. Ming Liao was a half-Italian, half-Ukranian man named Sam Mannino, who wasted no time going after Angus's jugular. "Do you understand the reason for this preliminary hearing, Mr. Wallace? The purpose of our convening this morning is to share the strength of our case with your barrister, so he knows the extent of the shit-storm you created for my client and the lengths we're prepared to go to make your life a living hell. For starters, we'll be moving your very public trial from this cozy Sheriff's Court in Inverness to the High Court in Glasgow in order to eliminate the biases of the plaid when we select a fifteen-person jury.

"On day one of the trial we will introduce evidence that shows you and your Highland Council cronies purposely deceived the public by concocting your little fairy tale about a second Loch Ness Monster. We will cross-examine the members of the Highland Council, effectually ending any future they might have had in holding an elected office, and then we'll introduce Exhibit A—the tool your EMT used on the carcass of an elk—I believe it's called a Jaws of Life—to make it appear as if the animal had been eaten. Then we will parade a day's worth of experts before the jury to demonstrate how your antics and false promises regarding your son's involvement in my client's upcoming venture in Antarctica ruined her expedition, costing her millions of dollars in investment capital.

"And finally, after the jury reaches the verdict of your guilt in this little civil matter, we will take every asset you own, including the resort on Loch Ness—which Dr. Liao will personally burn to the ground. Worst of all, your fellow Highlanders will curse you and your clan until the end of days for the financial ruin your lies will deliver unto the Great Glen. And then, Mr. Wallace, then I'm going to push for criminal charges that will consume every waking moment of your barrister's miserable life.

"How's that sound to you, *laddie?*"

"Sounds as if yer skat momma's still mad at me for defecating in her mouth the day ye was born."

That didn't go over well with the judge, but my father knew a dog-and-pony show when he saw one. I guess he figured there was no harm in stepping in more shit before they presented their backroom offer to Maxie.

"They want you, Zachary. They want your signed commitment to copilot the submersible into Lake Vostok. In exchange, they will drop all charges, and there will be no press conferences to derail the symposium. Oh yeah—and your pay will be reduced by five thousand dollars to cover the money wired to Angus. As your barrister I strongly urge you to sign the papers so we can get the hell out of here."

"You're not my attorney, Maxie, you're his." I turned to Brandy and saw disgust in her eyes.

My father looked into my eyes and saw fear. "Oh, come on. It's a bloody lake. Not like yer goin' down in yer birthday suit."

"Why does it seem like every time you're in a courtroom, I get it up the ass?"

"Maybe ye like it there?"

"He's all yours, Max. Come on, Brandy."

"Come on where? Ye heard tha' barrister. By the time they're through humiliating yer father, no tourist in their right mind will come tae the villages. I'm none too happy aboot this, Zachary, but Angus is right—ye got tae go."

"Listen tae yer wife," the old man gloated.

"Shut yer pie hole, ye old bampot," Brandy snapped. "Before my husband signs his name tae anything, I've a few conditions myself. First off, ye'll be moving Alban intae the hotel immediately, so's True can take proper care of him over the next five months."

"The Crabbit... in my resort... the resort he cursed when we broke ground?" Angus was about to lose it when he saw the look in Brandy's eyes. "Aye, whitever."

"Second, when September comes 'round and it's time for Zachary to go to Antarctica, True goes with him."

Now it was my best friend who protested. "Me? In tha' icebox for six months wit' a bunch of boring old men? Are ye tryin' tae neuter me, Brandy girl?"

"I'm trying tae neuter that Chinese vixen. Yer there tae prevent any alone time between Zachary and Dr. Liao before they descend intae that lake. So help me God, True MacDonald, if I hear my man so much as sits next tae her at breakfast, I'll skin the two of ye alive—starting with yer short and curlies."

5 months later...

6

August, die she must. The autumn winds blow chilly and cold;
September, I remember. A love once new has now grown old.
— Simon & Garfunkel, *"April Come She Will"*

13 September

For five months Vostok hung over my existence like a death sentence handed down by an oncologist. It greeted me every morning when I awoke, and it haunted my last thoughts before I succumbed to sleep.

What exactly was I afraid of? Being the anal-retentive left-brained thinker that I was, I mentally cataloged my fears into more easily digestible categories for self-analysis.

Fear of Separation: Six months would be a long time to be separated from my family. William was rapidly passing through infancy into the terrible twos, and each day seemed to introduce us to another facet of his burgeoning personality. I simply couldn't get enough of him and arranged for my sabbatical from Cambridge to begin in June so I could spend the summer with him and Brandy back in Drumnadrochit.

I had read that Antarctic missions were especially hard on marriages, and mine was already strained. Though we had reconciled, it was painfully obvious that Brandy felt threatened by Ming's combination of looks and intelligence. Not that my wife wasn't smart or pretty—she was both. But she lacked a formal education and never had the opportunity to go to college, something Ming and I shared. As spring bled into summer, Brandy grew increasingly more temperamental, actually believing that my father and I had conspired to get her to accept my excursion to Antarctica by using the "infamous Wallace cunning."

In her own way, Brandy eased my burden. By the time September rolled around I couldn't wait to get out of earshot of her accusations—not a good way to part.

Was I interested in the exotic Dr. Liao? I'd be lying if I said there wasn't an attraction, but Brandy was still my girl.

Then again, six months was a long time.

Back to my list.

Claustrophobic Fears: This was the dark cloud that had hung over my existence since I'd drowned and been revived in the Sargasso Sea. Despite Hintzmann's assurances, the reality was that our three-man submersible would be smaller than the *Massett-6*, the sub that had cracked open at a depth of 4,230 feet.

Imagine taking a twenty-hour road trip without being allowed to stop and stretch. To prepare myself, I created a mini-sub cockpit out of cardboard and sat in it for three- to five-hour stretches. Willy would climb in my lap with his favorite book, *Goodnight Moon*, and we'd read together and fall asleep.

What can't be simulated are the effects of a trillion-ton frozen ceiling of ice more than two miles thick. To reach Vostok's frigid waters would require us to plunge down a laser-melted hole that would reseal behind us. The pressure capping our 13,100-foot-deep entry point would generate 4,000 to 5,000 pounds per square inch of pressure on our sub—a pound of pressure for every dollar Angus had been advanced out of *my* paycheck.

Thanks again, Pop.

Adding to my fear of enclosed spaces was the fact that, save for the sub's internal displays and external lights, we'd be operating in complete blackness. If the power went out, or if we hit something, *or if something hit us...*

That last thought led to my final category of fear: Irrational Fear of the Unexpected. It included encounters with hydrothermal vents that spewed water hot enough to melt the seals on our sub and regressed into alien algae blooms that could clog our engines.

And, of course, there were lake monsters.

Two years had passed since I'd nearly died in the jowls of one monster. Though I seriously doubted anything larger than a slug occupied Vostok's waters, we would be entering an unexplored subglacial lake one hundred and forty miles *longer* and thirty miles *wider* than Loch Ness, energized by the same geothermal vents that had induced life on our planet 3.8 billion years ago.

Who knew what was down there?

A sane person would have walked away from this potential train wreck. Yet as much as I dreaded the trip, the scientist in me couldn't wait to explore Vostok.

The more I researched it, the more I realized the lake was a gift to science and scientists throughout the world. To be among the first three humans to venture into its untarnished waters would cement my reputation forever.

Named after the Russian outpost established in East Antarctica in December of 1957, Lake Vostok was first theorized by a Soviet scientist named Peter Kropotkin, who made an aerial observation of an island of flat ice sandwiched around mountainous drifts. Two years later another Russian, Andrey Kapitsa, used seismic soundings to measure the thickness of the ice sheet around Vostok Station and hypothesized the existence of a subglacial lake. Still, few believed the lake could be liquid until the 1970s, when British scientists performing airborne ice-penetrating radar surveys of the plateau declared the unusual readings indicated the presence of liquid freshwater in Vostok's vast basin. In 1991, a remote-sensing specialist from the United States directed the ERS-1 satellite's high-frequency array at Vostok, confirming the British surveys.

More of a subterranean cavern than a lake, Vostok was divided into two deep basins by a ridge. The northern basin plunged thirteen thousand feet; the southern basin reached twice that depth. The ridge itself was situated in seven hundred feet of water and, as incredible as it seemed, harbored an island.

82

* * *

The weeks of summer flew by. To my father's credit, his "monster mania" had resurrected tourism in the Great Glen for at least one more season, turning a potential economic disaster into a windfall. In fact, more tourists visited Loch Ness that summer than any other location in all of the United Kingdom or Europe.

But the "Hero of the Highlands" never apologized to me for his deeds or for the potential dangers associated with my upcoming deployment. And when the day finally came to say goodbye, I refused to see him.

For the hundredth time that summer, I read my infant son his favorite book as I rocked him to sleep in his stroller by the ruins of Urquhart Castle. *"In a great green room, tucked away in bed, is a little bunny. Goodnight room, goodnight moon... ."*

Brandy and I spent that last hour holding hands. Then the taxi arrived and it was time to go. I absorbed one last memory of those green hills, the gray cliff face, and the foam spraying off of the tea-colored waters, and asked my Maker to bring me home again to my wife and child—just not in a box.

True climbed in the back of the cab and slapped me hard on the knee. "So? How soon do ye want to get shitfaced?"

"As soon as we get on the plane."

* * *

Our flight out of Inverness was scheduled to depart at five o'clock on a Sunday evening, beginning the first leg of our journey—a twenty-seven-hour trip that included stops in Birmingham, Paris, Santiago, Puerto Montt, and finally Punta Arenas, Chile. After spending a day recouping in the southernmost city in South America, we would board a seaplane for King George Island, where a cargo plane would be waiting to fly us across the continent to Davis Base in East Antarctica. From there we'd have another day to adjust before flying out to the new bio-dome being erected over Lake Vostok.

Lying back in my first-class seat next to my snoring friend, I closed my eyes and attempted to organize my mental notes on our frozen destination.

At just over eight million square miles, Antarctica was bigger than both Australia and the United States combined, with ninety-seven percent of its land mass covered by an ice sheet that averaged two miles thick. The only continent not to possess an indigenous human population, Antarctica was divided into three distinct sections: its east and west regions and the peninsula.

A short flight for tourists arriving from Chile, the Antarctic Peninsula, nicknamed the "Banana Belt" by snarky scientists, included the South Orkney Islands and South Georgia. The peninsula's climate was mild compared to the rest of the continent and was home to a myriad of summer wildlife that included seals, whales, birds, and the emperor penguin. The male emperor penguin was the only warm-blooded animal that remained in Antarctica throughout the winter months. Their job: to stay on land and keep their offspring's egg warm by covering it with a flap of abdominal skin. While the females swam off to warmer waters, the males huddled in groups in sub-zero conditions, often going nine weeks or more without eating.

And here I was complaining about a twenty-hour sub ride.

West Antarctica occupied the landmass below the peninsula and was separated from the larger eastern region by the Transantarctic Mountains, TAM for short. It possessed two immense ice shelves: the Ronne and the Ross, the latter being home to McMurdo Station and its four airfields, owned and operated by the United States.

East Antarctica was the largest of the three regions and spanned two-thirds of the continent. It stretched from the TAM clear to the eastern coastline and encompassed the South Pole. A desert of ice, East Antarctica was the coldest, most desolate location on the planet.

Being in the Southern Hemisphere, Antarctica's spring and

summer, and its extended hours of daylight hours, were the reverse of Scotland, running from October through February. Darkness arrived in March, and the temperatures plunged another forty degrees. The mean annual temperature at our East Antarctica destination was minus fifty-six degrees Fahrenheit. We could hope for summer highs in November and December approaching zero degrees.

The coldest temperature ever measured on Earth was a boneshattering minus 135.8, recorded in East Antarctica… at Russia's Vostok Station.

After twenty hours in the air, the last plane ride of our first leg of travel touched down at the Presidente Carlos Ibáñez del Campo International Airport in Punta Arenas, Chile, just after seven o'clock in the evening. Exhausted, True and I collected our luggage and stepped outside into the frigid night. A taxi took us to the Blue House, a hostel Ming's assistant had booked us into for our stay. The moment my head hit the pillow, I passed out. Not even True's grumbling snores could keep me awake.

* * *

The southernmost city in the world, Punta Arenas is known as the gateway to the Chilean Antarctica. Perched on a hillside overlooking the Straits of Magellan, the Spanish town is a mix of colonial architecture and low-rise buildings with colorful metal roofs. Miles of gridded streets face the sea. Windswept grasslands and sheep ranches sprawl to the east, spectacular fjords and glaciers to the west.

True and I rolled out of our beds around noon, more from hunger than a restful sleep. Following the advice of the hostel owner, we bundled up in our ski jackets and wool hats and walked along the wide avenues past street vendors until we arrived at a stone building that was home to la Luna, a popular tourist spot. True ordered the crab casserole while I had scallops stewed in a garlic sauce, and we drank until we were tipsy.

The night and its drop in temperature arrived early. We

shopped, checked out the seaport, and ate dinner in a pub where True attempted to bridge the language gap with our Portuguese waitress. Reminding him we had a noon flight, I returned to our room alone and called Brandy from a land line. Forgetting about the time change, I woke her from a sound sleep and caught hell for being drunk.

Two days down, 182 to go.

* * *

My first official trepidation of the trip began when I walked across the runway beneath a low ceiling of dark clouds and saw the twenty-six-passenger Aerovías DAP seaplane rocking with the weather. A rough take-off and instantly it seemed we were flying over the Magellan Strait and Tierra del Fuego Island past Cape Horn. We dipped and rose with each gust, the pilot momentarily derailing our thoughts of crashing by pointing out a stretch of shoreline that was known as a whale graveyard, the bones of the dead leviathans cast up on the rock-strewn beach by the heavy currents.

The winds grew nastier as we flew over the Drake Passage, one of the more volatile waterways in the world. It was here that the depths dropped in excess of sixteen thousand feet—roughly the distance Ben Hintzmann and I would soon be plunging through ice. True and I watched the turbulent surface. We saw whales breaching and schools of dolphin torpedoing through the deep blue sea as, high overhead, our plane pitched against the elements. Before long, small islands of ice began appearing below, progressing into frozen sculptures of towering white and turquoise and blue, carved by the wind and shaped by the water. These were followed by flat city blocks of snow that quickly occupied the horizon.

After a harrowing five-hour flight we descended to King George Island.

* * *

Located seventy-five miles north of Antarctica, King George

86

Island was the largest of the South Shetlands, an island chain that extended away from the peninsula into the Southern Ocean. Still in its final weeks of winter, King George's surrounding seas remained fragmented with tabular acres of ice undulating beneath an early evening overcast sky.

Dressed in thermal underwear, jeans, gloves, wool caps, sunglasses, and our expedition jackets, True and I stepped off the plane into the elements and realized our attire was barely serviceable for the "Antarctic tropics," let alone what awaited us at Vostok. Trudging over a pebble-covered frozen dirt runway in our boots, we hurried past two abandoned Russian amphibious haulers on our way to the airport terminal, the skin over our exposed faces tightening painfully as it froze.

Gasping for breath, I paused. Up on the hill to our left, overlooking the airfield, was a Russian Orthodox Church that appeared like something out of an Alfred Hitchcock movie. True nudged me and pointed to our right.

We were being watched.

Penguins. Ten to fifteen of them stood on the packed snow like a welcoming party. From their markings I surmised they were chinstrap penguins. As we watched, three more suddenly popped out of an unseen ice hole in the water straight onto their feet, standing with their wings extended as they cooled off from their swim.

Unlike the penguins, True and I were not doing well in the freezing cold. Ducking against the wind, we continued across the unpaved airfield to the airport terminal.

Waiting for us inside was a fit-looking man in his twenties. Around his neck hung an I.D. badge that read Caner Gokeri—Davis Station.

"Caner? Zachary Wallace. This is my associate True MacDonald. Are you our liaison?"

"Yes, sir. And it's pronounced John-Air Go-Carry. It's a Turkish name. There's a Hercules C-130 transport on loan from the

Uruguayan Air Force waiting to take you to Davis Station, but before you board I've been instructed to outfit you for the weather."

"Glad you said that. It's pretty damn cold outside."

Caner smiled. "This is balmy compared to where you're going. Summer runs from mid-November through mid-February on the ice, and even then you'll be lucky to hit minus twenty. If you gentlemen will follow me, I've borrowed one of the lounges to get you suited up."

Caner told us he was a graduate student in the United States studying marine biology and was a fan of my work. He had been at Davis Station for a year, earning his keep as a cook while completing research in the environmental sciences. "Most of the people working at ice stations have college degrees, yet few of us ever end up doing scientific work related to our field of study. More important than publishing a research paper is just *being here*. There's simply no where else like it."

We followed him through the near-deserted terminal and down a corridor, stopping at a closed door labeled AUX-3. Keying the lock, he led us inside.

The smell of breakfast hit me first, the aroma coming from heated trays of food occupying a foldout table. Laid out on several other tables were neat piles of clothing and an assortment of gloves and boots. "This is ECW gear—Extremely Cold Weather clothing, designed especially to handle prolonged exposure to the elements. In addition, I personally customized a few items based on my own experiences on the ice. Vostok-cold requires extra care. For instance, I sewed fleece patches onto the quad section of your thermal underwear."

"What in God's name for, lad?" True asked, his mouth stuffed with scrambled eggs.

"There's a condition we call 'Antarctic thigh,' which is severe frostbite of the quads. It's caused by walking into the wind. And the wind gusts will also take your gloves and mittens, which is why I've sewn on elastic loops that connect them to your ski jacket. I also added kangaroo pouches in your thermal layers to store batteries and snacks. The key to staying warm out on the ice is layering your clothing loose enough to create insulating pockets of air. Too tight and you get frostbite. Go ahead and eat. Then we'll repack the belongings you'll be taking with you into Antarctica-friendly duffle bags."

An hour later we had stuffed ourselves with food, used the bathroom, and had completely reorganized our gear, eliminating most of the clothing we had brought from Scotland. Caner had us stow these items in our suitcases, which would be locked away at the airport and reclaimed in six months when we passed through on our return trip home. In its place were an assortment of lighter weight thermal undergarments and waterproof leggings, baggy pants shells, fleece trousers and sweaters, and two bright-orange jumpsuits designed to deflect the wind. We packed everything in duffle bags except for what we'd be wearing on the flight over. Stripping down to our boxer shorts, we redressed in layers, zipping ourselves up in the orange jumpsuits. On our feet we put two pairs of socks and double-lined rubber-insulated boots, and on our hands skin-tight gloves and elbow-high mittens. A wool scarf, wind-shielding snow hat, and tinted goggles completed the outfit, sealing every inch of exposed flesh on our bodies.

Slinging our bags over our shoulders, we grabbed our new ski jackets and followed Caner outside to an awaiting four-wheel-drive jeep, its rear axle sporting triangular-shaped traction belts, its front outfitted with skis. He drove us to another runway where a C-130 transport was being loaded through its rear cargo hold. Maneuvering around pallets of supplies, he parked as close as he could to the open entrance.

"This is as far as I go, gentlemen. Find a seat on board and try to catch some sleep. Oh, and be sure to remove your boots. This is a lightly pressurized transport plane, and your Wellington boots, unlike your feet, aren't designed to expand."

Accepting his parting gift—a set of earplugs—we exited the

jeep and made our way up the ramp with our gear and into the body of the military-outfitted Hercules. We passed the in-flight bathroom (a port-a-potty strapped to a cargo palette at the center aft of the plane) and located two vacant spots on rows of bench seating that faced one another. Stowing our gear, we removed our boots and sat, leaning back against a wall of webbed straps like paratroopers. Our window—one of only six in the cargo hold—was a mere four inches in diameter.

True leaned over and punched me on the shoulder.

"Ow. What was that for, you big lummox?"

"That was for marrying my sister and gettin' me stuck on this ridiculous trip."

Men in beards as thick as True's filed in along either side of us, squeezing us in like sardines. Some were private contractors, a few were scientists, and none seemed especially happy to be on board.

Another twenty minutes passed before the cargo hatch was closed. A few minutes later the plane rumbled across the gravel and dirt tarmac, gaining lift on its massive wings. The noise from the Hercules's four engines sent True and me on a pocket-to-pocket search for our earplugs.

For the next third of a day, we slept and woke in our throttling, pitching funhouse of steel and humanity. I cursed my bladder, which forced me to inch my way through rows of dozing bodies only to enter a tilted toilet shed of sloshing urine and excrement, wedging myself in as I peeled away three layers of clothing just to free my organ and pee—all while the cargo hold rose and plunged beneath me like a bucking bronco.

Three times I repeated that journey, four hours I slept, and True punched me twice more before we mercifully landed at Davis Station on the eastern coast of Antarctica.

7

Davis Station, East Antarctica

Barely awake, I grabbed my gear and followed True down the rear exit ramp of the aircraft, only to have my unprotected eyes assaulted by a brilliant hazy-white wonderland of ice. Seconds later, a forty-mile-an-hour gust of minus twenty-seven-degree wind blasted us in the face with a flurry of frozen crystals and abominable cold.

True turned to me and I could read his thoughts: *Welcome to East Antarctica— asshole.*

The two of us struggled to position our goggles on our faces as the other passengers pushed by, shaking their cloaked heads at our lack of preparedness.

Once I could see through my tinted eyewear, I stepped down from the plane and onto the frozen runway to get my bearings. Prydz Bay was to my left. I knew it was the bay because there was a massive tanker frozen in its icy grip. Beyond the ship were jagged hills that I learned were actually the tops of icebergs. Had the vessel not been there, the alabaster geology would have looked no different than the rest of our surroundings, and I wondered if any rookie expeditioners had ever taken a wrong turn off the base and simply walked out to sea.

To my right was the plane's exodus—sixty-plus passengers making their way to a series of lime-green-colored metal buildings connected by an enclosed walkway.

I followed True, using his girth to shield me from the wind.

Waiting for us inside, checking names off of his clipboard list, was the Davis Station flag officer, a senior geologist named Kyle Trunk.

"Names?"

"Zachary Wallace and True MacDonald."

The scientist's hazel eyes took their inventory. "Well, well, so the hotshot marine biologist and his Scottish lackey have finally—"

The flag officer never got out the word *arrived*. Having spent most of the last seventy-two hours cramped on planes while he was forced to remain sober, True was in no mood for a fraternal tongue-lashing.

Smiling, he grabbed a fistful of the man's crotch and squeezed hard. "Now, who are ye callin' a lackey, laddie? Don't ye ken who I am? I'm the prince of Scotland, and it would be best for your future kin if ye bloody well treated me as such."

The scientist's face flushed purple as he gurgled a frightened, "Sorry."

True released him. "Now be a good boy and show us to our rooms. I'm in need of a shyte, shower, and sleep."

Kyle Trunk backed away. "Davis rations its water supply. Showers are limited to one per person every three days for a maximum duration of three minutes."

"Three minutes? Tha's barely enuff water tae clean my pecker. The bloody place is surrounded by ice. Why don' ye jis melt it?"

"We have to conserve fuel. There's a bar in the Rec Room across from the mess hall. Why don't you let me buy you gents a drink when I'm through checking in guests?"

"We're only staying the night," I said, stepping between Kyle Trunk and True. "Our destination's Vostok."

"Change of plans. We have you scheduled to stay at Davis for two weeks. Captain Hintzmann's orders."

* * *

I found Ben Hintzmann in the mess hall eating lunch, the chin hairs of his beard specked with cream drippings from the bowl of New England clam chowder he was gulping down.

"Hey, Doc! Welcome to the ice. You look 'episched.'"

"*Episched?*"

"Sorry, I've been out here way too long. 'Exhausted, finished, dead and done for.' It's Antarctic slang. Hope that transport you rode in on was carrying fresh fruit and veggies. We had none of it this winter, and yours was the first plane of spring. I'd kill for boiled potatoes and carrots."

"The dude with the clipboard and attitude said we're not flying out to Vostok for two weeks. Why not?"

"Consider it a blessing. The weather out there makes Davis look like a fall day in Manhattan. There were delays in erecting the dome, plus the crates with the Valkyrie units only arrived two days ago. While Ming organizes her team, I'll teach you how to pilot the *Barracuda* here in Prydz Bay."

"The *Barracuda*? Is that the name of our submersible?"

"That'd be her, a narrow three-man acrylic vehicle featuring two Valkyrie lasers, one mounted on each flank. The generators necessary to power those puppies will remain on the surface, attached by fiber-optic cable, but the *Barracuda* will house miniature fuel cells capable of powering one four-hour laser burn—enough to get us topside in case of an emergency. Feel better now?"

I smiled. In fact, I did feel better... a lot better. The possibility of having our sub detach from the Valkyries' power supply unit had been among my worst fears. Apparently, Hintzmann's too. He had addressed it, and now I could rest more easily.

"I'm feeling episched, so I'm going to bed. Wake me in a day." Stealing Ben's soup, I raised the bowl to my lips and drained it, then headed off to my living quarters, a private room *negotiated* by my Highland "lackey."

* * *

Thirty hours later, True, Ben, and I stood on the frozen

waters of Prydz Bay beneath "manky" skies. *Manky* was Antarctic slang for overcast weather, apparently a common occurrence along the coast. A team of Chinese technicians from nearby Zhongshan Station used six-foot-long bog chisels to test the thickness of the sea ice before bringing out the *Barracuda*. "More than three whacks to get through and it's safe to walk on," Ben informed us. "Less than three and you double-time it back to where you came from."

After ten blows the ice failed to crack open, forcing the Chinese to use their chainsaws to open a twenty-by-fifteen-foot hole to access the sea.

Ben expected our days inland at Vostok would be "dingle"—good weather, good visibility. "On a dingle day it's time to play; wake up to a mank and the day will be dank."

Worse than a mank was a "hooley"—an Antarctic blower, also known as a katabatic wind. Formed when cold air descends onto the ice cap, it spreads along the ground like a relentless snow-blowing storm and can last for days.

I wasn't particularly excited about meeting a katabatic, but I rather enjoyed the Antarctic slang, which was far different from the Highlander vernacular, yet just as alien. Created by the OAE's (Old Antarctic Explorers), the vocabulary attempted to simultaneously label and judge everything Antarctic, from the extreme conditions to the people who visited.

I learned quickly that rookies were chastised until they earned respect, and respect translated into time on the ice. Summer visitors earned far less respect than winterers, and as such, True and I were identified as "hordes"—less than welcome newbies.

Before he had gone to bed in his "pit-room," True had stopped by the bar for his promised nightcap. The general rule at bases is that you only drink what you bring, but Kyle Trunk was treating. Exacting his revenge, the flag officer offered the big fella a vodka on the rocks, the rocks being natural Antarctic ice, a substance that dates back hundreds of thousands of years and contains captured bubbles of environmental gas that, when warmed with alcohol, pop. Hangovers induced from "poppies" were particularly onerous, and when True awoke he had a bear of a headache. Seeking caffeine, he found his way to the mess hall where another officer presented him with a mug of coffee known as a "grumble bucket." It seemed like a nice gesture until True drained the cup to find a lurker at the bottom of the unwashed container.

Welcome to the ice, ye Summer Jolly Merchant!

Ben was classified a "fidlet," a winterer entering his first summer. On our jeep ride out to the bay, he taught us two new words he had learned his second week on the ice.

A "slot" was a crevasse formed when a glacier, moving over the underlying bedrock, cracks open from the top down to form a pie-shaped wedge. Being "slotted" is what happened to Ben's Australian guide when the man stepped onto a bridge of wind-blown snow that collapsed into a twenty-foot-wide crevasse.

"It happened so fast," Ben said. "One minute he was walking back to the sled to grab a pair of binoculars, the next he was gone. I heard him scream a full thirty seconds before his body slammed into a tight wedge a mile and a half down—a nightmare known as "corking in." Poor bastard died down there, all busted up in the darkness while we tried to reach him. Slots scare the hell out of me. Everyone's got to be roped in on the open ice. And don't think you're safer in a vehicle either; jeeps get slotted, too."

Standing out on the frozen waters of Prydz Bay eliminated the risk of being slotted, but not the risk of freezing to death. Ben informed us that Antarctic seawater averaged twenty-seven degrees, a sub-freezing temperature made possible due to the high salt content, which lowered its freezing point several degrees. "The human body can withstand about thirty seconds of exposure in water that cold before the muscles seize and cease to function. You'll survive fifteen minutes if you are bobbing in a life vest. Either way, your blood feels like it's turning to lead."

It was into these sub-freezing waters that Ben and I would be taking the *Barracuda* on its maiden voyage. With all the ways one could die in Antarctica, we were about to toss the dice on another—an untested machine.

Even so, the moment the tarp was removed from the submersible I couldn't wait to get started.

Ben was right; the *Barracuda* was nothing like the three-man sub I had drowned and nearly died in two years ago. Sleek and torpedo-shaped, the watercraft reminded me of something you'd find on the Bonneville Salt Flats, only with a windshield that extended all the way to its front bumper. Inside this four-inch-thick acrylic pod were three rotatable seats, placed in tandem with their own command centers. I was assigned the forward position, Ben the center, and Ming in back, allowing her to control the sub's collection tubes and grabbers. The two Valkyrie units were mounted along either side of the vessel like missiles, the collector arms and storage bins located aft of her wings, folded out of the way by her keel. The bow was reinforced, narrow, and hydrodynamic, the outer chassis surrounding the cockpit painted dark neon blue, rendering her invisible in the deep blue sea.

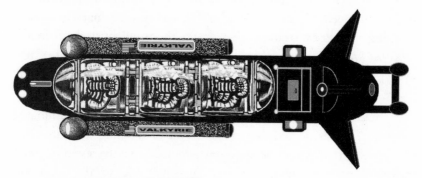

Ben stood next to her like a proud papa. "Stone Aerospace designed her shape so that she'd slide through the lasered ice funnel like a greased dart. Once we enter the lake, the wings hyperextend away from the chassis to give us more stability. We lose a bit of protection going with an oval interior pod instead of a standard sphere, but she still withstood eight thousand psi during lab tests, which is forty percent more than Vostok's surface pressure and twenty percent more than the lake's maximum depth. The acrylic is composed of quartz Lexan.

"Forward and aft ports house our high-definition night-vision cameras and broad-spectrum floodlights, in addition to the sonar array and hydrophone mics. Body panels are composed of titanium and a composite material called Isofloat, developed by the Aussies to withstand water pressure in excess of fifteen thousand pounds per square inch. Behind the cockpit is an accessible storage area that holds eighteen lithium-ion batteries. The engine pumps out four hundred and fifty horsepower and runs on rechargeable batteries and hydrogen cells, and I can't wait to see what she does when we let her run in open water."

"Why'd they make her so narrow?"

"Had to. Ice penetration rate is inversely proportional to the square of the diameter of the vehicle. Every time you double the vehicle's diameter, you increase the power requirements by four times. Once we're in Lake Vostok, we'll be running autonomously. Of course the beauty of the design is that we'll still be able to suck power from the surface generators."

"Unless the fiber-optic cable snaps."

"Even if that happens, we're still self-sustained for up to twenty hours at maximum cruising speed. Stop being such a naysayer. If you're still scared after all these precautions, then maybe the real problem is that you need to grow a bigger pair of balls."

True stepped between us, shoving Ben backward toward the hole in the ice. "Listen tae me, *sub pilot*. I witnessed our boy here descend intae Loch Ness to bait himself to a fanged beast forty feet long, wearing nothing but a Newtsuit—nearly got himself swallowed whole. When *you* pull a stunt like that ye can go 'round setting the standard for scrotes. Until then shut yer yap hole, or I'll shut it for ye."

Ben grinned nervously. "Personally, I have no intention of ever using a dive suit to perform an endoscopy on a fish."

True continued advancing, backing Ben closer to the edge of the rectangular hole in the ice.

"Oh, sorry. I can tell by the empty gaze in your eyes that my endoscopy reference went completely over your thick head. See, True, an endoscopy shoots a probe down your esophagus. In your case, however, I'd recommend a colonoscopy... to see what crawled up your ass."

True pushed Ben again, causing the heel of the sub pilot's right rubber boot to skid out over the rectangular hole in the ice.

"Hey, uh... Doc. Wanna call Thor off of me?"

"His name is True and he doesn't appreciate American sarcasm. For the record, neither do I."

Balancing on one leg, Hintzmann was no longer smiling. "I'm warning you, Doc. Call Haggis Harry here off before someone gets hurt."

True looked back at me and winked.

Oh, geez.

"True, don't."

But True did. He shoved Ben in the chest with both hands—only Ben was too quick. He grabbed the big fella's wrist and elbow as he dropped to one knee and took out his knees in a ju-jitsu move that sent my friend sprawling headfirst into the sea with a tremendous splash.

The Chinese laughed.

I ran to the edge of the hole as True surfaced, his face pale, his eyes wide in shock as he gasped for breath, his mitten-covered hands unable to grip the edge of the ice to pull himself out.

"Zach... help... me!"

"Give me your hand!"

Ben held me back. "There's no leverage, he'll pull you in." He signaled to the Chinese, who were already attaching a nylon rope to the back of the jeep.

I grabbed the free end and made a quick noose.

Barely able to keep his head above water, True managed to reach one dripping-sleeved arm up to me. I slipped the noose around his wrist and pulled tight.

Seconds later the jeep's driver moved slowly ahead. The slack tightened and hoisted True up and out of the hole like a sedated walrus.

I stepped over the shivering Scot and untied the line. "Hang in there, buddy, we'll have you warm in no time." I helped him up as the Chinese wrapped him with blankets and guided him into the front passenger seat. The driver hit the gas and headed back to Davis Station.

I confronted Ben. "That wasn't necessary."

"Learn this now; I'm a survivor. Your friend will be fine, but if he comes after me again with that crazed look in his eye I'll put him in the hospital for the duration of this mission and it'll be on your head. Now you wanna take this little girl out for a test drive or not?"

I glanced back at the submersible. The Chinese handlers were opening the sleek machine's interior pod. "The front seat is mine?"

"Best seat in the house. The first two cockpits have dual controls. The middle console has the master override. It's easier if you remove your boots before you climb in. Once we crank up the heat, we'll stow our jackets in back."

Following his advice, I climbed into the forward cockpit, noticing my bow compartment and grey leather bucket seat were sunk a foot below Ben's, sort of like the cockpit of an Apache helicopter. Sacrificing warmth for comfort, I removed my jacket and buckled the safety harness so that the dual straps crossed my chest in an X configuration.

"Get in already; I'm freezing my ass off."

Ben climbed in and hit a control switch to close the hatch. When it sealed, he buckled in and then pointed to a power switch on my forward dash. "Care to do the honors?"

I removed my mittens and pushed a gloved index finger to the control.

The pump-jet propulsor engine growled to life beneath us. The vents blasted us with cold air, forcing me to use my jacket as a blanket.

"Give it a few minutes. It'll warm up." Ben pointed to a joystick attached to my right armrest. "The joystick controls direction, pitch, and yaw. Flip the toggle switch up and the system activates. I have to power mine off to activate yours. There are two foot pedals on the floor. Each controls one of the props."

He pointed to the center of my dashboard at a sonar array. "Headphones are on that hook by your right knee. Ever use sonar before?"

"Assume I know nothing."

"Okay, I'll teach you once we're moving. Ready to go?"

"That's it? Isn't there some kind of checklist you need to go over?"

"What'd you have in mind?"

"I don't know. Should I buckle these straps dangling by my legs?"

"Seems like a good idea." I heard him buckle his.

"What about the rest of these controls? I'd like to know how to use them, just in case something happens to you."

Ben smirked. "What's going to happen to me down there that isn't going to happen to you?"

"I don't know. You could have a stroke. The point is I want to be prepared."

"That's the problem with you eggheads; you always have to read the instruction manual before you test drive the car. Me? I prefer to hit the highway and learn on the job."

Rapping his knuckles on the glass above his head, Ben gave

one of the techs a thumbs-up.

I held on as the four men pushed us toward the freshly carved rectangular hole in the ice. "This is how you're going to launch us? By pushing us in like… like my father taught me how to swim?"

"Yours did that, too?"

"Oh, geez!" I gripped the seat as we plunged bow-first into the dark blue world, our weight distribution continuing our forward roll into a full somersault as we fell like a sinking dagger.

With a sickening *crunch,* the Lexan dome struck bottom. Naturally buoyant, the sub bounced upward, only to be spun and inhaled by a powerful current that grabbed our inverted vessel and propelled us along the bottom.

I saw ice and then I saw stars as the *Barracuda* plowed bow-first and upside-down into the narrow space between the molar-shaped underside of an iceberg and the silt-covered sea floor.

"Well done," I said, the blood rushing to my face. "I hope this death trap has a reverse gear."

"Sit tight, I got this." Ben tapped the thrusters, attempting to torque us free, only to jam the inverted starboard fin in deeper.

"You're a maniac. No wonder the Air Force gave you the boot."

"Hey, you don't know shit about it, so shut up. And this little setback, it's all part of the learning process. Get the kinks out. We'll be out of here in no time."

"Maybe we can get a tow from a passing flock of penguins?"

"Stop talking and let me think."

"See, that's the trouble with you action-types, there's always time to think *after* you get your big balls caught in a vice."

"Yeah, but—"

"Butts are for crapping. Answer my question. Does this acrylic coffin have a reverse gear or not?"

101

"I was going to say you first have to manually reverse the drive shaft."

"Which I'm guessing you don't know how to do."

"It was on the top of my to-do list. There's a manual in the compartment by your right knee. Make yourself useful."

I fished the thick booklet out, my head throbbing. "Oh good, it's in Chinese. What's Mandarin for dickhead?"

"Screw the reverse gear. I'm powering up the Valkyries."

My pulse raced. "Have you ever done this before?"

"I haven't done any of this before. Should I give it the old Ivy League try, or would you prefer to just sit here until our air runs out?"

"Okay, okay. But *listen* first. Don't try to blast out the Holland tunnel. Just melt enough ice so that we have room to spin around in a tight circle and get out the way we came in."

"Got it."

"No, you don't *got it*! Evaporate too much ice in these conditions and it will create a vacuum effect which could suck us in deeper beneath the iceberg."

He paused as my words sank in. "Tap it and turn. Got it."

"Not yet, you don't. This has to be done simultaneously. One of us works the laser; the other jams one foot pedal down to the floor while turning the joystick hard to the same side. But only just enough to turn us 180 degrees, or we'll spin right back where we started, only deeper."

The berg groaned around us, sending the internal pod's psi readings from green to orange.

"Okay, Zach, which one do you want to do?"

"Give me the laser."

"I wanted to do the laser."

"What are you, a five-year-old? We need you to steer the damn sub. Now show me how to use the Valkyrie."

He pointed to an instrument panel on the center console. "The red light means the unit's powering up. When it turns green, engage the lasers by pressing these two buttons. Press them again to stop the beams."

I activated the fuel cells and waited, the blood rushing to my head, sweat dripping down my neck into my scalp. "Okay, it's green. You ready?"

"Yeah. Wait, quick question. If we're upside down and I want to turn us counterclockwise—"

"Tap your left foot on the throttle and follow it with your joystick."

"Which is now on my right, right?"

"Right. I mean, yes."

"Okay, we blast on three. One... two ... "

I stole a quick glance at the starboard Valkyrie, its business end glowing red.

"Three!"

I pressed both buttons. The sea boiled in a veil of orange bubbles as we spun hard seventy degrees counterclockwise and jammed, the wounded iceberg groaning above our feet. We continued firing and throttling until our field of vision yielded deep blue again.

The submersible leaped into the void. Ben executed a quick semi-barrel roll, which returned our world right-side up, then stabilized our yaw by extending the vessel's pectoral fins.

For several moments we simply laid our heads back and breathed as the sub rose slowly in neutral.

We both jumped as the acrylic dome above our heads collided with a ceiling of sea ice.

"Want to teach me how to use the sonar now, or would you rather wait until you plow us into a wall of glacial ice?"

For the next forty minutes, Ben taught me how to distinguish objects in the sea using active and passive sonar, as well as how to comprehend the sub's fuel gauge, battery range, and life-support system readings.

Finally feeling more like a copilot than a passenger, I called out obstacles on sonar while Ben steered us through a frozen labyrinth.

What was it like to dive the Antarctic sea in a submersible? In a word: breathtaking. The extreme cold was an exotic entity of nature that affected everything around us. As sea ice, it formed a seemingly endless ceiling that resembled an overcast December sky, its thicker patches dark and gray, its thinner veils streaked in bolts of neon-blue sunlight. Brine channels hung surreally from the frozen surface like hollow stalactites, their tubular openings bleeding liquid saline into the clear blue underworld.

Below us, bright pink starfish and clumps of anchor ice that resembled crystal tumbleweeds spotted a silt-brown bottom. Every so often a sea urchin or a rock would seem to defy gravity and rise from the sea floor, shanghaied to a glob of ice whose buoyancy would pin it to the ceiling.

Touching the inside surface of the acrylic pod, I could feel the penetrating cold held at bay by technology. Listening to the sea, we heard strange chirping sounds, the mating calls of Weddell seals mixed with the rumblings of grounded icebergs. In the coming weeks the sea ice would crack open and release these masses from a winter's purgatory, and their roots would plow the bottom as they flowed out of Prydz Bay, ripping out long gashes that would create new havens for marine life.

Leaving the bay, we headed out to the open ocean. The sea ice dissipated, and our surroundings became liquid blue. Pinging the area, I detected something immense floating on the surface a mile to the east. It was a tabular berg, the largest type of iceberg. Formed when large portions of an ice shelf break off and drift free, these glacier-like ice sheets can span several square miles, their sheer white cliffs towering hundreds of feet above the surface and reaching a thousand feet below.

Ben surfaced the sub so that we could take a look. The berg was a plateau of ice as big as three aircraft carriers, its waterline ringed by a turquoise lagoon, an effect created by its submerged alabaster mass. A twenty-foot ledge, forged by lapping waves, hung over the surface.

The face of the berg was mesmerizing—a two-hundred-foot-high curl that resembled a tidal wave frozen in time. Dark blue ice rose from the sea to form its textured vortex, melding into glistening clear ice capped by its snow-covered lip.

Antarctic clear ice was the oldest ice on the continent, its presence on the tabular berg tracing back to the glacier that calved it into Prydz Bay. Over eons, tons of snowfall had accumulated and had been compressed on the glacier. Air bubbles trapped in the ice were squeezed out, rendering the ice as clear as crystal and as old as half a million years.

The blue ice was a phenomenon associated with melting and re-freezing, a process that forced out trapped air, allowing the blue color in the visible light spectrum to pass through while blocking the red color.

Circling the tabular berg, we came upon a third color: green.

As glaciers cross the Antarctic continent, their roots crush and absorb minerals from the underlying bedrock. When the ice melts, phytoplankton feeds off the minerals and grows. In turn, krill feed on the phytoplankton, and penguins, seals, and whales feed on the krill.

The Antarctic food chain would not exist without its glaciers.

Hours later, we came across the top of that food chain.

We had been following a pair of minke whales. Thirty feet long, these ten-ton baleen mini-giants were less than half the girth of their rorqual cousins, the humpback and fin whales, and were quite plentiful in Antarctic waters. Ben was keeping us within visual distance of their white underbellies when a dozen blips suddenly popped onto my sonar screen.

Orca.

The wolves of the sea circled the minkes, separating the smaller female from its mate. Two big male orcas remained on the periphery, breaching high in the air to flop hard onto the surface as if to mark the kill zone.

The assaults were carried out by the juvenile killers and a few of the adult females. Over the next forty minutes, we watched from one hundred and seventy feet below the blood-drenched surface as the remaining minke fought to breathe—until one of the big bulls landed on its back in an attempt to drown it.

I turned in my seat and jumped, confronted by a black-and-white monster whose emerging presence occupied the entire starboard side of the acrylic glass. The bull killer whale stared at me as if we were a threat to its pod's dinner.

The sea became alive with squeals and clicks as the pack's males echolocated us. A nerve-racking game of cat-and-mouse ensued as the two six-ton predators bumped and prodded the *Barracuda* with their snouts until we vacated the area.

Dusk came quickly, offering us an opportunity to practice piloting in the dark. Ben engaged the exterior lights while I used the sub's sonar to guide us west through the shallows of Prydz Bay.

Four hours and twenty minutes after we had tumbled into the sea, the *Barracuda* leaped out of the water and slid onto the ice. Physically exhausted, Ben and I climbed out of the submersible and into the back of an awaiting snow vehicle while our underwater vessel was loaded onto its trailer.

* * *

We continued this training regimen over the next week, alternating our roles until I became a competent pilot. During this time, True occupied his days "recouping" in the company of a Swedish weather technician named Jennie Backman. I was thankful for her distraction.

Then on day eight, we received a radio communiqué from Vostok Dome, and everything changed.

8

Vostok, East Antarctica

Earplugs, bench seating with webbed backs, tiny windows, and a ride that induced hemorrhoids, we were back onboard another C-130 transport, this time bound for our final destination—a minus-forty-degree desert of ice located a thousand miles to the southeast of Prydz Bay.

Vostok. After six months of head games and fears, I was finally on my way. And I was truly excited. Perhaps it was the past week of training with Ben, but my attitude and confidence level had changed. The simple truth was that Vostok really *was* the holy grail of science, an unexplored frontier that could potentially reveal how life came to be on Earth. For whatever reason, Ben and I had been chosen among thousands of explorers to be its Neil Armstrong and Buzz Aldrin, and my ego was running wild.

The call from Ming Liao had upped the ante. Something had happened on the first Valkyrie drone launch, an unexpected find. Ming refused to provide any details other than to say that she wanted her two pilots on site immediately.

True was brooding. He had not wanted to leave his new lover. Conversely, I hadn't thought about my family since arriving at Davis. Part of it was the mental and physical demands of learning how to pilot the submersible; part of it was my own acceptance of the mission.

The gray-haired Russian scientist seated across from True and me had been staring at my face ever since we had taken off. Twenty minutes into the flight, he leaned toward me and shouted over the engine noise, "You are Wallace, yes?"

"Yes."

"Mikhail Kopilevich, geologist. This will be your first time at Vostok?"

"Yes. What about you?"

He snorted. "Eighteen summers on top of four winters. My first trip from Mirny Station was in winter on supply tractor. It took us entire week to travel thirteen hundred kilometers in minus twenty-five degrees Celsius. You know what is minus twenty-five degrees Celsius?"

"About minus seventy-eight degrees Fahrenheit." I leaned in. "How do you Russian scientists handle such extreme cold?"

He winked. "We know survival secrets."

"Anything you'd care to share?"

"First, you share something with me. Why does Chinese woman exclude my country from this new field operation? Without Russian Antarctic Expedition there is no Vostok Station. There is no discovery of lake."

"From what I understand, the coalition scientists involved in this new research station were afraid your team was not adhering to strict contamination protocols. You used Freon and kerosene to lubricate your borehole. Some of these chemicals tainted the bore samples and could have breached the lake."

The geologist snapped. "We stopped borehole before we reached lake! Vostok is under tremendous pressure. On breakthrough, water will rush up borehole, freeze, and seal chemical fluids."

"It's not my expedition, Dr. Kopilevich. I'm simply an invited guest."

"I think you are more than invited guest, Dr. Wallace. You should know new equipment is developed by St. Petersburg Nuclear Physics Institute to ensure lake remains uncontaminated upon intrusion. Visit our station; I will give you personal tour."

"Thank you."

"Consider this gift from new friend." The Russian reached

into his bag and removed a thirty-ounce tub of butter. "When Vostok weather becomes too cold, eat fistful of butter. It will make you warm inside."

* * *

Standing on an ice runway two hours later, I seriously contemplated scooping a mittenful of butter into my mouth.

Vostok greeted us with a punishing forty-mile-an-hour katabatic wind that dropped minus thirty-eight into another realm of cold. It abused our carefully planned layers of Extreme Cold Weather gear and seeped into our bones. It formed *snotsicles* on my upper lip and pelted my tinted goggles with shards of snow.

Dragging our duffle bags, we waddled like penguins to an awaiting bright red truck as our team of Chinese technicians loaded the crate containing the *Barracuda* onto a sled.

The Hägglund was a Swedish snow vehicle with cab space for eight passengers and a trailing sled that could tow up to two tons. Powered by a Mercedes turbo diesel engine, the truck rode on four rubber tracks and a loose suspension system that gave us a nauseating herky-jerky ride, made worse by its twelve-mile-an-hour maximum speed.

Forty torturous minutes later, we arrived at the dome.

The structure that housed the expedition was a three-story-high, three-hundred-fifty-foot-in-diameter geodesic dome, its gold-painted roof composed of an array of trianglular panels that were far more stable than the standard rectangular-cut structures. Highly resistant to snow, ice, and wind, the dome needed no internal columns or interior load-bearing walls, and required less power to heat than box architectural designs. Erected using prefabricated components, it could be disassembled if need be and moved quickly, which was a major consideration when taking into account the fact that Vostok's waters were spread out over 6,060 square miles. Different sections of the lake could produce vastly different discoveries—and life-forms.

110

Finding life in Vostok depended on two major issues. The first dealt with how the lake had formed. Was it simply a basin that had filled with meltwater fifteen million years ago, or had it been a flourishing natural lake that rapidly froze over during Antarctica's last major climate change? Geologists examining satellite photos generally agreed that Vostok's shape and location rendered it a natural rift lake, formed thirty million years ago when tectonic forces had split open to forge a long, narrow water basin. Surrounded by the East Antarctic highlands, Vostok's surface waters would have frozen over quickly when temperatures dropped, potentially entrapping its aquatic life-forms.

This led to one of the key questions our expedition had been organized to answer: had complex life-forms survived?

Most species found on Earth rely on food sources dependent on photosynthesis, the process by which plants make energy from sunlight. Vostok's waters were isolated in darkness, and yet in both the deep ocean and certain rift lakes, unique ecosystems had evolved based on a process by which certain microbes created energy through a chemical reaction called chemosynthesis. The process began when geothermal vents released superheated chemical-laced waters rich in hydrogen sulfide into the lake or sea. Chemosynthetic microbes spawn microbial mats, which in turn feed plants and grazers such as snails, limpets, and scaleworms. Fish consume the grazers, predators eat the fish, and suddenly you have the foundation of an entire ecosystem devoid of sunlight.

* * *

Our truck parked before the main entrance of the dome—a prefabricated aluminum structure that served as a weather room. Grabbing our gear, we braved the wind for another twenty strides and hurried inside, our boots tracking snow onto the rubber mats.

A sign was posted in English, Chinese, German, and French:

All Personnel must DEGOMBLE before entering dome.

Ben translated. "They want us to brush off the powdered

111

snow."

True took the opportunity to slap the back of my headgear clean of debris. "Wouldn't want ye tae mess up the dome, Dr. Wallace."

"True, if you're that unhappy being here, then just go home. Or catch the return flight back to Davis and carry on with the Swede. I really don't need a 260-pound babysitter with an attitude."

The big fella thought for a minute, then grinned. "Nah, I'll stay. Maybe Dr. Liao needs tae be degombled, ye think?"

"By you?" Ben blurted a sarcastic half-laugh. "Pal, she's so far out of your league you can't even see the playing field."

"A hundred dollars against your thousand says we bed together at least once before the mission is through."

"Done!" Ben shook True's hand. "I'll say this for you Highlanders—you aren't afraid to go down swinging."

"And I say him that's born to be hanged will never be drowned."

Having degombled, we entered the dome.

The temperature inside was a balmy thirty degrees, the air warmed by portable blowers, the ice covered by plywood sheets. Mobile lights pointed up at the domed ceiling, cabled to power generators that lined the periphery.

Ming had organized the facility into quadrants. Accommodations for her crew and the dozens of participating scientists were relegated to Tent City, an assortment of colorful nylon tents clustered by nationality. The smallest were single crawl-ins; the largest were six-person walk-ins with extended porches and multiple storage areas.

A mess station was set up next to the living areas. Crates held frozen microwavable meals, and coffee and hot beverages were available around-the-clock, provided one supplied his own mug and utensils. Folding tables and chairs accommodated diners and poker players. A row of port-a-potties lined the dome wall next to a supply trailer and first-aid tent.

The last two areas were devoted to science. Mission Control consisted of two long rows of folding tables that held three computer stations, a rack of video monitors, and a half-dozen crates on skis supporting the generators that supplied power to the Valkyrie units. An Army tent erected behind the command post doubled as a meeting area and Ming's sleeping quarters.

The last quadrant was almost completely occupied by a portable lab contained in an inflatable Level-3 containment bubble.

These four sections, each of which occupied about half an acre, surrounded a much larger central work area of exposed ice cordoned off by neon-orange fencing. Towering two stories above this site stood a gantry designed to hold our submersible.

Ben pointed to the chaos of twisted steel. "The *Barracuda* will be suspended nose-down for our launch. About a mile into our descent they'll begin pumping water into the hole to re-seal it behind us. We can't enter the lake until the hole is frozen over, otherwise the pressure will blast us back into the dome like Old Faithful."

I turned to see Ming exit the Army tent. She was wearing an orange fur-lined parka, jeans, and white "bunny boots" insulated with wool felt. Seeing us, she waved, a smile stretching across her tanned face as she approached.

Ben and I received bear hugs, True a nod. "Isn't this exciting? There's a briefing scheduled in my tent in one hour. Are you hungry? Let me call my assistant. She'll show you to your tents, and you can get something to eat before the meeting."

Using her walkie-talkie, she summoned a brown-eyed, blonde-haired American woman in her mid-twenties, sporting a track star's physique and a sorority girl smile. And just like that, True's attitude changed. "Gentlemen, this is my research assistant, Susan McWhite. Susan, this is Dr. Zachary Wallace, Captain Ben Hintzmann, and ... "

"Finlay MacDonald. But the ladies all call me True because

113

the rumors, well, they're all true."

Susan blushed as True kissed the back of her glove. "You're a feisty one."

"And a man who loves a good wager," added Ben.

"Susan, please show our guests to their tents. Make sure Dr. Wallace and Captain Hintzmann get something to eat before they join the briefing; we could be a while."

"Yes, Zachary. You and Captain Hintzmann go on without me." True winked. "Dr. Liao and I have a lot of catching up tae do."

"Mr. MacDonald, every person on this base has two jobs, yet you don't seem to have any. Susan, would you assign Mr. MacDonald to a task that fits his particular skill set?"

"Yes, ma'am. Let's see, sheepherding is out … "

True grinned. "This one's a pistol. I may have tae marry ye. But no worries, Ming, darlin', ours will be an open marriage."

* * *

Susan led us to three double-occupancy nylon tents set up in the English-speaking section of Tent City. "These three are yours. Inside you'll find sleeping bags, pillows, extra blankets, coffee mugs, and eating utensils. We're under strict water rations, so safeguard your silverware. Anything else you need," she glared at True, "any *supplies*, just see me."

We stowed our gear, then followed Susan to the dining area.

She hung back to speak with me. "Ming didn't mention it, but I'm a marine biologist specializing in cetaceans. I know you invented an acoustic lure for a giant squid. Did you ever think about creating something similar for humpback and gray whales?"

"Actually, I'm more interested in intra-species communication, especially among orca. Last week while we were training, Ben and I witnessed a pod of orca attack and kill two minke whales. The coordination of the hunt was incredibly

114

efficient.

"But now let me ask you something, Susan. As a cetacean expert, do you accept Darwin's theory that whales used to be land mammals? I believe in the first edition of his *Origin of Species* he claims the ancestors of whales were a race of bears, though the accepted natural-selection species is now a wolf-like carnivore called a *Mesonyx*."

"Honestly, Dr. Wallace, I've always disagreed with Darwin on this one. The first whales appeared about fifty million years ago. By most accounts there would have been tens of thousands if not millions of whales in the sea. That adds up to a mass exodus of a land species to a radically different environment. What would have caused it? And how do Darwin's theories regarding natural selection account for the incredible adaptations and mutations needed to change a relatively small land animal into a fifty- to one-hundred-ton leviathan able to swim deep in the ocean? The skeletal and physiological changes alone are collectively beyond reason, and yet we're expected to believe these evolutionary changes happened in only five to ten million years? Ridiculous."

"For the record, Susan, I agree. But I'd still like to hear your explanation."

"It's simple really. The ancestors of modern whales were prehistoric fish. Take *Leedsichthys*. Here was an eighty-foot prehistoric gill-breather with massive pectoral fins. Subtract the gills and add lungs and a blowhole and you have a humpback whale. Whale sharks siphon krill in a similar manner to baleen whales; orcas possess jaws similar to most sharks. Other than the manner in which the species breathe, the differences are subtle. Yes, the tail movements are different, but the horizontal movements of a fluke are an adaptation conducive to breathing above the surface. Which is easier to accept: that a *Leeds* fish could lose its gills and evolve a blowhole and lungs or that a four-legged wolf-like creature could shed its fur, alter its entire physiology, and increase its size a hundred fold to become a whale?"

"Point taken. But why would a fish become an air-breather in the first place?"

"Adaptations are necessitated by changes in diet and environment. I just think it's easier to accept an aquatic animal evolving an alternative means of processing oxygen and carbon dioxide than a wolf or bear entering the sea, losing its fur, limbs, and pelvis and growing a fluke."

"Want tae ken whit I think?" True interrupted, not waiting for a reply. "I think deid is deid. A million years from now, no one's gonna care if I breathed out of my mouth or my arse, or if Susan's eyes were slanted different than Ming's. What matters is love and who ye share yer sleeping bag with tae keep ye warm."

"Yes," I replied, "but I bet you'd care if a million years from now some archaeologist claimed your ancestors were English."

"Or jackasses," muttered Ben, a bit too loud.

"Excuse me, friend, but this is an A and B conversation, so C yer way oot of it."

I stepped in between them, guiding True to an aluminum vat filled with pea soup. I ladled us each a mugful while he filled our other cups with hot chocolate. "Ease up with the sexual connotations, big guy."

"I'm jist playing. Whit are ye doing?"

"I'm not doing anything."

"Oh, please. *To be honest, Susan, I'm more interested in intraspecies communication, specifically among orca.* Maybe ye can tutor her later in yer tent."

"She's a grad assistant studying to be a marine biologist. We were talking shop."

"Sure ye were. Jist do me a favor, and next time ye engage a woman not my sister in conversation, ask yerself if yer tryin' tae impress her with that big brain of yers, or the wee small fella dangling between yer legs."

* * *

Scientists, academics, and technicians from China, Australia, the United States, Canada, New Zealand, Britain, Germany, Japan, and France filed into the Army tent, quickly claiming one of the thirty folding chairs placed in a semi-circle facing a dry erase board. There may have been delegates present from other countries, but those were the only flag patches on ski jackets I could see from my vantage.

Missing from the meeting were members of the Russian Antarctic Expedition.

Ben and I found empty seats in the back, next to a large satellite photo of Lake Vostok taped to an easel. A white circle marked the location of the drone.

Ming was in a heated discussion with someone on her walkie-talkie. Ending the conversation, she took her place at the front of the tent. "Good afternoon. Dr. Jokinen is in the lab, finishing the analysis of water samples taken two days ago from Valkyrie Unit-1. While we are waiting, I'd like to introduce Dr. Zachary Wallace, our lead marine biologist, and Captain Ben Hintzmann, our submersible pilot."

Ben and I gave curt waves from our seats.

A silver-haired American turned to face us. "Kevin Coolidge, United States Geological Survey. With all due respect, Dr. Liao, most of us here agree it's way too early in the game to be sending a manned submersible into Vostok. NASA spent a lot of R and D money to develop their fleet of ROVs, as I'm sure these other marine science foundations have as well. Why risk your life and the lives of these two gentlemen when a sortie of drones can be deployed to cover a far larger area and bring back ten times the amount of raw data?"

Heads nodded in agreement.

Ming Liao seemed unaffected by her mutineers. "Dr. Coolidge, in preparing for this mission, I've formed a basic understanding of how remotely operated vehicles are designed. There are two forces in play that affect the stability of any object immersed in water: the center of buoyancy and the center of gravity. The distance between the two determines the vehicle's ability to remain upright, the drone's neutral buoyancy being a key factor in maintaining its maneuverability. It is a delicate balance and an important one. A bottom-crawling ROV that cannot sink is as useless as a drone that cannot maintain neutral buoyancy."

"Appreciate the lecture, Dr. Liao, but let me assure you, these ROV's were thoroughly field tested before they were shipped to Antarctica."

"Yes, but they were tested in freshwater tanks. Preliminary lab results indicate Lake Vostok is a hypersaline environment."

The news stunned the crowd, setting off a dozen side conversations.

The USGS administrator whistled for quiet. "How the hell is that possible? This is an inland rift lake, at least partially fed by meltwater."

A female scientist in a white lab coat and orange parka entered the tent.

Ming waved her to her side. "Dr. Helmi Jokinen is overseeing the analysis of subglacial lake chemistry. Dr. Jokinen?"

The Finnish biologist looked like a deer caught in headlights. "Yes, sorry for the delay. To respond to Dr. Coolidge's question, Lake Vostok is situated on a mineral bed. Residual salts from ancient oceans have rendered it a hypersaline chemocline. For those of you giving me strange looks, chemoclines are found in meromictic lakes—lakes with layers of water that do not intermix. The culprit in the case of Vostok is the presence of geothermal vents that release superheated mineral waters from out of the East Antarctic rift. Because of these vents, Vostok's waters run warmer the deeper you go."

I glanced at Dr. Coolidge, who seemed caught between frustration and an attraction for the Scandinavian scientist. "If you could give us the density readings, that would help."

"Yes, well, the density of fresh water to which your drones were set was 1.00 gram per milliliter. A typical density for salt water is 1.03 grams. The sample we drew from Lake Vostok measured 1.07 grams per milliliter. In short gentlemen—and ladies—as configured, your drones don't possess enough ballast to sink in this particular saltwater environment."

The USGS representative shook his head as he pulled his cell phone from his jacket pocket and turned his back to the biologist. "Gene, it's Kevin. We got us a major clusterfuck out here under the dome. Lab reports indicate Vostok is salt water. Contact NASA and tell 'em they need to recalibrate the ROVs' buoyancy gradients using water density markers set at 1.07 grams per milliliter."

Dr. Jokinen waited awkwardly while similar calls were made in half a dozen different languages. "For what it's worth, Dr. Coolidge, I suspect the Russians already knew this."

"Of course they knew it, only someone decided not to invite them to the party."

Ming smiled curtly, her almond eyes livid. "Is that all, Dr. Jokinen?"

"No, ma'am. The Russians and other experts had assumed Lake Vostok to be an oligotrophic extreme environment, meaning one void of nutrients. In fact the exact opposite appears to be true. Upon entering the lake, the Valkyrie drone passed through a brown algae field commonly associated with kelp. So far we've identified

119

five different genera of kelp that trace back to the Miocene era and are most likely being nourished by hot springs flowing out from the geothermal vents. Two of the genera—*Nereocystis* and *Macrocystis*—are fast growers known to produce dense kelp forests along the coast of Norway, flourishing in water temperatures between forty-three and fifty-seven degrees Fahrenheit. These kelp forests function as a food source for tens of thousands of invertebrates, not to mention thousands of aquatic species. To say the least, this is a huge discovery, the foundation of what could very well be a flourishing subglacial food chain."

With Dr. Jokinen's words, the aura inside the tent seemed to change. All eyes fixed on Ming Liao, awaiting her orders.

"Do what is necessary to re-ballast your drones. Dr. Wallace, Captain Hintzmann, get some rest. Our submersible is scheduled to make its first descent in the morning."

9

"I give myself very good advice, but I very seldom follow it."
—Lewis Carroll

Try as I might, I couldn't sleep.

Wrapped in my sleeping bag atop a nest of blankets, alone in my tent yet at the mercy of lights and voices and the occasional echoing *clang* of construction, I could not shut down my mind.

How did Neil Armstrong manage to sleep the night before his Apollo 11 launch? Was he on caffeine when he took his historic walk on the moon?

Minutes became hours, the glow from the battery-powered alarm clock advancing steadily until I freed myself from my goose-down cocoon at 3:42 a.m., my frustration getting the better of me. Even if I were to fall asleep now, I'd barely get four hours of rest.

Finding my boots, I tugged them over my wool socks, unzipped the tent, and emerged into the light, making my way through an alley of tents to the first-aid station.

I found the physician asleep on his exam table, his security tag identifying him as Zeb Gnehm.

"Excuse me? Yo, Doc. Some help, please?"

The physician sat up, bleary-eyed.

"Sorry to wake you, but I can't sleep and I need to be able to function in four hours. Could I get a sleeping pill or something?"

Dr. Gnehm responded with a contagious yawn. "Are you allergic to anything?"

"Not that I know of."

"Ambien works well, but you shouldn't take it if you'll only get half a night's sleep. Same with Lunesta. Best to go with either

Rozerem or Sonata, both of which stay active in the body for only a limited amount of time."

"What's *he* on?" I pointed to Ben, who was passed out on a cot, headphones over his ears.

"Hintzmann? He's on a prescription for Desyrel. It's an anti-depressant used for anxiety. How about a Valium?"

I popped the pill and returned to my tent. I zippered myself inside my sleeping bag and grew more irritated as my bladder reminded me I should have visited the port-a-potty while I was up.

Looking around the tent, I spotted a half-empty container of Gatorade. Two long swigs drained the wide-mouth bottle, which accommodated me just fine as I refilled the plastic jug with urine.

Relieved, I crawled back inside my goose-down womb, the digital clock winking 4:12 at me as the Valium pulled me under....

* * *

"Zachary, you're not thinking, son. Wake up."

I opened my eyes to find my mentor seated in a canvas folding chair. Joe Tkalec's brown hair was long and Albert Einstein wild, his matching goatee showing a touch of gray. His kind yet inquisitive brown eyes were magnified behind the same pair of rectangular glasses he had worn every day while teaching middle school science.

Transferring to a new school is never easy, especially when coming from another country in the middle of the academic year. I arrived in America with a Highland accent as baggage and a ninety-five-pound physique. It was deer hunting season—and I was Bambi.

Mr. Tkalec shielded me from the abuse. He helped me to overcome my accent while encouraging my love of marine biology by allowing me to borrow books and research papers from his personal library. His roommate, Troy—a retired semi-pro football player—introduced me to weight training and conditioning drills when I was thirteen. His coaching tips helped me to earn the starting halfback position on our high school football team.

Joe remained my mentor throughout my teen years and helped me get into Princeton. It had been three years since we had last talked.

122

What was he doing in East Antarctica?

"Listen to that katabatic wind, Zachary. It sounds like an earthquake, like machine-gun fire pelting the outside of the dome."

"Why are you here, Joe? Did you travel all this way to wish me luck? You know, if it wasn't for you, I probably wouldn't be here."

The kind eyes vanished. "Now that's a helluva thing to say. I trained you to think like a scientist, not a reality show buffoon. First, that nonsense back at Loch Ness— and now this? You disappoint me, Zachary."

I sat up, my heart racing. "But I resolved the identity of the Loch Ness Monster. I thought you'd be proud."

"Proud: Derived from the word pride, *as in self-pride, the abuse of which amounts to ego. Yes, son, you resolved the mystery of a large biologic inhabiting an ocean-access lake and then identified the species and the circumstances which led to its extraordinary adaptations. Only you weren't satisfied, were you? You went after the creature by using yourself as bait. Do you think I would have been filled with pride at your funeral? Is that why I encouraged you to become a marine biologist, so that one day I could brag to your wife and child at your gravesite how I had mentored you back in school?*

"And Vostok—where's the scientific method in this mission? You should be launching a thousand drones into the lake, shooting video, and taking water samples to analyze every square mile of its Miocene elements. There'd be enough data to study for the next twenty years. Instead, you fell for the lure of stardom, choosing to risk your life in a manned submersible just so you could say you were the first. That's what I'll say at your eulogy: 'Zachary Wallace, best student I ever had, and the first schmuck in history to die exploring a subglacial lake.'

"There's no science in committing suicide, son. At the end of the day, it's a selfish act that leaves behind only sorrow. You need to wake up, Zachary. Wake up... ."

"Zachary, wake-up!"

I was dead to the world, my brain encased in wet cement; yet through the inebriated fog, I felt a smooth velvet tingling of delight working its way around my groin, and through its arousal I awoke from my drug-induced stupor.

Then I realized the hand rubbing the inside of my thigh didn't belong to my wife, and my eyes flashed open in sudden panic.

True stood over me, a shit-eating grin plastered over his face. "Ken that would wake ye. So who was ye dreamin' aboot? Ming or my sister?"

"No one, you big douchebag. What time is it?"

"Time tae get dressed. Ye launch within the hour. That yer Gatorade? "

"Yeah, but don't put your lips to it. I can only imagine where they were last night."

"If yer referring to one Ms. Susan McWhite, she prefers her men scrawny and smart. Here's tae ye." He unscrewed the lid and took a big gulp, his eyes bugging out as he gagged on my urine.

I smiled. "If you're hungry, *lad*, I can shit you a turd sandwich to go with it."

* * *

The subject of bowel movements always comes up for astronauts and submersible pilots. Occupying a cramped cockpit over an extended period of time requires proper preparation. It was one thing for Ben and me to use a urine bottle and pop a few pills to temporarily shut down our bowels while we dove in Prydz Bay; Vostok was an entirely different mission. Each dive would average between fourteen and thirty hours.

Upon arriving at the dome, our submersible techs had swapped the *Barracuda*'s leather bucket seats for advanced models with built-in waste-collection systems. A suction hose disposed of urine into a cache beneath our seat. Bowel movements required the removal of a section of the seat, exposing a wastehole a third the size of a normal toilet. A privacy curtain separated Ming's cockpit from ours. I won't provide the rest of the gory details other than to say the three of us ingested plenty of large intestine suppressants in the hope of rendering the matter moot.

To utilize the waste-collection system required wearing a specially designed jumpsuit with easy access panels. Thus was born the ECU: Extreme Conditions Uniform. Lightweight and flexible, the ECU had panels in all the right places and contained built-in sensors to monitor our vital signs, an internal heating unit with a scalp-tight hood with ear holes for our headphones, and circulation cuffs fitted around the biceps, thighs, and calves, which inflated and deflated periodically to prevent cramps and blood clots.

Having consumed our pre-launch meal and used the toilet one last time, Ben and I emerged from our tents in our black ECUs like two modern-day Ninja.

Ming was dressed in her bodywear and looked incredible. Her technical team led us to the gantry where the *Barracuda* was suspended horizontally in its harness with the acrylic cockpit open. We climbed into our assigned seats while our techs plugged the hoses from our uniforms into their appropriate sockets.

True held up his iPhone to snap a photo. "For Brandy and William… and the *Inverness Courier*."

For some reason, my thoughts turned to my old science teacher, Joe Tkalec.

True clicked off a few shots. "Oh, and ye'll be happy tae learn tha' Susan found me the perfect job. I'm working with the team that'll be sealing yer borehole. I equate it ta givin' Antarctica a suppository, followed by a frosty enema chaser."

"You're a class act, Finlay True MacDonald."

We both smiled, but there was a look in my friend's eyes that I'd not soon forget. It was the same look of worry I had seen moments before he launched me into the depths of Loch Ness.

* * *

Ming was a combination of nervous and giddy. Before settling into her cockpit, she offered each of us a yellow pill. "It's just a little something to relax you. After all, there's nothing for us to do during the descent, which will take hours."

Having still not fully recovered from the Valium, I passed.

Ben pocketed his.

The three of us went through our checklists with the Mission Control techs while a small crowd gathered outside the gantry fencing. At 10:05 a.m. we received clearance to launch. We rotated our seats one hundred and eighty degrees to face astern.

Our pod's hatch was sealed, causing my heart to flutter. A moment later the gantry activated, rotating the harness vertically so that the *Barracuda*'s nose was pointed at the ice, placing us on our backs like astronauts launching into Hell. We adjusted our harnesses, tightening any slack.

"This is Vostok Command. Captain Hintzmann, you have clearance to activate your Valkyrie lasers."

"Roger that, Vostok Command. Activating Valkyrie units on my count: Three... two... one... activate."

The two tubes on either side of the sub ignited, the lasers' heat reflecting crimson against the ice, which was already steaming. We dropped two feet, then two feet more so that we were now ground level. Then we slipped beneath the ice, continuing a rough, herky-jerky descent as the frozen surface crackled and screamed in protest beneath the intense heat.

A borehole gradually opened beneath us. The melt and drop averaged four to six feet every ten to twenty seconds with an occasional stomach-wrenching drop into free fall.

I turned in my seat to take a look below. The ice bled like a fading sunset, slush splattering against the cockpit windshield. Every once in a while a dark pocket would open and we'd drop twenty feet, only to stop suddenly, the jolt absorbed by our cushioned bucket seats.

I checked our depth gauge after thirty minutes: 1,029 feet.

Vostok was 13,100 feet beneath the ice. At our present rate of descent, we wouldn't reach the lake for another seven and a half hours.

Ben's voice came over my headset. "How are you holding up?"

"I'll need some aspirin before this journey's through. How's Ming?"

"Sleeping like a baby. I meant to ask you; Dr. Ahmed claimed there was air in Vostok—how is that possible?"

"It's the sheer mass of the ice sheet. The pressure squeezes oxygen and nitrogen molecules trapped in the ice below and releases them into the lake. Vostok has been experiencing this gas exchange for millions of years. I wouldn't be surprised if we found pockets of atmosphere. Of course, if there are any organisms alive down there, they would have adapted to this unique oxygen—"

"Enough already, you're wearing my brain out. I'm popping one of Ming's pills. Wake me when we get there."

He was snoring less than ten minutes later.

The slush washing against the bow settled into a soothing rhythm. Curling on my side, I closed my eyes…

* * *

The wind whipped through the Great Glen, lapping white water across Loch Ness's foreboding surface.

True helped me with the dive suit, a heavy contraption that seemed more suited for space. "I'm beggin' ye, Zachary, don't go down there. Jist marry my sister and leave the Highlands behind ye forever."

"The creature's trapped, True. I need to free it or kill it. It's the only way to get these night terrors to stop."

"All right, then. Find the entrance to that underground river and use yer explosives before that thing gets a whiff of ye." True double-checked my dive suit, then peered into my helmet. "For a runt, ye got big balls. Better grab hold of 'em."

He disconnected my support cable, and down I went, dropping through Loch Ness's frigid waters like an anchor. The beam from my forward light cut through the darkness, revealing a tea-colored world, but everything seemed to be spinning.

"Speak to me, Zachary."

"Dizzy, I'm just a little dizzy."

"That's because yer spinning on yer cable. Look inside yer headpiece. Just below yer lower jaw you'll see a set of gauges. Check yer compass, it's in orange. It shows direction and course, sort of like a submarine. Press on your thrusters and come to a complete stop. Then call out yer depth to me."

"Two hundred thirty feet."

"Have ye stopped spinning?"

"Yes."

"Good. Now ease off the thrusters and continue descending while callin' out yer depth."

"Four-sixty. Five hundred feet. Five-forty—"

"Don't get cocky. Keep it slow and steady. What do ye see?"

"Not much. Even using my light, visibility's less than fifteen feet. Outside the beam, the water's pitch-black. I just passed seven hundred feet. The water temperature's a chilly thirty-eight degrees, but I'm fine. I can see the bottom. It's a muddy, flat expanse littered here and there by petrified clumps of Scotch pine. The trees are embedded in the soot, belching streams of gas. Their branches are covered in plankton. They're reaching out for me like the rotting arms of Loch Ness's dead…

"Jesus, what am I doing down here?"

* * *

"Jesus, Zach, whit are ye doing down there?"

My eyes snapped open, True's voice beckoning in my ear. "Sorry, I must have fallen asleep. Where are we?"

"Fifty feet from splashdown. Command shut yer sub down half an hour ago. The borehole's checked out solid above ye. I imagine they'll be allowing you tae proceed."

"Ben, wake up. We're here." I kicked the back of his seat with my foot. "Ming, you awake?"

128

She yawned and stretched as our headsets reverberated in our ears. "*Barracuda*, this is Vostok Command. We're ready for you to reignite the Valkyrie units. Are you ready to make history?"

Ben responded with a yawn. "Roger that, Vostok Command. Reigniting Valkyrie units on my mark. Three... two... one... ignite."

"Confirm ignition. Forty feet until splashdown ... "

"Zach, activate our exterior lights."

"Twenty feet ... "

"Hey, Zach, since you're in the nose cone, I guess that technically makes you the first man down. Since Ming's the first woman, where does that leave me?"

"Playing for sloppy seconds, I guess."

"Ten feet until splashdown. Here we go, people. Eight... five... two ... "

With a final *craaaaack* the layer of ice beneath us peeled away, and suddenly we were free-falling backward in darkness. My stomach lurched and my heart pounded in my chest as I waited for a splashdown that wasn't coming.

Ming screamed over the whistling of the submersible's aft wings cutting through the air.

Ben yelled, "Hold on!" three times before we finally struck water, our submersible plunging bow-first into Lake Vostok.

10

"If you drink too much from a bottle marked 'poison,'
it is almost certain to disagree with you, sooner or later."
—Lewis Carroll

The *Barracuda* plummeted through a blackness that seemed to reach out at us. After what felt like a two-hundred-foot dive, we leveled off, orientated in the pitch by the soft glow of our command console's lights.

I unlocked my seat and rotated it to face forward.

"Zach, how far did we fall?" Ben asked.

I checked my depth gauge, which was resetting to accommodate our new liquid environment. "According to my instruments, we're eighty-seven feet beneath the surface of Lake Vostok."

"That's not what I asked you. I asked how far we *fell.* In case you two still haven't figured it out yet, we weren't supposed to free fall out of the ice sheet. The ice sheet was supposed to be pressing against the lake's surface!"

I realized he was right. "Bring us to the surface. Let's take a look."

Ben shut down the lasers and powered up the submersible's engine while Ming tried the radio.

"Vostok Command, this is Dr. Liao. Do you have a fix on our position?"

"*Barracuda*, this is Victor Lopez in navigation. It looks like you may have overshot your targeted submergence point. We're waiting for a satellite pass to track your exact location. ETA is twelve minutes. Keep your lasers on so we can locate your heat signature."

"Acknowledged. We'll use the time to collect a water sample."

"Overshot our targeted submergence point? What the hell does that mean?" Ben ranted as he reactivated the Valkyries, the sub's exterior lights guiding us to the surface. "If you ask me, it sounds like somebody topside screwed the pooch. My money's on the dumb Viking."

"Shut up, Ben." I watched our bow lights' beacon cut a path through the clear, dark waters until our nose popped free of the surface.

We were surrounded by a dense fog. I aimed our starboard light overhead, but the beam failed to reach the bottom of the ice sheet. "It's gotta be up there somewhere."

"Zach, use the sonar to ping the ceiling."

"That won't work."

"Yes it will. The computer can calculate the distance between the air and the ice by the time it takes the sound waves to hit the ice sheet."

"Do it, Zach," Ming chimed in.

I positioned my headphones over my ears, activated the sonar station and pushed the red ACTIVE button, sending a loud *ping* echoing across the surface in all directions.

The acoustic reflection bounced off the ceiling, and the computer pinpointed the bottom of the ice sheet—112 feet above our heads.

Ben swore from his perch behind me. "A hundred and twelve feet. Houston, we have a major problem."

"Captain, please calm down. Whatever the problem is, we'll resolve it."

"Ming, in order to return to the surface we were simply supposed to activate the lasers and launch bow-up out of the water. As the hole opened Vostok's water pressure would drive us straight up like a geyser. That entire premise was based on the ice sheet being accessible. A 112-foot ceiling isn't accessible. Are we supposed to grow wings and fly up to it?"

"Stay calm," I said, my pulse pounding. "We know the first Valkyrie went down and came right back up. That means the bottom of the ice sheet isn't uniform."

"Zachary's right," added Ming. "We simply need to locate the first drone's exit point."

"All right, Doc, I'm buying what you're peddling, but riddle me this: if the *Barracuda* launched from the same starting point as the Valkyrie, then how did we end up here, wherever here is? Something must have altered our trajectory."

"Agreed, but remember the Valkyrie drone is basically a tethered laser with no variables to account for. The *Barracuda*'s trajectory is subject to a thousand possible weight displacements during the descent. Even the three of us leaning to one side could have caused us to deviate miles off course. In a worst-case scenario we can always have Vostok Command send down a second unit so we can track its splashdown. We'll be fine."

Ben exhaled a sigh of relief. "I knew there was a reason I brought you along."

Waves lapped against the *Barracuda*, rocking us gently. For a long moment the three of us remained quiet, listening to the darkness. A roll of thunder echoed in the distance, the ice sheet rumbling overhead as it inched its way east toward the sea.

If there were a more isolated spot on the planet, I couldn't imagine where it might be.

After a few minutes, Ming activated her sampling unit and siphoned six ounces of lake water into a collection tube for computer analysis. "Water temperature is thirty-seven degrees Fahrenheit."

Ben tapped his fingers. "Who cares about water temperature? Cold is cold, what did you expect?"

He was annoyed, anxious to hear back from Vostok Command. Defending Ming, I replied, "Water temperature is important because it governs the kinds of organisms that can live in Vostok. The presence of zooplankton and phytoplankton—even insects and fish—all thrive in different temperatures. Chemical reactions generally increase in higher temperatures. The freezing temperature would indicate there are no geothermal vents present in this area. Ming, what about E. coli?"

"Bacteria readings are still processing. Nitrogen and phosphorus concentrations are low, as we would expect. The pH is 7.1, highly conducive for fish."

"Fish?" Ben forced a laugh. "Hate to tell you, but I don't see so much as a speck of pond scum, let alone a fish. Seems like your people dropped us into a dead zone."

"Ben may be right," I said. "Bacteria count is near zero. Sorry to disappoint you, Ming, but if there are fish in this lake, they aren't defecating in it."

"Maybe they're using a toilet," I heard Ben mutter.

"*Barracuda*, this is Vostok Command. We have acquired your position. You can power down your lasers. As we suspected, your trajectory was altered during your descent."

"Altered how?" Ben asked.

"We're still working the numbers, Captain. You were right on target for the first twenty-seven hundred meters. Somewhere around that mark the sub passed through a magnetic anomaly that veered you off-course. The affected area spans a sixty-five-by-forty-seven-mile section of the plateau that separates the lake's two basins. There was too much interference for us to catch it from up here, and your suit sensors indicate you probably were asleep during the event."

"How far off course are we?"

"We have you 152 kilometers southwest of your extraction point. That's about ninety-four miles."

133

Ben slapped his palms to the acrylic dome above his head. "Helluva job, *amigo*. Your team aimed for the moon and landed us in Cleveland. We're lucky we even hit water."

Ming smacked the pilot on the back of his head. "Victor, can you pinpoint the source of the anomaly?"

"We're still working on that. I'm downloading the SAT image to the *Barracuda*'s computer. We highlighted your location and the extraction point as references. As you'll see, you're in the southern basin, separated from the northern basin by the Vostok ridge. Somewhere along that rise is the source of the anomaly. We suspect the ridge is part of an impact crater from an asteroid. Celestial impacts often magnetize the geology—that's how they located the crater in the Gulf of Mexico from the asteroid that killed off the dinosaurs."

A black-and-white photo pixilated across our computer screens. The image was generated from sensory equipment aboard *Onyx* and *Lacrosse*, a series of terrestrial reconnaissance satellites launched into orbit thirty years ago and only recently declassified. The satellites were equipped with synthetic aperture radar and other sophisticated instruments designed to see through cloud cover, ocean, ice, and even soil.

The *Onyx* satellite had pinpointed our sub by our lasers' heat signature. The SAR unit had generated the view of Vostok's topography.

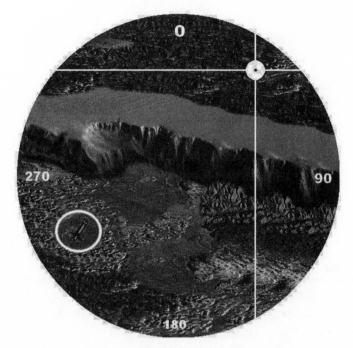

"Captain, we suggest you set a course on heading zero-three-seven. If you average twenty knots, you should reach the extraction point in less than five hours. That will give your team nine hours to collect water samples and explore Vostok before you need to start your ascent."

"Roger that, Lopez." Ben brought the sub about until we were pointed on our northeasterly heading, cruising along the surface at twenty knots.

I laid my head back, staring at endless mist as we plowed through perpetual darkness. I could have used my nocturnal glasses, but there was nothing to see. We had just pulled off an incredible engineering feat, gaining access to a lost world preserved beneath fifteen million years of ice, and yet somehow I felt disappointed.

What had I expected? What would have made me happy? Traces of fecal matter from a prehistoric trout? Perhaps a fossil or two?

One thing is for sure: we weren't about to find anything along the surface.

"Ben, any objections to checking out the bottom?"

"What for?"

"Maybe we can find some fossils."

Ming raised her head from her computer. "Yes. Very good, Zachary. I wanted to collect silt samples anyway."

"You two do realize the depths in this basin exceed twenty-five hundred feet?"

"It *is* a submersible," I said, winking at Ming. "You're allowed to get it wet."

"Suddenly the Sargasso survivor is a daredevil? Okay, Doc. As my tenth-grade English teacher said to me before she popped my cherry, 'Hold on, kid, I'm goin' down.'"

I grabbed onto the padded leather support handles as the bow dropped away into a near-vertical descent, the depth gauge's numbers advancing rapidly.

Four hundred feet…

Seven hundred feet…

"Easy, Captain, there's no rush."

"What's wrong, Doc? I thought you were an adrenaline junkie."

One thousand feet…

At 1,340 feet I felt the hull groan, the acrylic emergency pod wobbling under the sudden wave of pressure.

Ming reached forward and gripped the pilot's right arm. "Slow it down or Zachary will pilot the sub and you can catch the next cargo plane back to Wisconsin."

Ben eased up on the throttle, altering our angle of descent. "No worries. I was just seeing what this vessel could handle. That's standard operating procedure on a maiden voyage—part of my job."

"And part of my job is to minimize the risks to the crew.

Zachary, are you all right?"

Ugh. "Fine, thank you, Ming." *Yes. Thank you, Ming, for emasculating me in your penis-shaped submersible. And thank you for hiring an ego-driven headcase who managed to get himself kicked out of the Air Force for mistakenly entering a sovereign nation's air space. And thank you, Angus, for once again screwing up my life.*

As we passed two thousand feet, Ming squealed something in Chinese. "Zachary, I just took another water sample. The temperature has dropped to minus sixteen degrees Fahrenheit, with total dissolved solids exceeding two thousand miligrams."

I turned to face her. "We're entering a hypersaline chemocline. Vostok is a mineral concentrator. Remember, it's connected to Antarctica's oceans by a subglacial river. Residual salts have become trapped over millions of years, concentrated along the bottom. Lake Bonney works the same way; it has a temperature of minus twenty-three. Don Juan Pond is liquid at minus twenty-two. I wouldn't be shocked to find weird microbial communities thriving down here."

Geez, Wallace, you are such a nerd.

The tea-colored waters in our headlights grew more turbid as we descended, and the current increased, forcing Ben to decrease his angle of descent.

By the time we reached 2,185 feet, the *Barracuda* had nearly leveled off, the depths sweeping us north in the belly of a seventeen-knot current.

Ming aimed her keel light at the bottom, her underwater camera revealing a smooth, gray bedrock lake floor littered with fossils.

"Captain, slow down. I want to take a look. I want to collect samples."

"In this current?"

I shook my head. "Just come about and put our bow into the current. Haven't you ever changed a sail before?"

"Not in a sub, smart-ass."

Ben executed a bone-jarring turn, the current buffeting our craft until our bow was pointing south, our propulsors neutralizing the force of the water. Maintaining a forward speed of twenty knots, we cruised slowly over the ancient bottom, the treasures of the long-lost Miocene era appearing on our video screen.

For the next half an hour, we worked our way over unrecognizeable shards of bone and rock that were hardly worth the journey—until the remains of an ancient water creature blanched white in our keel lights.

Its backbone stretched before our widening eyes, each form-fitted vertebra as large as a bowling ball. I estimated the spine to be forty feet long, and then I saw the size of its skull and the adrenaline started pumping.

In November of 2008, paleontologists excavating a dried lake bed in Peru had stumbled across the fossilized remains of an undiscovered sea monster that definitely ranked up there as one of Nature's all-time killers. From the partially preserved skull, teeth, and mandible, they knew the creature had been enormous, as long as sixty feet. The cranium's curved basin suggested it harbored a spermaceti organ—a series of oil and wax reservoirs separated by connective tissue, theorized to be a resonance chamber used by cetaceans for echolocation.

The owner appeared to be the ancestor of a sperm whale, with one major anatomical difference—the Miocene killer had possessed a lower jaw that was far wider than that of its modern-day cousin, giving it a bite that rivaled *Carcharodon megalodon*, its chief competitor.

After much debate the excited researchers settled on a name for their mammalian monster: *Livyatan melvillei*, combining the Hebrew spelling for the biblical *Leviathan* with the surname of Herman Melville, the author of *Moby Dick*. It was a fitting title for an ocean predator that had not only owned one of the most vicious bites in history but also the largest teeth, some of which measured fifteen inches.

I had no doubt that the skull and jawbone lying twelve feet beneath our keel belonged to this Miocene monster. But why had these ocean-dwelling whales entered Vostok? Had something enticed them to venture upriver into a saltwater lake? Was it a survival instinct, a search for prey... *or something else entirely?*

The teeth were enormous, cone-shaped, and twice as long as an ear of corn. Ming quickly located a tooth that had belonged to the beast's lower jaw and decided she could acquire it using the sub's claw.

Ben disagreed. "The current will snap the claw like kindling."

"Nonsense. It will hold."

"It's too risky. If it bends you won't be able to dock the arm. And if you can't dock it, it will interfere with our ascent. Tell her, Zach."

But I was no longer listening to them, for the emptiness that had occupied our sonar monitor was no longer empty, the vacuum of space replaced by three distinct blips—

—and they were headed our way.

11

Blee-bloop... blee-bloop... blee-bloop ...

It was a freakish sound, almost like a water jug expelling its contents, and when I heard it in my sonar earpiece I nearly passed out from the blood rushing from my head.

Imagine surviving a plane crash, only to find yourself on another commercial jetliner years later hearing the captain announce, "Sorry folks, we just lost one of our engines. Prepare for an emergency landing." You'd feel your whole body go numb because you know what's coming, and it's seriously bad news as you ask yourself, "What the hell am I doing back on a goddamn plane?"

In my case it was a sub, and I knew what was coming because I had heard the *blee-bloop* sound on sonar in the Sargasso Sea just before I drowned. The Navy guys had named this unknown species "the bloops" because they weren't whales or sharks or giant squids, and their internal respiratory organs created a *bloop* sound on sonar. Having survived the encounter, it was my unfortunate fate to discover Nessie to be one of their kind—a predatory fish that had grown very large after becoming trapped in Loch Ness when an aquifer had collapsed, cutting off access to the ocean and her migratory pattern. Thus spawning a legend.

And now we were about to meet her ancient Miocene cousins.

Ben grabbed his headphones. "Where are they?"

"Approaching from the northwest on course two-eight-five. These are big, nasty predators, and we seriously need to leave. Like now!"

"How do you know they're predators?"

"You read my book. Don't you hear that *bloop* sound?"

"No. All I hear is Ming scraping that damn claw along the

140

bottom. Hey, Ming." He reached over his seat and grabbed her arm, getting her attention. "Zach says we've got biologics on sonar."

"Really? This is incredible. How far away are they? Can we catch up with them? We absolutely need to get them on video."

"Maybe I'm not explaining this right. These predators are thirty to forty feet long, and they're stalking us, Ming. Now get that claw docked. Ben, are you driving, or am I?"

"Just tell me a direction."

I stared at the sonar screen. *They're coming from the northwest. Southeast distances us, only we need to head north to get to the extraction point*

The creatures were closing fast, and I couldn't think.

"Zach?"

"Come about. We'll let the current take us north. No engines for now; we need to sneak past them. Ming, enough with the damn whale tooth!"

"Give me twenty seconds. I've almost got it in the catch basket."

I turned to Ben for help. "Remember that creature that choked on the croc? You're about to meet his great-grandkids."

"To hell with that!" Strapping himself in, Ben turned the sub hard to starboard, spinning the *Barracuda*'s bow to the north.

Ming swore in Mandarin. "I lost the tooth!"

"Dock that arm and strap in. Zach, you sure about these lights?"

"Yes— no. Wait. Keep them off for now, but be ready to turn them back on. Everyone quiet. Ming?"

"You wanted me to dock the arm; it's docked."

I listened on sonar, my eyes following the bloops. We were going to cross paths any second, only there was no way to know if they had heard us turn into the current.

Eight hundred feet...

The respiratory sounds grew louder. There were three of

them, an adult and two gurgling offspring.

Four hundred feet...

They were slowing.

They're unsure. They can't detect us with the engines off.

The current swept us closer to where the creatures were circling.

Two hundred feet...

Remembering my night-vision goggles, I reached into a cushioned compartment on the right side of my command center and retrieved them. I placed them over my eyes and the blackness was stripped away, replaced by an olive-green world—

—and a serpent-like creature looming before us that was clearly *not* my Nessie.

This one was far worse.

It was just as long at thirty to forty feet but far thicker in girth. Its hide was covered in thick slime that reflected our lights from its dark undulating coils. A vertical fin ran the length of its chocolate-brown body to the tip of its tail. The mouth was hideous, rimmed with curved, stiletto-sharp teeth set outside the jaw like the oversized fangs of an Angler fish. The snout was square, its volcano-shaped, pale-pink nostrils opening and closing as it inhaled the current.

Like its modern-day relative, it was a species of giant eel, only it possessed fore-fins—gruesome clawed appendages its ancestors probably once used to climb onto land.

Oh, yeah, and it was electric.

From its gilled neck to its tail, along its flank it possessed bioluminescent cells that generated yellow zaps of electricity, which radiated signals like an alien vessel—a light show, no doubt, designed to mesmerize its prey.

I was already mesmerized in fear. "Ben, full throttle!"

As Ben stamped down on both propeller pedals, I powered

on the exterior headlamps and aimed the beams at the creature's eyes—only I couldn't find its eyes. In my haste I had accidently powered on the Valkyries, and before I'd realized my error we had shot past the Miocene nightmare's snapping jaws.

A flash of horizontal lightning revealed the second creature lurking in the darkness off the starboard bow. It was as large as its sibling and appeared to be communicating to it using its bioluminescent cells.

Life and death is separated by a moment. When predator meets prey and there is no escape—the fly caught in the spider's web, the desert mouse stung by the scorpion, the seal suddenly crushed inside the jaws of a great white shark—the end happens in a startling microsecond.

It was as large as its sibling.

And in that microsecond of clarity, I knew the hyperflexed mouth that suddenly bloomed out of the darkness directly ahead belonged to the adult and not the juveniles. She could have been eighty feet or a hundred. It didn't matter. The seal doesn't think about the length of its killer when it's being eaten; it's more of a how-did-this-happen moment.

We were swallowed whole—shot right into the creature's outstretched jaws and down its gullet!

Before we could scream or yell or react, the *Barracuda* was soaring through a river of water down the creature's throat.

Before we could fathom where we were, we found our vessel being squeezed by internal esophageal muscles that bulged and prodded and clenched the submersible in an attempt to stymie our resistance.

Before we could sanely deal with our insane situation, the Valkyrie lasers scorched the stomach lining and evaporated the creature's digestive organs—along with blood, arteries, sinew, all of it—as the *Barracuda* exploded out of our would-be killer's new arse.

The entire journey lasted seconds.

The three of us yelled and laughed and whooped it up, leaving behind thirty tons of writhing, gurgling sushi for the monster's two orphaned goliaths to consume—Only the creatures ignored their dying parent and came after us.

Ben quickly maneuvered the sub back into the current and accelerated. "I'm pushing thirty knots and can't seem to lose them. Suggestions?"

Before I could reply we heard a metallic *pop* at the ship's tailfin.

"We just lost our umbilical cord," Ming announced.

My gaze shifted nervously from the sonar array to my monitor, the real-time images coming from the *Barracuda*'s aft camera. The night-vision lens had a restricted field of view and showed open water, but my sonar painted the two creatures as they independently swooped in and out from the perimeter, riding the current like dolphins as they gauged how best to attack their fleeing prey without getting seared by our laser's afterburners.

"Doc, we got a serious problem. Losing the umbilical means we're self-contained. If I don't shut down the Valkyries soon, there won't be enough juice left to make the ascent."

"Do it."

Ming's voice crackled over our headphones. "I think that should be my decision, Zachary."

"Actually, it's mine," Ben said, powering down the lasers.

Sensing the threat was gone, the two beasts grew more aggressive. Surfing the current, they attempted to snatch us in their awful jaws, each attempt inching closer to our hull.

"Doc, I can't hold them off!"

My mind raced. *They should have backed off by now. Why aren't they tiring? Oh, hell.* "Ben, get us out of this current. We need to wear them out."

He pulled back hard on his joystick, bringing us up and out of the river flow.

Propelled by the seventeen-knot current, the two eels shot past us. I picked them up on sonar six hundred yards to the north, registering the disturbance as they left the flow to reengage the hunt.

Ben wasted no time in changing course, taking us on a westerly heading at twenty-five knots.

The creatures pursued us for close to two minutes before the costly expenditure of energy forced them to give up the chase. They faded into white noise as they headed south, no doubt to feed upon the remains of their mother.

"We lost them."

"Thank God. So that's what you dealt with in Loch Ness?"

"No, not quite. Ben, we're on the wrong heading. We need to be on zero-three-seven."

Ben banked the *Barracuda* hard to starboard, resuming the northeasterly course that would bring us to the extraction point.

Ming's voice crackled loudly over my headphones. "Zachary, this is incredible beyond our wildest expectations. Did you ever imagine we'd discover such creatures in Vostok?"

Ben mumbled, "If he did, do you think he'd be here?"

Ming ignored him. "Zachary, how could anything so large have survived down here?"

I laid my head back and closed my eyes, my nerves still jumpy. "Humans adapt to new environments by using our brains; animals adapt by evolving anatomically. When Antarctica froze over during the Miocene age, it was a gradual process, not a mass extinction event. Vostok has air and water—"

"And five thousand pounds per square inch of water pressure," said Ben, who did a double-take, squinting to read his atmospheric pressure gauge. "Correction. Make that thirty-nine hundred pounds of pressure. How'd that happen?"

"It doesn't matter. Eels are fish, and water pressure doesn't affect fish. Eels are also hardy creatures. No doubt they've become apex predators in this realm. The question is what else is out there that filled the gap between chemosynthetic bacteria and giant eels. Obviously there are still key pieces of the Vostok ecosystem that we haven't seen."

"What good is *seen* without evidence," Ming quipped. "The videocameras missed everything. No one is going to believe what we discovered if we cannot prove it."

"We've got more pressing problems," Ben said, ascending the sub until once more we were plowing the lake's surface. "When we lost our umbilical cord, we not only lost contact with Vostok Command, we lost our main power supply. We've got nineteen hours of air left, and at least five of them have to be used during our ascent. That leaves us fourteen hours to locate a section of Vostok where the bottom of the ice sheet and the lake's surface are within a ship's length of one another."

The weight of Ben's words sunk in. For the next thirty minutes we remained quiet, conserving our air supply while we watched the mist overhead, hoping for an ice ceiling to appear.

Instead, it started to rain.

12

"Raindrops keep fallin' on my head,
But that doesn't mean my eyes will soon be turnin' red,
Cryin's not for me ...
'Cause I'm never gonna stop the rain by complainin'
Because I'm free... nothin's worryin' me."

—B.J. Thomas

It began as scattered droplets and progressed steadily as we advanced on our northeasterly course. The rain, of course, was coming from the ice sheet above our heads. The question was: why was it melting?

"Surface water temperature is forty-nine degrees," Ming called out. "We must be passing over a geothermal vent field. Captain, take us back down to the bottom. If the vents are there, then we must be in the wrong area."

Ben dove the sub, and we officially entered the Miocene.

Before I could react to the blizzard of objects appearing on my sonar screen, a swarm of anchovies glittered silver in our lights, whipping themselves into a frenzied six-story tornado.

My heart palpitated a moment later when sonar detected a massive object rising at us from two hundred feet below the surface. Before Ben could swerve out of the way the water was teeming with salmon. Thousands of seven- to eight-foot-long scaly missiles pounded the sub like hail as they raced to dine at the all-you-can-eat anchovy buffet, their upturned mouths widening to reveal gruesome needle-sharp teeth.

We waited until the deluge of fish passed before continuing our descent. The deeper we ventured, the larger the species seemed to be. Albino sunfish reflected our lights like miniature moons, and tarpon as large as groupers swerved around our craft. A toadfish pressed against the acrylic glass, blocking my forward view. Its large, flat head was as big as a basketball, its wide mouth filled with blunt teeth, its slime-covered body tapering back to a plump belly and fan-like pectoral fins.

Dozens of blips appeared on my sonar screen and in our lights giant stingrays flew past us on majestic twenty-foot wings, the magnificent albino creatures swarming to feed upon a wounded sunfish. One of these not-so-gentle giants swooped in and snatched the toadfish in its vicious bat-like mouth, its pale body pressing against the pod as its sharp triangular teeth skewered its meal. For a nerve-racking moment, the stingray's wingspan enveloped the *Barracuda*, pitching us hard to port before it swam off.

Ming delighted as she documented our descent. Ben swore. As for me, I could only gaze in wonderment at this preserved time capsule from the past, the marine biologist in me questioning whether these animals represented true Miocene species that existed in Antarctica fifteen million years ago or whether we were looking at anatomical variations that were a direct result of adapting to the extreme conditions of this uniquely isolated environment.

The creative right side of my brain told my left, logical side to shut up and enjoy the show.

The enjoyment, however, turned to trepidation when the first sharks appeared. Using my night-vision glasses, I identified two different species of requiem predators. The first Carcharhinid was a twelve-foot oceanic whitetip. The second brute was a bull shark that was twice the size and girth of the *Barracuda*.

While both of these species had a reputation for following freshwater rivers inland to inhabit lakes, it was still shocking to find these ocean dwellers thriving in Vostok.

Ming called out the temperature as we passed twelve hundred feet. "Fifty-three degrees."

That settled my shark dilemma. It was not just Antarctica, after all, that had frozen millions of years ago; the oceans

148

surrounding the continent had also incurred a precarious drop in temperature. A river bleeding a warm-water current into coastal waters would have lured many ocean species.

I shuddered to think what else might be down here.

I got an answer as we passed sixteen hundred feet. A thousand shadows materialized all around us in every direction, becoming bulbous eyes and jaws that unhinged, and bizarre fish with needle-sharp teeth, many of which cast bioluminescent lanterns that dangled before their open mouths like bait. These were Vostok's deepwater creatures, Miocene mutations forced to adapt to the darkness and cold.

But not cold, for the water temperature was fifty-seven degrees and still rising.

As we descended to twenty-two hundred feet, a gray haze began to appear, chasing away Vostok's denizens of the deep.

At twenty-four hundred feet, the water temperature had risen to sixty-three degrees.

Forty more feet and I saw the first black smoker.

Hydrothermal vents were first discovered in the Pacific Ocean back in 1977. Since then, they had been found in every ocean as well as in certain rift lakes.

Vostok was just such a lake, formed when East Antarctica's crustal plates had separated, creating a valley that became the waterway's basin. The geothermal vents were switched on when cold water began seeping into cracks along the forming lake's floor. Heated by molten rock in the earth's mantle, the water mixed with oxygen, magnesium, potassium, and other minerals before being forcibly ejected back into the lake. Once this hot mineral soup met Vostok's cold, oxygen-rich water, it generated hydrogen sulfide, which in turn fueled bacteria—the foundation of the lake's chemosynthetic food chain.

Avoiding direct contact with the superheated discharges, Ben gave us a tour of the vent field, a petrified forest of volcanic chimneys that spewed billowing dark clouds of mineral-laden water, which spawned a thriving subglacial ecosystem. Piled along the base of these vents was a mosh-pit of life—crustaceans and shrimp, clams and anemone—everything white and twice the size of similar species outside of Vostok. Our sub rocked in eighty-nine-degree water as we passed over miles of vent fields, small fish feeding off the spaghetti-like clusters of tubeworms that grew in acre-size clusters.

"All right, Zach, Ming—we've taken a look. What say we move on before this mineral water clogs one of the engine's intake valves?"

Not waiting for our reply, Ben began our ascent as we continued our trek to the northeast.

We had journeyed another three nautical miles when we discovered another missing cog in Vostok's thriving ecosystem.

Upon reaching a depth of 420 feet, we discovered strands of what appeared to be kelp dangling across our cockpit glass. The higher we rose, the denser the growth, until we were surrounded by thick strands of algae.

As we continued our ascent, sonar revealed the lake's surface had been replaced by a thick algae mat that carpeted Vostok's lake for miles.

"This is bizarre," I said. "A kelp forest is usually rooted to the bottom. This forest is upside down. Its holdfast is growing out of the geothermal soil and algae that has accumulated along the surface."

Ben kept the *Barracuda* eighty feet beneath the mineralized surface, fearful of the Valkyrie units becoming entwined in long strands of kelp.

Everywhere we looked, there were fish.

Hundreds of Miocene rockfish dominated the shallows, their six-foot-long frames carrying a good hundred pounds. They must have been blind, for they remained unaffected by our exterior lights.

Their thick hides were a bright orange, rendering the inverted vines a Miocene pumpkin patch.

"This is incredible. Ming, I hope you're getting this. Ming?"

I turned to find her chair spun around as she hovered over the rear instrument panel. "It was recording perfectly until a few moments ago, but now the image is pixelating."

"It must be that magnetic interference. We're probably close to the plateau."

"Good," Ben said. "Once we cross the plateau we'll be in the northern basin, and the magnetic interference should pass. Looks like we won't be getting there along the surface, though. Guess it's back down to the basement."

"Wait," I said. "Are you able to get an atmospheric pressure reading?"

"Give me two minutes."

Before I could object, Ben had powered up the Valkyries, igniting the kelp strands in front of us. Within seconds we were rising through clear water, the lasers evaporating plants and barbequing fish as they burned a hole through the soil-covered surface.

Ming was livid. "You maniac. Look what you did!"

"What did you want me to do? We needed a place to surface, now we have one. No one needs to know."

"That is not the point. We did not journey into this pristine environment to destroy a fifteen-million-year-old ecosystem."

"Don't go all PETA on me, Ming. So I fried a few fish. Big deal. The dead will be eaten, and the algae will grow back."

Before she could retort, the *Barracuda*'s bow punched through the smoldering mattress of vegetation. The sub leveled out in the midst of a midnight fog swirling beneath a cloudlike ceiling of ice at least twenty stories high.

While Ben swore at the ice sheet and Ming swore at Ben, I used my night-vision binoculars to survey our new surroundings.

151

We were surrounded by a thick, undulating bed of vegetation. To the north the surface layer progressively expanded into a dark, lumpy moss and what appeared to be tens of thousands of snakes. After adjusting my focus, I realized they were roots growing out of the marsh. With no sun to reach for, the growths had twisted horizontally into thick briar patches, nourished solely by the chemosynthetic-rich soil.

Farther out still, I saw the dark silhouette of a rise.

Ben and Ming were still arguing in my headphones, distracting my thoughts. "Enough," I yelled, silencing the voices in my ears. "Ben, I thought the plateau that divides the lake's northern and southern basin was underwater."

"Depth is seven hundred feet, according to Vostok Command. Why?"

"Because there's a ridge out there preventing us from entering the northern basin, and it's definitely not submerged."

My two shipmates located their binoculars and panned the northern horizon.

Ming didn't seem too surprised. "At least three nations studying Vostok claim the lake has islands and tides. Perhaps these radar scans were completed at low tide and confused the partially submerged ridge for islands."

Ben angrily shoved his binoculars back in their pouch. "Maybe Vostok does have tides, or maybe somebody just screwed up. If a high tide is coming, it'd better get here soon. Otherwise we have about nine and a half hours to figure out how to cross a land bridge in a submersible."

"There's something else," I said. "The external air pressure has dropped again, this time from thirty-nine hundred psi to just over four hundred. That's a massive pressure differential."

Ming theorized. "The geothermal vents heated the water. The warmth melted the ice, which carved out the bottom of the ice sheet, creating more air space. That space filled with compressed

152

oxygen and nitrogen particles, which are perpetually being squeezed to the bottom of the glacier. It is this atmosphere that is counteracting Vostok's external pressure."

"That doesn't explain the magnetic interference that's scrambling your cameras. Ben, as much as I'd like to believe in the tides, I think you'd better take us deep. Maybe we can find an underwater passage that leads into the northern basin."

The *Barracuda* slipped beneath the algae mat and descended.

Dancing in and out of our exterior lights was bio-diversity on a scale I had never seen before. There was the kelp forest—a million inverted olive-brown tentacles swaying with the current. Then there were the kelp-feeders—anchovies and mollusks, along with countless other dark creatures. Finally, there were the packs of carnivore fish, their presence attracting a few rogue predators.

Perhaps it was to keep Ming on his good side, but Ben made a special effort to maneuver the sub so as not to disturb the wildlife. At one point he even diverted from our descent so that Ming could collect samples of kelp and several anchovies using a vacuum tube.

Having acquired living specimens seemed to lighten Dr. Liao's soured demeanor.

It took Ben twenty minutes to dive beyond the olive-brown tentacles of algae into open water.

For a long moment we hovered, gazing at the abyss. Particles of brown soot and debris floated past our lights like dark, mesmerizing snowflakes. My eyelids grew heavy. I yearned for sleep.

"Guys, I'm wiped. Maybe we ought to sleep in shifts."

"Go on, Doc. I just popped a caffeine pill."

"Get some rest, Zachary. I will monitor the sonar array."

The *Barracuda* leaped ahead, jumping from three knots to twenty within seconds. Brown flakes flew past the acrylic glass like a dirty blizzard.

Settling back in my seat, I closed my eyes…

13

"This anomaly is so large that it cannot be the product of a daily change in the magnetic field."
—Michael Studinger,
NASA project scientist mapping Lake Vostok's magnetic anomaly

PING.

PING... PING... PING.

The acoustic disturbance jump-started my heart like a bad alarm clock. Locating my headset, I spoke into the mouthpiece, the soothing calm of my catnap eradicated. "What's wrong? Ben, why are you pinging?"

"We've reached the southern face of the ridge. You were right; the plateau runs straight up to the surface. Ming suggested we go active on sonar to see if we could find a breach in this underwater gauntlet."

I stole a quick glance at my control console. The depth gauge read 817 feet. Using my night glasses, I glanced out to starboard. We were heading west, moving parallel to an imposing cliff face covered in algae.

"How much of the plateau have you surveyed on sonar?"

"Only about four miles, but we're pinging every three hundred feet. All this algae deadens the sound."

Ming set off another ping. I switched my headphones to SONAR, following the rippling sound wave on my monitor as it reflected off the plateau, my eyes catching a blip dancing in and out along the right edge of my screen.

"There's something registering on our acoustic periphery."

"Tell me it's an underground river."

"Sorry. It's a biologic. Not a small one, either."

154

"How big?" Ming asked.

"I don't know. Maybe ten meters. It's about a kilometer to the west, hovering along the face of the plateau close to the surface. But stay calm. For all we know, it could be a giant sea cow. They were pretty common during the Miocene."

"A sea cow? How do you know that? Did you hear it mooing?"

"Take it easy, Ben. The way it's moving along the rock face suggests it's a plant-eater."

Ben stared hard at his sonar screen. "Ming, ping again."

The *gong* raced out in all directions, the reflection appearing on our monitors. A bright line swept clockwise across the grid, illuminating the blip to the west—along with a second object rising slowly away from the bottom a thousand yards south of our position.

Oh, hell.

"Zachary?"

"Yes, Ming, I saw it. Ben, bring us as close to the plateau as you can, then ascend the sub so that we're on an intercept course with that first blip. Ming, no more pings."

"That second blip—it's a predator, isn't it?"

"I think so."

"How big?"

"Trust me, Ben, you don't want to know."

Ben quickly closed the distance to the plateau so that the sub's starboard tailfin was within six feet of the rock face. Keeping our speed at fifteen knots, he ascended the *Barracuda* steadily from its eight-hundred-foot depth, his voice grumbling in our headphones. "I took this mission hoping to find fifteen-million-year-old mollusks, not thirty-foot lake carnivores."

"The thirty-footer is a vegan. It's the second creature we have to worry about." My eyes remained focused on the second blip on the monitor, still rising beneath us.

Ben would not let up. "You're assuming it's a predator. Tell me why."

"It moves like a carnivore. I think it's been stalking us. It's also fifty to sixty feet long, which renders it a threat."

"Another eel?"

"No, Ming. Eels prefer the cold. This creature was warming itself in the vent field like a reptile raising its body heat in the sun."

Ben veered us away from an outcropping of rock. "Bastard, you know what this is. He knows, Ming."

I ignored him, my attention focused on the second blip, which had suddenly increased its speed. "It's making its run. Okay, the first blip is grazing beneath the surface about a thousand feet to the west. Ben, you need to circle it without spooking it."

"What the hell for?"

"There's an old saying: when a hungry bear chases you through the woods, you don't need to be faster than the bear to survive—"

"—you just have to be faster than the next guy. Doc, I like the way you think." Ben accelerated after the first blip as the second blip accelerated after us.

We were two hundred feet below the surface, kelp whipping past our acrylic glass dome, when we heard a distinct cry over sonar.

"What the hell was that?"

"That, Ben, was the other guy. Come to course three-zero-three. Range to target is 260 feet."

He accelerated.

Three minutes later we sighted the first blip. It was moving through kelp ninety feet below the algae-covered surface. An adult female, she was thirty-two feet from her snout to her whale-like fluke, her bulbous body weighing well over ten tons. Her calf was a

156

third her girth, its bulk partially obscured in a cloud of its own blood.

"It appears to be a giant manatee."

"Same family, Ming. Essentially, it really is a Miocene species of sea cow."

"Look at those sharks circling below. All that blood in the water is like a dinner bell."

"The mother is trying to push her calf back to the ridge."

"She'll never make it," I muttered.

As we watched, an eleven-foot bull shark darted in from below like a missile and savagely tore a hunk of blubber from Junior's gushing belly. The calf cried out again, its almost human-like wail magnified in my headphones. Dozens of sharks were now circling below, hundreds of salmon soaring in and out of the chaos of blood and blubber to snap up morsels.

It was a Miocene feeding frenzy.

Then the second creature arrived, and this one scared the Highlands out of me.

14

"It would be so nice if something made sense for a change."
—Lewis Carroll

"Ben, it'll be focused on the calf's blood, so move us away slowly. Ben, are you listening?"

Maybe it was the unnervingly quick exodus of the other predators; maybe it was the fear experienced during our confrontation with the eels, but instead of heeding my advice Ben opened the engine up full-throttle.

As I feared, our sudden movement attracted the trailing predator.

Hugging the plateau, Ben raced the sub to the west, and the creature closed the distance from below.

Ming tracked it on her aft camera, the image partially scrambled from the magnetic interference. "Ben, it's gaining. Do not slow down. Why are you slowing down?"

"Outcroppings. I can't react that fast."

"Then move us away from the ridge!" I yelled.

"I can't. It has the angle. It'll cut us off. How close is it now?"

"Eighty feet."

Ming screamed, "It's coming up beneath us!"

Ben pulled back hard on his joystick, accelerating toward the surface at a steep angle as he ignited the Valkyries. The twin lasers burned through the thick ceiling of vegetation and suddenly we were airborne, soaring high over the algae-infested lake.

I caught a fleeting glimpse of coastal marshlands on our right just before the *Barracuda*'s keel slapped down hard against the unyielding chaos of roots and sulfur-rich soil carpeting the surface.

With the sub resting on its belly, the lasers burned nothing but air and darkness.

We were marooned.

Before I could contemplate our situation the vegetation mushroomed as the creature's snout, skull, and upper body breached beneath us.

Purussaurus!

My brain went numb as the forty-ton caiman thrashed and rolled and obliterated the mattress of minerals, churning millions of years of growth into liquefied muck.

Our vessel slipped sideways back into the swamp and found water. Ben slammed his right foot to his pump-jet propulsor controls, sending us into a barrel-rolling descent just as an eight-foot-long lower jaw snapped at our starboard wing, its fangs catching only vegetation.

The Valkyries opened a sizzling path in the olive-green kelp forest as we zigged and zagged our way through an underwater maze of jungle.

Following our trail, the Miocene monster stalked us like a hungry tiger.

Glancing at my sonar screen, I saw where Ben was headed and nodded tersely.

Fifty yards... thirty ...

The giant caiman's frightening head, as big as a tractor trailer, closed on our aft monitor.

Twenty yards... ten... !

We swerved to starboard, and the creature turned with us, its head rolling sideways as its jaws widened—

Crunch!

The *Purussaurus* engulfed the dead juvenile sea cow, along with the two whitetip sharks that were feeding upon its gushing remains. The giant croc slowed to swallow its meal, circling its kill zone lest another challenger enter.

Ben laid back in his seat, sweat pouring down his face. "Take over, Zach. Shut down the lasers. Keep us heading west. Ming... I deserve a bonus."

The Chinese beauty leaned over her console and kissed his forehead.

I engaged the controls and shut down the Valkyries, my eyes catching the air supply gauge as it inched below seven hours.

* * *

We were down to five hours and twenty-two minutes when Ming and I heard the faint sound of rushing water over our headphones. Sonar tracked the sound to the west where a channel of current appeared to be rushing inland. The surface above us had no vegetation, the waves far too violent to allow anything to accumulate.

I roused Ben from his sleep. "We found something, a channel running inland. If the river cuts across the plateau it could empty into the northern basin."

"What happens if it strands us in the shallows and we beach? You want to be the one who gets out and pushes?"

Ming interjected, her tone soothing. "Ben, we have followed the plateau for twenty miles. From the satellite images we know the rise is at least thirty miles wide. Perhaps there is another inlet somewhere, but if we do not begin crossing the plateau soon we will run out of air."

The pilot nodded. "I'll take the conn. Zach on sonar. Once we move into the channel, I want you to go active to gauge the depth. If it seems deep enough we'll give it a shot. If not, we head back and continue the search. Agreed?"

"Agreed."

Ben took a moment to relieve his bladder using his plastic-bottle urinal. Then, taking over as pilot, he ascended the sub into the channel.

We surfaced into a swiftly moving deluge, driven by ten- to twelve-foot waves that lifted our craft and nearly tossed us over the first curl.

Ben accelerated ahead of the next swell, offering us a glimpse of what lay ahead.

The water was being channeled between two headlands, seven- to ten-story cliffs that jutted out into the lake. The waterway was as wide as an eight-lane highway, but its length and depth were impossible to gauge.

I waited until we were closer to the whitewater entrance before going active on sonar.

The acoustic *PING* rippled across the channel, its reverberations painting the waterway's topography. The river swept inland another half-mile before the shallows appeared, where the depths reduced from seven hundred feet to eighty-five feet—certainly deep enough to accommodate our tiny sub.

The sonar signature disappeared into white noise as the river turned to the northeast.

Ben kept us in the middle of the channel. Volcanic cliffs rose to either side of the sub, waves crashing against the base of the plateau.

As we ventured farther inland, a blip appeared on my screen as something massive rose off the bottom.

"Zachary, what is it?"

"From its size, I'd guess another *Purussaurus,* or maybe the same one. It's still in the vent field, but it's ascending toward the channel."

Ben cursed under his breath. "In for a penny, in for a pound."

The *Barracuda* accelerated through the chop, our propeller's signature lost in the whitewater.

"Talk to me, Zach. Can that croc follow us inland?"

"Yes, but that doesn't mean it will. The entrance is plenty

deep. I can't see anything beyond the first curve. It's getting a bit rough topside."

"Got it." Ben dove the sub, killing our external lights in favor of his night-vision goggles. A Miocene river bed appeared below us in bright green, littered by harrowing outcroppings and boulders that churned the surface at twenty-three knots.

My pulse raced as the *Purussaurus* entered the channel.

We followed the waterway inland for several miles, the canyon's walls gradually settling along either side of us into a rocky embankment, the volcanic rock slick with algae.

The sound of rushing water grew louder in my headphones until I was forced to pull them away from my ears. "We're either approaching rapids or the dispersal zone of a waterfall. Can you back us off?"

"Negative. We're caught in its vortex. There's no room to come about. Hold on, boys and girls, we're going through."

A thunderous echo of water reverberated through the *Barracuda* as the river curved to the east, slinging us sideways and grinding the keel against unseen rock as we spun downstream through subglacial rapids, the whitewater tossing our submersible about like a log.

Closing my eyes, I held on in the turbulent darkness, waiting for the sudden rush of freezing water as our inverted cockpit repeatedly bashed against unseen rocks. I thought about Brandy and William and cursed the selfish decision that defied my own fear and intellect. Most of all, I cursed Angus for having manipulated me.

Who was I kidding? The decision to accept the mission had been mine to make. I had forfeited happiness for a shot at immortality, and for that I would pay the ultimate price.

Emptiness replaced fear as I realized I'd never hold my beautiful bride again, never play ball with my son, never walk him to school or watch him grow up or graduate or raise a family of his own. With my death, those responsibilities and the rewards that came with parenthood would be passed on to his mother and whomever she chose to fill the void I was about to leave in her life.

These toxic thoughts were shunted as an unseen force drove us bow-first into the river bed. I heard Ming cry out as the sub's tail rose behind us, the river pinning us upside-down at a nauseating angle for untold torturous minutes.

Locating our exterior lights, I powered them on to reveal our bow now wedged tightly in an underpinning of rock and held fast by the force of the current. Through my moans and the thunderous current, I heard Ben yell, then felt his grip on my shoulder. "Release your harness and climb up here with me and Ming."

With trembling fingers I pried open the latch to my harness and tumbled out of my seat onto the now-slanted roof of the acrylic pod. Crawling on my belly, I made my way into Ben's cockpit.

Ming remained suspended upside down in her seat, her wavy brown hair dangling from her scalp.

"Zach, we're caught in a sieve. There's a hole in the rock where the river flows through. The sub's pinned by the current. We'll die down here unless we can free ourselves."

"How?"

"I shifted the prop's gear into reverse. I'll gun the engine and try to rock the sub enough to catch the main current with our tailfin. Climb back into Ming's cockpit. Use your weight to help sway us back and forth. If that's not enough, be prepared to slam your body against the highest point of the sub."

I nodded and then crawled into the rear compartment. "Ming, you okay?"

"My head hurts. Please hurry."

Ben reached up to his command console's joystick and revved the propeller in reverse, pressing foot pedals with his free hand to get the sub to rock. I tried to shift my weight with each roll, but it wasn't enough to free the bow.

"Zach, when I say jump, jump up and grab hold of the back

163

of Ming's chair. On three. One... two... three!"

Reaching high overhead, I slid my hands along the base of Ming's chair and jumped just as Ben rocked the sub in the same direction. For a surreal moment I seemed to defy gravity as the *Barracuda*'s tail caught the current, which pried the bow free and flipped us into the river's powerful vortex.

Flung head-first into darkness, I slipped into its warm embrace.

15

I opened my eyes and was surrounded by darkness. The heavy rush of the river was gone, replaced by the pitter-patter of raindrops splattering across a metal surface somewhere above my head. My skull throbbed in pain. Reaching for the source, I felt blood pooling behind my neck.

I tried to move, but my upper body was pinned by an immoveable object. Slipping close to panic-mode, I twisted my head free and managed to sit up, my eyes latching onto a blue LED light that slowly orientated me.

You're in the forward cockpit. The sub's upside-down.

"Ben?… Ming?"

No reply.

Feeling beneath my inverted chair, I found an emergency kit and a flashlight. Crawling on my hands and knees along the cold curvature of the acrylic dome, I squeezed myself into the middle cockpit and found Ben lying face-down, either unconscious or dead.

I reached for his right wrist and felt a pulse. Using the light, I did a quick search for open wounds as I roused him. "Ben, wake up. Come on, rise and shine."

He coughed, groaning as he rolled over. "What happened?"

"I don't know. The current freed us, but I have no idea where we are. The sub's on its back."

He sat up, striking his head on the pilot seat's inverted joystick. "Ow. Why'd the engine shut down?"

"I don't know. Wait here, I'm going to check on Ming."

I crawled back to her cockpit. Still strapped in her seat, she was suspended upside down and appeared to be unconscious. Reaching up, I opened the latch to her harness and let her lithe gymnast's body slide into my arms.

"Ming, you okay?"

"Zach, forget her. I need your help."

I laid her down gently on the cockpit's inverted ceiling and crawled back to Ben's compartment. "What's wrong? Are we powerless?"

"If we were powerless, we'd be dead. Hear that humming? That's our lithium-ion batteries."

"How long will they last?"

"Longer than us, I'm afraid." He pointed to the inverted air gauge: 147 minutes.

My limbs began to tremble, fear pushing my mind toward a place that I knew would end badly.

"We're in a bit of trouble here, Zach. The river left us high and dry on its bank. We need to find a way to maneuver the *Barracuda* back into the water, then manage our way across this plateau into the northern basin and locate our extraction point. Allowing for a minimum ascension of thirty minutes, we need to accomplish all that, well, pretty damn fast."

"The river must be close. Maybe we can roll the sub manually, like a log."

"You're reading my mind. First things first, we need to retract the *Barracuda*'s wings. I'm seeing double right now, so maybe you can locate the stabilizer controls on my command console."

Balancing on my knees, I used the flashlight to search the control panel. "Got it."

"Beneath—I mean above—the stabilizer are two small T-bars. Pull them toward you and the wings should retract."

Locating the devices, I gave them each a sharp tug.

166

A whine of hydraulics joined us in the darkness as the wings retracted, sending the *Barracuda* barrel-rolling down an embankment.

There was nothing to grab hold of, just dizzying darkness and painful bumps and an elbow to the head that drew stars. With a jarring *thud*, we stopped, the sub landing right side-up.

Ben and I moaned as we disentangled ourselves in the narrow cockpit. Crawling over his dashboard, I dropped into my leather chair and closed my eyes against the vertigo and a nauseating drop in blood sugar. Feeling for my personal storage area, I removed a bottle of water and a bag of trail mix and ate.

"Zach, use your night glasses. See if you can find the river."

"We're in the river," Ming said, groggily. "The water is gone."

I searched for the night-vision goggles, put them on, and stared out of the bow at the alien landscape. We were in a gully as wide as a city block, its depths tapering down two stories. The surging rapids had been replaced by a three-foot-deep trough of water, interrupted by patches of volcanic rock and mud.

"Ming's right, Ben. We're in the river, but the water's gone."

"Gone? How? Where did it go?"

"Vostok has tides," Ming reminded us. "We left on a full moon. Perhaps we are experiencing the effects of— "

"Come on, Ming. Full moons don't cause a fifty-foot drop between high tide and low tide. Tell her, Zach!"

Ben was losing it.

So was I.

My eyes locked on the LED instrument panel before me, hoping to steady the vertigo.

"Zach, what's your external pressure reading?"

I glanced at the gauge, blinking several times. "This can't be right. The gauge must have broken when we flipped. I've got 228 psi. What could be causing it?"

"It must be it," Ming muttered.

Ben turned around, suddenly animated. "I knew it! I knew you were MJ-12."

"I don't know what you mean, *Captain.*"

"The hell you don't. Why don't you tell Dr. Wallace what's causing this magnetic interference? After all, that is why we're here."

"What's he talking about, Ming?"

"Nothing. It is simply a theory."

"A theory... really?"

"Ben, take it easy."

"No. No, I want to hear about this theory—the theory that funded this expedition. Isn't that right, Dr. Liao?"

"Ignore him, Zachary. My sponsors funded this historic mission to advance science."

"Your sponsors, of course. Tell us about your sponsors. Agricola Industries, for instance. Why would a private Canadian firm specializing in tar sand technology invest over half a million dollars in an exploratory mission of a subglacial lake? Doesn't make much sense until you do a little digging and learn that Agricola was bought out two years ago by ITT. Have you ever heard about ITT, Zach?"

"Why don't you tell me *after* we figure a way out of this mess?"

"They're big in transportation and energy," Ben said, "but their strength lies in the aerospace and defense sector. This is a company whose CEO met with Adolf Hitler prior to World War II, whose subsidiary owned a twenty-five-percent share of the German aircraft manufacturer that built Luftwaffe fighter planes. To show you how well connected they are, ITT received $27 million in restitution from the United States for damages inflicted upon their Luftwaffe plant as a result of the war. What a set of balls on these guys. They invest in our enemies, then sue America for fighting their German allies. And the bastards win! They were involved in the 1964 CIA coup in Brazil, the 1972 Republican National Convention scandal, the 1973 Pinochet coup in Chile, and in 2007 Ming's sponsor became the first major defense contractor to be convicted of criminal violations of the U.S. Arms Export Control Act when they transferred classified information about laser weapon countermeasures to China."

"How do you know all this, Ben?"

"It's public record."

"Let me rephrase that. *Why* do you know all this?"

"I know it because their defense sector is a front for MAJESTIC-12, a tightly wound group of puppet-masters who profit from war and are committed to maintaining the status quo when it comes to our energy supply. Big Oil, Monsanto, the military industrial complex, and a select group of bankers... don't roll your eyes, Zach. I'm not a conspiracy theorist. Discover a new clean-energy source that can free us from fossil fuels and these boys will deny you a patent, steal your technology, and crush you like a bug. There's a reason they're funding this little venture, but it has nothing to do with marine biology. Oh, and you can bet the farm it was their GeoEye-1 satellite that pinpointed our location when we splashed down a million miles off-course."

The satellite... Vostok Command can't send help unless they know where we are!

Spinning my chair back around to my command console, I powered up the Valkyries, creating a heat signature for their thermal imaging sensors.

Ming and Ben continued wasting our air supply. "My job in organizing this venture, Captain, was to procure enough funds to cover the technological expenses. So what if a defense contractor invested in our mission?"

"Vostok's huge. Yet somehow you managed to select a splashdown site where the magnetic anomaly is at its strongest?"

"It's a geological phenomenon. I'm a geophysicist."

"A geophysicist who recruited Zachary Wallace as a front, to fool the Russians into believing the mission's aim was to discover new life-forms. Of course, you never said what kind of new life-forms."

The conversation was getting heated and more than a little weird. Perhaps I might have cared had we not been running out of air.

Thick droplets of water rained down from the ice sheet, dropping out of a dense fog. The river bed twisted up ahead to the right. Beyond that, we'd probably never know.

What if there was water around that bend?

My eyes returned to the gauge monitoring the exterior pressure. *How much could the human body handle? The ice sheet was obviously off the scale, but 228 psi— that equated to free diving in about 350 feet of water. The world record for free diving was about 420 feet. I was certainly no diver, but leaving the sub wasn't about holding my breath, it was about being able to handle the extreme pressures that would be squeezing my ears, sinus cavity, and lungs—something I had faced years earlier when our submersible had suddenly cracked open in the depths of the Sargasso Sea.*

If water was out there, could we drag the sub to it before our air cavities ruptured?

I was about to broach the subject with my bickering shipmates when we felt the river bed beneath us rumble.

Silence took the sub. I quickly shut down the Valkyries while Ben extinguished our exterior lights. Huddling in the dark, the three of us searched the landscape using our night-vision goggles.

The reverberations were getting closer, and then a creature appeared over the rise and I forgot all about venturing outside.

It was a *Purussaurus*, a pregnant female, I surmised from its labored gait. Staking out a sand-covered expanse close to the river bed and less than fifty yards from our sub, the eighteen-ton prehistoric crocodile began digging a hole with her clawed hind feet while her enormous tail swished back and forth, flicking debris in every direction.

Ben backed away from the glass. "Mother of God... I seriously need to be drunk."

Sand rained across the pod, obscuring our view. I heard Ben offer Ming something. A moment later, he leaned over into my cockpit and passed me an open whiskey bottle. "A gift from your Viking pal. Go on, it'll make it easier."

I took a long swig and passed it back to him. "I feel like such an arse. For the first time in my life, I had it all—the girl of my dreams, a son, a prestigious job. Why'd I do it?"

"You're a scientist; you did it for the work."

"No, it was my stupid ego. Over three thousand people have climbed Mount Everest, hundreds have been in space, but Vostok—I wanted to be the first, the Neil Armstrong of subglacial lakes, the marine biologist who ventured back in time."

"I suppose that makes me Buzz Aldrin. Want to know why I took this mission?"

I glanced at the air gauge. "You have fifty-seven minutes, go for it."

Taking the whiskey again from Ming, he took a long swig. "I'm a fighter pilot. It's in our blood. My grandfather flew B-29s over Normandy; my dad flew F-16s during Desert Storm. Even my best friend, John Rodsenow, flies test planes for Skunkworks. The Air Force was all I knew."

The sound of dirt piling up on our hull grew more muffled as our burial deepened. I wanted to scream.

Instead, I grabbed the whiskey from Ben and swallowed until my stomach burned. "Sorry. You were saying?"

"Everything started with my grandfather. After WWII he was transferred to Wright-Patterson Air Force Base and OSI, the central investigative agency for the Air Force. Did you know the United States Air Force wasn't even established until 1947? That was the year an unidentified airborne object crashed on a ranch in Roswell, New Mexico. My grandfather was part of the official investigation, assigned to Project Grudge, which later became Project Blue Book. Data was sent to his office for analysis: reports of sightings, radar signals—all made by reputable people like military pilots and radar techs and police officers. Back then, no one had ever even used the term UFO. OSI kept a lid on everything."

"Wait," I said. "Are you seriously talking about UFOs?"

"Says the man who hunted the Loch Ness Monster. Sorry, 'biologic.' Wouldn't want to paint you as a nutjob. May I finish my story?"

"Do I have a choice?"

Ben ignored me and continued. "My father, Lieutenant Colonel Mark Hintzmann, experienced two close encounters. The first happened fourteen months after he retired from piloting jets. At the time, he was training as an aircraft control and warning operator stationed at the 753rd Radar Squadron at Sault Sainte Marie, Michigan. One night his phones lit up with calls from cops who claimed they were chasing three UFOs from Mackinaw Bridge up I-75. Dad checked his radar and sure enough, there they were.

"There were no written instructions for how to deal with a UFO, so my father called NORAD's chief of staff, a Major General Todd Coleman. Dad told Coleman there were two inbound B-52s en routed to Kincheloe Air Force Base minutes away from a head-on encountered with three UFOs and asked what he should do. The general ordered the bombers diverted to another AFB; then he told my father that if any reporters or cops asked, he was to tell them there was nothing on radar and to keep everything to himself.

"A few years later, Dad was stationed at Nellis Air Force Base in Nevada. Cool place, Nellis, very high security. It's the site where my buddy tests highly classified aircraft, designed and built by Lockheed Skunkworks. Anyway, one night around one-thirty in the morning, my father was walking back to his barracks when he noticed a crowd had gathered, everyone watching the northwest sky. Dad looks and sees flashing lights moving at incredible speeds that he estimated to be well over three thousand miles an hour. But here's what really blew him away—the UFOs would trek across the sky at super-high speeds, then suddenly stop dead and change directions. They were moving and changing directions so quickly that Dad said they were leaving blurs of light in the sky. As he and the others watched, these E.T. vessels aligned with one another to form a circle in the airspace just east of the Groom Lake Flight Test Facility, more commonly known among us alien conspiracy guys as Area 51. The UFOs began rotating in their circle when *poof*—they suddenly disappeared.

"Dad hurried inside to check with the radar techs on duty, who confirmed seven UFOs were flying back and forth through the radar beam, with an eighth vessel hovering at about eighty thousand feet. Everyone was watching it onscreen. It remained stationary for a good ten minutes, and then slowly descended until it dropped off the radar. It disappeared for another five minutes, then instantly re-appeared at eighty thousand feet, again just sitting in the sky, completely stationary. On the next radar sweep it showed up again, only now it was two hundred miles away. It hovered there for another ten minutes before repeating the pattern two more times."

We were down to our last fifty-two minutes of air, yet I was on the edge of my seat, buzzed and listening. There was nothing to question here. Ben was repeating classified information on his deathbed before all three of us suffocated.

Ming was listening too. "What happened over Pakistan?"

Ben turned to her, close to drunk. "Give me a kiss and I'll tell you everything."

She leaned over his seat, and I became the third wheel as they made out in the darkness.

I stared at the air gauge: forty-three minutes.

After a minute Ben continued his story. "Pakistan. In the fall of 1998, I was assigned to an air division in the Persian Gulf. I had all the top security clearances and was one of the control officers who had access to the nuclear launch authenticators. One night our radar detected a UFO hovering over a Pakistani nuclear site, and yours truly was sent to be our eye-in-the-sky.

"This wasn't our first close encounter with E.T.s over nuclear facilities. Many insiders shared the belief that it was our nuclear tests, combined with the bombings at Hiroshima and Nagasaki, that summoned them to Earth in the first place. Over the years I'd seen top secret SAT photos taken of both U.S. and Soviet nuclear sites. Sometimes in the process of verifying a SALT Treaty we'd find objects in those pictures that shouldn't have been there. In fact, on my first tour in the Middle East I was briefed about a 1976 UFO incident over Tehran. Two F-4s from the Iranian Air Force had tried to intercept the E.T. vessel. When the Iranian pilots turned on their fire control systems, their electrical systems went out, and they had to return to base.

"Anyway, I was in my jet approaching Pakistani airspace when I received word that the UFO was hovering a thousand feet over their nuclear facilities and everything had gone black—no power. Since the Pakistani radar was dead, my supervisor decided it was politically safe to take a closer look. I executed a steep dive and leaped down from forty thousand feet. I had the UFO painted on my radar; I could see his lights in the distance. Then I saw it—a saucer as big as a city block with a four-story-high dorsal-fin-shaped conning tower. At least that's what it looked like to me. The vessel was hovering over the nuclear weapons facility while four Pakistani JF-17 interceptors bore down on us from the southeast. Without warning, the UFO took off like a speeding bullet and disappeared into orbit, leaving yours truly in Pakistani air space on Pakistani radar over their powerless nuclear weapons facility.

"The Pakistan government blamed the United States, and I took the fall. A falsified psychiatric evaluation all but sealed my doom. Six months after I received my walking papers, a guy named Steven Greer contacted me.

"Dr. Greer had left his career as an ER physician to dedicate

174

his life to persuading military and government officials to come clean about UFO sightings—not just to convince the public they were real and meant us no harm, but to release extraterrestrial technologies, which the military industrial complex had been suppressing, that could supply society with an endless supply of free, clean energy. In 1993, Greer had met with a group of military advisors to find a way to poke holes in the dam of secrecy and disinformation that had obscured the truth about extraterrestrial contacts since 1947.

"Greer had been selected to carry the disclosure baton for multiple reasons, not the least of which was the access he gained to military and political leaders. He and his lawyer used the Constitution to create a legal loophole in the Classified Information Nondisclosure Agreement signed by all military and civilian personnel with top-security clearances. Greer was able to convince hundreds of individuals with top secret clearances who'd had encounters with UFOs to come forward to testify on May 8, 2001, at the National Press Club Meeting in Washington, D.C., at an event called *The Disclosure Project*.

"Armed with classified photos and testimonials from hundreds of seasoned Intel and military commanders, pilots, and NASA and FAA officials, Greer put together the briefing materials requested by President Clinton. He personally briefed James Woolsey, Clinton's first CIA director, along with the heads of the Defense Intelligence Agency, members of the Senate Intelligence Committee, and a select number of congressmen. To his shock, Clinton was denied access to MAJESTIC-12, which was operating on an annual multi-billion-dollar black budget, free of congressional oversight. Greer learned that there is a shadow group—a cabal—made up of the four largest banks, which also own and operate the four largest oil companies. These cartels work hand-in-hand with the defense industry and orchestrate the wars that finance their entities. They own every major newspaper, magazine, radio, and television network, which allows them to black out news stories that run counter to their enterprises. When inquiries are made, people turn up dead, and no rank is too high to be assassinated. CIA Director William Colby agreed to support Greer's investigation—until his body turned up in the Potomac River.

"That was a warning to Clinton and other members of the cabal who might think of defecting. President Obama received his warning while in Norway to receive his Nobel Prize. On December 9, 2009, MJ-12 fired off a scalar burst over Oslo from one of their satellite weapons. A scalar weapon uses gravitic waves to vaporize targets, and the Norway blast left behind a blue spiral in the night sky that was witnessed by thousands. Obama was put on notice that he may be President, but the cabal is still in charge. This group has one singular objective—to acquire E.T. technologies for weapons applications while keeping a tight lid on clean, unlimited power-generating systems that would essentially solve the planet's energy crisis and put the fossil-fuel industry out of business. The powers-that-be don't want that... do they, Ming?"

"No."

My eyes widened. "This is true? This conspiracy stuff is real?"

She nodded. "I was sent to East Antarctica to determine the feasibility of accessing Lake Vostok from Prydz Bay. The Loose Tooth Rift is opening above a subglacial river that runs west beneath the Avery Ice Shelf before forging south to connect with Vostok's northern basin. As for your involvement, Ben is right; we used the discovery of the Miocene fossils as an excuse to mount an exploratory mission into the lake. And your presence legitimized the ruse."

"I don't get it. What ruse? What mission?"

Ben took another swig of whiskey and passed the near-empty bottle back to Ming as another swath of sand rained down upon our sub. "A few years ago SOAR, the Support Office for Aero-physical Research, sent a reconnaissance flight to conduct magnetic resonance imaging over Antarctica. When they flew over Lake Vostok, their magnetometers went nuts. Scientists from Japan and Germany later confirmed the presence of a magnetic anomaly in the subglacial lake along a rise located in its eastern sector. The affected area spans a sixty-five-mile radius. Whatever's responsible for throwing us off-course probably packs enough juice to power every city in the world for the next hundred years."

"That doesn't mean it's an extraterrestrial spaceship."

"What else could it be?"

"Any one of a dozen things—from a localized variation in the earth's magnetic field to the magnetism of the geology due to the impact of an asteroid. Antarctica got walloped by a huge one about 250 million years ago—killed just about every life-form on the planet."

"Believe what you want, Zach. Eighteen months ago, my buddy at Skunkworks told me he saw engineering schematics for a thirty-seven-foot submarine named the *Tethys*. He told me it was a black-budget project designed for one purpose—to access Lake Vostok by traveling *beneath* the East Antarctic ice sheet through a network of subglacial rivers. The sub's bow is equipped with a Europa-class Valkyrie laser, an energy-sucking beast designed specifically for Jupiter's frozen moon. The E-class is powered by its own nuclear reactor that superheats its exterior hull plates. The conductor plates are composed of a calcium isotope that can maintain temperatures of fifteen hundred degrees Fahrenheit without compromising the metal."

"And your friend saw this sub being built?"

"No, just the plans. The moment it gets funded, Dr. Greer will go public with photos of the E.T. ship I was assigned to bring back with me."

Ming drained the remains of the whiskey. "The Chinese have a similar project in development. The project gets funded or derailed based on my report."

"So you used me, the two of you. Thanks for nothing."

"Sorry, Doc."

"Zachary, if it means anything to you, your family will be compensated."

I thought of Brandy raising William alone and teared up.

Ben whispered something to Ming. Then I heard him climb back into her cockpit.

A million lightyears from home, sitting alone in ·the dark, I watched the minutes count down, still too sober to cope with what was coming—the futile gasps, the panic. I thought of Brandy and our final minutes alone together by Urquhart Castle. I thought of William—

—my memory disrupted as the sub started rocking and filled with the sound of Ming and Ben groaning.

Great. My last few minutes on Earth will be spent listening to these two getting it on in the backseat.

The cockpit began spinning in my head.

Less than six minutes of air left.

I decided to record my final goodbyes on the *Barracuda's* black box and my audio journal before I lost consciousness.

"This is Dr. Zachary Wallace. We're marooned on Vostok's plateau, caught in a low tide, our air supply nearly exhausted. Please tell my wife that she was the only woman I ever loved. Brandy, please forgive me for not being a better husband. To my son, William: Willy, I was so blessed to have met you. I wish... I wish I had the chance to see you grow up. I wish there was a happier ending. Just know that Daddy loves you so very much and that I'll watch over you and Mommy from heaven. I promise."

The countdown approached two minutes.

I closed my eyes against the whirling darkness.

"Brandy, when you see Joe Tkalec, please tell him that he was a great teacher and I should have been a better student. This whole mission, it was ego-driven. Had I acted like a real scientist instead of a celebrity—so stupid, so selfish. Forgive me."

AUDIO ENTRY: FINLAY MACDONALD

25 SEPTEMBER 01:26 HOURS

Testing... test. This is Finlay MacDonald, True tae my Mukkers. If yer hearin' this, then I'm deid or worse. Or maybe I'm just prepping fer my *own* memoir... seemed tae work for my friend, Zachary Wallace.

Zachary's the reason I'm recording this entry, which I hereby authorize to serve as my *Last Will and Testament*, whereas I leave all my worldly belongings tae my sister, Brandy MacDonald-Wallace, and her son, my nephew William. Brandy, be sure tae check my savings account, as there's a sizeable deposit jist come in. Which leads me tae tonight's adventure and why I'm blabbing intae this device like a schoolgirl on prom night.

As I dictate this story, I'm confined inside an ADS. An ADS, William, is an Atmospheric Dive Suit tha' looks like something an astronaut might wear fer a walk on the moon. Being self-contained and pressurized, it protects the diver against extreme pressures and the bends. But it's a bit like carrying a cow tae market, so the joints have oil in them tae assist with movin' aboot.

The ADS I'm standing inside of right now is called a SAM suit, which is a newer, less confining version of the JIM suit I once made my living in, workin' oil rigs in the North Sea. I was a deep-sea plumber of sorts, fixin' leaks in two hundred meters of water. Not a job fer the squeamish.

Wouldnae recommend this job neither, truth be told. The SAM is packed inside an aluminum pod slightly bigger than our fat Aunt Lizzy's coffin. The pod's attached to a sled, and the sled's attached tae a torpedo-looking laser device called a Valkyrie which, as I speak, is burnin' its way through a bloody mountain of ice wit' yers truly stowed and towed as baggage.

Ben Hintzmann, tha' bloody bastard, the moment I saw him I teld Zach he was too full of himself tae be trusted as a pilot. Made a muck of this mission, he did. Now yers truly has tae take the plunge intae Antarctica's frozen arse like a warm suppository jist tae save my boy and keep my sister from bein' a widow. Bloody hell.

Jist so ye ken, Brandy, t'was the gents from NASA who recruited yer brother fer this rescue mission and not Ming Liao's team. The eggheads woke me up from a hard night's sleep tae tell me they had lost contact with Zachary's submersible, which had run aground. "Run aground?" says I. "How do ye run aground in a bloody subglacial lake?"

The lead gent, whose name fer any lawsuits was Stephen Vacendak, yammered about tides and volcanic rock and such, and then he put it simple: either we get Ming and the boys some air, or they'll be deid by mornin'.

Next thing I ken, I'm bein' dressed and hustled out of the dome intae the frigid night. A helicopter lands and they shove me in the cargo hold. Vacendak, who's apparently a colonel, talks tae me aboot his kayaking and mountain climbing adventures in some place called Ketchum before he hits me with the mission. "It's easy," he says. "The laser burns through the ice, towing the supply sled and pod. You'll be inside the pod wearing the ADS. The laser, sled, and pod are attached by steel cable to a surface winch. Once the laser melts through the ice you'll be lowered to the lake's plateau. Touch down, climb out, and we'll direct ye to the sub.

"Power is the first priority. You need to connect the fiber-optic cable to the *Barracuda* so we can remotely open the aft hatch and give you access to change out the sub's empty air tanks. Once you save yer friend, you'll need tae reverse the cable

180

connections. The Valkyrie is the first thing we're hauling up tae the ice sheet, followed by the sled and your pod. You'll be topside before the hole freezes over."

Maybe these rocket scientists took me for a dumb Highlander, but I had questions—like exactly how long will I be cramped in the pod, to which he says, "Not long at all. We've already burrowed through, so you'll shoot straight into Vostok. Simple."

"Simple?" I says. "Colonel, simple is pickin' yer nose. Carrying yerself inside an ADS on land is more akin tae pickin' yer mate's nose whilst the two of ye are riding high-speed motorbikes down a mountain road. One wrong move and yer on yer belly, pinned under the suit's weight."

Then this Colonel Vacendak fella says, "True, we'll make it a risk worth taking." And he offers me money tae rescue yer husband. Good money. Well, that got me tae thinkin'. First off, this entire rescue operation required serious planning and preparation. Second, ye don't come tae Antarctica with a SAM suit unless ye've got an experienced diver to use it. Which means the hole they already burned through must've had a diver on-board, which makes me Plan-B, which means Diver-A failed in his attempt... which means he's dead.

So's I teld the Colonel, "Look, lad, I love Zach like a brother, but seein' how I'm the only qualified diver on this entire bloody continent, ye'll be payin' me triple fer my services, with half tha' money wired intae my account *before* I climb intae that sardine can of yers." And he agrees without batting an eye.

Vacendak had the money wired intae my bank account before we landed in the middle of nowhere, on a desert of ice beneath a night sky sparkling with a billion stars. I climbed out into minus fifty-seven-degree temperatures and a wind that caught the open cargo hold and nearly blew the chopper over.

Two men in orange extreme weather gear grabbed my arms and led me tae a configuration of three trailers positioned bumper-to-bumper to form a triangle. In the space that separated them was a three-story, silo-shaped enclosure. There was also two trucks holding them large satellite dishes.

They led me inside the nearest trailer and through a control room to the central area, which was the launch site for the Valkyrie sled. The SAM suit hung upright on its support post like a scarecrow, its aluminum skin reflecting the portable overhead lights. As the NASA lads stripped me down tae my thermals, a serious-looking woman with brown hair and blonde highlights joined us.

"Mr. MacDonald? My name is Ashlynn Archer, and I'm here to brief you."

"I've already been briefed, lass," says I, "but do it all again if ye think it'll help."

"I'm not an engineer," she says. "I'm an animal behaviorist."

25 SEPTEMBER 05:02 HOURS

Sorry, Brandy, must've dozed off. Standing inside the SAM suit in this coffin is nae tha' bad. Sorta like bein' in a grinding, lurching down-elevator. However, there's lights and snacks and water inside my SAM suit, and a video monitor that plays movies. I fell asleep watching *Caddyshack.*

There's a window above my head. All's I can see is meltwater and ice and darkness. My helmet is off, held loosely and tilted so I can see the depth gauge, which reads 3,682 meters. Guess I'm nearly—

—ahhh... ! Bloody hell! I jist went intae freefall oot the ass-end of the bloody ice sheet. Cable must've caught. Now we're swaying and lowering through whit looks like a gray fog.

Thankfully, my left knee caught the helmet. I'm puttin' it on now. I'll record my internal communications and replay them for ye on the return trip, God willing.

25 SEPTEMBER 05:13 HOURS (Internal Recording)

"Mr. MacDonald, how was the ride?"

"Tha' last drop near give me a heart attack. How's aboot ye call me True, and I'll call ye Ashlynn."

"Mister—True—we're lowering you to the surface. Let us know the moment you touch down, and we'll do our best to keep your pod upright to make it easier to exit. When you're ready to exit, let us know and we'll open the pod's bay doors."

"Understood. Okay, I'm doon, but I'm leaning. Ashlynn, darlin', have yer team take up a meter of slack before I fall oot and cannae get up."

"Stand by. How is that?"

"Better. Thank ye, darlin'. Ye can open the doors now. Activating my night vision. Looks like I landed in a gully... shite."

"What's wrong?"

"I think ye dropped me intae the river bed. I jist sank knee-deep in mud and sand. Where's the bloody sub?"

"Eleven meters on heading two-six-three. Before you head out, be sure to bring the air tanks with you."

"I'm opening the storage container now. Six air tanks on a sled. Ye NASA folk think of everything."

"True, don't forget the fiber-optic cable. The adapter plug is attached to the back of the Valkyrie."

"Got it. I'm proceeding on heading two-six-three. Stand by."

"True, you're breathing very hard. Your heart rate is over one-seventy."

"Try... walking... through sand... up tae yer knees... in a metal suit."

"Can you see the sub? It should be right in front of you."

"It's not here. Wait... there's somethin' buried. I think it's the sub. Ashlynn, the sub's covered. Can't find the arse end tae load the air. Give me a moment tae rest."

"No! True, listen to me. There's a good chance they're already out of air. If this rescue is going to happen—"

"There's water streaming around my legs. Holy shyte, looks like the beginning of a flash flood."

"True, the tide's rising. In a few minutes you'll be underwater."

"Water's clearing the debris off the sub, but I'm sinking deeper. Where's the bloody outlet for the fiber-optic... ? There ye are. Ashlynn, be a good lass and take up the slack from the cable before my ride home's washed away."

"Acknowledged. True, describe what's happening."

"The water's knee-high. I nearly lost the air tanks beneath the sub. Plug's now locked intae the outlet. Ye should have power to the sub."

"Yes, we've reestablished contact. We're opening the chassis now."

"Okay, lass, I'm in. Six empty tanks. Popping out the cylinder in slot number one... tha' was easy. Bugger! Havin' trouble lifting the replacement with this bloody clasper. Come on, ye bastard. Okay, tank one's connected."

"Roger that. Opening tank one now. Good job, darlin'."

"You sweet vixen. I ken ye liked me. Stand by, this river's

184

startin' tae float the boat. Tank two and three are in. Talk tae me, sweetie. Tell ol' True whit ye like aboot me."

"I like my men rough and tough."

"An' I like my women wit' blonde streaks in their hair. Four's in. Ah, shyte! Come on!"

"What's wrong?"

"Five's jammed, and the water's gettin' deeper."

"Skip five. Replace six and get the hell out of there!"

"Right. So? Does the carpet match the drapes?"

"Get back up here and maybe you'll find out."

"Ugh. The water's pushin' up the back of my SAM suit, pinning me tae the sub. Okay, six is in. Seal the—ahhhh...   bloody hell!"

"True, are you okay?"

"I'm neck-deep underwater...   both legs stuck in the mud. The current's too strong."

"Don't fight it; use it to push you up the bank. True?"

"Stand by. Okay... okay. Found some rocks. I'm underwater, fightin' my way up the northern bank... . so tired. Head's above water again...   twenty paces from the Valkyrie. Everything's danglin' above the river. Ashlynn, I'm going tae wade downstream. When I say, get yer lads to let out the slack, and I'll try tae grab hold of the bloody laser."

"True, don't go out too far. You'll get swept away."

"Fortunately, old True's got a lot of experience fighting currents. Okay, darlin', I'm in the shallows...   let it oot slowly... slowly...   tha's good. Here comes the Valkyrie...   got it. Ashlynn, give me five meters of slack, so I can lay everything oot on the river bank and realign the cable."

"You sound exhausted. Let me walk you through it. Tell me

185

when you have everything laid out."

"Done. But I cannae stand much longer."

"True, don't rest now. Can you see the cable? Disconnect it from the pod, using the snap hook."

"Bloody hell, the thing's frozen tight. River's rising up the bank. Might... might have tae take a raincheck on us, darlin'."

"True, focus! Align your pincers and open the snap hook. Do it!"

"Okay, I did it. Now whit?"

"Now you need to snap it in place on the Valkyrie. There's an eye-bolt located just behind its laser... True?"

"Got it. Whit's next?"

"Unclip the cable connecting the sled to the bottom of the pod. Rotate the pod 180 degrees, then reconnect the cable. This way you'll make the ascent head-up... True? True, don't go to sleep on me!"

"Sorry, jist dizzy. Water's ankle-deep. Got the cable free. Reconnecting the pod, window-up. What's next?"

"Seal the storage compartment of the sled, then get inside the pod and we'll haul you topside."

25 SEPTEMBER 06:22 HOURS

Back inside the pod now, Brandy girl. Can't believe whit jist happened.

When I went tae seal the storage compartment on the sled, my eyes caught sight of somethin' the rising river had exposed from beneath the sand. Oh, Brandy, it was incredible—an egg as big and oval as a ripe watermelon. Pliable like rubber. Clear and green as snot. And when I lifted it from the sand, I felt something alive wobblin' from inside.

186

Whit kind a prehistoric creature could it be? Whit if I could bring it tae hatch in Loch Ness? Would it bring the crowds back when it grew up, or would it eat them? Whit if we built a secure pen tae house the big fella?

I removed my flashlight from my utility belt and tried to look inside the egg. I could jist make out the creature's long neck, four webbed feet, and a long tail.

Good God, Brandy, I found me a plesiosaur egg.

Like a bairn on Christmas morn, I gently packed junior intae the sled's empty storage compartment, dumping arms full of sand along the edges tae secure it before sealing it shut.

"True, what's taking so long? Get in the pod."

"Easy Ashlynn, jist checking the cables."

"Get in the pod now—there's something large approaching your position."

Two awkward strides felled me to my knees. Unable tae stand, I crawled over tae the pod on all fours and flopped inside onto my back.

"I'm in, Ashlynn. Shut the bloody doors!"

The pod's bay doors slowly rotated into place.

I shook in fear, feeling the ground reverberating beneath me as Momma Plesiosaur approached."

"'Take up the slack, Ashlynn. Take it up now!"

A long moment's delay, then my head raised and the pod lifted off the ground. I waited until the hydraulic lock sealed the compartment shut before I peered out the glass using the helmet's night vision.

We were rising quickly, swaying some seventy feet off the ground when the monster suddenly appeared in the darkness below and leaped for the pod, nearly stopping my heart. I couldnae make oot Momma Plesiosaur's features, but her skull was as long as my body and her nostril big and round and it came within a bairn's breath of striking the pod. When she hit the river, the splash flung muddy water ontae the glass.

I laid back inside the SAM suit and removed the helmet, my pulse pounding. *"Ashlynn, any word from Zachary?"*

"Not yet, but he's alive. We're registering pulses from all three of the crew on their ECU jumpsuits."

"Thank the Lord."

"True, did you see it?"

"See whit, lass?"

"I thought maybe you saw the biologic; it was fairly close to you."

"Sorry, darlin', maybe next time."

Water and ice flowed past the window, signifying the beginning of my ascent. That's when my mind started thinkin'.

I ken I could git the egg back tae the dome, but how could I git it tae Scotland? It'd have tae be smuggled oot of Antarctica and taken back tae the U.K. in a private charter. The job called fer someone who was resourceful, devious, and lacking in all morals."

"Ashlynn, is it possible tae make a phone call from yer command post when I return?"

"I just might be able to arrange that. Who are you calling—not your wife?"

"No rings on these fingers, darlin'. No, it's a business call. I need tae speak wi' Angus Wallace, Zachary's father."

16

… Dr. Wallace, Captain Hintzmann, please respond. Vostok Command to Dr. Liao, Dr. Wallace, Captain Hintzmann, please respond…

The voice was muffled in a subconscious encased in sand. Gradually, the grains dropped away, and the voice grew louder until its persistence became maddening, an irritant demanding my attention.

I opened my eyes, confused by the brightness of the LED lights and the cool air blowing on my face.

"This is Vostok Command. Dr. Liao, Dr. Wallace, Captain Hintzmann, please respond."

My arms and legs were down there somewhere, refusing to cooperate as my mind tried to convince me to hit the snooze button.

Then an explosion of sound shocked me out of my paralysis.

Before I could test my new-found limbs, a concussion wave swept the submersible up in its vortex and flung me out of my seat.

The sub surfaced. To my horror, I found myself staring between swells at the female *Purussaurus*. The fifty-foot crocodilian was upstream, scrambling onto its belly, its attention focused somewhere overhead. Jaws fixed open, the giant caiman hissed as it reared back on its hind legs, balancing on its thick tail.

For a brief moment I thought the croc would leap. Instead it remained coiled and disappeared from view as the river's current swept us around a bend.

"This is Vostok Command. Dr. Liao, Dr. Wallace—"

"This is Wallace, stand by." I leaned over my seat to check on Ben. He was lying on the floor, unconscious.

Reaching to his command chair, I flipped the toggle switch on his joystick, relegating control of the submersible to my cockpit.

Strapping myself in, I started the *Barracuda*'s engine and resurfaced the vessel, keeping our nose pointed downstream.

"Vostok Command, this is Dr. Wallace. What the hell happened?"

"Wallace, this is Colonel Stephen Vacendak at Vostok Mobile Command Post One. Your vessel ran out of air. We were able to resupply you with five fresh tanks and reconnect your umbilical cord. For the duration of the mission you'll be communicating directly with me."

"Understood."

I heard a moan as Ben awoke. "Ugh. My head feels like it was used as a bowling ball. Ming, you okay? Get dressed."

The privacy curtain to Ming's cockpit was pulled open. Ben climbed over the back of his seat into his cockpit. "Zach, why are we alive?"

"Ask Colonel Vacendak."

"Where's that damn urine bottle? And who the hell is Colonel Vacendak?" Ben put his headphones on. "Hello?"

"Captain Hintzmann, this is Colonel Vacendak in Mobile Command Post One. Are you inebriated?"

"Inebriated? Hell no, I'm shitfaced drunk. Now who the hell are you and how is it that we have a Mobile Command Post that I never knew about?"

"You'll be briefed at the appropriate time. Is Dr. Liao all right?"

"Yes. What happened, Colonel?"

"We sent Dr. Wallace's friend on a rescue mission."

"True was down here?" I glanced back at Ben. "Where is he now?"

"Mr. MacDonald is en route back to the surface in a Valkyrie tow pod. For now, we want you to relinquish command of the *Barracuda* to us. We're going to remotely guide you across the plateau through a maze of waterways, then into the northern basin to your extraction point. You have just over nineteen hours of air in your tanks, but we anticipate having you topside in twelve. Any questions?"

"It's Dr. Wallace. How do we relinquish command?"

"First, you'll need to give control of the vessel over to Captain Hintzmann. Hintzmann, there's a red button under a plastic cap beneath your console. Pop open the lid and press the button to activate the remote. Once we take control, your computer screen should change to a GPS map of your surroundings."

Ben flipped the toggle switch on his joystick, regaining control of the *Barracuda*. "Is that it, then, Vacendak? One dive and Dr. Wallace and I are done?"

"We'll be asking you to complete one last task before your ascent, otherwise we want to analyze the discoveries you've made and determine the safest course of action before we send another team down there. Obviously, no one anticipated such an active food chain in Vostok; we'll have to reevaluate the mission. For now, just sit back and leave the driving to us."

"It's all yours, pal." Locating the master switch, Ben flipped open the plastic cap and pressed the button. Seconds later, our joysticks and foot pedals synchronized as Vacendak's team took control, accelerating the sub along the surface.

My night-vision goggles revealed our river had settled into a relatively calm waterway. According to our GPS feed from Vostok Mobile Command, the tributary would flow to the northeast, where it would drain into its far larger parent river.

The riparian zone we were moving along was similar to a shoreline one might find in Tibet's Mekong River, a barren stretch of volcanic rock that served as a flood plain during Vostok's mysterious high tide. Vegetation was almost non-existent, limited to an occasional patch of Matgrass, a brown meter-tall weed that fed off trace chemicals in the water. Other than that, the Miocene plateau was desolate; more of a drainage area than an ecosystem

191

save, of course, for the birthing zone of its giant prehistoric reptilian population.

After twenty minutes, moonscape-like features rose gradually from the river to meet the valley's watershed, a stretch of volcanic rock six stories high, the flat snow-covered plateaus created by the faulting and rifting occurring beneath East Antarctica. The ice sheet hung less than thirty feet above these mountain tops and its proximity dropped the valley's exterior temperatures well below freezing.

The thermostat would continue to drop as we distanced ourselves from the geothermally heated waters in the southern basin.

Ben tapped me on the shoulder, his index finger over his lips, indicating that I shouldn't talk. He handed me an instruction booklet where he had written a message in pen:

Colonel Vacendak is MJ-12. He's guiding us to the E.T.
I took the pen and booklet and wrote: *Suggestions?*
Ben responded: *MJ-12 wants info, not eyewitnesses. Trust no one, including ML.*

An hour later, the tributary merged with its parent river, and the landscape changed radically.

The waterway was several miles wide, its depths dropping more than 740 feet—as deep as Loch Ness. It was this body of water the Russians and Japanese must have analyzed when they had taken readings of the plateau. The river's dark waters ran a bone-chilling twenty-nine degrees, and snow covered the shoreline as far as my night-vision glasses allowed me to see.

We made two very startling discoveries in this frozen lost realm: the first was the existence of mammals.

Lazing about across the snow-covered banks by the thousands were a Miocene species of elephant seal. The males we spotted were few in number, but massive—thirty feet long and easily weighing more than six tons. Each bull perched upright on its blubbery hind quarters and was surrounded by a harem of females, their hides as white as the snow they were nesting upon. Every so often one of the males would jut its head back and bellow a primordial call throttle toward the ice-capped ceiling, the sound echoing across the valley.

The elephant seals were not the only mammals present. Before I could even contemplate their existence, the sub was swarmed by a greeting party of twelve-foot-long albino Weddell seals. Within minutes the carnivores went from curious to aggressive, bumping the submersible with their one-ton bodies, forcing Ben to take control of the *Barracuda* from Vostok Mobile Command and guide the sub into deeper water.

He had to alter our course again when a gray-white tornado of krill rose from the depths directly beneath us. The presence of these alabaster crustaceans quickly attracted a stubby species of dolphin, their muscle-bound hides completely black, giving them a decided advantage in this albino-dominated ecosystem.

"Guys, this makes no sense. Mammals can't survive in Vostok; they possess air cavities. The extreme pressures would burst their lungs like a ripe tomato."

"Zachary, what about those sea cows we saw in the southern basin?"

"Check the video, Ming. You'll see the species had evolved gills; they were breathing underwater. These mammals are clearly breathing air." I glanced at my control console. "Ben, what's your exterior pressure gauge reading?"

Ben shot me a look that translated into *play along.* "My gauge must be broken. It's reading two atmospheres, which we both know is impossible."

"Maybe, but it does explain how these mammals are able to inhabit this section of Vostok."

"Vostok Mobile One to Captain Hintzmann."

"Hintzmann here."

"Captain, we need you to restore control of the *Barracuda* to our remote pilot."

"As soon as we feel it's safe. Seems the wildlife down here are getting a bit frisky."

I flipped the toggle switch on my radio. "Mobile One, this is Wallace. Colonel, we're approaching a magnetic anomaly that appears to be responsible for equalizing atmospheric pressure. Assuming it's the magnetized remains of an asteroid, I'd prefer to give it a wide berth. You never know how these things might affect the sub's controls."

"We concur with your theory, Dr. Wallace; however, we feel the risk is minimal, and there's only one way into the northern basin. Just out of curiosity, Doctor, what makes you think the magnetic interference is coming from an impact zone?"

"Two hundred and fifty million years ago another asteroid, much larger, struck East Antarctica and wiped out ninety-nine percent of the life-forms on the planet. The impact crater was discovered beneath the ice sheet in Wilkes Land, which is about six hundred miles to the south."

"Is there anything you don't know, Dr. Wallace?"

"Yeah, I don't know where True is."

"He arrived topside eight minutes ago and is in the capable hands of my assistant, Ashlynn."

"That's my boy."

"Captain, six-point-five kilometers due east of your location is the entrance to a bay. Enter the waterway and return control of your vessel to our pilot. There's one last thing we need you to investigate before we guide you to the northern basin."

I glanced over my shoulder at Ben. "Can you give us a clue here, Colonel?"

"You'll be briefed at the appropriate time. Stand by."

The three of us remained silent for the next fifteen minutes as we made our way east, three hundred feet below the surface. Ming seemed especially distracted. Perhaps she had regrets about giving herself to Ben, or maybe she knew what the Colonel's "last thing" was.

Leaning back in my seat, I gazed out into the dark waters with my night glasses, listening to the distant chirps of the Miocene seals over my headphones. For the third time in my life, I had escaped almost certain death—the fourth time, if I included my final encounter at Loch Ness. While each circumstance had been different, I realized there was a common thread that ran through them: ultimately I had chosen to place myself in danger.

This realization made me ponder whether I had a death wish.

A strange sensation of déjà vu made me think of Joe Tkalec.

When was the last time I had spoken to him? Three years ago... a few days after my near-death experience in the Sargasso Sea.

My mind was adrift as I nonchalantly stared at the blip now appearing on my sonar screen. *Joe had chastised me for pushing the dive limits of our three-man submersible just so I could lure up a giant squid.*

"Yo, Doc? Are you seeing this?"

Was it my fault the pilot had died? Should we have surfaced the moment the biologic blooped in my headphones? If only we had gone active on sonar... realized their size and numbers—

Without thinking, I pressed the red button marked ACTIVE.

Ping.

"Zachary, what are you doing?"

"Huh? Sorry. There's something out there, I just thought ... " My eyes widened as data compiled on my screen. "It's a biologic. Range: 1.4 kilometers to the east. Depth: 833 feet. Geez, this thing is big."

"Another crocodile?"

"No, Ming. These waters are way too cold for *Purussaurus.*

Ben swore. "Any good news?"

"The good news is it isn't coming after us."

"Yeah, well, maybe you shouldn't have let it know we're

here."

I was about to retort when a flesh-tingling *zzzzzzzzzt* sound rattled the cockpit's dome. My stomach knotted. "I think I just screwed the pooch."

"What was that sound?"

"We were just echolocated. Ben, kill the engine."

"Damnit." Ben powered down the propulsors, allowing the neutrally buoyant sub to rise slowly to the surface.

"This is Colonel Vacendak. Why have you stopped?"

"We were just echolocated by a biologic, a Miocene sperm whale."

"Wait... that fossil we saw?"

"Easy, Ben. So far it's staying deep."

"But we're not. The moment we hit the surface, the river's current will carry us east again."

"Dr. Wallace, the biologic is circling between you and the entrance to the bay."

"Thank you, Colonel, we know."

"We suggest you wait until you get closer and then accelerate past it into the bay. We can guide you into the shallows where you'll be safe."

I turned and looked at Ben and Ming. "It's worth a shot."

The *Barracuda* continued to rise. As it drew closer to the surface the current swept us up and carried us east at seven knots.

Another tingling *zzzzzzzzzt* rattled the sub.

I listened intently on sonar. "Damn. It's either feeding along the bottom or waiting in ambush. I can't tell which. Twelve hundred feet until we pass over it. Hang tight, Ben."

"Captain Hintzmann, once you're in the bay, relinquish command and we'll remotely guide you to your destination. No worries; we'll see you past this little speed bump."

"Obviously you didn't see the size of the little speed bump's

196

teeth. Zach?"

"Stand by. Eight hundred feet."

Zzzzzzzzzzzzt.

I heard Ming cry out in the darkness.

"Three hundred feet. It's gotta know we're here. Ben, restart the engine but don't hit the gas until I say."

"Just keep in mind this monster probably has another gear, too."

"Two hundred feet. It's getting agitated... It just went vertical. Shit, it's fast. Gun it!"

I clenched my teeth and cursed myself as the propeller struggled to catch water a second before the back of my head hit the seat and we shot ahead—

—the surface behind us erupting.

I turned to see a white lower jaw and abdomen rise majestically from the depths.

Livyatan melvillei... This is insane.

For a spellbound moment the hundred-ton bull whale seemed to defy gravity. Then it collapsed belly-first in the water, its tidal-wave splash crashing over our acrylic cockpit. By the time the creature attempted to echolocate us again, we had entered the tributary doing thirty knots.

Ben continued on a northerly course for another three miles before he was convinced we were sufficiently safe enough to warrant turning the sub over to Vostok Command.

"It's all yours, Colonel."

I grabbed for the handrail as the *Barracuda* rolled into a steep dive, avoiding islands of ice. We accelerated through the depths, our sonar now thankfully biologic-free.

The sub surfaced thirteen minutes later. Our night-vision glasses confirmed we were now in a bay. Ahead was a peninsula, or perhaps it was a small island; it was hard to tell, as the coastline was partially obscured by mist. A snow-covered mountain towered seven stories above sea level, its peak reaching half the distance to the ice sheet ceiling.

Two hundred yards from shore our vessel suddenly accelerated through the ice-riddled surface, heading straight for land without any signs of slowing.

"Easy, Colonel, slow down!" I tightened my harness seconds before the *Barracuda* skidded out of the shallows and slid into a snow drift with a teeth-rattling *thud*, our impact chasing off a quartet of beefy female elephant seals.

"What the hell, Vacendak!"

"Sorry, kids, but we needed to get up a head of steam to beach your craft. Dr. Wallace, this island is the source of the magnetic interference that has equalized the pressure of the ice sheet and has enabled life to flourish in this section of Vostok. Before we pilot the *Barracuda* to your extraction point, we need the three of you to establish a sensory array around the base of the mountain."

I shook my head in disbelief. "Colonel, you don't seriously expect us to go outside, do you?"

"The pressure's normal in this area of Vostok; there's no danger."

"Apparently, you didn't see the size of the creatures you just scared off."

"The *Barracuda*'s exterior lights will keep them a safe distance away. I assure you, Dr. Wallace, it's perfectly safe."

"How could you possibly know that?"

"Let me rephrase that: setting up a sensory array on this island will be far safer than what you've already experienced. Dr. Liao, inside the storage compartment behind your seat you'll find a duffle bag containing Extreme Weather Gear, climbing axes, boots, and backpacks for each of you. Inside each pack is eighty feet of nylon rope, night-vision goggles, a night-vision monocular lens, bottled water, a first aid kit, and a lead case the size of a small poster tube. Do not open these tubes until you arrive at each of your designated coordinates, as they contain the sensory instruments. Inside you'll find a telescopic aluminum antenna capped by a small metal octagonal unit the size of a golf ball that will feel warm to the touch. But do not touch it; the reason it's warm is because the exterior casing is composed of plutonium."

"You exposed the three of us to plutonium?"

"The plutonium keeps the unit heated against the elements. I can assure you, Captain, the lead casing more than contained any harmful radiation."

"How are these sensory units powered?" I asked.

"A radioisotope thermoelectric generator provides electricity to five sensors designed to monitor everything from atmospheric pressure changes and energy fluctuations to magnetic variations. A computer vision system will create 3-D thermal images while another instrument uses x-ray diffraction to determine the mineral composites within the asteroid impact zone."

Ben winked as he passed me one of the neon-orange nylon backpacks, along with extreme weather pants, gloves, a hat, spiked climbing boots, and a jacket. There was also a combination magnetometer, GPS unit, and Geiger counter—all contained in a unit the size of my cell phone.

I tested the latter, just to make sure the plutonium canisters were doing their job.

We dressed quickly while the Colonel downloaded coordinates to each of our GPS units. "The first site must be established three-point-seven kilometers to the north at an elevation of seventy meters above sea level. Dr. Liao will remain at the first site while Dr. Wallace makes his way to the northwest coordinates, and Captain Hintzmann heads to the northeast. Once all three devices are powered up and the array triangulates, we'll send a signal through your GPS units to regroup with Dr. Liao. Return to the sub, and we'll have you at the extraction site in just under an hour. Are we ready?"

"Hell, no." Reaching above his head, Ben unlocked the hatch and popped open the acrylic dome.

A blast of subzero air forced me to quickly zip my jacket and mask my face. Ming passed her backpack to Ben, who then helped her out of her cockpit.

Adjusting the straps on my climbing boots, I exited the sub, purposely spiking Ben's leather seat with my steel cleats just for good measure before securing the hatch.

17

"I have seen so many extraordinary things, nothing seems extraordinary anymore"

—Lewis Carroll

I stood between Ben and Ming in our frigid surroundings, the three of us sharing the same sense of awe the Apollo 11 astronauts must have felt when they first set foot on the Moon, the same emotional rush a mountain climber experiences upon reaching the summit at Everest. For several minutes, we simply allowed our senses to partake of our Miocene world as we stretched away thirty-plus hours of cramped muscles. We inhaled Vostok's air, smelling its high oxygen content, registering a trace of dizziness in its purity. We listened to the ice sheet as it crackled and groaned and rumbled high overhead, its pitted foundation trickling droplets of water, each liquid discharge congealing during its twenty-second descent into golfball-sized meteors of slush. These semi-frozen projectiles delivered a painful wallop when they found their mark and were impossible to dodge, forcing us to cover our heads with our backpacks.

The ski goggles Colonel Vacendak had supplied us with were equipped with night-vision lenses, which painted the environment olive-green, adding a surreal alien element to our surroundings. Somewhere to the north a snow-covered mountain towered like a smaller version of the Matterhorn, its base enshrouded by fog.

The snow beneath our feet had been crushed by the elephant seals. We could smell the oily musk secreted by their blubber as it mixed with the saline bay waters lapping behind us along the shoreline. Yet, while the atmospheric pressure was tolerable, the electromagnetic elements in play were far from static. They caused our flesh to tingle and our hair to rustle beneath our hoods.

Removing the multi-purpose instrument from my jacket pocket, I attempted to use the global positioning system to get a fix on our first target. When the compass scrambled, I switched to the magnetometer, which registered 175,000 nanoteslas—the equivalent metallurgy of the New Orleans Superdome—about what you'd expect from an asteroid impact site.

Ben handed each of us a climbing axe and flashlight, both items trailing a cord that attached to our jackets' belts. "We'd better rope up. Zach, you take the lead. Then Ming. I'll bring up the rear. Use the handle of your axe to test the ice ahead of you. You hear something crack, back off fast."

Ming and I removed the ropes from our backpacks. I used mine to link my belt with Ming's. She attached her line to Ben, so that between us we shared 160 feet of nylon cord.

I set out from the shoreline, the metal spikes in my climbing boots slipping on the flat stones hidden beneath the packed snow. The herd of elephant seals grew restless as we approached, the adult females snorting and growling but yielding enough ground for us to slip past their beachhead and around a few boulders to where a thirty-degree slope led up to the base of the mountain.

Virgin snow greeted us as at an elevation of forty-five feet, our boots sinking in up to our calves… then our knees. Each step became its own adventure, the physical exertion forcing us to transfer the packs to our backs in order to use our arms for balance.

Extreme cold breaks down the body's reserves. My breathing became labored. My muscles trembled. My pulse became a heavy, rapid thud. I could feel frostbite exploring my feet, making my smaller toes tingle.

I heard Ming behind me. She was struggling as the slope grew steeper. Our pace slowed as we had to tug her along a few times to prevent a prolonged rest.

We entered a fog bank, a heavy white mist that seemed to stagnate over the base of the mountain. Over the next hundred yards, I became immersed in its emptiness, the mountain disappearing behind the mist and the knee-deep snow barely visible from one stride to the next. It was a complete whiteout except, of course, it was pitch-dark—olive-green in my vision. I would have lost it mentally had Ming not offered an occasional tug on the rope to reassure me I was not alone in this madness.

All but blind, I feared we could be walking in a giant circle, until I felt rock beneath my boots, the ground solidifying with each step. Another fifty feet elevated me above the fog, and I found myself at the base of the mountain, staring up at its snow-covered peak. Leaning against a boulder, I checked my GPS, which indicated I was in the green zone for Target One.

Ming joined me. She was shivering badly, approaching the threshold of hypothermia. Dropping to her knees in the snow, she handed me her sensory instrument. "Plant it for me. I'm too weak."

I unscrewed the lead cap and popped out the device, careful not to handle the octagonal-shaped plutonium unit. Stretching out the telescopic antenna, I plunged the pole's spiked end into the earth and snow, twisting it back and forth like a beach umbrella to deepen the hole before filling it in. After testing the stability of the pole, I powered on the sensory device.

Other than a reassuring hum, nothing happened. *And nothing will until all three sensors are working and the array is established, dumb-ass.*

I was taking another reading from the magnetometer when Ben emerged from the fog. He was sucking in lungfuls of air, on the verge of hyperventilating. "This… is… batshit crazy. Ming… you okay?"

She shook her hooded head no.

I pulled Ben aside. "Ming's close to hypothermia. The way I see it, we have three choices. We can leave her here while we plant the other two devices, in which case her core temperature will continue to drop and she'll probably die before we make it back to the sub, or we can send her back to the sub *now* while we plant the other two devices."

"What's the last option?"

"The three of us head back to the sub now and tell the Colonel to go fuck himself."

Ben gazed at the mountaintop. "Ordinarily I'd vote for the last option, but there are ramifications. Whatever's out here, it's been generating incredible gobs of energy for fifteen million years, which means the three of us are standing on top of the single most powerful thing in the solar system, besides the sun. Agreed?"

"No, but go on."

"My point is that an operation with a payoff this big is strictly black ops, which makes our Colonel Vacendak, at the very least, a Skunkworks engineer or, worse, a MAJESTIC-12 senior officer. Either way, if Vacendak suspects that we know what's really down here, you and I just became expendable. I'm not talking dishonorable-discharge-with-an-extended-stay-in-a-mental-asylum expendable. We'll simply disappear, and Vacendak will inform our next-of-kin we died in Vostok."

I felt lightheaded. "So what do we do?"

"We have to plant the other two devices, otherwise the Colonel won't take us to the extraction point. Send Ming back to the sub, and you and I play it dumb. There was just a mountain covered by snow. We planted the devices and left."

"No big deal. That's all there is as far as I can tell."

He nodded toward the summit. "Look closely. Hidden beneath all that ice and snow is the mast of an extraterrestrial vessel."

I looked, but all I could see was volcanic rock covered by snow.

He's obsessed. Don't argue. It's minus thirty degrees and Ming's dying. Humor him, plant the devices, and get the hell out of here.

"I'll get Ming started back down." He unclipped his rope from his harness.

"Ben, wait. Maybe you and I shouldn't split up. It might be safer if we hit the remaining two sites together."

204

"According to the GPS, the remaining targets are three kilometers from here. Roundtrip, that's just under a four-mile hike for each of us, plus the return trip back down the slope. If we did it together, we'd end up having to circle the entire base of the mountain, doubling our journey. That equates to an extra hour or more in this cold. All things being equal, I'd rather get the job done sooner alone than face freezing to death in pairs."

"And if one of us gets back here first? Do we wait for the other guy before we head back down, or do we meet at the sub?"

"We wait. Let's say fifteen minutes. If the other guy doesn't show up by then, we'll meet at the sub." He held out a gloved hand. "See you back here in thirty minutes."

"Or less." We shook on it; then he was off, setting a quick pace to the east.

I returned to Ming, detaching the two climbing ropes from her harness. "Ming, you can't stay out here. Do you have the strength to make it back down to the sub on your own?"

She nodded and stood. "Getting down is far easier than climbing."

I coiled one of the two lengths of rope, shoving it inside her backpack. "Follow our tracks; they'll take you right to the sub."

She offered me a pained smile and a thumbs-up; then she set off.

I coiled my rope and stowed it in my backpack as I watched Ming head slowly toward the fog bank. Then I climbed to the base of the mountain and headed west.

Mountain. *Not* alien spaceship.

As intriguing and believable as Captain Benjamin Hintzmann's close encounter stories had been, once one removed the storyteller's embellishments I knew there was a reasonable explanation for everything.

The same could be said about Lake Vostok's extreme variations in pressure. Magnetic anomalies in Antarctica were far from unusual, and an asteroid impact in a volcanically active region would yield a powerful magnetic resonance. As far as I was concerned, establishing a sensory array around an impact zone was standard operating procedure.

No, what concerned me wasn't the Colonel, it was Ben. The captain's behavior was anything but S.O.P. for a former member of the U.S. Armed Forces. Pilots simply didn't abandon their wingmen to turn the mission into a race. They stuck together against the elements, even if it meant walking a few extra miles in extreme weather conditions.

Yet Ben had not only preferred to separate, he'd seemed eager to go off on his own.

He thinks there's a spaceship down here, and he means to prove it to the world. Maybe he'll find an entrance inside. He'll snap a few hundred photos with his iPhone and send them off to Steven Greer and the rest of the E.T. screwballs in hopes of reclaiming his career.

The sudden realization of Ben's circumstances gave me pause.

He's a lot like I was. After the Sargasso Sea incident, my career was in serious jeopardy. When Angus tricked me into testifying at his trial, and the Inverness judge practically stripped me in court to reveal scars from a childhood attack on Loch Ness, my name was reduced to a punchline on late-night television. All my hard work and field research as a marine biologist—down the drain. My reputation was destroyed, my career in ruins. In the end, I had done exactly what Ben was attempting to do now: prove to the world he was right.

Feeling like the world's biggest hypocrite, I picked up my pace.

* * *

Twenty minutes passed. I had managed to forge a path as close to the base of the mountain as possible, taking advantage of the patches of exposed rock, but as I neared the area targeted on my GPS I was forced to move farther out, exposing myself to snow drifts and unseen crevasses. I was shivering badly, and my resolve was weakening.

The designated site was another thirty feet or so down a steep embankment. I stared at the spot.

Ten more paces across virgin snow. Three minutes max to set up the sensory device.

The air was thick and static, the snow muffling all sound. I remained motionless, listening to my rapid breaths, my life reduced to the emerald-green boundaries within my goggles.

I was hesitant. I was afraid.

What if the snow was over my head? What if I couldn't make it back up the hill?

Remembering the rope, I retraced my steps up the embankment to a cluster of boulders located at the base of the mountain, the smallest of which outweighed me by a solid ton. Removing the nylon rope from my backpack, I tied off one end around the nearest boulder and clipped the free end to the belt around my waist.

Feeling more confident, I backed down the hill, moving beyond my own tracks as I watched the GPS screen in my gloved hand.

I was chest-deep in snow when the target finder finally blinked green.

Working quickly, I freed the sensory device from its lead case, extended the support pole to its maximum length, and tomahawked the antenna into the snow drift so that only the octagonal sensor was showing.

I powered up the unit. Feeling a bit dizzy from the high oxygen content, I paused to rest while the sensory array triangulated.

I gazed overhead as the ice sheet rumbled like an approaching storm. Inching its way east toward Prydz Bay, the thirteen-thousand-foot-thick cap of packed snow was a living entity that affected the entire planet. For fifteen million years its weight had been held in check by an unseen magnetic source, and in the battle for supremacy, the resultant equilibrium had carved out a neutral zone where life had continued to flourish. Even now, the weight of the glacier was squeezing billions of gas particles of oxygen and nitrogen into the lake just so its trapped inhabitants could breathe.

Breathe.

Breathe, Zachary, breathe!

"Huh?" I raised my face out of the snow and gasped a breath.

Something had happened! Why couldn't I see?

For a terrifying moment I thought I had gone blind. Then I realized I had lost my night-vision goggles. A horrible pain radiated from my chest, the tightness clenching me beneath both armpits.

I was spinning, dangling from the rope in complete darkness. Reaching out, I brushed a rock face. That's when I realized what had happened—I had fallen into a crevasse.

How deep was the fissure?

Without my night-vision goggles, I couldn't see my own two hands in front of my face.

Cold, scared, and disoriented, I did the only thing I could: I climbed.

Using the rope for support, I walked my way up the rock face using my spiked boots. The rope was eighty feet long, but half its length remained topside so it only took me a few minutes to reach the ledge.

Sensing a change in the air current, I pulled myself out of the crevasse and onto my heaving chest.

For a desperate moment, I blindly felt along the snow for my goggles. Remembering the flashlight, I felt for its cord and powered on the light.

The beacon cut a narrow swath through the darkness. The crevasse at my back ran north-south, cutting a jagged eight- to ten-foot-wide gap fifty feet or so below the base of the mountain. The rift appeared to have swallowed the sensory device—and me with it.

Why had it opened? Could the sensory array have triggered it?

I shone the light down its gullet. The walls of the crevasse descended four or five stories, ending in a pile of snow.

Aiming the beacon ahead of me, I searched again for my goggles. Tracing the impression my body had left as I slid into the crevasse led me to them, the snow around them streaked with blood.

Touching a gloved finger to my running nose, I realized I was bleeding from both nostrils. Using my scarf, I wiped the goggles clean and put them on, then pinched my nose to stop the bleeding.

The crevasse appeared to circle the base of the mountain. A fog had formed, generated by the warm air escaping from the rift. The mist was so thick that my light couldn't penetrate it, but the sound did.

The growl was guttural, a predatory snarl that snapped my head around.

Heart pounding in my chest, I stared at the wall of fog that separated the edge of the crevasse where I now stood from the base of the mountain. I heard the animal's clawed feet moving over the rocks as it approached. I sensed its enormity as its front paws crushed snow. It was tracking my scent, drawn to my blood.

Cold sweat beads dripped down my face. I reached for the climbing axe resting by my right thigh and gripped its handle in both gloved hands.

Batter up, Zach. Just like hitting a fastball.

The next sound that came was a bloodcurdling cry, accompanied by quick strides through the snow that backed me toward the crevasse.

I saw the beast charge out of the mist—

And jumped!

I don't know how far I fell. All I know is that one minute I was falling feet-first and then I jerked to halt as something large and musky and covered in fur hurtled past me, howling as it clawed at the sheer vertical walls of the rift.

I heard it hit the ground below, the impact followed by a second and more solid *whump*, which drove the air from its lungs and the life from its body. Its death silenced the fissure, save from my own strained wheezing.

Reaching out, I managed to dig my spikes into a ledge, relieving the stress of the noose around my upper body. Still gripping the flashlight, I aimed its beam below.

The animal had struck the bottom of the chasm and had broken through to an immense cavern running below the crevasse. Even more bizarre, the hole it had opened up was radiating light. I removed my night-vision goggles, the luminescence appearing violet.

Reaching for the GPS instrument in my jacket pocket, I set the device to take Geiger readings and held it out, fearful of radiation.

The needle never moved.

Had it not been for that mysterious vein of light, I would have climbed out of the fissure and set off for the rendezvous point.

But why rush back? Hadn't I come to Vostok seeking knowledge about our past, looking for undiscovered life-forms? I was in no immediate danger. Vostok Command was certainly monitoring my vital signs through the sensory junctions of my ECU jumpsuit. And the Colonel wouldn't allow Ben to leave without me.

Climb down, take a quick look, and then leave.

I looked up, inspecting the interior of the crevasse through my night-vision goggles. The rift narrowed considerably to my left, enough so that I could wedge my body between the two walls and free climb up using my axe and cleats. That was important, as I might need the rope to climb out of the cavern. That meant climbing out of the crevasse, freeing the rope, and climbing back down to explore the subterranean opening, a chore that exhausted me just thinking about it.

Climb out and reevaluate.

I plunged the spiked end of the axe into the rock wall and, using my cleats, squeezed my way up the narrower section of the chasm, testing my climbing abilities. With a bit more effort than I'd anticipated, I reached the top and pulled myself over the ledge, breathing hard. My quads had done the brunt of the work, and my legs were shaking with the effort.

Surrounded by the dense fog, I was also vulnerable to another attack.

Shyte or git aft the toilet, Wallace.

Using the blade of the axe, I sliced through the last forty feet of rope, leaving the rest intact to ascend the embankment. Gathering up the line, I shoved it in my pack and eased myself feet-first over the ledge of the fissure.

Going down proved far easier than climbing up, and within ten minutes I was standing about fifty feet below the surface. Lying on my belly by the edge of the seven-foot-long hole, I removed my goggles and ducked my head inside. It was a vast ice tunnel, its walls perfectly circular and radiating blue.

Blue? I thought it was violet? Had the color changed, or was it my perspective?

My first impression of the cavern tagged it as an ancient lava tube that most likely led to the base of the mountain, an extinct volcano.

I estimated the drop from the bottom of the crevasse to the bottom of the ice tunnel to be thirty feet. Getting down was easy, getting up would be a bitch. The rope wasn't exactly the kind I had been forced to climb as a teen in gym class, and bundled in extreme weather gear, already exhausted, left me with a nightmarish thought of being stranded in a damn ice tunnel.

Having already cursed my own stupidity back in the sub when we nearly suffocated, I thought was *why risk it?*

But what about that blue glow?

Triboluminescence is a geological feature of both sphalerite and tremolite. Friction applied to these two minerals actually causes the rocks to glow. It was certainly feasible that the lava tunnel was composed of one or both of these minerals, and that the blue hue was simply caused by the surrounding ice thawing and refreezing, something that had occurred God knows how many times since Vostok had been sealed.

Satisfied with my game of cause and effect, I stood to begin my ascent when the tunnel's luminosity changed from its blue hue to emerald green.

Dumbfounded, I knelt by the hole and looked inside again. There was no mistaking it, the color had changed.

Lucky bastard... looks like you're going in.

Removing the rope from my backpack, I tied a grapefruit-sized knot at one end and then wedged the ball inside one of the narrow gaps chiseled into the bottom of the rift. I tested it and the anchor passed. Still hesitant, I tied another eight knots in the rope to give myself something to grip during my climb.

Satisfied I could negotiate the climb, I dropped the line into the ice tunnel. It came up short, but it was a manageable reach.

Grabbing hold of the first knot down, I lowered myself through the hole, climbing down hand over hand like I used to do in tenth-grade phys. ed. So intent was I on not falling that I only took in my surroundings once my spiked boots hit bottom.

The curved tunnel walls dwarfed me. One end ran south in the direction of the bay, the other north toward the mountain.

Two paces to my right was the dead animal.

It was four-legged and gruesome. Half the size of a bear, it had thick reddish-brown grizzly fur but was more dog-like in its appearance, with canine teeth that stretched outside its jowls, a long rodent-like tail, and limbs designed for lumbered sprints through the deep snow.

I confirmed its identity as an *Amphicyonid*, an extinct species of bear-dog. It was an apex killer during the Miocene. The males were bigger and nastier than the females, and this one must have weighed between two and three hundred pounds.

Ignoring the urge to check its sex, I gazed from one end of the luminescent-green tunnel to the other. Maybe it was fatigue, maybe it was the high oxygen content, but choosing a direction seemed a mental chore I hadn't the strength to complete. So, I yelled out, "Which way, José?"

The tunnel to the north brightened from green to light green to yellow.

What? It's communicating with me using the colors of the electromagnetic spectrum.

Stepping over the dead predator, I headed down the northern section of the shaft, feeling lightheaded and a bit like Alice as she made her way into the rabbit hole. Of course, Alice's rabbit hadn't tried to bite her head off.

I had walked about a hundred yards when the light changed from yellow to orange.

AUDIO ENTRY: FINLAY MACDONALD

25 SEPTEMBER 12:17 HOURS

I'm back onboard a transit chopper, Brandy girl, my precious bundle of joy hidden beneath my seat.

T'was no easy thing. The ride up through the ice sheet was a rough grind. Ashlynn Archer managed tae keep my mind off me bein' sealed in an armored suit in a coffin while the laser burned through four kilometers of ice. I was unconscious when they finally pried me loose.

I awoke in Ashlynn's sleeping bag with an I.V. feedin' fluids intae my veins. The Colonel stopped by tae offer a congratulatory handshake. He told me Zachary was safe and tha' they no longer needed my services.

Ashlynn arranged for a helicopter tae take me back tae the dome for proper medical attention as soon as my I.V. drained. Fine by me, only I needed tae smuggle the egg oot of the Valkyrie's storage compartment. Feigning fatigue, I teld Ashlynn tae return tae duty whilst I rested.

The moment she was gone, I yanked oot the I.V. and searched her quarters for something tae hide the egg inside of. I found a bathroom towel and a backpack filled wit' paperback books. I emptied the lot, then tossed the towel in the backpack and found my way back tae the Valkyrie pod and sled.

Fortunately, the egg was where I had left it. Wrapping it snugly in the towel, I shoved it in the backpack and stowed it under my ski jacket and ECW gear that was piled atop a folding chair. Then it was back tae bed where I waited for Ashlynn tae return.

25 SEPTEMBER 2:09 HOURS

Good news and bad. The good: I'm back in the dome, and the backpack is in my tent. I've spoke tae Angus in our own special Highland code. He's over the moon and is makin' arrangements tae fly intae Davis Base aboard a charter paid for by whit he referred tae as "private investors."

The bad news: Zach's gone missing.

18

"Curiouser and curiouser."
—Lewis Carroll

It was Sir Isaac Newton, the man who formulated the theory of universal gravitation, who first discovered that sunlight passing through a prism revealed the colors of the electromagnetic spectrum.

The human eye perceives only visible light, which lies in a very small region of the spectrum, each color possessing a different wavelength. From shortest to longest the rainbow runs red, orange, yellow, green, blue, indigo, and violet. The human eye cannot see wavelengths outside this spectrum. Ultraviolet radiation has a longer wavelength than violet light, and infrared radiation has a shorter wavelength than red light. White light is a mixture of every color of the visible spectrum. Black is the absence of light.

Sunlight, our most important source of energy, consists of the entire electromagnetic spectrum. Violet and blue wavelengths scatter across our atmosphere more efficiently, but the sky looks blue because the sun emits more energy as blue light than as violet and our eyes are more sensitive to its wavelength. Grass and leaves appear green to us because green is the only color not absorbed by the leaves. The sun's scattered wavelengths shorten at sunrise and sunset, producing orange and red hues.

* * *

My heart pounded with adrenaline as I moved through the ice tunnel, my eyes darting from the pulsating orange light ahead to the Geiger counter in my gloved right hand.

Just a quick look. One quick look and I'll have enough information to theorize cause and effect. Then I'm up the rope and climbing out of the chasm,

216

and we're back in the sub and en route to the north basin. Up the ice sheet and I'm done. Done with Vostok, done with Antarctica and its insane cold. Then it's home to Brandy and William.

Wary of the time, I started to jog, counting each ice-crunching stride to gauge the distance back to the rope.

Twenty-one... twenty-two... twenty-three...

It was a surreal feeling, the color as dazzling as a tropical sunset, the cavern's solitude violated only by my metal spikes digging into the ice.

Eighty-six... eighty-seven... eighty-eight...

By the time I arrived at the end of the tunnel, the ice was glowing red.

Wheezing cold air from my esophagus, I bent over and paused to rest, my eyes tearing, the goggles pinned against my neck. The tunnel ended ten paces ahead. The light originated from a meter-high ten-pointed figure, the upper three sparks white, the middle six blinking crimson, the bottom one violet.

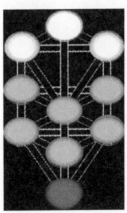

The pulsating marker was embedded in metal, part of a massive object that spanned the entire opening of the tunnel and beyond, the dark mass entirely encased in ice except for the glowing panel.

This was no asteroid. This was an object not of our world.

217

How long had it been here? Was it still functioning? Was it the source of the magnetic interference?

Remembering the Geiger counter, I scanned the icon, which registered no radiation.

My adrenaline pumping, I approached the ten-pointed figure, which seemed strangely familiar to me. I had seen it before.

But where?

Moving closer, I noticed a light mist rolling off the unpolished surface. Removing my right glove, I held my palm close to the six red points of light, registering a radiating warmth on my flesh.

I hesitated, then reached to touch the three white points of light—

—and was inhaled into darkness.

* * *

I opened my eyes to warmth and shadows, half-expecting to be confronted by any one of a dozen extraterrestrial sci-fi scenarios, from being surrounded by high-tech control consoles and three-dimensional holographic computer displays to finding myself imprisoned in a barless cage while other captive humans were strapped to exam tables awaiting lobotomies or anal probes... whatever was on the menu.

Based on the I.Q.s of the stereotypes who always seemed to be the ones abducted, the differences between the two procedures weren't that far off.

I heard a chuckle in the darkness, and then a single red candle flickered to life, revealing a wall of books.

And Joe Tkalec!

My middle school science teacher and mentor watched me from his favorite easy chair in his home library and smiled. "I always enjoyed your sarcastic wit. Are you comfortable in this setting?"

I was seated on the padded rocker where I had spent numerous hours reading after school. "How did you— Wait. That icon, it probed my mind and my memories, didn't it? Hope that's all you probed."

The entity appearing as my mentor smiled. "Anal probes... as if exploring the human rectum could reveal the meaning of life. You do realize all of those ridiculous stories were the result of a disinformation campaign executed by your military intelligence operatives to scare the public about extraterrestrial activities."

"Yeah. I mean, sure. Why would an advanced species travel lightyears to probe a redneck's asshole?"

"You're wondering if this is real or a dream. For now, let's call it a lucid dream."

"Sounds like you're playing a mind game. Is that what this is?"

"Not at all. My role is to provide you with the information you desire. We felt that communicating with you in a familiar setting would be far less distracting than revealing your true surroundings."

"So, if you're not really Joe Tkalec, what should I call you? How about Alien Joe? Where am I, Alien Joe? Is this your spaceship?"

"It is more of a portal. Think of it as a spaceship if it makes you feel more at ease."

"A portal bridges the gap between two distinct places. Assuming I'm physically still in Antarctica, then where are you?"

"I'm here with you, only not in a physical sense. We're communicating using the universal consciousness."

"Yeah, yeah. But this ship was built to travel. Where did it come from? Where's your home world?"

"Does it matter?"

He had a point. What difference did it make what star system his planet belonged to? The fact is he was here, at least mentally.

Alien Joe seemed to be reading my thoughts. "Human travel moves from point A to point B on a linear realm. Think beyond this."

My head was swimming with a million thoughts.

Am I awake? What the hell is a lucid dream? Is there a purpose to this? He said it was a portal, only we're both here in Antarctica...

"You're referring to trans-dimensional travel. Theoretically, it's the only way to travel beyond the speed of light."

Alien Joe smiled. "Very good, but let's refine your conclusion. Travel pertains to an act of physical movement; movement invokes the passage of time, which is a component of the physical dimension. As we speak, you and I occupy a higher dimension where time does not exist. I mention this to ease your mind about hastening your journey back to the submersible. Time is not passing in the physical sense while we are conversing, so don't feel pressured. Let me also assure you that you are not being held captive. Simply express the desire to leave, and you'll find yourself back in the ice tunnel and on your merry way."

"Will I remember any of this?"

"No."

"Then what makes it real?"

"The implications of our communication are very real."

Settling deeper into the seat cushion, I began to rock, finding the familiar action soothing. "You say we're in a higher dimension. It doesn't feel any different."

"Do you hurt?"

"No."

"Yet you were experiencing physical discomfort before you entered the ice tunnel."

"But if this was a lucid dream, I wouldn't be shivering or suffering from frostbite or aching muscles or joint pain. Or even hunger."

"Good point."

"How many dimensions are there? Are they all like this?"

"You studied quantum physics at Princeton. How many dimensions are there, Zachary?"

That's why the icon seemed familiar!

"Ten. There are ten dimensions, at least according to superstring theory. And they're arranged just like that icon glowing on your—your front door."

Ten golfball-sized sparks of energy appeared between us, hovering four feet above the wooden floor in the same alignment as the icon, only now the three upper dimensions were burning white, while the middle six were flowing with the colors of the spectrum—red to orange intoyellow, followed by the darker green, blue, and indigo hues. The lowest dimension, our physical dimension, remained bathed in violet.

"Interpret what you see, Zachary."

"Energy. It seems to be flowing through the ten dimensions in accordance with the electromagnetic spectrum, from the three upper worlds into the bundle of six, and from the six to the one, the physical world."

"Very good. White energy encompasses the inclusive spectrum. Darkness, defined as the absence of light, generates an eleventh dimension, which we do not access. What else can you theorize through your observations?"

"While the purest energy is abundant in the upper three dimensions, by the time it reaches our physical world it's been filtered considerably. The wavelengths are longer and yet weaker, as if by design."

"Excellent. And why is that significant?"

"Less energy imposes limitations."

"And what limitations might be imposed on a physical being such as yourself?"

"You really do sound like Joe."

221

"Answer the question, please."

"Sure. Wouldn't want to *waste your time*." I burst out laughing, feeling giddy.

And there it was—the answer he was trying to coax out of me.

"My own mortality. In the physical world we face the threat of dying every day. You can add to that disease, pain, hunger, hatred, injury, loneliness, and sorrow. Do you experience any of these things on your world, Alien Joe?"

"We did, but not anymore. We evolved."

"You're immortal?"

"The soul is immortal. Physicality imposes limitations that can be overcome."

A chill ran down my spine. At least I registered the sensation as such. "Alien Joe, why are you here?"

"I am here because I chose to communicate with you. Why are you here, Zachary?"

"I'm here because I sought answers about life by exploring the past. Now that I've been given access to an advanced intelligence, I need to know more. How did you evolve as physical beings? Does it have something to do with this energy that is flowing down through the ten dimensions of existence? Where's this energy originating from? What does it do? How can we access it?"

"You say you seek answers about life. What you truly mean is existence: why are we here? What is our purpose?"

"Tell me."

"How can I tell you that? My purpose is different from yours."

"Then tell me, does God exist?"

"Define God."

"The Creator. The entity that was here before there was a

222

here."

Joe closed his eyes and rocked. "Let's play our old game of cause and effect. How was the physical universe created?"

"The Big Bang."

"If energy flows from the higher dimensions into the physical universe, then which came first, the energy or the Big Bang?"

"I suppose the energy."

"Then imagine, if you can, the entirety of existence before the *here* as pure, infinite, conscious energy. And in this infinity of conscious energy, there was the essence of the energy's DNA, an essence which gave it an all-consuming desire."

"What desire?"

"The desire to share."

"Share what? What can energy— Oh, you mean immortality."

"Far beyond immortality, Zachary. We're talking about everlasting, unimaginable fulfillment. But there is one problem: sharing requires a receiver. And so this vast all-consuming conscious energy created another consciousness to receive its energy. Let's think of this second consciousness, this creation, as a vessel. With the creation of the vessel, the conscious infinite energy could experience its own fulfillment by sharing, and the vessel could receive fulfillment by receiving. And everything worked, until—"

"Until what?"

"Until the receiver wanted to experience what the energy, its creator, felt. It wanted to feel the desire to share. You see, even though it was created to *receive* energy, the vessel was made from the energy's essence, endowing it with a like desire to share. But unlike the energy, the vessel hadn't earned its fulfillment. Imagine, Zachary, that you were given every accolade as both an academic and an athlete, and yet you had never earned those honors. Remove the trials and tribulations that lead to success and you are left with emptiness. That's how the vessel felt.

"Seeking to earn its fulfillment, the vessel did the only thing it was capable of doing—it shunted its creator's flow of energy. And in doing so, it shrank to a singular point of existence.

"The creator energy understood what its creation desired. Because the energy loved the vessel unconditionally, it gave its creation the opportunity to earn its fulfillment. The vessel reopened, and energy rushed in until the vessel burst."

The entity appearing as Joe Tkalec stopped rocking and opened its eyes. "Zachary, tell me again how the physical universe came into being?"

"The Big Bang."

"Describe the event."

My scalp tingled as I suddenly comprehended what I was being told. "The Big Bang was the sudden expansion of a singularity of inconceivable energy containing protons, neutrons, electrons—all ejected into the vacuum of space."

Alien Joe nodded. "And now you know cause and effect. The event that shattered the vessel and expanded the physical universe also gave order to the upper dimensions so that the flow of energy might be veiled."

"Why veil it?"

"Think of the upper dimensions as everlasting fulfillment and the physical universe as the arena where that fulfillment had to be earned. This is what the vessel desired."

My mind was reeling. "Okay, so if the conscious energy is what we collectively refer to as God, what was the vessel?"

"The collective immortal soul in its unified state prior to the Big Bang."

I closed my eyes, attempting to absorb everything I had just heard. "Well, then, organized religion sure screwed that creation story up. Chalk that one up to quantum physics."

"The primer of existence is communicated to every physical species, including yours. Humans were given the information 3,409 Earth years ago."

"Really? I'd love to see it. Is it buried somewhere?"

"The information was encoded into the Old Testament's original Aramaic, transcribed on Mount Sinai to the entity Moses. Fourteen centuries later, the information was decoded and recorded in the text referred to as the Zohar."

"So all those hokey Bible stories were just written as an excuse to encrypt the info contained in our owner's manual? What are Adam and Eve supposed to represent?"

"Protons and electrons—the male and female aspect of the atom."

"Nice. What about the creation of the world in six days?"

"Six days refers to the bundle of six dimensions. The only creation is the vessel of the unified soul. The physical world is not the real reality. The physical world is the lucid dream where fulfillment must be earned."

I felt dizzy. "Why am I here?"

"That remains to be seen."

"Whoa, now hold on a minute, Alien Joe. You've made it a point to tell me that time has no bearing in the upper dimensions. If that's true, and quantum physics seems to back that theory, then you not only know what happened in the past, you know what will happen in the future—my future. You knew I'd be exploring Lake Vostok, which means you purposely left this portal under the ice sheet for me to discover and access. I want to know why."

Alien Joe rocked in his easy chair, his demeanor unaffected by my rants. "Your observations are correct. Time has no bearing in the upper worlds; therefore, this moment, and everything that follows, has already occurred numerous times before, all with varying results but similar outcomes. Do you know what a multiverse is, Zachary?"

"It's a quantum term, referring to the choices we make in life. Each choice theoretically creates its own universe."

"Correct. Now tell me why this spaceship is here."

"It's here because I am here.You knew I'd be here, which means you need me for something."

"Correct. And that need begins *after* you survive Vostok."

"Then I guess I'll be on my way. The sooner I get out of this freezer, the sooner I see my family... and a good psychiatrist. Not that anyone would believe this. Hell, I don't believe it."

"Unfortunately, Zachary, you have yet to experience a multiverse where you survived."

The blood rushed from my face. "What does that mean? Did I fall into another crevasse? Did another bear-dog get me? Give me a mulligan, Alien Joe, a do-over."

"As I said, everything that follows has already occurred numerous times before, all with varying results but similar outcomes. In the end, you never made it out alive."

I stood, unable to contain my anxiety. "Are you here to save me?"

"That is something only you can do."

"All right, whoever or whatever you are, you must have a good reason for arranging this little rendez-vous. So tell me, Alien Joe, what's your end game?"

The entity stopped rocking. "The end game, Zachary Wallace, is the survival of your species."

19

*"Well that was the silliest tea party I ever went to.
I am never going back there again!"*
—Lewis Carroll, author - *Alice in Wonderland*

My heart pounded with adrenaline as I moved through the ice tunnel, my eyes darting from the pulsating blue light ahead to the Geiger counter in my hand.

Just a quick look. One quick look and I'll have enough information to theorize cause and effect. Then I'm up the rope and climbing out of the chasm, and we're back in the sub and en route to the north basin. Up the ice sheet and I'm done. Done with Vostok, done with Antarctica and its insane cold. Then it's home to Brandy and William.

Wary of the time, I started to jog, counting each ice-crunching stride to gauge the distance back to the rope.

Twenty-one... twenty-two... twenty-three...

It was a surreal feeling, the deepening blue light fading to indigo, reminding me of my descent into the Sargasso Sea three years ago, a dive that had ended badly.

Eighty-six... eighty-seven... eighty-eight...

The tunnel dead-ended ten paces ahead, the indigo glow originating from sapphire formations embedded in the volcanic rock. Using my climbing axe, I chipped loose some of the zinc-laden ore and examined it in my gloved palm.

Sphalerite. Just as I thought.

Angry at having wasted so much time and energy, I jogged the quarter of a mile back down the tunnel. By the time I reached the rope, I was light-headed and dizzy, the stench of the dead bear-dog by my feet nauseating me.

Don't stop now. You can rest in the sub.

I don't know why I moved just then. Perhaps it was my proximity to the animal's mouth, perhaps divine intervention, but when the creature snapped at my right ankle it missed. By the time it had pulled itself up on its forelegs to pursue me, dragging its broken hip, I had the climbing axe in my hand.

Swinging the handle like a baseball bat, I sliced open the bear-dog's throat, splattering blood across the far curved wall.

Wasting no time, I reached for the highest knot on the rope I could grab onto and fought my way up arm length by arm length, clenching my spiked boots around the nylon cord for some kind of leverage. My limbs were shaking by the time my head poked above the fractured ceiling into the crevasse's frigid darkness.

Crawling out onto my belly, I rolled onto my back, panting as I adjusted the night-vision goggles over my tear-filled eyes. Snot froze on my upper lip as I gazed up at the steep chasm walls and the climb that awaited me.

How easy to just close my eyes and disappear.

Goodnight, moon. Goodnight, William...

No!

Grunting back to life, I forced myself onto my knees and crawled over to where the rope was anchored. I tugged repeatedly in an attempt to free the knot, only to grow frustrated.

Screw it, you don't need it. Leave it for the next schmuck.

Regaining my feet, I removed the climbing axe from my backpack, squeezed myself between the chasm walls, and set my spiked boots, pushing my way up the parallel rockfaces.

Grunting, wheezing, leveraging myself up three feet at a time.

Keep your moaning to a minimum. If one bear-dog was out there, then there must be others.

I reached the summit more quickly than expected and listened before I climbed out.

228

Before me were my own snowprints, matched by those of the bear-dog. I followed them to the remains of the rope, then pulled myself up the incline through the waist-deep snow until I was again standing at the base of the mountain.

Checking my GPS to make sure I was heading southeast, I set off at a steady pace, my toes aching with the cold.

How much time had elapsed since I activated the sensory device? Twenty minutes? An hour? Was the damn thing even working, or had it been swallowed by the crevasse?

Vostok rumbled overhead, startling me.

I picked up my pace.

I limped the last half-mile. The first sensory device was there, but no Ben. Without waiting, I worked my way down the slope to the white fog bank.

Able only to make out the tracks directly in front of me, I made my way slowly through that blinding mist, each step bringing me closer to the warmth of the sub, making me want to run. I held each breath in anticipation, knowing that another bear-dog could be locking onto my scent and sounds, stalking me through the fog.

I listened for its telltale growl and heard only the ice sheet crackling. And then a yellow mist blossomed into a humid, sulfurous belch, and I froze.

It was the crevasse. The opening encircled the entire base of the mountain. Had I not smelled the sulfur, I surely would have fallen in.

I backed away and followed the chasm until I located a narrower gap that I could safely leap over. Then I continued down the snow-covered slope, wary of each step.

Another fifty paces brought me beyond the fog. Before me were the ice-laden waters of the bay. My spirits rose when I saw the *Barracuda*'s external lights on the shoreline, my homing beacon. Detouring around a herd of sea elephants, I darted from one rock formation to the next, doing my best not to stir the four-ton beasts.

And then I stopped. Not far from the sub was a figure, waiting in ambush by a snow-topped boulder. From this distance I couldn't be sure what it was.

Slowly, quietly, I removed the flashlight from my backpack and aimed the beam.

"Ming?"

She was on the ground, leaning back against the rock. I shone the light in her face and saw open eye slits behind the goggles. I shook her, feeling the stiffness of rigor mortis.

There was no telling how long she had been dead, but from the tracks in the snow it appeared as if she had been dragged.

A flashlight beam danced on my jacket, beckoning me to the sub.

I hurried over as the cockpit dome popped open.

Ben looked up from the center seat. "Where the hell have you been?"

He was ghostly pale, his eyes wild from loss of blood. His lap was covered in it, the wound gurgling beneath the jumpsuit's torn left pant leg where he had attempted to tie a tourniquet.

"What happened?"

"I set my device, then waited for you where we left Ming. When you didn't show, I headed down the slope. I heard this growling, only I couldn't see anything because of the fog. So I started running. Something chased after me. It knocked me down from behind. The snow was deep, and that saved me. As it rolled over to come after me again, I swung the climbing axe with both hands and split open its skull.

"It wasn't until I left the fog behind that I realized the bastard had bitten me on the leg. Must have gotten my femoral artery. Tried to make a tourniquet, but all I had were shoelaces. Can you find something?"

I pulled off my scarf. Trying my best to be gentle, I worked the length of wool beneath Ben's leg as he moaned, his eyes rolling

230

up as he passed out.

I tied a knot and then searched the sub for something resembling a stick. Finding Ben's backpack, I opened it—

—and found the sensory device, still in its lead case.

"Lying bastard."

Discarding the plutonium device, I slid the narrow length of lead between the wound and scarf and twisted it tight, eliciting a grunt from my patient. Locating his scarf among a pile of discarded clothes in Ming's seat, I secured the tourniquet in place.

I glanced back at Ming's remains. Taking her body back with us was a sentimental gesture, but served no purpose. The sub would be lighter without her.

Moving to the bow, I pushed the *Barracuda* backward down the shoreline and into the icy waters, and I climbed inside the cockpit. I sealed the dome and attempted to start the engine.

Nothing happened.

It must still be on remote pilot.

The radio crackled. "Vostok Mobile Command to *Barracuda*, Colonel Vacendak here. Report, gentlemen."

"Wallace here. Captain Hintzmann's been seriously wounded, and Dr. Liao has died of hypothermia. I'm suffering from exhaustion and mild hypothermia. Start the engine so I can crank up the heat."

The sub powered on, sending a rush of cold air pouring out of my vent.

"Dr. Wallace, what happened to the sensory devices? We're registering Dr. Liao's device. Your unit appears to have been activated but isn't tracking—"

"I lost it when I fell into a crevasse. Screw your damn instruments and get us to the extraction point before Ben bleeds to death."

A moment's pause. "I'm sorry for your loss, Dr. Wallace. I'm

231

going to turn you over to Captain Eric Schager, whom I've instructed to pilot you out of that maze into the northern basin. We'll have a medical team waiting for you back in the dome."

"Thank you." I laid my head back, then peeled off my gloves. Raising my dripping wet left boot, I attempted to unbuckle the straps with my half-frozen fingers.

"Dr. Wallace, this is Captain Schager. I'm tracking your position using our SAT feed, but there are going to be biologics along the way that I can't see. I can take you safely out of the bay and back to the main river. After that it would be best if you piloted the sub under my direction."

"I'll do my best. But right now I can't feel my feet."

"Acknowledged. Coming to course zero-eight-four. Dive to sixty feet and proceed at ten knots. Call out if you see anything I should know about."

Dark, frigid water washed against the acrylic dome as the *Barracuda* submerged and moved at a steady pace through a black sea.

Locating my night glasses, I worked them into place with numb fingers that began registering pins and needles of circulatory pain.

Blooming into view off our starboard bow was an albino elephant seal the size of a cement mixer.

Too tired to say anything, too exhausted to care, I barely gave it a glance as I held my hands to the hot air now pumping out of my console.

* * *

A powerful rush of current shook me awake. We had reentered the main river, its easterly flow sweeping us along at twenty knots.

I searched my snack stash and quickly consumed an apple and a bag of trail mix between two orange juices. My bladder signaled it was back on the job, and with a bit of aim and effort I

232

managed to relieve myself in a plastic urinal.

"Dr. Wallace, are you ready to take over?"

"Two shakes."

I took three, capped the bottle, rezipped, and adjusted my headphones. "Standing by, Captain."

I felt the console's joystick come to life in my right palm, the foot pedals responding beneath my throbbing, frostbitten feet. I had managed to peel off the climbing boots, but left my socks on, afraid of what lay beneath.

As instructed, I followed the main river, trekking east for several miles.

"Dr. Wallace, in half a kilometer you'll come to a tributary off your portside bow. Follow that waterway; it flows into the north basin."

"Acknowledged."

The swift current bled north into a deepwater inlet, and I knew the basin had to be close. And then my headphones were accosted by clicks, the bizarre underwater acoustics coming from multiple contacts in the river directly ahead.

I slowed to five knots, my heart pounding in my chest.

Ben moaned something in his delirium.

"Shh!"

"Are we topside yet?"

"We're en route to the extraction point. Be quiet. Something's between us and the northern basin. Whatever they are, there seems to be a lot of them."

"I'm dying back here and you're messing with more fish? Just pound the horn and scare 'em outta the way."

Before I could stop him, Ben overrode my sonar control, switching from passive to active a second before he repeatedly pinged the depths.

Ping... ping... ping...

233

I unclipped my harness and leaned over the back of my seat to his console, grabbing his wrist before he hit the device again. "Are you nuts?"

"Take me home!"

Leaving me no option, I punched his wound, the pain rendering him unconscious. Wheeling back around, my eyes focused on the sonar monitor as my hands worked at re-securing my harness.

They had been sleeping upright in the water like sixty-foot logs. Now, as their brains awoke, the pods of *Livyatan melvillei* mothers and calves began bombarding the river with bursts of echolocation that rattled the sub like a giant tuning fork.

Z*ʑʑʑʑʑʑʑʑt*… *ʑʑʑʑʑʑʑʑʑʑʑt*…

I turned to starboard as a two-story, charcoal-gray head charged out of the murk. The creature's ivory-colored lower jaw was stretched open, its conical teeth as big as dinner plates.

Stomping on the throttle, I shot away from the monster's maw a split second before it snapped shut on the *Barracuda.*

The depths before me were a swirling freeway of converging masses, impossible to track on sonar or see through my night vision.

Operating purely on adrenaline and fear, I executed a tight U-turn and raced back in the direction we had come from, drawing the chaos behind me into an angry pod of Miocene sperm whales. Sonar quickly distinguished parent from calf, and I realized the pinging had disturbed a sleeping nursery. As the cetaceans closed behind me into a protective pod, I dove straight for the bottom, executing a tight barrel roll into a 180-degree turn, slingshotting past the confused behemoths, just missing being swatted by a fluke the size of a garage door.

With nothing but open water ahead of me, I raced over the plateau's cliff face into the northern basin, feeling giddy over having survived yet another confrontation with death.

"This is Schager. That was some maneuver. Now, if you are through teasing the wildlife, come to course zero-three-seven. The extraction zone is less than six kilometers away."

Seeking to gauge the ice sheet, I surfaced. The frozen ceiling was sloping closer to the water line, but was still forty feet overhead.

"Schager, the ice is too high to reach."

"Be patient. You haven't reached the extraction zone. Stay on course. The ice sheet will drop, and the external pressure will rise. When your gauge hits 3,100 psi, the ice sheet and the lake's surface waters will be separated by less than five feet of air space. Dive the boat to a depth of three hundred feet, then ascend on a ninety degree vertical plane with both Valkyrie lasers on high. As soon as you pop up out of the water you'll melt ice, and the external pressure will force the *Barracuda* up into the hole you've created and drive you straight up through the ice sheet. By the time the water freezes behind you and reseals the hole, you'll be halfway home."

Zrrrrrrrrrrrrrrrrt!

The acoustic jolt was far more powerful than the others, reverberating inside my skull and throughout the *Barracuda*. I searched for the source on sonar, but it was too late.

The bull leviathan breached beneath the *Barracuda* and took the submersible sideways in its powerful jaws. I experienced the sensation of being lifted into the air as our exterior lights illuminated a pink mouth and rows of brown-stained teeth.

And then a deafening *craaaaaack* popped my eardrums, and a shock of icy water blasted me in the face as I was tossed sideways into death's crushing embrace.

20

"Life, what is it but a dream?"
—Lewis Carroll

I opened my eyes to warmth and shadows, and then a single indigo candle flickered to life, revealing a wall of books and the alien resembling Joe Tkalec.

"Welcome back."

"I died again, didn't I?"

"A skill you have become quite adept at. So far you've bled to death in the ice tunnel, frozen to death resting in one crevasse, broken your neck when you fell into another, drowned twice, and now been eaten by a giant aquatic mammal. Six wavelengths, six multiverses to alter your destiny—all resulting in six deaths."

"Maybe if you actually allowed me to retain the slightest bit of memory … "

"Zachary, I've explained the rules regarding free will. Vostok is a test, to see if you are worthy of accessing the portal.

"Once more into the breach?"

"Isn't there something you can offer me?" I asked. "The slightest clue? Even the real Joe Tkalec wouldn't sit back and watch me suffer like this. I feel like an animal caught in a trap."

"Then act like one! An animal caught in a trap would chew off its leg to free itself."

"Is that it, then? Is that the secret to our survival as a species?"

"No." The entity appearing as my mentor stopped rocking. "Zachary, do you remember how you used to solve a Rubick's Cube? Six sides, kept in flux, each move affecting at least three

236

other sides. In every moment of existence there are varying moments within the spectrum of free will. You can remain in the mainstream or venture out into the radical, but each decision will create a domino effect upon the next. To survive Vostok's darkness, you must figure out how to curve the elements that have brought about your death into a pathway that leads to your survival. That is the means to revealing more light, more energy. You'll need this light to access the portal.

"You've methodically exhausted six of the seven accessible dimensions of the energy spectrum, leaving only violet, the last wavelength. The ice tunnel will collapse behind you as you leave, sealing off further communication. If you perish this time around, I cannot save you."

* * *

My heart pounded with adrenaline as I moved through the ice tunnel, my eyes darting from the pulsating indigo light ahead to the Geiger counter in my hand.

Just a quick look. One quick look and I'll have enough information to theorize cause and effect. Then I'm up the rope and climbing out of the chasm, and we're back in the sub and en route to the north basin. Up the ice sheet and I'm done. Done with Vostok, done with Antarctica and its insane cold. Then it's home to Brandy and William.

Wary of the time, I started to jog, counting each ice-crunching stride to gauge the distance back to the rope.

Twenty-one... twenty-two... twenty-three...

The indigo hue deepened to violet, reminding me of my fateful descent into the Sargasso Sea three years earlier, a mission that had led to my second drowning—a near-death experience that had changed my path in life.

Would this present decision alter my path again?

Not likely, it seemed. The tunnel simply dead-ended in a slab of volcanic rock.

I switched the Geiger counter to the magnetometer, the

needle going haywire.

A magnified asteroid impact crater, just as I thought. What a waste of time. You let Ben and his crazy stories get inside your head.

Without warning, the violet light disappeared, and the tunnel swallowed me in its all-consuming blackness. I fumbled with my night-vision goggles. My surroundings reappeared in a faint olive-green, but everything felt different—cold, dead—and a surge of claustrophobia unleashed a wave of anxiety that sent me sprinting back down the tunnel.

I made it to the rope and immediately started to climb. I was halfway up when the bear-dog revealed itself to be alive, raising its head and upper body off the ice, crying out in pain.

The animal's hip was broken. Had I delayed my ascent it might have caught me in those sharp canine teeth.

I left it there, howling in the darkness, its cries of pain echoing through the ice tunnel. It was still crying out as I reached the hole in the crevasse.

I paused. Even though the animal had intended to kill me, it was clearly suffering.

How could I just leave it like this?

Easily, I told myself. If you climb back down to put it out of its misery, you're using up precious energy. Think about William.

I did.

And that's why I climbed back down.

The bear-dog seemed to sense that I was there to help. It laid its head down, panting in pain.

Trembling, I gripped the axe.

The first blow caused it to spasm.

The second ended its suffering.

The ice tunnel began to reverberate.

I leaped for the rope, a rush of adrenaline driving my arms and legs. I saw ice collapsing around me like a shattering mirror as I pulled myself out of the tunnel and up into the crevasse. Dragging myself to my feet, I swung the axe, burying its blood-covered spike into the rock overhead, climbing up the parallel walls with my boots.

I felt the tunnel collapse beneath me, swallowing the floor of the chasm. I cursed my foolishness, an insane act of kindness toward an animal that had been crippled as it had tried to eat me.

Managing my way out of the fissure, I hoisted my quivering body onto the snow-blanketed mountainslope. Shaking with exhaustion and spent nerves, I retraced my footprints to the remains of the rope and pulled myself up the steep incline through waist-deep snow until I was standing at the base of the mountain. Heading southeast, I set off at a quick pace, my feet numb beneath me.

I covered the distance so fast that I actually passed Ming's sensory device. It was only after I came upon Ben's spikeprints that I realized I had gone too far.

I was surprised to come across a second set of boot prints.

Ming? Why had she set off after Ben? Maybe she had been too scared to descend through the fog alone?

I followed the pair of footprints another thirty yards in search of return tracks, but found none.

That was a problem. If they had gone off together and still hadn't returned, then something had happened to them.

They probably planted Ben's device together, then found another way back to the sub after the crevasse opened up.

Wanting to believe that, I retraced my steps and descended into the fog bank.

I was fifty paces in, working through three feet of snow and near-zero visibility, when I caught a whiff of something that smelled like rotten eggs.

Sulfur?

I turned away from the scent, diverting down another path, a shortcut that brought me out of the fog. Below were the dark waters of the bay. As I began my descent, I saw the light.

At first I thought it was the *Barracuda*, only the light was moving, following a course parallel to the shoreline. Removing my backpack, I located the night-vision monocular. Powering it on, I slid my goggles down to my neck and held the lens up to my right eye, zooming in on the light.

It was Ben, and he was dragging something behind him.

Ming?

Tucking the lens in my jacket pocket, I returned the night-vision goggles to my eyes and hurried down the slope, my galloping movements through the snow startling a harem of forty or fifty female sea elephants lazying about the shoreline.

A chorus of belches and burps alerted the male. The ten-ton bull charged out of the shallows, a rolling mass of angry white blubber.

Seeing the beast, Ben ducked behind a boulder.

I stopped running, my heart racing as I found myself confronted by a creature roughly the size of a cement mixer.

The animated mammal pounded its fore flippers in the slush and shook its head, so that its three-foot-long proboscis sprayed me with snot and salty lake water, but the bull never advanced.

Nor did I.

After several bouts of snorting and belching, it rambled off to join its harem.

I met up with Ben, who was kneeling by Ming, checking her pulse as she rested with her back against the rock. "Is she alive?"

"Barely. Let's get her inside the sub."

"Ben, you're bleeding."

"Huh? It's nothing. I packed some snow on it. It looks a lot worse than it is. Grab her other arm."

He tried to lift her as he stood, only to drop to one knee.

"Guess I hurt it worse than I thought."

"Wait here." I half-dragged, half-carried Ming to the sub. Laying her down, I activated the hatch, then stripped her of her backpack and lifted her into her seat, buckling her in. I tossed her pack in the storage compartment and went back for Ben.

He had stripped off his own pack and was examining his wound. Blood was everywhere, dripping from a jagged six-inch incision along his upper left thigh.

"Looks like you nicked your femoral artery; we need to get a tourniquet on this. How'd you do it?"

"Fell on my climbing axe."

I shouldered half his weight, hustling him over to the sub, fearing what the scent of his blood might be attracting. He moved to climb inside the middle cockpit, only I stopped him. "You can't operate the thrusters with one leg. Get in my seat; I'll man the master control."

I helped him into the bow cockpit, then foraged through Ming's backpack to find something to make a tourniquet. Removing her rope, I tied three feet of cord tightly around Ben's wound, the pain causing him to pass out.

Moving to the bow, I struggled to push the *Barracuda* backward down the shoreline and into the water. I made it halfway to the waterline before I had to rest.

Leaning against the sub, I looked back and saw the bear-dogs. The adult was sniffing and pawing at the blood-drenched snow, her offspring following the trail toward the sub.

I gripped the bow and pushed.

I could see the charging adult in my peripheral vision as my boots hit water. Another shove and I climbed inside, my feet straddling Ben as the animal struck the sub.

The bow spun in the water.

I fell into the middle seat and managed to seal the dome as the predator stood up on its hind legs and pawed at the acrylic,

241

pushing us into deeper water.

I tried the engine.

No power.

For a second, I panicked; then remembered Vostok Command had us on their override.

The radio crackled. "Vostok Mobile Command to *Barracuda*. Colonel Vacendak here. Report."

"Wallace here. Captain Hintzmann's seriously wounded, and Dr. Liao's in bad shape. We're all suffering from exhaustion and hypothermia. Start the engine so I can crank up the heat."

The sub powered on, sending a rush of cold air pouring out of my vent.

"Dr. Wallace, what happened to the sensory devices? We're registering Dr. Liao's and your devices, but Captain Hintzmann's was never activated."

"I'll ask him about it when he comes to. Right now you need to get us to the extraction point before he bleeds to death."

A moment's pause. "Dr. Wallace, I'm going to turn you over to Captain Eric Schager. He will pilot you into the northern basin. We'll have a medical team waiting for you back in the dome."

"Thank you." I laid my head back, then peeled off my gloves. Raising my dripping wet left boot, I attempted to unbuckle the straps with my half-frozen fingers.

"Dr. Wallace, this is Captain Schager. I'm tracking your position using our SAT feed, but there are going to be biologics along the way that I can't see. I'm going to take you out of the bay at five knots just to make sure that whale's moved on, but don't go active on sonar."

"Acknowledged." I struggled to remove my climbing boots so I could warm my feet, hoping the pain of their thawing out wouldn't affect my piloting.

The *Barracuda* submerged, moving at a slow pace through the black sea.

Rotating my seat around, I leaned over the aft console to check on Ming. Her breaths were shallow, her lips violet-blue.

Climbing back with her, I stripped off her coat. Searching through the storage compartment, I located a wool blanket and wrapped it around her, then used the aft compartment's microwave to heat some water for tea.

"Ming, sip this." I held the cup's built-in straw to her lips, but she was unresponsive.

I pressed the hot plastic to her face, and she moaned but still wouldn't drink.

I took a long sip myself, reminding me of the emptiness in my stomach.

Gently lifting her left leg, I unlatched her boots and gently worked them off. I peeled her wool socks from one blue bare foot and then the other. Her toes were dark purple with frostbite. Warming my own hands with the cup, I sandwiched her foot in my palms, transferring the heat. I repeated this with the other foot, which was in far worse shape. She'd probably lose her two smallest toes.

Then I saw the ECW iPhone case lying on the seat.

It must have fallen out of her jacket pocket when I pulled it off her. Obviously, there was no reception in Vostok, but there was the device's camera.

I removed the phone from its extreme weather case and pressed PHOTOS.

What in the hell… ?

21

"Well, now that we have seen each other," said the unicorn,
"if you'll believe in me, I'll believe in you."
—Lewis Carroll

The images were of the southeast face of the mountain, the photos taken from an elevation halfway up the snow-capped peak. Ben was in most of the photos, which were shot from below as he made his way up to the summit, a climbing axe in each hand.

They were working together.

The first dozen shots zoomed in on his ascent. The rest attempted to capture an object he had exposed at the summit.

Find Ben's camera. He'll have taken the money shots.

"Dr. Wallace, you have reentered the main river. I need you to take over."

"Stand by."

I climbed over the aft console to the middle seat. Searching through Ben's stash of food, I consumed a container of raisins and a protein drink to raise my blood sugar and stave off the hunger pangs. My bladder signaled it was back on the job. Wincing at having to share Ben's plastic urinal, I relieved myself.

"All right, Captain, I'm ready."

I felt the console's joystick come to life in my right palm, the foot pedals responding beneath my thawing feet. Following the main river, I kept our speed at ten knots, allowing the current to carry us.

We had traversed several miles when Vostok Command relayed new instructions.

"Dr. Wallace, in half a kilometer you'll come to a tributary off your portside bow. Follow that waterway; it flows into the north basin."

"Acknowledged."

The swift current bled north into a deepwater inlet, and I knew the basin had to be close. And then my headphones were accosted by clicks, the bizarre underwater acoustics coming from multiple sonar contacts in the water directly ahead.

I slowed to five knots, my heart pounding in my chest.

Ben moaned something in his delirium as he regained consciousness. "Are we topside yet?"

"We're close to the extraction point, only something's between us and the northern basin. Whatever they are, there seems to be a lot of them."

"To hell with 'em. Just pound the horn and scare 'em outta the way."

Before he could switch our sonar from PASSIVE to ACTIVE, I overrode his console. "Stay quiet. It could be another whale."

In fact, there were dozens of them, and they were bobbing vertically in the water, taking long, rhythmic breaths as they slept. The adult sperm whales were all female, their hides lead-gray or black except for an albino pigment that bleached their bellies and terrifying lower jaws white. The borders where dark met light were patterned differently, serving to distinguish one *Livyatan melvillei* from the next.

The young bobbed next to their mothers, many suckling in their sleep.

Using only my night-vision glasses, I maneuvered between these living logs of blubber at a crawl. The females were about forty feet long, their enormous heads comprising a third of their anatomy and half their mass. Husking breaths echoed in my headphones, the sounds coming from blowholes positioned at the very upper left corner on the top of their skulls. The eyes were elliptical and

245

remained closed, situated in the middle of that tremendous head, followed by the ear hole and a relatively small swim flipper. A dorsal hump separated the box-shaped upper torso from the powerful tail, the flukes divided by a median notch.

We passed close enough to one female to glimpse deep prune-like wrinkles running down her dark back.

The calves were longer than our sub, weighed over a ton, and were mostly albino.

It took more than fifteen minutes to pass through the forest of sleeping whales. Finally, we were through, moving past the plateau's cliff face into open water.

"This is Schager. Well done. You've entered the northern basin. Come to course zero-three-seven. The extraction zone is less than six kilometers away."

I kept the Barracuda ninety feet below the surface, maintaining our northeasterly heading at twenty knots. I was beyond tired and kept nodding off every few seconds, my drooping head snapping me awake.

"Wallace, it's Schager. There's two things you need to know. Dr. Liao has passed away—"

"Huh?"

"—and your sonar just detected a very large blip."

I glanced behind my seat at Ming, then back at my sonar monitor. The blip was shadowing us, matching our course and speed as it moved along the bottom, 1,266 feet below the surface.

It was another *Livyatan melvillei*. A bull, most likely the elder male. Sonar estimated his length at a staggering ninety-three feet, his girth at forty to fifty tons.

"Schager, how close are we to the extraction point?"

"Less than two kilometers. Vostok's external pressure is rising as the ice sheet drops. Keep it nice and easy, I want you to descend to three hundred feet as you power up both lasers. Then turn the sub back over to me. Once you reach the extraction zone,

I'll launch you on a ninety-degree vertical plane and begin a countdown.

"At zero you'll pop up out of the water and melt the ice directly above you. The hole you've created will cause a vacuum effect, and the low external-pressure zone you create above you will suck the *Barracuda* straight up through the borehole, forcing the sub up through the ice sheet. By the time the water freezes behind you and reseals the hole, you'll be halfway home."

Zzzzzzzzzzzzzzzt!

"Shit." I pushed down on the joystick, watching in horror as the blip rose away from the lakebed to meet us.

"Okay, Moby Dick, let's see if you like *my* noise." Going ACTIVE, I let loose a chorus of *pings*, backing the monster off.

"Schager, you there? I'm at three hundred feet. Lasers are powered up and on high. Turning over control on my count: three... two... one!"

I pushed the button beneath my console... and prayed.

"Cease all sonar pings and hold on to your balls."

I stopped pinging and gripped my armrests as Vostok Command rolled the *Barracuda* into a steep 2-G ascent, driving us back into our seats while slingshotting us into a vertical ascent.

"Two hundred feet until surface. Counting down: five... four... three—"

Zzzzzzzzzzzzzzzt. Zzzzzzzzzzzzzzzt.

"—two... one!"

We launched out of the water and instantly hit a ceiling of ice, only we never actually *hit* the ice. It simply washed away into a progressively evaporating tunnel of mist and water while a geyser exploded upwards through the borehole from behind the sub, driving us faster, its wave pushing past around our acrylic dome.

"Congratulations, gentlemen, you've achieved orbit and are headed home. Stand by, Colonel Vacendak wants to speak with you in private. See you topside. Schager, out."

247

I hyperventilated gasps of relief as I checked my depth gauge, which was already resetting to accommodate the ice sheet. A little less than four thousand meters, about thirteen thousand feet, until we surfaced. Ascending at a steady fifty feet per minute, I estimated our ascent would take a little more than three hours.

And then we stopped moving.

I checked the Valkyrie gauges. "Something's wrong. The lasers powered off."

Colonel Vacendak's voice crackled over the radio. "Good afternoon, gentlemen. I thought we might have a private conversation before you arrived topside. Answer my questions honestly, and you'll enjoy a steak dinner on me. Lie to me, and you'll end up as dinner for that magnificent creature still circling below."

The engine shut off. A wave of queasiness hit me in the gut as the *Barracuda* plunged twenty feet tail-first through a funnel of icy water.

The propeller re-engaged, the spinning blades halting our descent.

I heard Ben wheeze a pained breath.

"This is Wallace. Quit your head games, Colonel. Captain Hintzmann's in no shape—"

"Captain Hintzmann is dead."

"What?" Unbuckling my harness, I stood on my seat and leaned over to check on Ben. His face was ghostly pale, his eyes glazed over. I checked his neck—no pulse.

I flopped back in my seat, feeling numb. "Take me home... please. I'll do whatever you say."

"Glad to hear it, Dr. Wallace. Did you know the captain and Dr. Liao were working together?"

Don't tell him about the photos.

"What do you mean by working together? Aren't we all working together?"

"You're lying, Dr. Wallace. I think you know exactly what I mean."

Damn uniform. It's registering my heart rate. Vacendak's using it like a lie detector. Don't get excited. Take slow easy breaths. Answer in truths that keep him off-balance.

"Yeah, so they had sex. So what? We thought we were going to die. Why do you give a shit? Don't tell me you're a jealous lover."

I climbed back to Ming's cockpit and glanced outside the ship at the tailfin. The umbilical gave the Colonel complete control.

Was there any way to disconnect it?

"Zachary, when you ventured down that crevasse, what did you find?"

"I didn't venture, I fell."

"And?"

"The crevasse led down to an old magma tunnel."

"Nothing unusual?"

"There was a glow, I went to check it out. It was caused by a vein of sphalerite. It's a mineral that, under pressure, creates its own illumination. The force of the crevasse opening generated friction. By the time I left, it was dark."

"I see. And this glowing tunnel, where did it lead?"

"It dead-ended at volcanic rock. Why are you asking me this?"

I gripped the seat, clenching my teeth as the propeller ceased and the sub dropped another thirty feet.

"Are you insane? Bring me back up to the surface, you psychopath!"

"Zachary, did you know that the suit you are wearing contains sensors that allow us to track all sorts of things. For instance, changes in your blood pressure told us the moment you had descended another two atmospheres to access that tunnel. Thirty-three minutes elapsed between the time you went down and whe you climbed back up."

"Now you're judging my climbing skills?"

The rope!

Climbing back into the third seat, I removed the eighty-foot coil of nylon from Ming's backpack.

"Time, Zachary, can be deceiving. As you probably know, time is a concept limited to our physical third-dimensional perspectives. It doesn't exist in a fourth-dimensional vortex—say, a wormhole. Or, theoretically, a vessel capable of interstellar travel."

"Colonel, no offense, but if you want my opinion about quantum physics, we could just as easily have this conversation back in the dome."

I proceeded to loop the end of the rope around Ben's upper body and the chair, using them as an anchor. I looked back, estimating the distance from the bow cockpit to the sub's tailfin.

Wallace, this is insane.

"Zachary, one of the injections you and your deceased colleagues received prior to your descent was a microscopic probe that calculates blood circulation. It takes approximately sixty seconds for a human heart pumping at an average of seventy beats per minute to circulate an adult's six liters of blood. According to Dr. Liao's monitor, her blood circulated thirty-two times from the moment you set out to explore that tunnel until the moment you ascended. Captain's Hintzmann blood volume circulated forty times, the higher rate due to his exertion while he was doing a bit of rock climbing."

Measuring six armlengths of rope, I tied the cord around my chest and climbing belt.

"Zachary, your reading was quite a bit different. According to your sensor, your blood circulated 1,127 times, the equivalent of just over eighteen hours of heartbeats."

"What?" I paused from knotting the rope. "How is that possible?"

"It's possible only if you had entered a portal to another dimension."

I wanted answers, but first I needed control.

Grabbing the MANUAL EMERGENCY HATCH, I pulled the lever.

A blast of icy water shot into the cabin as I dropped feet-first past Ming and into the flooded borehole, the dark shaft of ice illuminated by the sub's exterior light and my night-vision goggles.

Dangling by the *Barracuda*'s tailfin, pinned between the sub and a geyser of pressurized thirty-seven-degree water, I held my breath and felt for the umbilical cable. Locating the plug, I attempted to brace my stocking feet against the slippery chassis, cursing myself for not having worn my spiked climbing boots.

Realizing what was happening, the Colonel ignited the Valkyries, attempting to toss me from the rising sub or burn me alive.

The heat evaporated the water around me and warmed my body as I yanked the plug free.

The lasers abruptly ceased.

In the same amount of time it took the Big Bang to explode in a vacuum of space, my ears popped as a vacuum of ungodly pressure flung me back into the aft compartment and slammed the acrylic cockpit shut.

A hundredth of a second later, a geyser of water erupted around the sub, launching it another thirty feet before pinning it, bow-first, against the slush-filled roof of the borehole.

22

"Sentence first, verdict afterwards."
—Lewis Carroll

I opened my eyes to bone-chilling darkness. A sonic buzz rattled my ears. Disoriented, I fumbled my way around like the lone survivor in a plane crash, orientating myself by identifying the dead.

Persistence persevered over panic, and I managed to locate the night-vision goggles and power up the sub.

That was the extent of the good news—that I had regained control of the *Barracuda*. Everything else was bad.

I was trapped in a submersible, lodged in a borehole surrounded by ice. My air gauge had dropped below eleven hours. Calculated for a crew of three, I guessed my supply would last a solid day. More troubling were the batteries. Power levels were down to seventy-six percent. That was sufficient if I was merely piloting the vessel, but the Valkyries would drain that quickly.

Stay calm. Think it through. There are two ways out of Vostok. You can try ascending using the lasers and see how far you make it, or you can attempt to locate that subglacial river that runs out of the northern basin and forge a trail beneath the ice sheet all the way to Prydz Bay.

Eight hundred miles in twenty-four hours, squeezed beneath the ice sheet in total darkness without a GPS?

That was suicide.

The depth gauge indicated the sub was only eighty-seven feet above the lake, leaving 13,012 feet of ice overhead. Using the computer, I calculated the power requirements. Even in a best-case scenario, the Valkyries would run out of juice 1,244 feet short of the surface.

Either way, I was a dead man.

Frustrated, angry, and overwhelmed with fear, I pounded the back of my skull against my chair's headrest. My decision to pull the umbilical and regain control of the ship had been foolhardy and not very well thought out. By severing communications, I had lost the ability to negotiate with the Colonel for my life. In effect, I had regained control and condemned myself to be buried alive in ice.

How had I managed to find myself in this predicament? The Colonel had threatened to kill me, *for what?* Because a sensor in my bloodstream indicated I had spent eighteen hours hanging out in another dimension. The whole thing was so ludicrous it seemed laughable, only the Colonel actually believed it enough to erase my existence.

So instead, you did the job for him, asshole.

I glanced at Ben's lifeless body still tied to the seat in front of me. Leaning over his body, I loosened his bonds and searched his pockets. I located the iPhone in his jumpsuit and powered it on to check the photo bucket.

As I had suspected from Ming's images, Ben had climbed to the mountain's summit with a sense of purpose.

There were only two photos. The first revealed an icon embedded in what appeared to be a dark metallic surface. Based upon the climbing axe in the shot, the figure appeared to be about a meter-high and featured ten glowing fist-size objects set in triangular pairings. The upper three were white, the middle six were red, and the one on the bottom was violet.

The second image was blurred and had caught the side of Ben's face as he had fallen from the face of the summit.

I returned to the first photo.

I've seen this configuration before…

It took me a few minutes to blurt out the answer, my voice sounding muffled against the tinnitus. "Quantum physics… string theory. The alignment of the ten dimensions."

String theory was an attempt by physicists to find a single

equation that would unite gravity, electromagnetism, and the strong and weak nuclear forces. While these fundamental forces acted separately, quantum physicists believed that moments after the Big Bang these phenomena were unified through interacting strings. For their theory to make sense, existence needed either ten or eleven dimensions, with six of them curled up or *compactified*.

The icon Ben had photographed appeared to fit that description.

I stared at the image, my mind growing desperate.

Whatever was buried beneath the snow and rock appeared to have a power source, and power was what I needed right now.

What the hell? Freezing to death seemed a better way to die than suffocating in the dark surrounded by dead bodies.

First order of business: get out of this borehole and back into the lake.

Activating the aft camera, I zoomed in on the funnel of ice below the sub. To my surprise, the shaft had already frozen over.

I powered up the Valkyries. The lasers melted the ice ahead of the sub, but with the borehole clogged with ice, the lake and its pressure had been effectively cut off, holding me eighty-seven feet above Lake Vostok.

"I'm trapped!" I pounded my fists against the armrests, constricted by the nylon rope still tied around my chest.

The animal caught in the trap will chew its own foot off to survive...

I stopped, my mind racing.

I've had crazy ideas before, and almost none have ever worked out. The last crazy idea had occurred two years ago in Loch Ness when I decided the creature needed to be set free.

Correction: My last crazy idea had occurred to me when I yanked out the sub's umbilical cord, severing my communications with Vostok Command.

Shut up and do the math. It's eighty-seven feet down to the lake. The rope was eighty feet. That'll leave you seven feet short, plus another few feet to bait the trap.

Step One: Attach one end of the rope to the sub's tailfin.

Locating my spiked boots, I struggled to get them over my toes, which had become painful pins and needles. Loosening the rope from around my chest, I positioned it around my waist and then climbed back to the third seat, trying my best to avoid looking at Ming as I popped the cockpit hatch.

A shrill whistle greeted me, the pressure howling up through the borehole loud enough for even my damaged ears to hear. A cold spit of moisture rose with the updraft, convincing me the ice below hadn't fully solidified.

That was encouraging.

Walking backward out of the cockpit, I straddled the sub's tailfin, the ice cracking all around me. I undid the loop and secured the end of the rope to the tail assembly, then climbed back inside the sub and resealed the hatch.

So far, so good. Now for the rough part.

Climbing up to the middle seat, I leaned over the bow seat and unwound the rope from Ben's corpse. Blood poured from the severed femoral artery as I dragged his remains into my cockpit before heaving him into the rear seat next to Ming.

I fashioned a noose out of the end of the rope and slipped it over Ben's head first, then Ming's, binding them chest to chest.

Then I searched for my axe.

God forgive me.

I popped open the hatch. Positioning both bodies on the edge of the sub's chassis, I slit Ming's belly open with the climbing spike, gagging as I eviscerated her.

The deed done, I lowered the two bleeding corpses over the side, guiding them past the tail assembly before releasing them.

The 310-pound flesh missile free-fell twenty feet before striking ice. I heard muffled crackling sounds as I hurried to reseal the hatch.

Strapping myself in my middle seat, I waited.

* * *

Eighty-seven feet...

If the ice had not fully formed, there was an outside chance the remains of my two companions could plunge all the way to the end of the rope. In that case, the tail assembly would snap and they'd drop another ten to fifteen feet into Lake Vostok, igniting a geyser of water that would free me from the borehole.

I wasn't counting on that.

The minutes passed slowly. I had all but given up when I felt the sub reverberate. The moment passed. Then something struck the ice sheet from below with a tremendous wallop.

Seconds later, a geyser of frigid lake water raced up the shaft and plowed into the *Barracuda*.

I waited until the pressure equalized. Then, having already shifted the propeller shaft into reverse, I maneuvered the sub backwards down the flooded borehole.

The two corpses floated up and struck the tail assembly. I drove them back down the shaft, my eyes shifting from the depth gauge to the aft camera.

Descending to the bottom of the ice sheet, I pushed the bodies through the hole. They fell six feet into the lake and floated away while I kept the *Barracuda* inside the borehole and waited, my eyes focused on the video monitor.

A dark mass passed below.

It had not been the combined weight of the two bodies that had cracked the ice, it had been the *Livyatan melvillei*. Lured to the hole by the blood and innards pouring out of the bottom of the ice sheet, the ninety-foot, fifty-ton Miocene sperm whale had breached, bashing its enormous skull against the opening of the partially clogged shaft.

Now the bull wanted its meal.

I shifted the propeller back to FORWARD and held my breath as the rope went taut, dragging the sub backwards out of the borehole and through the lake on a Nantucket sleigh ride, as the male *Livyatan melvillei* swallowed my deceased colleagues' remains whole.

23

The whale dragged the *Barracuda* backward into the depths until the nylon rope snapped and cast the sub adrift.

In darkness, kept at bay by the soft glow from my command console, in a quiet violated only by the fading buzz in my damaged ears, I found a moment's solitude. Exhausted, beaten to the point of surrender, I wondered what more there was to fear. Not death. Death was simply a passing, the process of the soul shedding the burden of flesh and life's imperfections with all its scars and pains and sorrows.

Death was the great unknown. It was the perpetual fear of dying that made living hard. Vostok had immunized me, for I my head I had died so many times over the last forty hours that my mind's eye had gone blind to its anticipated horrors.

The sub drifted and so did I, in and out of sleep, until the demands of the flesh said, "Enough! Drink, eat, piss, remove these tight boots from your throbbing feet. Get back into the game, Wallace! God didn't spare your sorry ass to sit on the sidelines and wax poetic. Find a reason to live."

Unzipping my coat, I reached inside the breast pocket of my extreme conditions uniform and removed a wallet-size photo of Brandy holding William.

Get back in the game.

Placing the photo on my console, I stripped off the neoprene undergarment, ripping the tiny electrode connections from my skin. Shedding the undergarment meant I'd be losing some body heat when I left the sub, but it was better that the Colonel and his team believe I was dead.

MAJESTIC-12 was one threat. The other, besides my diminishing air supply, was the bull sperm whale. It was still out there, but it had just fed.

If I kept my pace slow and steady...

I redressed in my long johns and every article of extreme weather gear I could find, then I started up the engine. The GPS unit was useless, but by reversing the sub's last course I was able to plot my way back to the bay with little effort.

I wiped blood from my night-goggle lenses and adjusted them on my face. Then I dived the sub to three hundred feet, set my speed to ten knots, and engaged the auto-pilot.

* * *

"Huh?"

Exhaustion and a steady ride had gotten the better of me. I opened my eyes, stunned to find the nose of the *Barracuda* beached before a restless herd of sea elephants. Having fallen asleep before reaching the plateau, I don't know how I had managed to cross the *Livyatan melvillei* nursery without disturbing the females. Perhaps they had been feeding when I had passed through the channel. Perhaps it was divine intervention. But somehow I had made it all the way back to the bay.

Climbing over my seat into the aft compartment, I searched the backpacks for supplies. I had my climbing axe, magnetometer, three flashlights, and, to my surprise, Ben's sensory device. Leaving the Colonel's instrument behind, I packed the other items into my bag, along with water, snacks, and the two iPhones. Gingerly sliding my thawed feet into my climbing boots, I zipped up my jacket, secured my facemask and hat, and bound and wrapped every inch of exposed flesh before slipping on my gloves. Ready for the cold, I popped open the cockpit's hood.

Vostok greeted me with a golfball-sized chunk of hail that

splattered across the *Barracuda*'s bow.

I dragged, pulled, and pushed the sub out of the water and onto the beach, then resealed the hatch, having decided to leave the bow lights on. Yes, I needed to conserve the batteries, but power was useless if a six-ton sea elephant decided to squat on my submersible as a nest.

Locating Ben's and Ming's imprints in the snow, I followed the tracks to the northeast.

The path my deceased companions had used on their return to the sub kept to the coastline as it circled the island around to the east, then south. Though a bit longer, it was far easier to negotiate, and even as I began the ascent up the base of the mountain, the snow accumulation at its worst was only calf-deep. The fog bank was barely intrusive.

What did I expect to find? An ancient spaceship? A gateway to a parallel universe? To be honest, I had no clue. All I knew was that Ben and everyone else in charge of this expedition had gone to great care and expense to access this snow-covered mountain, and I needed to know why.

I had crossed the fissure and had reached the base of the mountain when I remembered the magnetometer. Retrieving it from my backpack, I powered it on.

What in the hell...

The instrument registered 305,000 nanoteslas, a huge jump from the reading I had taken hours earlier on the shoreline with Ben and Ming.

Seeking answers, I pocketed the device and gripped my axe. Approaching an exposed section of rock, I repeatedly struck the volcanic geology with the spiked end of the climbing tool. A dozen whacks and I had chipped away an eight-inch-wide, six-inch-deep divot. Turning on my flashlight, I shined the light upon the hole.

The exposed surface was dark and rough, possibly uniform. It was too hard to tell from the small sample size.

A strange tingling sensation gave me pause just then, and I realized the hairs on the back of my head were rustling beneath my wool hat.

I turned slowly and saw the bear-dog. Having followed my trail through the snow, it was watching me, growling in the darkness, its eyes glowing olive-green in my night-vision lenses.

Seven to ten strides up the slope and it would be on me.

Gripping the axe tightly, I spun around and slammed the spike as high as I could into the rock above my head. I pulled myself up so that the toe of my right boot found the divot, my left hand searching for a ledge as I heaved myself off the ground.

Don't look back. Just climb!

I managed to dig the cleats of my left boot into the snow-covered rock by my waist and drove the climbing spike higher, pulling myself up and just out of range of the animal's snapping jaws.

I gasped heavy breaths through my mask and looked down. The predator was standing on its hind legs, clawing at the rock. My muscles were trembling with cold, fear, and fatigue. Balancing on my perch, it was just a matter of time before I'd lose my balance.

Above me awaited a precarious four-story climb up a thirty-degree twisting rock face covered in snow. I doubted I could make it up, but given the choice between the vicious predator and falling to my death, I decided to climb.

Hugging the wall, I wiggled the climbing spike free and struck blindly above my head. Testing the grip, I shifted my weight to my left leg, dug my boot into the snow and pulled myself up another three feet.

Wheezing breaths, rotating grips. Teary eyes blinking, snot freezing cold in my mask. The growls below faded, muted by the snow crunching against my jacket and pants. Where was I going?

Give it up. One last heave away from the mountain and it'll be over.

My gloved hand found a hole in the packed snow. Glancing over, I saw frozen spike marks, the trail zig-zagging to my left.

Ben's tracks.

Looking up, I saw something glowing.

Adjusting my course, I assaulted the summit with renewed vigor until I found myself staring at a dark, rough, exposed metal surface displaying ten radiant orbs. Ben had left one of his climbing axes behind when he had fallen. I worked my gloved left hand into its loop and pulled myself up so that I was eye-level with the violet, light positioned at the bottom of the icon.

And then something strangely familiar happened. The ten luminous objects bled the colors of the spectrum, from red to orange to yellow, darkening to green and blue, and indigo to violet before consuming me within their warm radiant light, which simultaneously blinded me and absorbed me into—

—energy.

24

"It's no use going back to yesterday, because I was a different person then."
—Lewis Carroll

I can't say for sure whether I opened my eyes because I don't remember having shut them. All I remember is that one moment I was freezing, trembling, exhausted, and cleaving to the side of a snow-capped summit—the next, my consciousness was consumed by ten glowing orbs, which condensed into one warm, white, soothing light.

There was no pain or fear, no growling predators or ice sheets, nor was there my physical being. I just seemed to be floating merrily along. I think I was even giggling.

Am I dead?

A red dot appeared. Lacking the perception of either below or above, the singularity simply grew larger until it became a doughnut-shaped object. As it continued to magnify, its details became clear and I could see three circular ring plates divided by blue magnetic fields. As the object expanded beyond my field of vision, its gaping hole swallowed me, changing my view from outside to inside, so that I was now in the center of the ring.

My entire 360-degree field of vision was occupied by rollers, tall canister-shaped, magnetized columns of metal that were rotating around the innermost ring like ponies on a merry-go-round. Though the rollers were revolving at an incredible speed, their velocity was such that they remained uniformly visible, like the rotating blades of a helicopter. This effect allowed me to count twelve of them, aligned side by side within the innermost ring. Held in place by the lower and upper plates, the twelve rollers were not actually touching the plates; instead they were floating upon a magnetic field like a high-speed monorail.

Most bizarre. As my consciousness hovered in the ring's hole, I could feel a rush of negatively charged electrons racing through the positively charged core. How did I know these particles were negatively charged? I have no idea. But in my present state of existence I found that I could *sense* it, just as I sensed the electrons forming pairs within the gap, then compressing as they rushed outward into the rotating rollers. There was a powerful magnetic field in play, created by the alternating alignment of the poles in both the rollers and the plates. And I realized it was the outward flow of these paired bosons that was causing the twelve cylinders to rotate within the inner ring plate.

Hitching a ride along the electron current, my consciousness was inhaled through a magnetic layer that carried the particle stream through a second ring plate that was even larger than the first. There were more rollers here, and they revolved even faster.

Exiting out of the second ring, the stream of electrons passed through a layer that tasted of copper before accelerating into a third and final ring plate, this one composed of even more rollers whirling at an even faster velocity.

I realized then that I was touring an electrical generator, a never-ending circuit of electricity powered solely by the internal tensions of the atoms themselves—atoms whose negatively charged electrons were being perpetually drawn into the device's positively charged neodymium core like bees to honey. There was no build up of heat, no fuel expended, nor toxins released. Powered by the infinite ocean of atoms that surrounded us, the alien device was, quite simply, a source of endless, clean, free energy.

As these thoughts came to me, I felt my consciousness drawn out of the centrifuge and away from the shrinking power generator, so that I was again gazing upon its ring plates. The object progressively grew smaller until it shrank once more to a red singularity and disappeared.

And as it disappeared I felt my own atoms reappear, gaining mass as I re-entered the physical dimension, materializing inside the private home library of my mentor, Joe Tkalec.

The moment I saw the alien entity, I remembered everything—every missing minute of existence, every experienced death, culminating into the now.

"Welcome, Zachary. But not 'welcome back.' Tell me why."

"*Welcome back* refers to a past moment lived. Had I actually experienced any of those moments other than this last one, I would not be here."

"Correct. And yet you experienced all of them, each choice creating its own branch of reality, each decision generating its own parallel universe. In some of these universes, you never made it back to your submersible. In others you returned injured, only to find Ming dead and Ben piloting the sub. Countless parallel universes created by a multitude of choices, and yet in only one distinct set of circumstances did the life of Zachary Wallace culminate in his returning to the mountaintop. And because time and existence are dependent solely upon the consciousness of the observer, all of the other multiverses have now disappeared."

"Or have they? Do you remember our discussions about the two theories of time?"

"I remember discussing McTaggert's theories with Joe…"

"How can you be so sure I'm not Joe?"

"Stop it."

"What if I told you I am your old mentor and friend, that I was summoned to this moment by the same forces responsible for your being here? Only your belief system is preventing you from accepting me as the real deal, despite the fact that your five senses tell you I am Joe Tkalec."

"Common sense tells me you're not."

"Funny. Common sense tells me that I am the real Joe and you are Alien Zachary."

"It's your show, pal. You want to waste time playing mind games, go for it."

"But the physical dimension is riddled with mind games. Take our sense of sight, for instance. Tell me, Alien Zachary, how does the human eye see?"

"It doesn't. Images are constructed in our brains based on electrical signals sent from our eyes."

"So then, if we *see* a Miocene sperm whale, in reality the whale is the electrical signal interpreted by our brain."

"Your point being?"

"What if everything that surrounds us, everything we perceive as matter, is also simply an electrical signal? How would you know the difference? The human brain, after all, is designed to interpret electrical signals sent from our five senses. How do we know an external world even exists? What if our perceptions are originating from another source, the same source responsible for our dreams? According to quantum physics, matter doesn't even exist; the material world is simply an illusion, an electrical signal perceived by the brain to convince the soul that the universe is real."

"Guess that's why I became a marine biologist and not a quantum physicist."

Joe smiled. "We'll table the subject of reality for the moment and talk about time."

"What's the point? You told me time doesn't exist in the

266

upper dimensions."

"True, but before you access the portal, you need to understand that time is not an absolute."

My heart raced. "I'm to use the portal?"

"Or perhaps you already have?"

"Maybe you are Joe. He used to drive me crazy with his riddles, too."

"And perhaps you really are the skinny runt I took under my wing as an eleven-year-old import from Drumnadrochit. Ah, but what if I hadn't? Would you have still been a scientist? Would you have gone on to Princeton? Married your childhood sweetheart? If my roommate Troy hadn't trained you as an athlete, perhaps you would have drowned in the Sargasso Sea. The person you are today is based on a million variables, all manipulated by your conscious thought."

"How is that possible?"

"It begins with desire and setting goals, and all the hard work and perseverance you demonstrated in both academics and athletics, but it goes way beyond that. All matter possesses a frequency. The atoms that make up matter are fluctuations of energy within a huge void. What appears solid to your senses is a construct of how your brain interprets the frequency of those electrical signals. Change the frequency and you change both matter and energy. The soul achieves this through conscious thought.

"Young Zachary Wallace desired to be a scientist. The intensity of that desire affected Joe Tkalec, and the protégé *magically* has his mentor. Young Zachary was bullied in seventh grade by a ninth grader, and the exposed weakness created a desire to lift weights. Enter Troy and his conditioning regimen. New parallel universes divert from the old as you learn the game of football. Would you have become a marine biologist without my involvement? A running back without Troy's coaching? Perhaps. But of all the possible outcomes you could have experienced, the ones you did experience resulted from the ability of your consciousness to alter the frequency of matter—the so-called aligning of the stars. The phenomenon is real, and those who discover how to control it can remove the chaos associated with existing in a dimension so far from the energy source. Then again, others can abuse their conscious thoughts for themselves alone, creating chaos.

"Now let us add the variable of time to the equation. Recite the two theories of time authored by the philosopher John McTaggert."

I sat back in my cushioned chair and rocked. "McTaggert's A-Theory stated that the only real time is the present. The past is gone and the future exists only as a probability distribution, a potentiality of the possible things that can happen. Since the future isn't set, it's not real."

"And his B-Theory?"

"That the past, present, and future all co-exist simultaneously. Since the past determines the future, everything that has happened since the Big Bang was predetermined. Quantum physics is based on B-Theory, that everything that could possibly happen has already happened, or, as you say, time is dependent upon the observer."

"And what do you say, Zachary? Is it possible to alter the present by changing the past?"

"I don't know. If you were to go back in time forty years and murder my father, then you would have changed my birth parents. Still, who's to say I would have turned out any different? My new father might have been a womanizing alcoholic just like Angus. If everything is predetermined, then you might board a different train but all tracks lead to similar outcomes. In the scheme of things, consciousness may not have the big effect you're alluding to."

"Let's hope you're wrong." The entity appearing to me as Joe Tkalec closed his eyes and rocked quietly.

Joe or Alien Joe, I knew better than to interrupt.

He opened his eyes. "Zachary, in a previous communication

we discussed the frequencies of the ten dimensions and how their wavelengths—let's call them vibrations—corresponded to different colors of the electromagnetic spectrum. There exists an eleventh dimension exiled from the ten, a dimension associated with darkness, which is defined by the absence of light. The darkness feeds off the slow, dense vibrations generated by negative energies: fear, ego, lust, greed, hatred, and violence.

"A very radical alternate reality is threatening to bring chaos to the physical world. It is being driven by a fear-based dichotomy, dictated by a minority that is controlling the masses through their desire for the accumulation of matter."

"You mean money. Why would a species capable of interdimensional travel give two shits about a bunch of greedy rich people?"

"The negative elite responsible for creating these fiefdoms are destabilizing the natural order of things. By unknowingly feeding the darkness, they are generating random shifts that have self-organized into higher complexities, creating chaos. We will show you the particular chaos that concerns us, so that you can decide whether you are the one who can help alter the collective consciousness."

"More riddles. And don't think I forgot what you said about Moses on Mount Sinai. If that was a portal, then he should have foreseen his people losing faith while he was getting the Ten Commandments."

"That was an encoded story. The Ten Commandments were the ten dimensions; the gift was immortality. Moses denied the Israelites the gift when he realized they were not ready."

"So what's the gift I'm supposed to—oh no." I stopped rocking. I stopped breathing.

The generator...

"Free, abundant, clean energy for everyone on the planet. Yeah, Joe, that's a game-changer. And the negative elite, the fiefdoms, they're going to be a lot worse than the guys building the

Golden Calf. The idol worshippers of my time start wars to keep the status quo. Don't get me wrong, what you want to do is fantastic; I just don't think I'm the right guy. Maybe the president? Or Bill Gates?"

"The methodology and the means remain yours to decide."

"You're not listening. Bringing a product like this to market takes money, and I'm nothing but a piss-poor scientist. Until recently, the only thing I could afford to feed my family was mutton. Ever eat mutton, Alien Joe? It tastes like it sounds."

"Zachary, you used the analogy of multiple trains following converging tracks. Not all multiverses run together or even parallel. Some deviate radically from the norm. Humanity has shifted its collective consciousness to on the same track our ancestors found themselves on long ago. Unless diverted, the train will derail and take your species with it."

"Show me."

The room dimmed, and I felt myself growing lighter, as if gravity were leaving with Joe Tkalec and his library... and the density that was my atomic structure. And as my being again danced and flitted and floated about in the higher dimension, the dot reappeared. Only this time it was blue. The singularity grew larger until it became a ring that encompassed my entire field of vision, until its gaping hole drew me into the center, looking out at the spinning rollers.

As my consciousness hovered in the centrifuge's positively charged core, an image appeared on the wall of spinning rollers like a 360-degree movie screen. The projection showed a man who looked to be in his mid-forties, his hair silver-gray and long, pulled back into a tight ponytail. He was dressed in an expensive, charcoal-black Italian suit with a matching shirt and tie. He was seated in the back of a limousine next to an attractive brown-eyed blonde in her mid-thirties. The two of them were holding hands.

As I watched, the silver-haired man's eyes rolled up and he slumped over. The woman grabbed him and shook him and called out his name, but her words were distorted, rippling with echoes. Before I could comprehend what she was shouting, a tsunami of negatively charged electrons swept through my being and carried my consciousness outward through the portal's spinning inner ring. That's when I realized the man in the limousine was me.

Part Two
Endings…

25

"Zachary! Zach, honey, wake up. Driver, pull over!"

I opened my eyes, my brain buzzing with electricity, my body weighed down by a sudden sensation of gravity.

"Zach, are you all right?"

I turned and stared at my research assistant and lover, and the buzzing stopped.

"Susan?"

"Thank God. I thought you were having a stroke." Susan McWhite, Ming Liao's former assistant, turned to the dangerous-looking fellow in a buzz-cut and dark suit leaning inside my open window. "Jim, tell the driver we need to skip the hearing and get Dr. Wallace to a hospital."

I turned to my head of security. "It's okay," I said. "I'm just tired from the flight. How soon until we arrive?"

Jim Clancy checked the GPS on his watch. "Twenty-eight minutes. You sure you're okay, boss? You look kinda pale."

"I'm fine."

The armed bodyguard waited until I closed the window before signaling to our motorcade over his radio. Then he climbed back into the front passenger seat, and we continued our journey through the District of Columbia.

* * *

The Subcommittee on Energy and Power falls under the auspices of the House Committee on Energy and Commerce, its congressional members exercising control over the broadest jurisdiction of any congressional committee on Capitol Hill. These powers include overseeing national energy policy, energy conservation and information, energy regulation and utilization, regulation of nuclear facilities and waste, the Clean Air Act, and all related Homeland Security issues.

Democrats sat behind a stretch of elevated wood-paneled tables at the front of the assembly room. Chairing this morning's event was Congresswoman Cassandra Boyd of Texas's twelfth district.

I found myself seated at a small table on the assembly room floor next to my attorney, Scott Schwartzberg, whose team of litigators occupied the first row of seats behind us. Behind them were my fellow defendants—inventors, scientists, and entrepreneurs. The rest of the galley overflowed with private citizens, all of whom had to pass through security.

I wondered if the members of the media who were seated on the floor by my table had been subjected to similar scrutiny.

Scott pointed out the woman seated behind my research assistant. "Jaqui Billups; she's from the *New York Times*. She's been hounding me all week to set up an interview. Next to her is Dawn Warfield, a video columnist from *The Huffington Post*. She wants to do a podcast before we leave the building."

"I'll do the *Post*. Forget Billups. The CIA will redact anything positive in her article. What about *60 Minutes*?"

"I'm still waiting for a confirmation."

Congressman Boyd took her place behind the dais, adjusting her microphone. "The subcommittee will come to order. This morning we're going to hear statements from members of the science community who oppose H.R. 1691, the Alternative Energy Fraud Act, sponsored by Congressman Jaime Watkins of Kentucky, and our esteemed co-chair, Lorey Schmidt. This much-needed piece of legislation will protect investors who have lost vast sums of money to charlatans who claim to have designed clean, abundant, and non-polluting energy sources, only to learn later that they were duped.

"Our first witness is Dr. Zachary Wallace. It should be noted for the record that Dr. Wallace is not a physicist. He is, in fact, a marine biologist who earned his fifteen minutes of fame resolving the monster mystery at Loch Ness. Seven years ago, Dr. Wallace survived a manned descent into Antarctica's Lake Vostok. When the mission lost its funding, Dr. Wallace returned to his teaching position at Cambridge. At some point he left the university to work with John Searl, the British inventor who is best known for the Searl Effect Generator, a device Searl claimed could levitate like a flying saucer, though conveniently it was never filmed doing so. Dr. Wallace refined the design so that it functions as an electrical generator. He then used investor capital, most of it coming from the Tanaka Institute, to fund his own company, Wallace Energy, a privately held corporation with headquarters in Edinburgh and San Francisco.

"Dr. Wallace, you have been granted five minutes to explain to the subcommittee how this device works. Then we'll open it up to questions."

I waited while a large flatscreen television was rolled into position before the assembly and powered on. Using a DVD remote, I pushed PLAY.

Appearing on screen was a doughnut-shaped metal disk the size of a dinner plate. Spaced out along its surface were three one-inch-wide rotating rings.

"Energy surrounds us. The challenge is to convert it to power, defined as voltage multiplied by current to equal wattage. This is the Vostok, a closed-circuit perpetual generator. It produces a quantum vacuum flux field using zero point energy. It is powered by the electrons that perpetually surround us, producing clean and unlimited electricity. As you can see, its doughnut-shape design contains three circular ring plates. Held within these ring plates are rollers, each the size of a D battery. These rollers, along with their ring plates, possess a magnetic north and south pole. As a result, the rollers float on the magnetic field without actually touching the ring plate.

"The process of rapidly circulating these rollers around the ring plates in order to generate electricity begins when one powers up the positively charged neodymium core. Negatively charged electrons immediately rush into the device, where they join together to form boson pairs. The pairs compress and then exit through the central core to the first outer ring, where they cause the twelve rollers to accelerate to speeds averaging 250 miles an hour. From there they pass through a magnetic layer that both excites and pulls them through the second ring, where they cause these rollers to revolve at a velocity exceeding 600 miles an hour. Finally, the electrons exit to the copper emitter layer, where they join trillions of other boson pairs in ring three, spinning these rollers at over 1,500 miles an hour.

"A switch directs the generated electricity through standard coils, completing the electrical circuit. Unlike conventional generators that heat up after prolonged use, the Vostok remains cool no matter how long it runs. There's no fuel needed and no toxins released. The unit is powered solely by electrons entering it and the unit and the internal tensions of the atoms. It is, literally, a source of endless clean energy."

Several subcommittee members stood and applauded, irking their chairman who looked down her nose to address me. "Theories are different than working models, Dr. Wallace. Where's your prototype?"

My blood pressure ticked upward. "In fact, Chairman Boyd, we had thirteen working models of varying sizes and outputs that were all beta-tested. Three were designed to power cars and trucks, two for trains, and two larger models for commercial jets. The rest were designed to power single-family homes and high-rise commercial structures. Our entire manufacturing plant in Edinburgh ran on a single unit no larger than this table."

"And where are these prototypes now?"

"Perhaps you should ask the two CIA agents, posing as technicians, who stole the prototypes from our R and D safe shortly before my Edinburgh factory burned to the ground."

"Sir, you dare to accuse the CIA? Where is your proof?"

"You mean that I was robbed, or that the thieves were CIA agents? Maybe they were MAJESTIC-12. Does it matter? Whoever they are, they're being funded by Congress with zero oversight. These guys make their own rules and don't care who they hurt."

The chair held up a CD file. "The official report indicates the fire was a direct result of your invention overheating."

"The *official* report, congresswoman, was prepared by the same investigative firm who cleared British Petroleum in last year's oil rig explosion in the North Sea."

"Why is it, Dr. Wallace, that every inventor who fails to produce a working model of their so-called 'new energy technology' always has a conspiracy story to tell?"

"My story's real. So is the security tape of my safe being robbed, which we posted on YouTube—until the network was ordered to remove it. I guess triple-X videos are fine, but energy systems corrupt the minds of our youth."

The audience in the galley stood up and applauded.

The chair banged her gavel for quiet. "Does anyone have a question for the witness? The chair recognizes the junior congressman from Montana."

Justin Willems nodded to his colleague. "Thank you, Ms. Chairman. Dr. Wallace, I'm impressed by the Vostok, and I've always supported alternative energy. The problem you seem to have is credibility. Sex scandals, accusations of financial abuses. Even your partners, the Tanaka Institute, have been named as defendants in a series of lawsuits—"

"The Tanaka Institute is an investor, Congressman Willems. The Taylor family runs an aquarium that features the most dangerous predators that ever lived. Sometimes accidents happen.

279

But Jonas Taylor and his wife, Terry, are good, moral people who I'm proud to be associated with. As for my own credibility, none of the accusations made about me are true. This is all part of a disinformation campaign that began two years ago, shortly after we made a technological breakthrough that allowed us to adapt the Vostok power generator to motorized vehicles, directly threatening Big Oil's stranglehold on the transportation industry.

"A short time later, unsubstantiated rumors were circulated on the Internet and various news organizations that I had used investors' monies on lavish trips to Beijing, which wasn't true. Then a former associate went on a news show and accused me of rape, which led to her giving birth to her daughter. She sued me for $20 million. The woman's attorneys were paid from a private offshore fund. The DNA evidence acquitted me, but my reputation was soiled. Weeks after the trial, I began receiving death threats and had to hire a private security team. The paranoia helped to end my first marriage.

"For the record, these same strong-arm tactics were used on Professor Searl, who was poisoned while eating in a diner with Intel agents posing as investors. Dr. Searl was wrongfully imprisoned, and all of his equipment and papers were destroyed. Similar things have happened to other courageous citizens and inventors like T. Townsend Brown, John Keely, Victor Schauberger, Otis Carr, and Dr. Steven Greer. It seems like every time a scientist or private company attempts to market a device that threatens the fossil fuel industry, the powers that be strike back without mercy."

While I was speaking, Chairman Boyd handed a note to an assistant, who took a roundabout route before slipping it to the court stenographer.

My attorney immediately grabbed my microphone. "Excuse me, Chairman Boyd. May I inquire what was in the note your assistant just handed to the stenographer?"

The congresswoman's cheeks flushed. "The official transcript of these hearings is not the appropriate venue to cite innuendo. As such, I asked that the witness's last statement be stricken from the record."

The members of the galley lost it. Shouts and threats and catcalls rained upon the members of the committee—along with several shoes.

It was exactly the response the chair had hoped to elicit. Within minutes, security had cleared the hall of all visitors.

With order established, the hearing resumed. "The chair recognizes Congressman James Hinks from New Mexico."

"Thank you, Ms. Chairman. Dr. Wallace, I've been reading stories about lawsuits filed against your company by the Chinese and Australians, something about fiduciary claims on behalf of investors who funded your Vostok mission years ago. Could you expand on that?"

"Congressman, the lawsuits are ridiculous and unfounded, and that's all I'm at liberty to say."

"Then you're denying this technology originated from an extraterrestrial spacecraft abandoned in Lake Vostok?"

Scott Schwartzberg took the microphone. "Congressman, my client is not at liberty to discuss proprietary claims from the lawsuit you mentioned, or any of these other ridiculous claims. The underlying issue here is whether the Vostok works. It does. Whether its designs were inspired by collaborations with Dr. Searl, Dr. Wallace's pet goldfish, or little green men has no bearing on this hearing."

The scientists in the galley laughed. A few members of the subcommittee smiled.

Not Congressman Hicks. "You may well find my line of questioning amusing, but in New Mexico we take these matters quite seriously. There have been fourteen incidents of UFO sightings in the last four months, and some have suggested these sightings have coincided with the testing of your devices—something to do with accessing a trans-dimensional conduit, I don't know exactly. So I ask you again, on the record, have you ever seen or had access to an extraterrestrial spacecraft?"

Scott Schwartzberg leaned over again to instruct me.

"Dr. Wallace, why do you need your attorney's help to answer a simple question?"

"Because it's not a simple answer, congressman. The very nature of asking me about extraterrestrials characterizes my work as fringe science. It's not. Have I personally witnessed an unidentified flying object? The answer is no. Do I believe they exist? Having listened to the sworn testimonies of several hundred high-ranking military officers, jet fighter pilots, and commercial airline pilots—all of whom claim to have seen these E.T. vehicles—I'd have to say yes.

"The military must think they exist, otherwise why spend hundreds of billions of taxpayer dollars building top-secret underground facilities in the southern desert of Nevada. Again, none of this has anything to do with the Vostok power generator, which absolutely works. If it didn't, why would Peter McLaughlin, the former CEO of General Motors, have offered us a three-billion-dollar contract two years ago to produce Vostoks for a new line of passenger vehicles?"

Congressman Brian Ullom motioned to the chair to respond. "If that's true, Dr. Wallace, then why did General Motors cancel the deal?"

"They cancelled because the United States Patent Office refused to issue patents for our design. In fact, the patent office has turned down patent requests for over five hundred alternative energy devices, many of which, like the Vostok, would render fossil fuels obsolete. It also doesn't help our quest to take our company public when members of this very committee threaten to issue a Section 181 order, as per title thirty-five of patent law that allows for military seizure in the event that we ever do receive a patent. You see, Congressman Ullom, the real reason we're still polluting our air and biosphere with carbon dioxide and why wars continue to rage in the Middle East is not because we lack energy solutions. It's because the concept of free, clean energy threatens Wall Street and its six-hundred-trillion-dollar derivatives and commodities market. That's who your subcommittee should be protecting the American public from, not us."

* * *

Three hours later, Susan and I walked out to a late October afternoon and were greeted by a brisk wind and a wild crescendo of cheers. A sea of humanity spread out before the entrance of the Rayburn House Office Building, covering Independence Avenue all the way to Union Station and beyond. A million strong, maybe twice that, based on a quick glimpse down the mall. Thousands bore handheld signs expressing *Thank You, Dr. Wallace* and *Free Us from Big Oil* and *Save the Planet* a hundred different ways.

It was as gratifying as it was frightening. I was completely at the mercy of the crowd and every wacko with a gun.

At the Capitol building a stage had been set up facing the mall. Jim Clancy grabbed one arm and Susan the other as our security team surrounded me and pushed their way through the parting masses toward the podium. It was as loud as a college football bowl game, and I heard Jim shouting instructions about a bulletproof shield.

The shield was an eight-foot-high, three-sided Lexan enclosure that surrounded the podium. Jim opened the back panel and I ducked inside. There were no air vents other than a few slits atop the slanted ceiling, and the effect created a stifling silence.

"Good afternoon." My greeting repeated across dozens of speakers in a staggered delay throughout the mall.

Muffled by the bulletproof plastic, the crowd's response returned to me in waves, concluding with the distant din from the masses gathered around the Washington Monument almost a mile away.

"Imagine your home powered by an infinite supply of free, clean electricity. Imagine never having to fuel your car again. Imagine free public transportation, reduced manufacturing costs, urban areas with clean air, and oceans with reduced levels of carbon dioxide. The threat of global warming addressed, the threat of a war in the Middle East defused. Energy is the life-blood of civilization, the key to our survival as a species. For most of the last century, our fossil-fuel masters have used energy to maintain control of the masses. I say, enough is enough."

Staggered cheers moved across the multitudes, the sound reverberating off the surrounding buildings.

"The powers that be refuse to go quietly in the night. When we demonstrated the Vostok prototype, they offered me five billion dollars to buy the company. When I refused to sell out the people of this planet for a few trinkets of silver, they stole it. When we received funding to begin manufacturing our line of generators, they burned our factory to the ground. They play by their own set of rules, and—"

I paused. In the distance, the crowds gathered around the Reflecting Pool and Washington Monument were gesturing to something in the eastern sky. Like a stadium crowd doing the wave, section by section looked up and pointed.

I turned to see for myself, only my view was obscured by the Capitol building.

And then I saw it.

The vessel was imposing, as dark and wide as a B-2 Bomber, only saucer-shaped. It descended majestically and then hovered, motionless over the mall, as if it were going to perch on the tip of the Washington Monument. The teardrop belly was flashing lights and emitting a magnetic field that I knew all too well, and those people caught in its gravitational vortex found themselves levitating fifteen to twenty feet in the air.

The crowd went wild as hundreds pushed and climbed over one another to experience zero gravity within the UFO's shadow.

I stared at the scene, dumbfounded. Everything about this felt wrong. Through my own experience in Lake Vostok, I knew these

284

vehicles were organic in nature, flown telepathically by beings whose aura of sharing could be detected by humans involved in the close encounter. This was corroborated by the testimonials from military personnel who had been the first boots on the ground when a UFO had crash-landed.

This experience felt cold and calculated, and the way in which the E.T. moved seemed too mechanical.

It's not an E.T. It's an ARV—an Alien Reproduction Vehicle—designed by MJ-12 to fool the public!

I grabbed the microphone. "Run! It's not a real—"

What happened next occurred so quickly that only super-slow-motion replays of the historical event could reveal the truth, which is why they were subsequently banned and removed from both the television networks and the Internet.

That alone should have been enough to redirect the public's rage.

First, there was a loud humming noise. That was followed by a brilliant flash of light originating from the vessel's power source, immediately followed by an explosion at the base of the Washington Monument.

In the six seconds that followed, the world changed. That was how long it took the 555-foot tower to collapse, crushing and instantly killing more than one hundred people.

Flying rubble wounded hundreds more, and the panicked crowd increased that number into the thousands as people trampled one another to flee the area.

Concrete gravel struck the outside of my plastic enclosure as I watched the fake alien craft fly off. It did not slingshot into the atmosphere like the real thing. Instead it gained altitude like a helicopter before racing to the west.

Then the soldiers in black camouflage fighting gear arrived. I saw Jim Clancy go down. Susan was carried off as smoke grenades closed the curtain on the scene seconds before I was dragged away.

285

26

"The only reason for time is so that everything doesn't happen at once."
—Albert Einstein

"True, don't do this!" I followed my best friend across the dilapidated harbor dock to the parking lot of the Clansman. Once the crown jewel of Loch Ness, the hotel and its waterside restaurant, had been bashed into a barely recognizable pile of brick rubble.

The sun had dipped below the Monadhliath Mountains. With darkness approaching fast, the crowd had swelled to several hundred men and women, many villagers openly carrying shotguns. They stood solemnly, watching as True and his deckhand, Jim Clancy, unloaded a two-hundred-pound cow carcass from the back of the former U.S. Army Ranger's pick-up truck.

"True, listen to me. There are better ways to kill this monster. Stuffing a dead cow with C-4 explosives and dragging it around Loch Ness—it's crazy. The croc's bigger than your boat."

"Nessie was bigger than my boat, too, but it didnae stop ye from diving the loch in a Newtsuit. Unlike ye, Zach, I brought this nightmare to the Highlands, and now I'm goin' tae end it."

True tightened a steel cable around the dead animal's neck while Jim slit open its belly, anchoring a plastic thermos packed with C-4 inside the ribcage.

"Secure the udder wit' those clamps, Jimmy, but let the entrails leak oot a bit. We'll need a good stench tae lure tha' bitch up from the bottom."

Turning to my right, I saw a BBC camera crew filming a female news reporter from behind a police barricade. Keeping my back to them, I eavesdropped on her while she read from a teleprompter:

"Its name was Purussaurus, *and it was a gigantic caiman, a prehistoric ancestor to the modern-day crocodile. Reaching lengths of more*

286

than fifteen meters, it lived in what is today the Amazonian rainforest but was eight million years agoa vast inland sea teeming with freshwater whales, giant turtles, and enormous rodents. How one of these monster predators survived to inhabit Loch Ness remains a mystery.

"It's a mystery that became public seven years ago when Highland resident Finlay McDonald found an ancient egg frozen in the bowels of Aldourie Castle, a three-century-old chateau that looms over the eastern shoreline of Loch Ness. An ancient aquifer connects the Moray Firth and the North Sea with Loch Ness beneath the castle grounds, and so it's not unusual to find sea creatures venturing inland. Still, no one had ever seen an egg quite like this.

"Footage of the egg's discovery went viral after scientists were astonished to discover a life-form still alive inside. Three months later the egg actually hatched, producing a living, breathing, four-legged, gilled reptile roughly the size of a Bassett Hound.

"The animal, dubbed Plessie by locals, was kept in the swimming pool at Nessie's Retreat, a luxury hotel located in the shadow of Urquhart Castle. Experts debated over the identity of the species, conducting daily examinations, while over four million visitors flocked to the Highlands that first summer to see the creature, which the hotel owner insisted was a Plesiosaurus.

"As the creature grew larger, it became apparent that Plessie was not a Plesiosaurus *at all, but a species of crocodile. Marine biologist Zachary Wallace added to the controversy by claiming the creature was a* Purussaurus, *an extremely dangerous predator that dated back to the Miocene era. Wallace warned residents that the pen would not be able to contain the animal, which now exceeded three meters in length and was predicted to grow five to six times that size. A larger containment area was cordoned off at Loch Dochfour, a narrow waterway at the head of Loch Ness, with a series of gates established to secure a seven-acre pen. An observation galley was erected in time for tourist season, providing visitors with a bird's-eye view of the pen's truck-sized occupant.*

"For the next four years, Plessie made the Scottish Highlands the number one tourist destination in the world, the crocodile surpassing sixteen

meters and weighing an estimated thirty tons, ten times the weight of a double-decker bus. During the warmer months, the croc spent its days sunning itself on the walled shoreline, to the delight of onlookers. At night and throughout the winter, she remained underwater in the muddy bog. When her handlers attempted to flush her back to the surface after a long winter's hibernation, they discovered that the underwater gate separating Dochfour from Loch Ness had been ravaged.

"A massive search began in the Great Glen. During the investigation that followed, one handler told authorities that three months prior to Plessie's escape, keepers had so feared the creature that they'd kept it on a steady diet of tranquilizers. As the weather turned cold, the croc, now a juvenile adult, spent more time underwater, gradually weaning its system off the drugs, affording it the opportunity to escape.

"Throughout March and into late spring, there were no sightings. Many believed Plessie was dead, poisoned by Loch Ness's heavy peat content. Others claimed the crocodile was secretly being fed from Aldourie Castle's subterranean caverns. Water bailiffs reported that the local deer population no longer crossed Loch Ness. When a reptile claw footprint measuring two meters was found on the shoreline near Foyers on May 29, residents grew worried.

"The first probable attack on a human being took place two weeks later, when the remains of a fishing boat piloted by Glasgow resident Martin McCandless washed up on the shores of Tor Point. Police painted a grim picture. The creature had bludgeoned the keel from below, sinking the vessel and taking its lone occupant. Still, with no overwhelming forensic evidence to indicate a change in the creature's diet, Inverness officials waited to exercise boating restrictions on the loch.

"On the evening of June 21, everything changed. Hours earlier, a small ferry had left the wharf located here at the Clansman Hotel. Returning from Fort Augustus loaded with thirty-seven passengers and three crewmen, the boat was passing Urquhart Castle when it was rammed from below with what many eyewitnesses described as the force of a locomotive. Though the boat took on water, the engines remained intact and the ship's captain managed to make it back to the dock. Then, as shaken passengers disembarked, Plessie surfaced half a kilometer to the north of where I'm

standing. Hungry from her long months of hibernation, the creature went after the fleeing tourists.

"The first victim was Magdalena Hicklen of New York. The South Bronx native, who had survived drive-by shootings and a counter-culture of drugs and crime, was vacationing in Scotland with her husband, Nate, and their young son, Spencer. When she saw the giant caiman coming down the A-82 highway, Magdalena yelled to her spouse to get the boy inside the hotel. Witnesses say the woman distracted the thirty-five-ton crocodile, ducking between parked cars before hurrying inside the Clansman's lobby herself. The enraged animal smashed through the entrance and emerged from the wreckage with Magdalena dangling from its mouth by her left leg. The woman thrashed and kicked the creature with her other leg but was unable to free herself as the giant caiman returned to the water and submerged with its meal, leaving behind a decimated hotel and locals fearing for their lives.

"Two more attacks have occurred since the Clansman feeding, all around dusk and at four- to five-day intervals. Lorey Schmidt was taken as she walked along the shoreline in Foyers, texting her girlfriend back home. Ernest Lazano was reported missing from Invermoriston, where he was staying at a bed-and-breakfast. His severed right arm was found thirty meters upstream from Loch Ness in the River Moriston.

"While members of Parliament continue to debate over whether to capture or kill the Purussaurus, *the man who discovered the egg has decided to take matters into his own hands."*

I followed True as he and Jim wheeled their bait back down the wharf to his boat. Jim clipped the end of a steel cable around the dead cow's neck collar while True used a hose to wash the animal's blood from his hands.

He grabbed my arm in a wet, vice-like grip when I tried to board the vessel. "Sorry, lad. You and Jimmy are stayin' here."

"True, there's no way I'm letting you do this alone."

"Yeah, there is. It's my fault all this happened, an' we both ken it. But before I go, there's one thing I need tae hear from yer lips: how did ye do it, Zach? How did ye escape from *Vostok* seven years ago?"

"I told you. I found the subglacial river and followed it all the way

289

back to the Amery Ice Shelf."

"Yer lyin', lad. Even if ye had a GPS that would 'ave worked beneath all that ice, the Barracuda *didnae have enough battery power left nor air tae breathe for ye tae complete the eight-hundred-mile journey. So how did ye do it?"*

"Don't get on that boat, and I'll tell you everything."

True smiled. "Ye don't ken yerself, do ye lad?"

He tossed me aside, then climbed aboard the twenty-eight-foot boat and gunned the engines, sending the cow carcass flying into the water past a stunned Jim Clancy. The two of us watched as True motored half a mile out before circling the bait into a tight figure-eight pattern.

That's when I knew...

There was one other craft tied off at the wharf—Brandy's old tour boat. The engine was shot, but the radio worked. I climbed aboard, hurrying to the pilothouse—

—Waaa-boom!

The blast tossed me to the deck. Seconds later, a bloody stew of flesh and innards rained across the windshield, adding a lasting stain to the boat, wharf, and tarmac.

I emerged from the cabin in a daze, Brandy's boat rocking violently beneath me. I heard the report of wood landing on the rock-strewn shoreline, so I didn't need to look out upon those tea-colored waters now running crimson, or inventory the collection of floating debris, to know what had happened.

I already knew.

I already knew...

I already knew...

"What did you know, Zachary?"

"Sir, he's still under the effects of the medication. It'll be another—"

"Wake him."

A rush of ice water blasted through my veins, forcing me to

swim to the light.

"Huh?" I awoke, disoriented. I was inside a chamber, seated upright before a machine that resembled something an ophthalmologist might use to examine one's eyes. My wrists and ankles were strapped to the chair.

Seated next to me was Colonel Stephen Vacendak.

27

*"In the councils of government, we must guard against the acquisition of
unwarranted influence, whether sought or unsought, by the
military-industrial complex.
The potential for the disastrous rise of misplaced power exists and will persist."*
—President Dwight D. Eisenhower

There were electrodes attached to my temples and forehead,
and an I.V. bag dripped into a tube in my left forearm.

"Dr. Stewart, your patient's out again."

*"Sorry, Colonel. We've got enough Dilaudid in him to numb a horse,
but I'll hit him with another shot of B12."*

*"I want him coherent, not in a stupor. Give him something with a little
kick."*

* * *

"Huh!"

My eyes snapped open. My heart was racing, my lungs
heaving to catch up. I was dressed in surgical greens, my wrists and
ankles strapped to a leather lounge chair.

Before me stood a big man about my father's age dressed in
surgical greens and a white lab coat. He had long, graying blonde
hair and a goatee. My eyes focused on his identification badge.

"Dr. Chris Stewart. Levels twenty through twenty-six."

"Good, the fog is lifting." I detected a trace of Scottish
Highlands tucked into the physician's British accent. As he backed
away, I realized I wasn't looking at him; I was watching a flatscreen
monitor on my left. The man's face suddenly multiplied, as if he
were looking into a mirror that was facing another mirror, only
everything that appeared on the screen was originating from *my*

vision.

"Let me turn that away from you, it's too disorienting." He pushed the monitor around on its swivel arm.

I heard a hiss of air pressure as a pneumatic door opened behind me. I caught a whiff of cheap aftershave and knew it was the Colonel.

He positioned a stool on my right and then spun my chair around to face him. "What did you know, Zachary?"

"I don't understand."

"In your last memory emergence you said, 'I already knew.' You were at Loch Ness, the day your best friend, True, died. What is it you knew?"

"That he wanted to die. That he was wracked with guilt over the deaths caused by the *Purussaurus*. I knew when I saw him circling in his boat that he had rigged the keel with explosives. How did you know I was dreaming of that day?"

He pointed to the optical scanner. "I know because this machine reads the electrical signals perceived by the brain and plays them on this monitor for me to watch. In the last seventeen days, I've dialed up every pertinent memory you've experienced, and it's been quite an adventure. Your life is a paradox, Dr. Wallace... No, let me rephrase that: Your death is a paradox. I've watched you die so many times that I feel I owe you flowers. From your drowning as a young boy in Loch Ness to your drowning in the Sargasso Sea, to at least a dozen horrible deaths in Lake Vostok. And yet, here you are."

"What's that supposed to mean? I had a few near-death experiences, so what?"

"Not near-death, my friend. You *died*."

I laid my head back, feeling lightheaded.

Dr. Stewart leaned in with an apple juice, which I sipped from a straw.

"Thank you."

"Let me know if you want more. And if you feel like you have to urinate, go ahead. We have a catheter in you."

I felt queasy. "Why am I here? Is any of this even real?"

"Good questions," the Colonel said. "Over the years, many individuals have experienced a close encounter with an extraterrestrial, either physical contact or a mind-to-mind interaction. What determines the extent of the experience is the level of consciousness of the E.T.; the higher the being, the more positive the interaction. Seven years ago you channeled soul to soul with the highest being our paranormal experts have ever found trace memories of in a close-encounter subject. That makes you a conduit into another dimension. As a result, your consciousness has the ability to selectively route your soul through a multiverse of infinite probabilities.

"Let me give you an example. On your ninth birthday you caught your father cheating on your mother. Incensed, you rowed out on Loch Ness by yourself to test your sonic lure. Your invention attracted a school of salmon, and one oversized Anguilla eel, which sunk your boat and left you flailing in near-freezing water. At that moment your consciousness created a dozen possible scenarios, all but one ending in your death. Call it multiple forks in the road. The thing is, your consciousness bypassed the eight-lane superhighway and followed a torturous dirt road, and the life of Zachary Wallace miraculously continued."

"So what? So I cheated death a few times. Every day, every person chooses between infinite possibilities. Some days we avoid death and never know it, simply because we took another route to work or didn't book a plane ticket or didn't trip on the cat and fall down the stairs. How is my life a paradox?"

"Because you're here. Because you made it out of Vostok alive when there wasn't an escape option—No, that's not true. *I* was your escape option. Unfortunately, Captain Hintzmann told you a conspiracy tale that obviously painted me as the bad guy. I'm not the bad guy, Zachary."

"Bullshit. You threatened to leave me stranded in the borehole."

"It was only a threat. I didn't trust the personnel inside Vostok Command, and I needed answers. I never expected you to climb out of the sub and disconnect the umbilical. That's what's known as being hero-stupid. Suicidal. And yet, in a hundred multiverses of death, your consciousness managed to find the one possible outcome that led you back to that extraterrestrial vessel. And that, my friend, was your emergence point into the higher dimensions."

Colonel Vacendak popped a straw into another box of apple juice and held it up to my parched lips. "You asked me what is real. Every possible outcome in our lives creates an alternate universe, and every one of them is real. Our consciousness selects the routes. Who knows, perhaps somewhere out there exist trillions of parallel universes and hundreds of each one of us living out these alternative lives. But I've spent the last two weeks scanning your memories, Zachary, and you never made it out of Lake Vostok alive.

"I know you think you piloted the *Barracuda* through a subglacial river. I'm also certain you're convinced that when you ran out of river and found yourself trapped, you were able to use the lasers to create your escape. But it never happened.

"That river you saw on the satellite chart, it wasn't complete. To make it out through the Amery Ice Shelf, you would have needed a hundred Valkyries powered by a small nuclear power plant. Not to mention air. The most you had left while the umbilical was still attached was twelve hours. Even with two completely functional lasers fed by an endless surface supply of power, it would have taken you eighty hours to cover eight hundred miles through near-solid ice. So how did you do it? How did you manage to get to Prydz Bay and the airfield at Davis Base to board your father's chartered jet, which just happened to be there to whisk True and his crocodile egg to safety?"

"I don't know. I was out of it. I spent a month in the hospital. I remember bits and pieces, but the rest is a blur. Yet I was there, and I'm here. I didn't die. You can't go from being trapped beneath the ice to Davis Station without the journey in between."

"Or maybe you can. Have you ever heard of quantum tunneling? No? When we examine the inner workings of an atom, we know that it is about 99.99 percent empty space. In fact, all matter is mostly empty space. So why, then, if that's true, can't we walk through walls? The reason is electrons. Electrons are tiny, but they pack a strong negative charge. These electrons are continuously moving around the circumference of the atom at the speed of light, repelling each other. It's their repelling charge that prevents us from walking through walls. Did you know we go through our entire lives without ever actually having touched anything? When we stand, the electrons in our shoes repel the electrons in the floor, levitating us about a millionth of a centimeter. Of course, you already know that from having spent the last seven years marketing an alien electron generator.

"Quantum tunneling is the quantum mechanical process by which a particle can pass between two separate points without passing through all the intermediate points. Extraterrestrial aircraft move from point A to point B in the blink of an eye, appearing to stop on a dime when in fact they're quantum tunneling. Oh, yes, we know a great deal about our alien visitors, and I want to share everything with you."

I stared hard into his eyes. "Why? So you can start some bogus space war predicated on a false flag attack that your phony spacecraft initiated? How many innocent people have to die so you and your big-oil allies can stay in power? These beings mean us no harm. Why do you want to kill them, too?"

"Don't be so quick to pass judgment. There's a reason they gave you access to the higher dimensions, and it wasn't so you could battle the Loch Ness monster and sell books."

He looked up at Dr. Stewart. "Give us some privacy, please.

I'll call you when I need you."

"Yes, sir."

I heard the physician leave, the door hissing closed behind him.

"I need to trust you, Dr. Wallace. More importantly, I need you to trust me. So I'm going to debrief you. In doing so, I'm going to reveal events so incredible they defy belief, things that are so shocking your first instinct will be to dismiss them simply out of self-preservation. The truth will sound like a combination of fiction and conspiracy theory, but it's absolutely real. To keep these truths from the public, the Constitution has been trampled upon and the United States government subverted. Good, moral individuals like yourself have been murdered, including a world leader who attempted to derail the people who now hold power. If someone of this man's stature was expendable, then you and I are barely an afterthought. And yet you may hold the key to saving our world, or destroying it. Thus, you need to know everything.

"Are we alone in the universe? Far from it. There are countless species out there vying to influence our evolution. The question now is whether humanity can survive the encounter. Although these visitations date back thousands of years, the first modern-day encounters occurred two years after the atomic bomb was used to end World War II. The crash outside Roswell, New Mexico, occurred when a new electromagnetic scalar weapon was switched on, causing two of the E.T. aircraft that were phasing out of super lightspeed to collide. Between January 1947 and December 1952, our EMP (electromagnetic pulse) weapon brought down thirteen alien spacecrafts: eleven in New Mexico and one each in Nevada and Arizona. Two other crashes occurred in Mexico and one in Norway. Sixty-five bodies were recovered, including one alien that was kept alive for three years. Of special importance was an alien craft, one hundred feet in diameter, recovered on a mesa near Aztec, New Mexico, on February 13, 1948. In addition to its dead crew, the vessel contained stored human body parts.

"In December of 1947, President Truman secretly approved Project Sign, a program that recruited America's top scientists to study the alien phenomenon. A year later Sign evolved into Project Grudge, which included a disinformation campaign known as Blue Book. Special Ops groups known as Blue Teams were trained and equipped to recover the crashed spacecraft and their alien crew, everything overseen during these early years by the newly formed United States Air Force and the Central Intelligence Agency, the latter created to deal exclusively with the alien presence.

"On November 4, 1952, President Truman established, by secret executive order, the National Security Agency. The NSA's primary task was to decipher alien communications and establish a dialogue with extraterrestrials. They were also charged with monitoring all communications worldwide for the purpose of gathering intelligence, both human and alien, and to containing the secret of extraterrestrials' presence. Truman's executive order exempted the NSA from all laws that did not specifically name the agency in the text of the law, essentially placing the NSA and its activities above the law, allowing them to operate free of oversight. President Obama learned this the hard way when he found out the agency was eavesdropping on the German chancellor without his administration's knowledge.

"Truman's actions created a plausible deniability buffer between the White House and the 'do whatever is necessary' tactics of his newly established intelligence agencies. In years to come, this order effectively prevented future presidents from accessing information from the intelligence communities regarding E.T.s. In other words, when it comes to aliens, these intelligence agencies report to no one.

"Truman's Secretary of Defense, James Forrestal, objected to the secret executive orders and was asked to resign. Convinced he represented a threat to their secrecy, the CIA tailed him around the clock. The resultant paranoia was diagnosed as a mental breakdown, and Forrestal was forcibly committed to the mental ward of Bethesda Naval Hospital, where he was isolated and denied visitors.

298

When Forrestal's brother notified authorities that he intended to remove James from Bethesda, CIA agents tied a sheet around the former defense secretary's neck, fastened the end to a room fixture, and threw James Forrestal out the sixteenth-story window. The sheet tore and the fall killed him, his murder made to look like a suicide."

"I don't care about your conspiracy tales, Colonel. I've heard them all before."

"Have you heard about the captured alien? He was a Gray. Grays come in different sizes, but they all share the same basic DNA structure. We've encountered reptile-like beings as well as humanoids, which we call Nordics. Each species has a different agenda, but I'll save that for later. The first Gray was called Ebe, short for Extraterrestrial Biological Entity. Like all Grays, Ebe was hairless, with a slightly elongated skull and big black eyes that had no exterior lids. A Gray's neck is centered at the base of its skull, giving the head a top-heavy, unstable appearance. Their hands are thin and double-jointed, possessing three long fingers and an opposable fourth digit.

"Ebe's sexual organs were internalized, but after two years of attempted communications, we were pretty sure he was a male. The alien's internal anatomy was chlorophyll-based, and it processed food into energy and waste material in the same manner as plants. It had to be kept in a Faraday chamber, which disrupted its ability to control electromagnetic currents. Otherwise, Ebe would escape by walking right through the walls.

"We learned a lot from Ebe, everything compiled into what became known as the Yellow Book. Unfortunately, the Gray became ill in late 1951. Medical specialists were brought in to treat him, along with a botanist. In a futile attempt to save the being's life and demonstrate our peaceful intentions to a superior race of beings, the United States began broadcasting radio signals into deep space. These distress calls, part of a project called SIGMA, went unanswered. Ebe died on June 2, 1952; Spielberg's movie E.T. was loosely based on these events.

299

"Fearing an alien invasion, Truman made sure our allies and the Soviet Union knew about the E.T.s and their technology. Because Congress couldn't be trusted, a small group of world leaders were organized to strategize how to deal with the threat. This ruling body became known as the Bilderberger Group, named after the hotel where they first met.

"The alien encounters grew more frequent in 1953 after President Dwight Eisenhower took office. To deal with the problem, Eisenhower appointed Nelson Rockefeller as chairman of a Presidential Advisory Committee on Government Organization. His first assignment was to create a secret task force.

"By 1955, the new entity, known as MJ-12, was placed in charge of all alien activities. The secret society included Nelson Rockefeller, Secretary of Defense Charles E. Wilson, CIA Director Allen Dulles, Secretary of State John Dulles, Chairman of the Joint Chiefs of Staff Admiral Arthur Radford, and FBI Director J. Edgar Hoover. There were also six men selected from the Council on Foreign Relations and six from a scientific group formed during the Manhattan Project, known as the JASON Society. Policies could only be mandated by a majority vote of twelve, thus the name MJ-12.

"Power breeds contempt, Dr. Wallace. Over the years MJ-12's top positions were dominated by members of the CFR and the Trilateral Commission. This group of elitists ruled in favor of its own special interests. Buoyed by Eisenhower's hands-off executive orders and Rockefeller's restructured government, this secret society had essentially been given the keys to rule the world, and they intended to shape it in ways that ensured they remained in power.

"Trillions of dollars have been secreted into covert funds over the years, to feed the military industrial complex without congressional oversight. Billions more were raised by exploiting the opium market. Working with South American drug cartels, cocaine shipments were brought by boat to offshore U.S. oil-drilling platforms, where CIA operatives would then transport them ashore with the rig's supplies, bypassing customs. New Orleans and California were the primary destinations, targeting minorities and the poor, an element the elite considered to be our nation's weakest links. Even today, the CIA controls most of the world's illegal drug markets, as well as its major newspapers and media outlets. Some of these vast appropriations were used to build elaborate underground facilities, supposedly to house the government in case of nuclear war. In reality, these bunkers are part of a plan known as Alternative Two. Alternatives One, Two, and Three are contingency plans that deal with the threat of an alien invasion.

"When President Kennedy learned what the CIA was doing, he threatened to shut down the agency, and with it MJ-12. In doing so, he underestimated the lengths the elite would go to, remain in power. If you believe that Lee Harvey Oswald and his magic bullet assassinated JFK, then I'm wasting my time with you. Most of the Warren Commission was made up of CFR members; you know how that investigation played itself out.

"There are secret underground military bases across the United States, including one in Fort Huachuca, Arizona, run by Army Intelligence, which houses nine extraterrestrial vessels and the remains of their crew."

"Is that where we are?"

"No, you're in Dreamland, better known as Area 51. We run a program here where our pilots test alien aircraft. We also run a fake test program to fool the public."

"You mean like the bogus alien craft you used to launch your false flag event?"

"That wasn't us. But I can see you don't believe me." He touched something in his right ear. It must have held a communication link because a moment later, the door hissed open and someone entered.

Her perfume arrived before I saw her. "Susan! Susan, are you all right?"

She knelt and kissed my cheek. "I'm fine. It's you I've been

301

worried about." She looked up at the Colonel. "You've accessed enough of his memories for a lifetime. I want these tubes taken out of him."

"In a moment. He needs to know who we are and where we stand."

Searching through a drawer beneath my table, she located gauze and tape and then set to work removing my I.V. tube. "Zach, MJ-12 fractured into two ideologies years ago. Our group is made up of intellects from the JASON Society and seeks peaceful relations with the E.T.s. The other group, composed of radical members of the Bilderbergs, Trilateral Commission, and CFR, seek to exploit the aliens' technology for their own New World Order."

I winced as the tube was extracted from my vein. "You're a part of this?"

"I was recruited into the JASON Society my senior year at Yale."

"What about... us?"

"I was told to get close."

"In other words you used me."

"Yes, but for the greater good. There's so much you don't understand."

"Try me."

Colonel Vacendak interrupted. "As I explained before, we've figured out how these saucer-shaped E.T. vessels appear to violate the laws of physics, hovering in mid-air and changing directions at will, moving at beyond-lightspeed. They're phase shifting in and out of a higher dimension, using a device similar to what you wanted to unleash upon the world, an energy device that creates a powerful rotating electromagnetic field that interacts with gravity. For some reason, the being you were in contact with seven years ago chose you to deliver it to humanity. Care to tell us why?"

"Maybe because it knew you and your kind would exploit it instead of share it, like the other assholes."

Susan stepped in between us. "The E.T. communicated with you while you were in a lucid dream state, something we refer to as a conscious-intelligent visual, or CIV. Existence is all about consciousness. Among higher souls like your alien friend, it transcends the limits of both time and space. While the Creator represents the absolute universal mind, physical beings like ourselves can tap into the same energy, or light vibration, to experience precognition, inspiration, intuition, creativity, and even remote viewing. This can be achieved because a link exists between awareness and matter. When you entered the ice tunnel, the purity of your consciousness allowed you to gain entry into the ship."

The Colonel nodded. "Tell him more about the different species we've encountered."

"Nordics are physical beings that resemble humans. They prefer to observe from a distance, though at times they've flown over our nuclear missile bases and short-circuited our weapon systems. They have communicated messages intended to awaken a spiritual evolution. Grays and Reptilians are darker beings who visit evolving worlds under the guise of serving as a 'mentor' species. They come bearing gifts, which they offer those who share the same negative vibrational frequencies as their own. Secret societies like the Bilderbergs, who are misled into bringing about mass destruction on a planetary scale, become their puppets.

"Zachary, a spiritual revolution is already upon us as the masses refuse to accept poverty, inequality, and endless war spawned by class warfare and greed. In order to control the populace, the elites have once again created the illusion of wolves stalking the flock, this time in the guise of aliens hell-bent on destruction. These contrived threats will lead to the forfeiture of even more personal freedoms, in this case the energy system you introduced to the public. It's a page straight out of the 9/11 playbook, except on a global scale, spawned by a Faustian agreement entered into between the elites and their alien counterparts, placing all of humanity in grave jeopardy."

"How is humanity in danger? And what does all this have to

303

do with me?"

"It had nothing to do with you," the Colonel said. "All we wanted you and your team to do was plant a few sensors around that damn ship and get out of Dodge. Instead, you triggered a portal that our alien visitors have been trying to access for years. If Susan and her fellow JASONS are right and some kind of cataclysm is going to hit—"

"Catacylsm? What kind of cataclysm?"

Susan held my hand. "Zach, honey, there was a reason you were contacted seven years ago in Lake Vostok. We believe an extinction event is going to happen in the near future. It could be natural or man-made, or induced by the E.T.s. To prevent it, we need to know what it will be and when it is supposed to happen.

"I'm sorry, baby, but we need to take you back."

28

"You're entirely bonkers. But I'll tell you a secret. All the best people are."
—Lewis Carroll

"Take me back where? To Lake Vostok? You're nuts!"

"Zach, the space-time portal you accessed allows you to move within the multiverses of your soul's existence. You can use the portal to access the future. Not only can you learn what disaster awaits us, you can determine the proper course of action that will save our species."

"And how the hell am I supposed to get back down into that godforsaken lake?"

"The Colonel will explain everything. For now, let's get you cleaned up and moving about."

I let out a loud yelp as Susan removed my catheter. She pulled loose the Velcro straps from my ankles and wrists, then removed the EKG tabs from my chest.

"Ow."

"Sorry. Try to stand."

I attempted to climb out of the chair, but my legs lacked the strength.

The Colonel summoned his physician, who returned with a wheelchair. "Susan, take him to the dining hall and get him something to eat. The transport leaves tomorrow morning at 0800 hours. I need him fit enough to travel."

"Twelve hours? I'll do my best. Zach, let's see if we can get some solid food into you."

Susan wheeled me out of the pneumatic door to an antiseptic-white, tiled outer corridor. We passed a dozen similar doors, each chamber's electronic keypad marked by either a green or flashing red light. I wondered who else they had hooked up to their insidious machines, whose memories they were probing.

At the end of the hall were three elevators. Susan swiped the magnetic strip on her identification card and pressed the UP button. The middle car arrived and she backed me inside.

We were on the twenty-third floor. The thirty-three elevator buttons were arranged in ascending order to reflect the subterranean location of our facility, the top floor listed as G.

She pushed SEVENTEEN. *"Zach, we're being watched. Don't react—I know you can hear my thoughts. I want you to tell me you'd prefer to take a hot bath to get your circulation going before you eat something."*

My pulse raced as I heard her words whispered into my consciousness. "Susan, if it's okay with you, I'd like to take a hot bath to get my circulation going before I eat something."

"Good idea. I'll take you to your quarters." She pushed FIVE.

The elevator passed the seventeenth floor and stopped on the fifth.

The doors opened and Susan wheeled me out to a seemingly endless corridor that felt more like a dormitory than a secured floor. Corkboards spaced at intervals along the walls held flyers advertising the week's schedule of social events. We passed a dozen rooms, a lounge, and a weight room before we reached Suite 514.

Susan indicated the keypad, and I pressed my thumb to it, unbolting the door.

The room brightened as we entered, revealing a small living room that looked out onto a dazzling view of a Mediterranean beach and an azure sea. The balcony door was open, venting the air-conditioned apartment with warm gusts of briny air. I heard the ocean washing along the shoreline and seagulls cawing—and none of it was real.

Susan shut the door of the video-screen balcony,

extinguishing the view.

"Zach, keep all verbal communication to small talk. Once we're in the bathtub, I'll answer all of your questions."

I caught myself nodding. "Uh, nice place."

"Let's get you into a hot bath."

I stood and leaned on her shoulder as she led me into her bedroom.

A queen-size bed faced bay windows that were part of the same holographic system as the balcony. There was a sound system and a flat-screen television. A wall of mirrors concealed a closet.

I stripped out of my surgical greens while Susan ran the bath water. My arms were covered in bruises from multiple I.V.s. My leg muscles had atrophied. Remembering the weight room, I decided a workout would follow my meal, if only to regain some strength to escape.

Susan was naked, waiting for me inside the whirlpool tub. "Come in and lean back against me. I'll massage your shoulders."

I climbed in and lay back against her breasts.

She wrapped her muscular quadriceps around my waist, running her hands along my groin.

I grabbed her wrists. *"Hey, knock it off! I want answers, like how we're able to communicate telepathically."*

"Now, don't react... I'm a Nordic."

I tried to sit up, but her legs were far too strong.

"I won't harm you. I'm here to help you, but you have to trust me. The Colonel lied. He needs you in Vostok to access the alien vessel. Once MJ-12 has access to the portal, they'll be able to time-jump, altering third-dimension reality. We can't allow that to happen."

"What's this 'we' stuff? You don't need me, Susan, you're Nordic. Destroy the damn portal and be done with it."

"We can't. The magnetic shield is far too strong. Even if we could destroy it, there's a hierarchy in play. The being that communicated with you

exists in the upper dimensions. When it comes to these higher-vibration entities there are no coincidences. The portal is in Lake Vostok because it knew you would be there. It offered you the gift of energy for a reason. If it knows what is to come, then we must trust it."

"And why should I trust you?"

"Nordics have been mentoring humans for thousands of years. The Mayan teacher, Kukulcan, was a Nordic, as was the Inca leader Viracocha. If Colonel Vacendak knew I was a Nordic, neither one of us would ever see daylight again."

"Where do Nordics come from? How long have you been on Earth? Were you born here?"

"I'll tell you everything, but you must remember we're being watched. Close your eyes." She kissed the back of my neck while massaging my shoulders. *"Life thrives in multiple plains of existence throughout the universe. Imagine each galaxy as a garden, most of its flowers cultivated within its central greenhouse. Star systems like yours, situated along the fringes of the galaxy, must be seeded for life.*

"Seeded how?"

"The process begins with water. Billions of years ago Earth was bombarded with asteroids and comets, each impact releasing moisture into the atmosphere along with the chemicals and amino acids necessary to foster single-celled organisms. Life took root almost four billion years ago; however, eons of evolution failed to produce a species worthy of harboring a higher soul.

"Cataclysms are a means of testing the worthiness of a species or merely starting over. The asteroid that wiped out the dinosaurs was intended to end their reign and pave the way for the ascension of mammals, primates, and finally primitive man. When it comes to hominids, Nordics are purebreds: our genome possesses DNA strands designed to adapt to each world's unique environment. Homo sapiens were selected for an interspecies breeding program designed to accelerate your hybrid faster up the evolutionary ladder."

"Why?"

"The purpose of existence in the physical dimension is to provide suitable harbors for the soul. Intelligence is a trait that blossoms when fertilized by a

higher species. Nordic hybrid development tends to follow similar progressions, spurred by adversity. Nomads forge clans and clans form alliances, usually out of the need for protection. Eventually, these unions expand to tribes, with the manner in which disputes are settled determining the potential reign of each budding group.

"Agrarian societies replace hunter-gatherers with farmers, stone tools with metallurgy, chaos with the rule of law. Chiefdoms and kingdoms are absorbed into geopolitical systems. Geographical territories are defined and redefined, with empires rising and falling as the world seeks equilibrium. Market-driven economies empower democracies over autocracies, with the availability of energy determining population levels, wealth, and military might.

"It is at this stage that every intelligent species either succeeds or succumbs to its own weaknesses. Technology is the great equalizer. As it evolves, global communication and information challenge the elite, the majority demanding freedom and an equitable share of a better life. The institutions in power either raise the standard of living among the masses or seek violent means to preserve the status quo. What's at stake is the future of the species.

"Equality is the key to survival, Zachary. It leads to free-market globalism and new energy systems that eventually unite the entire planet. Energy, both physical and spiritual, is what ultimately transforms a Type-0 civilization like yours into a Type-1 civilization. It is at this point that the dangers of splitting the atom are replaced by the threat of extinction. Cataclysms like asteroid strikes, caldera eruptions, lethal viruses, and ice ages induced by climate change will either unite a species or destroy it."

"Assuming we survive these challenges, what then?"

"Unity is what defines a Type-1 civilization. Societies thrive using clean, renewable energy. Type-2 civilizations are those which terraform other worlds within their solar system. Type-3 civilizations—the highest level attainable for third-dimension physical beings—have mastered zero-point energy and faster-than-light travel, uniting them with the community of intelligent beings in their galaxy.

"What prevents a Type-0 civilization like yours from evolving and ultimately surviving is the resistance by institutions to turning their power over to

the people. When economic tribalism dominates the political system, civilization reverts to a system of fiefdoms. Contempt divides the masses, and conflicts result in war and a deeper divide. When the first potential extinction event arises, the stagnating Type-0 civilization will always perish."

"And what is my role in this equation?"

She slid me around, slipping her tongue in my mouth. *"Colonel Vacendak and his MJ-12 brethren are convinced the space-time portal you accessed in Vostok will give them access to zero-point energy, a technology reserved for Type-3 civilizations. You must pretend to assist the Colonel—"*

"Susan, I'm not going back in that subglacial icebox. No way."

"You have to. The future of your species is at stake. It's the reason the Grays are here, the reason the trans-dimensional being sought you out." She gripped my face, staring hard into my eyes. *"Unless you act, your people and every air-breathing being on your planet will perish."*

29

"Heroism on command, senseless violence, and all the loathsome nonsense that goes by the name of patriotism—how passionately I hate them."
—Albert Einstein

Over the next twelve hours, I managed two meals, dedicated a few hour-sessions in the weight room working my atrophied muscles into shape, and spent a restless night curled in bed next to Susan.

Who was she? *What* was she? Frankly, I didn't care if she called herself a Nordic. It wasn't like she had two heads. What bothered me more was that our relationship had been strategic, not emotional. She had baited me into loving her to satisfy her species' agenda, and that meant I couldn't trust her.

They came for us at six in the morning.

Two armed security men escorted us up to the third floor to a chamber the size of a middle school gym. Members of the team that were being flown out to Antarctica waited in line to receive shots and collect their Extreme Weather Gear, most of the crewmen already dressed in nylon Bio Suits.

Dr. Stewart pulled us out of line and led us into a private room. We were handed dressing gowns and asked to strip down for our pre-flight exams. The "booster shot" into my right buttock administered the requisite biochip and tracer into my bloodstream.

We dressed in nylon navy-blue Bio Suits and boots, selected our breakfast from a buffet line, and ate. When we finished, our armed escorts took us down to Level 16.

Susan reached for my hand as we stepped off the elevator. *There's a Gray on this floor. You'll feel it reading your mind. Don't think about last night; focus on a distant memory.*

We entered a small room with porous steel walls that exuded an electromagnetic current that caused my hair to dance away from my scalp. Two chairs sporting wrist and ankle couplings were bolted to the white tile floor, facing dark glass that spanned most of the front wall.

Colonel Vacendak directed me to occupy the chair on the left, Susan the one on the right. I sat upright, wincing as my limbs were secured in place.

"My apologies, but this pre-flight pep talk could get emotional. Captain, are you carrying a firearm?"

The senior security guard nodded.

"I'm going to ask Dr. Wallace five questions. At the first wrong answer or his refusal to respond, you will shoot Ms. McWhite in the head."

The guard methodically removed his gun from its holster, coldly chambered a round, and then pressed the barrel to Susan's left temple.

I felt a wave of hot blood rushing to my face. "What's your problem, arse? Weren't you hugged as a child?"

"Question one: Dr. Wallace, is Susan McWhite able to communicate telepathically with you?"

I glanced at Susan, who was staring intently at the dark glass. "Yes."

A green light flashed on from behind the glass for just a blink.

Colonel Vacendak nodded. "So far, so good. Question two: Is Susan McWhite a Nordic?"

I felt myself shaking. "How the fuck would I know a Nordic from a human?"

A long moment passed before the green light flashed again.

"Your answer is deceptive, but accepted. Question three: Can I trust Susan McWhite once our team has gained access to the interdimensional portal?"

I stared at our reflections, registering a strange sensation inside my head that felt like icy fingers probing the crevices of my brain. I hesitated, knowing a truthful answer would condemn Susan as much as a lie.

And then another thought occurred to me, one that altered my interpretation of the question. *Maybe the bitch is setting me up again.*

I looked at Susan. "Yes, you can trust her."

The light flashed green.

Susan exhaled.

Colonel Vacendak's eyebrows raised. "Question four: Can I trust *you* once we're in Lake Vostok?"

I turned to face him. "No."

I didn't bother looking for the light.

"So far, you've been truthful, confirming things I already knew. And, by telling me that I can trust Susan, you've told me that you don't trust Susan. By now, you must have considered her role in the theft of the Vostok units from your warehouse safe?"

I closed my eyes. *"I trusted you, Susan. I loved you! How could you set me up like that?"*

"I'm sorry, Zach. But there are things in play that you can't see. If it means anything, I do care about you."

"Stay out of my head!"

The Colonel was watching us, smiling. "A lover's telepathic quarrel? If only we humans could handle them the same way. One day, perhaps, assuming we can survive what lies ahead. And that, after all, is the point of this mission, is it not? To see what catastrophe lies in wait for us, the very survival of an entire species hanging in the balance.

"This exercise served its purpose, I believe, for it made you realize that our Nordic friend here can't be trusted. And now I realize that if a come-to-Jesus moment arises in Lake Vostok that requires you to trust me to do the right thing, you no longer value Ms. McWhite's life enough to persuade you. So then, we'll need to up the ante. Question five: What do you value above even your own welfare?"

The Colonel signaled to the glass.

A moment later a hidden door pushed open along a sidewall, and another guard entered the room with a ten-year-old boy.

His hair was raven-dark like his mother's, and when William saw me, he ran to me and hugged me, curling himself in my lap. "Da, I don't like this place. Mum blames ye fer us bein' here."

I stared venom into Colonel Vacendak's eyes. "Where's the boy's mother?"

"She's safe. She's a handful, that one. Your son and ex-wife will spend the next few weeks with us here at Dreamland. Once you complete the mission, they'll be released unharmed."

"Why should I believe you?"

The Colonel signaled for the guard to remove Willy from my lap. He waited until the two had left the room and the door clicked shut before nodding to the guard aiming the gun at Susan's head.

"No!"

The muffled blast splattered a Rorschach pattern of blood, brain, and bone across the white tile.

I turned my head and puked up my breakfast.

"Trust is all we have, Dr. Wallace. Susan McWhite was a valued ally and friend. She was also my lover. If I was willing to sacrifice her life for the greater good, you have to trust that I won't hesitate to kill you and your family should you attempt to deceive me in Lake Vostok."

He turned to the guard who had shot Susan. "Have her remains taken to the seventeenth floor for dissection, then clean him up and get him aboard the transport."

"Yes, sir."

* * *

Thirty minutes later I rode the elevator up to ground level with my armed escort. A wave of early-morning Nevada heat greeted me as we entered a "scoot and hide" hangar the size of six football fields. Beneath the high roof I could see a slice of red rock, the mountains concealing the rising sun. To the west rose a cluster of radar antennas. To the north a building meant to resemble a mess hall was flanked by several antiquated housing facilities, and farther down the road, by a perimeter fence, stood a guard house.

The surface facilities were there for window dressing because Area 51 conducted most of its business deep underground.

Two long tarmac runways, constructed on a dry lake bed, ran parallel to the hangar. My escort led me to a Lockheed C-5 Galaxy, an immense military transport that dwarfed everything else under the roof. Painted in green camouflage, the plane—nicknamed FRED (Fucking Ridiculous Environmental Disaster) by its crew—had twelve internal wing tanks and was equipped for aerial refueling. The T-shaped tail towered three stories overhead, its nose and aft loading docks lowered open to receive its payload.

The payload was a thirty-seven-foot submarine named the *Tethys*, the very ship described to me seven years earlier by Ben Hintzmann. She had been named after the Titan goddess of freshwater rivers and streams, and the ancient sea that harbored prehistoric life 200 million years ago. The vessel had been designed for one purpose: to access Lake Vostok by traveling beneath the East Antarctic ice sheet through a network of subglacial rivers.

To accomplish this, the sub housed two ice-melting elements in its reinforced, chisel-shaped bow. The first was a Europa-class Valkyrie laser. Like the two Valkyries that had been mounted on the *Barracuda*, it was designed specifically for Jupiter's frozen moon. The E-class, however, was three times the diameter of its predecessor and was powered by a nuclear reactor.

To help the sixty-three-ton ship's twin engines propel the *Tethys* through the ice, the sub had been equipped with a bow and flat bottom composed of a calcium isotope, the plates of which could be superheated to temperatures exceeding fifteen hundred degrees Fahrenheit. The end result was a dagger-shaped vessel that melted ice like a hot knife through butter, keeping the submarine hydroplaning toward its target.

Technicians loaded the ship aboard the transport and secured it in chains. I boarded through the open nose to the forward passenger section, where seventy-two business-class seats were set in eighteen rows facing the rear of the aircraft. The plane was empty, the sub's crew still finishing breakfast. The guard stopped me at the third row and motioned for me to occupy a window seat while he took the aisle. Reclining the chair, I closed my eyes and tried to settle my nerves.

But the thought of William and Brandy held captive, along with the image of Susan's skull splattering across the white tile floor, wouldn't leave me. The guard's presence only added to my anxiety.

Unable to take it anymore, I stood and confronted the armed man. "I need something to put me out. Drugs, booze, a bottle of cough syrup—I don't care what it is, but I need it now!"

"How about I just punch you in the face?"

"Do it, arse. Then you can explain to the Colonel why his lead scientist can't function when we get to Antarctica."

Realizing he needed to deal with my issue, the guard radioed for a physician.

Ten minutes later Dr. Stewart was rigging an I.V. drip to service me in the first-row window seat. "This will put you in La La Land for a good fifteen hours. When you wake up, you can take these pills, one every four hours. Just make sure you eat something first." He slid the needle into a vein in my left forearm, securing it in place with medical tape. "By the way, I'm sorry about Susan. To waste a life like that... It's not why I joined MJ-12. All life is sacred. No matter the species, we're all God's creatures. Even the bloody Irish."

He winked, started the drip, and left.

VOSTOK

I reclined my seat, pulled the blind down over my window, and closed my eyes, allowing the liquid elixir to float me away.

30

Susan's soul came to me, only it was harbored in the physicality of another.

As was mine.

We were on a mountain bluff overlooking a tempest sea. The sky was violet, but not by dusk's cool touch, for the sun was still high in the sky. She was picking purple flowers that grew from vines twisted around branches of a scarlet oak, and the wind kept catching her tunic, causing the sheer fabric to bloom above her hips, revealing her naked torso to me.

"You're using the wind to tempt my loins." I said aloud.

"And why would I do such a thing? This is my fertile time, and the Council has placed yet another moratorium on conception. Or perhaps you've spent so much time in your cave that you haven't heard?"

"I am a scientist, Lehanna. The decree is in response to the latest Miketz update. The magma chamber's internal pressure has risen higher than our geologists predicted."

"How much longer do we have?"

"It's best not to dwell on predictions."

"Avi Socha, as your senior wife I need to prepare our home for every eventuality."

"The Miketz is a probability, not a certainty. It could still subside."

"How long?"

"Two solar orbits, with the pyroclastic blast most likely occurring before the spring harvest."

The new doomsday timetable hit her hard. "And how many escape ships has the Council commissioned for Charon's lower rungs?"

"So far, only sixteen—just about enough for a single tribe."

I watched as the sadness in her eyes changed to anger. "And for the Council?"

"They are keeping the number secret, but I sincerely doubt any of the Appointed Ones will be left behind."

"Sixteen ships... And the lottery determines which tribe will be saved, correct?"

"Or which seven hundred. To the Council the twelve tribes are simply a minority to be managed. Not that it matters. The transports only carry enough supplies to orbit Charon for one solar year. Most of us scientists in purgatory agree, the effects of the Miketz will render the planet uninhabitable. We need a new planet to call home, but none of the other worlds in this star system are capable of sustaining life. And the transports lack the technology to venture beyond the asteroid belt."

"What about Berudim? The Council believes the third world possesses water."

"Berudim's atmosphere is toxic. And the planet is far too close to the sun to inhabit. The Council is offering the people false hope in an attempt to maintain order. Lehanna?"

She was calculating odds. "Our tribe has a one in twelve chance of being chosen. We can increase those odds with a better harvest and by obeying the Council's new edicts. Avi, you've already been forbidden to practice the mystic wisdom. For the sake of our loved ones, I ask you now to end your midnight activities in the caves."

"It's not mysticism, Lehanna. Soul searching is a higher form of meditation which taps into the universal consciousness."

"It is heresy and a violation of Council law. If you are caught, our tribe could be excluded from the lottery."

"What good is it to be orbiting a dead world? If I succeed in communicating with my soul's future incarnates, perhaps they can provide me with the knowledge to prevent the Miketz."

"It's utter nonsense."

"Not true! In the past year, I have communicated with an ancient one whose physicality housed my soul long before me. He described Charon as it was a century before the Council divided our people into tribes. He taught me about the upper worlds, a wonderful existence our souls inhabit between incarnations.

319

Time does not exist in these other realms, which makes it possible for me to communicate with a future me."

"There is none after you, *Avi Socha!* This planet is doomed. Ours shall be the last generation to inhabit Charon. Now wake up."

* * *

"Hey, pal, wake up."

I opened my eyes. My face was covered in tears, my mind lost in a stupor. Everything was gone—the violet landscape, the ocean... the woman. Instead, four men in neoprene jumpsuits stood over me, chuckling, their presence anchoring me to my new surroundings, even as my growing wakefulness drained the memories from my bizarre out-of-body experience.

I was confused. I felt empty inside. Wherever I had been, I wanted to be back there. I *belonged* there.

I took a deep breath and smelled Susan. In the lucid dream, I had called her by another name. *Lehanna.* She had referred to me as Avi Socha. She had called the planet Charon. Was it a Nordic world? Had it survived the doomsday event we were talking about? Or was this a future event in a multiverse still to come?

No. Our conversation had been vocalized; there was nothing to indicate an evolved ability to communicate telepathically.

Try as I might, the memory of the dream dissipated too quickly to analyze. It was then I realized something was happening.

Dozens of crewmen were hovering by the windows on my side of the plane, many snapping photos with their iPhones. I raised the window shade and looked outside.

Sweet Jesus...

We were flying over water, the night illuminated by the patterns of light emanating from countless UFOs. Whether their intentions were to escort us to Antarctica or shoot us down, I didn't know. But they were everywhere. Some flew in formations of up to a dozen, while others zipped close to our wing and hovered, only to accelerate out of view. Then there were those that preferred the cheap seats high above our altitude, their lights appearing like stars. One massive triangular craft the size of a small city dominated the heavens. Every so often it would execute an incredible end-over-end 360 as if just to show us it could do it.

It was a mind-boggling, humbling, and surreal spectacle, and I might have actually enjoyed it had I not feared they were only here because of me.

31

"There is a force/energy/consciousness/divine thread that connects us all spiritually to something greater than ourselves."

—Oprah Winfrey

Fear shuts down the mind and paralyzes the body. It unleashes thoughts that smother reason and strangle hope, reducing consciousness to a dying ember.

Sitting on the transport, I realized that I no longer cared whether I lived or died. In truth, it was only the need to save William and Brandy that forced me to take another breath. Yet, even in my state of anxiety, I knew there was zero chance of Colonel Vacendak ever releasing any of us. The only thing keeping us alive was MJ-12's belief that my presence was needed to access the object in Lake Vostok. When the mission was finished I, along with my loved ones, would be disposed of as collateral damage.

Logic therefore dictated that in order to keep William and Brandy alive, I needed to escape.

That, of course, would be far easier said than done. Besides being guarded around the clock, there weren't many places one could hide in East Antarctica. Not to mention the interest of the extraterrestrials. They had been following our transport for the last twenty-four hours, and there was a feeling of trepidation among the crew regarding what they might do after we landed. Gazing out of my window at a spectrum of alien lights, I realized something far more important than that my miserable life was at stake, but it was unclear whether the aliens supported my return to Lake Vostok or sought to terminate it.

As my mentor, Joe Tkalec, used to say, "Don't accuse God of being a bad dealer until you play out the hand you've been dealt."

And then Lake Vostok anted up and the cards were reshuffled.

We were crossing over the South Pole, passing through neon-green curtains of energy that marked the Aurora Australis. Manifested by electrons accelerated by the solar wind colliding with protons and atoms in the upper atmosphere, the Aurora danced its charged waves across the midnight sky, the lime-green color defined by the presence of atomic oxygen over the pole.

Having passed over the bottom of the world, Colonel Vacendak ordered the pilot to adjust our course farther to the south and take the C-5 transport into a gradual descent. Many of the crew wondered why we were landing.

Twenty minutes later, we found ourselves soaring over a seemingly endless desert of ice at an altitude of six hundred feet.

As we passed over Lake Vostok, the buried magnetic anomaly seemed to reach up from the subglacial lake like an invisible hand. It shook the plane with vomit-inducing waves of turbulence. We pitched and dipped, our engines sputtered, and the lights went off several terrifying times. Yet this was nothing compared to what happened to our alien escorts.

Facing backward in my seat, I saw a mega-sized saucer trailing below our plane phase in and out before it fell out of the night sky like a bowling ball. Seconds later, it smashed sideways onto the ice sheet, blasting snow a hundred feet into the electrified air.

By the time I glanced out of the window at the other craft, it was raining UFOs.

Unable to match the power of the force field being generated from the buried vessel, the smaller E.T. ships went into free fall, crashing to the ice with thunderous wallops that could be heard and felt for fifty miles in every direction.

The alien craft high overhead broke formation and dispersed.

Having flown beyond the anomaly's reach, the pilot increased our altitude and adjusted our course to the northeast, heading back toward Prydz Bay.

Round One was over, and it was a clear victory for the Colonel.

* * *

We touched down on the rock runway at Davis Station ninety minutes later, everyone on board relieved to be on the ground, their fears now focused on a possible retaliatory response.

It never came. Ground radar indicated that the surviving E.T. vessels had moved into the stratosphere. After another hour of waiting, the Colonel gave the order to unload the *Tethys,* a process that would take two days. Then the submarine would be wet docked by her surface ship, which was still en route. In fact, the only vessel visible in Prydz Bay was a 319-foot-long hopper dredge that was slowly working its way toward the Amery Ice Shelf.

It was November 2, spring in Antarctica. The sun hung low in a hazy gray sky when I stepped off the plane, the sub-zero continent welcoming me back with a blast of minus-seventeen-degree wind. Dressed in full ECW gear, I followed my keeper across the tarmac like a penguin waddling after its mother, only I purposely lagged behind just to piss him off.

I was assigned a room at Davis Station and released on my own recognizance. With a biochip circulating in my bloodstream, I was hardly a flight risk. Besides, where was I going to go?

Yet, I did have a plan.

The E.T. vessels had disappeared into the ether once we'd begun our initial descent over East Antarctica. Assuming they had been there to escort yours truly to Vostok, perhaps a few of the more sociable aliens might wish to communicate with me in what the Colonel had called a lucid dream state.

Reaching out to communicate with an extraterrestrial is defined as a close encounter of the fifth kind, or CE-5 initiative. Developed and practiced by Dr. Steven Greer and his supporters, the protocol uses vedic-style meditation to initiate telepathic communication between humans and extraterrestrials, in order to forge a mutually beneficial, sustainable, and cooperative relationship between our species. According to Dr. Greer, once an E.T. exceeds lightspeed it enters a state of cosmic mind. Humans can therefore use coherent thought sequencing to interface with an extraterrestrial, causing the craft to actually vector in on the group's location through their collective consciousness, culminating in some incredible experiences. Not only have lights appeared out of the ether to signal to CE-5 practitioners, messages of peace have been downloaded to the human participants.

Greer found that there was a universal readiness among extraterrestrials to engage in peaceful communications with the common man rather than our appointed leaders, who have downed dozens of crafts using EMP weapons over the last five decades. There are no secrets when communicating through the conscious mind, so if a human participant possesses a dark agenda, contact is cut off. CE-5 participants believe warfare and the use of nuclear weapons have led to Earth's isolation, our visiting E.T. ambassadors seeing humanity as an aggressive, divided civilization armed with knowledge that could lead to self-destruction. As such, these entities are hesitant to share advanced technologies until a lasting world unity and peace is achieved.

The fact that one of them had chosen to share its knowledge with me gave me hope that I could use Greer's CE-5 protocols to communicate outside of Lake Vostok.

What was I hoping to accomplish? In truth, I didn't know. I felt desperate and alone, and Susan's murder had rattled my nerves. With my son's life hanging in the balance, I needed something—anything—that might give me an edge, be it information or a weapon… or an alien ally whom I could convince to free my family.

After consuming a mug of clam chowder in the Davis cafeteria, I returned to my room to change into my extreme weather gear. I was pulling on my boots when I heard a phone playing the Rolling Stone's *Gimme Shelter*, one of my favorite songs. Searching the room, I traced the sound to a cell phone stuffed inside my pillowcase.

A text had been sent.

Dragonslayer: FOLLOW THE SHORELINE NORTH AND AWAIT FURTHER INSTRUCTIONS.

My pulse raced. Only one person had ever called me Dragonslayer—my father.

I quickly finished dressing. Slipping the phone inside my jacket pocket, I left my room and headed out of the nearest exit, my face cloaked behind goggles and a ski mask.

It was dusk and curtains of green light were already forming in the eastern sky by the time I made my way down to the frozen surface waters of Prydz Bay. I followed the shoreline north as instructed, abused by a twenty-knot wind carrying a wind chill of minus thirty-five.

I heard someone trudging through the snow behind me. It was my guard. He was following me on a parallel course farther inland, trying to stay out of sight.

The cell phone vibrated in my jacket pocket. I pulled it out, using my body to conceal its light from my shadow.

WALK OUT ONTO THE BAY 200 PACES AND STOP.

The bay? They must be sending a helicopter. I glanced overhead, listening for rotary blades. *Would MJ-12 shoot it down? Did my intended rescuers know I had a tracking device circulating through my bloodstream?*

I hesitated, then turned and walked out onto the frozen bay. The ice seemed plenty thick, the spring thaw having gained little traction. Counting my strides, and trembling from the cold, I continued to scan the star-filled sky for my ride.

Two hundred paces brought me some distance from shore. The surface remained solid beneath my boots, but there was still no sign of a chopper.

The wind howled in my wool-covered ears, sweeping snow particles across the barren ice. Tugging my jacket over my buttocks,

I sat down and closed my eyes to attempt a CE-5 communication.

When it comes to meditation, I'm strictly an amateur. Hunkering down in the bone-chilling cold, I ducked my hooded head and closed my eyes, attempting to imagine the Milky Way galaxy and the spiral arm that harbored our blue speck of a planet. When that seemed silly—the E.T.s knew where I was, having just followed me halfway across the world—I shifted my internal eye to the patch of ice beneath me.

I don't know how long I remained in this position. I may have fallen asleep, but at some point I felt another presence.

Opening my eyes, I found myself surrounded by mist. Directly overhead, a triangle of light seemed to be materializing out of another dimension, along with the flat metallic bottom of an extraterrestrial vehicle. It had to be hovering incredibly close, for it blotted out the stars.

I registered a brief fleeting moment of elation, then sudden panic as the ice beneath me evaporated and I went under, my lung-collapsing yelp stymied by a mouthful of salt water. Rational thought left me as unseen tentacles dragged me deeper into water so frigid it curdled my blood into jelly and strangled my circulation. It was Loch Ness all over again; the darkness, the paralysis of cold, the mind-snapping terror. I caught a glimpse of an immense, dark object moving beneath me as a pink fluorescent light sparked to life before me, revealing a scuba diver.

He shoved a regulator into my mouth, the device attached to a small container of air.

Pinching my nose, I inhaled a dozen quick breaths, struggling to get them into my failing lungs. The diver motioned below to a bullet-shaped canister the size of a double-wide coffin. Grabbing my left wrist, he dragged me to it, the dark container yawning open like a clam as we approached. He laid me inside as another wave of anxiety hit.

He squeezed in next to me and sealed the canister by pressing a device attached to his buoyancy control vest. The moment the pod sealed, a blue light activated.

The diver held up a plastic card.

STAY CALM, ZACHARY.

The top of my head struck the inside of the container as the pod jettisoned through the sea and a second laminated card appeared before me.

POD WILL DRAIN IN 2 MINUTES. CORE TEMPERATURE DROP NECESSARY TO SHUT DOWN BIOCHIP.

I closed my eyes, comforted by my rescuer's knowledge of the biochip, my body convulsing in the twenty-nine-degree water.

Two minutes . . . 120 seconds.

119... 118... 117...

Coherent thought goes hand in hand with core temperature. Stray too high or too low and you start to lose it. You start to die. In a battle of neurological functions, my mind fought to maintain a foothold of sanity as my hypothalamus struggled to control my body's internal thermostat.

It takes a lot to overcome this almond-sized super-organ, but subfreezing water is its kryptonite, the effects rapid and catastrophic. Within seconds of submerging, my brain had ordered the capillaries in my skin to squeeze out the blood, pushing it inward to help maintain my core temperature, and thereby inflicting horrendous pain upon my pinched extremities in the process. My muscles tightened and contracted as hypothermia swept through my body. For the first minute my muscles fought back using high-speed involuntary contractions, but the heat generated through shivering required more blood, which accelerated the drop in core temperature.

100... 99... 98...

The muscles in my face were fluttering. The diver noticed and clamped his hand over my mouth to keep the regulator in place.

95... 94... 93...

My hypothalamus continued hoarding resources, the organ willing to sacrifice a few pawns and knights to save the king. My thoughts dulled, my mind slipping into a stupor.

90... 85... . . . . . 23...

My oxygen-starved brain struggled to keep me awake. Urine seeped into the canister, my flooded kidneys overwhelmed by an influx of fluids.

Just a quick nap...

The diver shook me awake.

What was a scuba diver doing in my bathroom stall?

Timpani drums throttled my chest as my heart became arrhythmic and limited the oxygen to my brain. I turned to my right and saw True.

"Relax, lad. Him that's born to be hanged will never be drowned."

"You big lummox. I'm not drowning, I'm freezing to death!"

"Aye. But yer not swinging from a rope, are ye?"

Suddenly my skin was on fire.

"True, help me! I'm burning up!"

"Nothing I can do, lad. Yer hypothalamus has blown a fuse. Paradoxical undressing, it's called. Yer brain's last-ditch attempt at saving yer arse. Look at ye, yer blue as a fish. Ye haven't even got a pulse. Yer not alive, but yer not quite dead either. Better pray yer rescuers ken enough tae warm ye slowly, or yer constricted capillaries will reopen all at once and cause a sudden drop in blood pressure that will send yer heart into ventricular fibrillation."

"True, are you here to take me to heaven?"

"If need be. For now, jist close yer eyes."

32

"How do you know I'm mad?" asked Alice.
"You must be," said the Cat, "or you wouldn't have come here."
—Lewis Carroll

I rode a wave of pain to consciousness but refused to open my eyes, afraid to see what monster was chewing on my extremities.

And then the monster spoke.

"Christ in Heaven, enough with the bloody whimpering. There's old women in the Inverness Polar Bear Society tha' jump in Loch ·Ness every winter's morn, and ye don't hear those daft bitches yelping. Open yer eyes."

I opened them as my father commanded. He was seated beside me, dressed in a wool sweater that matched his hair and beard, and his Gael eyes had fire in them.

"There now, tha's better. There's work tae be done if ye want tae see yer family again."

I sat up, looking around the small infirmary. "Where are we?"

"Aboard Jonas Taylor's boat, the *McFarland.* She's a hopper dredge. Been in these waters since before ye went missing in D.C."

"I don't understand. How did Jonas know I'd be in East Antarctica?"

"He didn't. I contacted yer friend after Doc Stewart let me ken where ye was bein' held and whit fer."

"Doc Stewart? You mean the English physician who worked on me back at Groom Lake? Angus, the guy's MJ-12. He's one of the bad guys."

"First, they don't call themselves MJ-12 anymore, it's SECOR, short for Security Organization. Second, Stewie's only part English; his father wore the plaid. And he's an old friend. We grew up together before he left the Highlands to join the RAF. Caught the UFO fever back in 1980 when he was stationed at a NATO air base in Suffolk—Bentwaters, if memory serves. It was right after Christmas when one of yer alien vessels appeared over Rendlesham Forest, jist east of Ipswich. According to Stewie, a triangular metal object lit up the entire forest with this brilliant white light. Lots of folk saw it, but the RAF made no claims. From tha' day forward Stewie worked tae get himself involved with the MAJESTIC crowd. I hadnae a clue he was stationed in Dreamland Base 'til he contacted me.

"Stewie told me this Colonel Vacendak is forcing ye tae lead him intae Lake Vostok. Stewie says most of these MJ-SECOR lads are secretly rootin' fer ye tae succeed in bringing these free energy devices out intae public. The problem is Big Oil and the sociopaths in SECOR like this Colonel Vacendak, who enjoy killing. It's the crazies tha' keeps the others in line. They'll kill my grandson and yer ex without batting an eye."

I shifted uncomfortably, my skin still burning despite the I.V. drip. "Angus, can Jonas get me into Lake Vostok?"

"Aye. He has subs on board, and they're equipped with those lasers tha' melt ice. We rescued ye in one of 'em."

"We? That was *you* in the dry suit?"

"Yes, Gertrude. And did ye have tae make such a fuss?"

"You try submerging in subfreezing water for that long and see how you handle it!"

"Stop yer whinin'. I told ye in my note, we had tae drop yer core temperature tae disable the tracking device Stewie shot intae yer vein. The Colonel's divers stopped searchin' for yer body an hour ago. They gotta think yer dead. Tha's whit we want."

Angus stood to leave. "Finish yer I.V., then get dressed and find yer way to the pilothouse. Jonas says he needs tae train ye

331

before he'll give ye one of his subs."

* * *

I had met Jonas Taylor and his friend James Mackreides eight years ago, shortly after my book, *The Loch*, was published. The Tanaka Oceanographic Institute had offered to host a public signing event at their California facility on the coast of Monterey. Constructed twenty-five years earlier by the late marine biologist Masao Tanaka, the Institute featured a man-made lagoon with an ocean-access canal that intersected one of the largest annual whale migrations on the planet. Designed as a field laboratory, the waterway was originally intended to be a place where pregnant gray whales returning from their feeding grounds in the Bering Sea could birth their calves. Masao was so convinced, his facility would bridge the gap between science and entertainment that he mortgaged his entire family fortune on the endeavor.

Instead, the lagoon would become home to *Carcharodon megalodon*, the sixty-foot prehistoric cousin of the great white shark.

Like *Livyatan melvillei*, megalodon was a Miocene monster believed to be extinct. Jonas Taylor had discovered them inhabiting the deep waters of the Mariana Trench while piloting a top-secret dive for the Navy. According to his testimony, *"I was staring out the portal at the hydrothermal plume when sonar picked up an immense object rising from below. Suddenly, a ghost-white shark with a head bigger than our three-man sub emerged from the mineral ceiling."*

Two scientists on board had died during an emergency ascent, and the deep-sea submersible pilot was blamed. Discharged from the Navy, Jonas decided to become a marine biologist, intent on proving the megalodon was still alive.

Seven years later, rising construction costs on the Tanaka Institute forced Masao to accept a contract with the Japanese Marine Science Technology Center. The mission: to disperse sensory drones along the Mariana Trench that would function as an early-warning earthquake detection system. To complete the array, D.J. Tanaka, Masao's son, had to anchor each drone to the trench floor using an Abyss Glider, a sub resembling a one-man version of the *Barracuda*. When several of the drones stopped transmitting data, Masao needed a second diver to help retrieve one of the damaged sensors.

He selected Jonas Taylor.

Jonas accepted the offer, desiring only to recover an unfossilized white megalodon tooth photographed in the wreckage. But the dive ended badly.

Jonas and D.J. came face to face with not one but two Megs. The first was a forty-five-foot male, which became entangled in the surface ship's cable. The second was its sixty-foot pregnant mate, which was accidently lured topside.

The Tanaka Institute took on the task of capturing the female. Jonas and Masao were determined to quarantine the monster in the whale lagoon, with JAMSTEC agreeing to refit the canal entrance with King Kong-sized steel doors.

The hunt lasted a month, culminating in an act that surpassed my own nightmare in Loch Ness. In the end, one of the megalodon's surviving pups was captured and raised in Masao's cetacean facility—and a monster-shark cottage industry was born.

Angel, dubbed the Angel of Death, was a 70-foot albino, so fearsome she was easily one of the most terrifying creatures ever to exist. The monster would earn the Tanaka-Taylor family hundreds of millions of dollars. She also managed to escape twice, birth two litters of pups, and devour no less than a dozen humans, five of them in her lagoon.

Yet people still lined up by the tens of thousands to see her, and they wept when they learned she had died. Angel had met her own Angel of Death last summer, following her most recent escape. She had been tracked to the Western Pacific and had been caught in open water in an industrial fishing net, where she became entangled and drowned.

At least, that was what the world had been told…

* * *

The rusted-white steel superstructure of the 319-foot-long hopper dredge *McFarland* towered five stories above the deck and nearly twice that over the waterline. Everything aft of the command center and crews' quarters was dedicated to the business of dredging. Built in 1967, the ship was designed to clear waterways of sediment by vacuuming up slurry—a mixture of sand and water—from the sea floor using two large drag arms. After being pumped through pipes, the slurry would be deposited in a hopper, a massive hold that occupied the mid- and aft-decks like an oversized Olympic swimming pool. The *McFarland's* hopper could hold more than six thousand tons of slurry and evacuate it in minutes through its keel doors.

The Tanaka Institute had purchased the *McFarland* a year after the U.S. Army Corps of Engineers had decommissioned the ship and three months after Angel had birthed her five pups in captivity. Jonas had been looking for a vessel large enough to safely transport the juvenile sharks to another aquarium, knowing the Institute simply wasn't large enough to house six full-grown megalodons.

It was still dark outside when I left sickbay and made my way to the bridge, the hood of the crewmen's jacket Angus had left me pulled tightly around my head and face, just in case the Colonel had one of MJ-12's satellites watching the boat.

We were headed north at three knots, the ship's bow maneuvering through lead-gray surface waters dotted with islands of ice. To port rose the snow-packed cliffs that dominated the East Antarctic coastline; to starboard, the dark horizon and open ocean. I paused at the guardrail to look down at the ship's main deck and its mammoth hopper. The open hold occupied the deck space between the bridge superstructure and the ship's bow. The 175-foot-long, 45-foot-wide, 55-foot-deep tub remained in the shadows, the machinery designed to stir the captured slurry long since removed.

Locating an interior stairwell, I ascended to the bridge.

The *McFarland's* command center seemed far too big for its solitary row of computer consoles. Large bay windows surrounded the chamber on all four sides, looking out nine stories above the ocean. There were two men inside. The boat's captain, a Georgia man named Jon Hudson, was at the helm. The other man sat at a chart table, studying a map of the continent.

Gray-haired and in his mid-sixties, Jonas Taylor appeared fit, but the dark circles under his eyes told a different story. Rising to meet me, he greeted me in a bear hug.

"Zachary Wallace, you look good for a guy who didn't have a pulse an hour ago. Sorry about the way we had to bring you aboard, but you're messing with an intelligence agency exercising a mercenary mentality. I guess that's a necessity when dealing with extraterrestrial threats."

"There is no extraterrestrial threat. The D.C. attack was a false flag event staged to look like an E.T. vessel."

"Staged by whom?"

I glanced at the Captain, whose back was to us. "Is there somewhere we can speak in private?"

"Captain, how far are we from the Amery Ice Shelf?"

"Just under five nautical miles. No close contacts on sonar or radar."

"All engines stop. The bridge is mine. Get some breakfast."

Jonas waited until the Captain left. "For the record, I trust the Captain."

"I have no doubt he's a loyal employee, but we're dealing with sociopaths. Killing is as natural to them as it is to Bela and Lizzy. If you have the information they want, they'll get it."

"*They* being MAJESTIC-12?"

"MJ-12 oversees the black ops weapon systems and the military bases. The guys calling the shots are a cartel of power brokers, bankers, and egomaniacs who think the rest of us are here to serve them. These are the same assholes that stole my Vostok generators and burned our factory to the ground. They act above the law, have no interest in improving the lives of the seven billion people on this planet, and don't give a damn that their organizations are destroying the earth's biosphere.

"And they kidnapped William and Brandy to force me to lead them back to Lake Vostok."

"Why? What's in Vostok?"

"I'd rather not say, but it's important enough that MJ-12 designed a sub to travel beneath the ice sheet through a network of subglacial rivers into the lake. Jonas, it's critically important I make it to Vostok before them."

Jonas scanned his chart, using a slide rule to measure distances. "Vostok's at least eight to nine hundred miles away. My Manta subs are equipped with Valkyries, but they don't pack nearly enough juice to take you that far."

"They don't have to. MJ-12's sub will lead me into the lake's northern basin. Once I'm there, I'll be able to overtake them and get to where I need to be before they do."

"And how will making it back to Lake Vostok ahead of these guys save William and Brandy?"

"Again, I'd rather not say. The less you know the better."

"It'll take you twenty to thirty hours just to reach Vostok. Maybe more. Who's your copilot?"

Angus must have been eavesdropping from the interior stairwell, for he came bursting in on cue. "I'm going with the lad."

Jonas and I looked at one another with the same startled expression.

"Wha's with the long faces? I can handle it."

"Forget it," Jonas said. "I have no interest in sponsoring a suicide mission. If this is really about saving your family, then let's go to the authorities. I campaigned heavily for the President, and the Institute was a major donor to his election campaign. One phone call and you'll be speaking with the national security advisor himself. "

"I appreciate the offer, Jonas, but these guys operate outside White House jurisdiction."

"Tell Jonas everything, lad. Him not knowing isn't going to matter tae these people. The moment they see the Manta, they'll realize he arranged yer escape."

I knew my father was right. "There's an extraterrestrial vessel in Vostok. It's unlike anything we've seen. Seven years ago I was allowed access."

"Allowed? By what?"

"An entity... a higher life-form. It shared the secret of zero-point energy with me. I need to destroy it before MJ-12 finds it. Once that threat is removed, I'll initiate a dead-man's trigger—a threat to expose Colonel Vacendak's entire operation if he doesn't release William and Brandy within twenty-four hours."

Jonas was about to respond when a man dressed from head to toe in ECW gear entered through an exterior door, blasting us with a gust of frigid air. As he stripped away his hood and mask, I could see it was James Mackreides, Jonas's partner at the Tanaka Institute—his most trusted friend.

Mac acknowledged me with a nod, then handed Jonas his binoculars. "The *Tonga* just came into view; she's headed toward Prydz Bay."

Jonas moved quickly to the starboard windows and focused on the dark horizon, using the night-vision glasses. "That's her, all right. Where's the *Dubai-Land*?"

"Out in front. I caught sight of her bow wake."

"If the trawler's out front, then David may already be in the water."

"I don't think so," Mac said. "They're using the two boats to drive the creature to the ice shelf. David won't launch until the *Tonga* drops her nets into the water."

I looked at Jonas, confused. "David? As in your son?"

Jonas let Mac answer for him. "Remember that arse marine biologist, Michael Maren? Before he croaked, he discovered the remains of an ancient sea called the Panthalassa, buried beneath the Philippine Sea Plate. After he died, his fiancée sold maps of the subterranean sea to a guy named Fiesal bin Rashidi. Bin Rashidi happens to be a first cousin to the crown prince of Dubai."

"The guy you sold two of the Meg pups to?"

Jonas nodded. "The crown prince is constructing a new theme park called Dubai-Land. The jewel of Dubai-Land will be an aquatic exhibit featuring a dozen of the largest viewing aquariums ever conceived."

"And what goes inside the other tanks? Creatures from this Panthalassa Sea?"

"That was the plan. David impressed the crown prince and his cousin with his ability to pilot the Manta subs. Against my wishes, he joined other trained pilots who were recruited to entice these prehistoric sea creatures out of the Panthalassa and into their nets. David and another young submersible pilot—a young woman—were trapped in a bathyscape. I used Angel to escort me down to them, where she squared off with another alpha female, a 120-foot *Liopleurodon*."

"My God."

"I managed to free the bathyscape from its anchors and float it out of the Panthalassa. Angel and the *Liopleurodon* followed us up. The Meg had the creature's neck in its jaws like a bulldog. Then the crown prince's tanker passed by, sweeping everything off the sea floor and into its wake, including the bathyscape. The two kids escaped. Unfortunately, David's companion didn't make it.

Mac shook his head. "David's first love. Bin Rashidi managed to tag the creature with a homing device before it swam off."

"David's twenty-one," Jonas continued. "He went through a lot. Losing someone you love in any manner is hard. The kid left

338

California seven months ago. We found out that he and a friend rejoined bin Rashidi's team assigned to capture the *Liopleurodon*."

"That's why you're in Antarctica…it prefers the cold water."

Jonas nodded, handing me the binoculars. I focused them on a set of lights growing larger on the eastern horizon, an oil tanker appearing out of the darkness.

"The tanker's called the *Tonga*. She's a Malaccamax VLCC, a very large crude oil carrier designed with a draft shallow enough to navigate the Antarctic coast. She's as big as they come, over a thousand feet long and two hundred feet wide. The crown prince had her scrubbed and refitted to haul his sea monsters. Inside the cargo hold are saltwater pens three times the size of our hopper. David told me they had already captured a *Dunkleosteus*, a sixty-five-foot *Ichthyosaurus*, and a *Helicoprion* shark."

"That's incredible. And these species all survived the trip to Dubai?"

"The Dunk was in its aquarium when David saw it; the rest I don't know about. Bin Rashidi's kept everything quiet, since he ordered his team to follow the *Liopleurodon ferox*. Moving out ahead of the *Tonga* is the *Dubai-Land*, a 280-ton fishing trawler. That's the hunter's boat. David's on board with one of the Mantas."

Jonas turned to Mac. "What's the status on our subs?"

"Number One is being recharged. Number Two is in the dry dock ready to launch."

"Inform Mr. Reed I want to be in the water in fifteen minutes. Zach, you're with me; it's time for your first piloting lesson."

I followed him out the door and down the steel stairwell, my heart racing.

33

"Why, sometimes I've believed as many as six impossible things before breakfast."
—Lewis Carroll

I followed Jonas into the bowels of the ship. Reaching the lowest deck, we made our way aft through a tight corridor, past the engine room to a watertight door.

WARNING: PRESSURIZED DIVE CHAMBER
Do NOT enter when red light is ON.

The light was off, the door open.

Jonas led me inside.

Perched on rubber blocks above a pair of sealed horizontal doors in the ship's keel was the Manta submersible. Aptly named, the hydrodynamic vessel was dark brown on top with a white belly, its body nine feet long with an eighteen-foot wingspan.

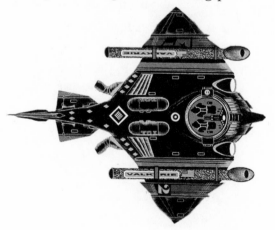

"She really does look like a giant manta ray. What's the hull made of?"

"Layered acrylic," answered a mechanic, his navy-blue jumpsuit and leather jacket stained with grease.

"Zachary Wallace, Cyel Reed, our chief engineer."

Reed snorted sarcastically. "One chief, no Indians. And still no damn heater down here. I had to pour boiling water over the starboard wing just to tighten the support struts on your damn laser."

Jonas examined the Valkyrie. "It came loose when I pulled out of a barrel roll. Think it'll hold?"

"Will it hold? Yeah. If you quit trying to fly it like an F-15. Weight distribution's off. You don't put a luggage rack on a Ferrari and expect it to perform. Barrel rolls or the ability to melt ice—pick your poison, J.T."

Jonas turned to me. "We can pull the Valkyries. It's your call."

"Melting ice is more important to me, especially where I'm going. Maybe the additional weight will help stabilize the sub in the currents."

"And maybe if I eat coal for breakfast I'll shit diamonds later," the mechanic scoffed. "Only I wouldn't bet my life on it. Anyway, she's ready to launch."

Four minutes later, I found myself seated in the starboard cockpit while Jonas methodically ran through an abbreviated systems checklist from the portside command console. "Hatch sealed. Life-support: go. Batteries: go. Back-up systems: charged. Valkyries: charged. Chamber is pressurized. Mac, are you online?"

"As always. Why does this feel like a bad déjà vu?"

"My life is one big déjà vu. How far away are bin Rashidi's ships?"

"The trawler's still a good four miles out. The *Tonga*'s changed course, moving south. As for the creature, there's nothing on sonar. Maybe they're just coming ashore to get supplies?"

"Maybe. Keep us apprised. Mr. Reed, *Manta 2* is ready for

341

launch. Flood the chamber."

Water rushed into the compartment, lifting the buoyant submersible off its blocks. Rusted hinges groaned as the keel's three-inch-thick steel doors opened beneath us, venting the chamber to the Southern Ocean.

Jonas maneuvered the two-man submersible out of the flooded dock, into the ink-black sea. Rather than power-on the headlights, he adjusted the cockpit glass to night-vision mode, our surroundings blooming into a tapestry of olive-green.

Below us lay a carpet of sea stars and urchins. Above, a blizzard of shrimp-like krill congregated beneath an island of surface ice. Seconds later the ocean rained emperor penguins, their tiny arms propelling them into the depths, their darting forms trailing bubble streams.

Jonas gave them a wide berth. "You ready to take over?"

"Give me a quick tutorial."

"Joystick steers, the two foot pedals accelerate the port and starboard propulsors. It's all about coordinating your limbs with your navigation console. Just remember green is right-side up, red means you are upside down. Switching control to your command console... now."

I grabbed the joystick while my feet searched for the foot pedals that operated the sub's twin thrusters. Within seconds our smooth ride became a herky-jerky nightmare.

Jonas pointed to my navigation monitor. "Watch the current, you're buffeting. The gauge will suggest a course adjustment."

I glanced at the reading and banked three degrees to starboard, the slight change smoothing out the ride. "It's an incredible machine. How much pressure can she handle?"

"More than Vostok can deliver. But I'm not sold on lending her to you just yet."

My stomach tightened. "Jonas, my son—"

"I don't see how getting to this alien vessel before MJ-12 will

342

force this Colonel to release Brandy and William. Seems like there's something you're not telling me. As for this E.T. who helped you seven years ago, how is that even possible? The ice sheet's been in place for millions of years. How could it still be around? For that matter, how important could its technology be? And depending on your father to function as a reliable copilot isn't exactly a selling point."

"Jonas, this extraterrestrial exists in the upper dimensions, where time has no relevance. It's the reason I know about zero-point energy. As for Angus, he can be taught to maintain the autopilot."

"Maybe. But this is more about your credibility, Zach. As someone who's been the target of smear tactics, I can discount the things I've read about you in the paper; however, strictly from a business perspective, we've already invested a lot of money in your energy company. With the Institute essentially out of business, the conspiracy stories are starting to wear a bit thin."

"Jonas, the generators worked. We still have the schematics and more than thirty countries who are ready to do business."

"Not anymore. While you were out of commission, NASA announced that the E.T. attack on the Capitol may have been provoked by gravitational fluxes caused by your Vostok generators, which affected the aliens' life-support systems. It's a lie, I'm sure, but it's an effective one. No nation on the planet will risk using your generator to supply power."

I felt exasperated. Once more, the powers-that-be had reasserted control over humanity's future.

Mac's voice over the radio interrupted my thoughts. "Jonas, another vessel just entered Prydz Bay. Looks like it's the support ship for that submarine Zachary described."

"Download its bearing to our navigation system. We'll take a look."

A line of position appeared on our monitors, connecting our present location with Mac's destination, the eastern face of the

Loose Tooth Rift.

* * *

For the next twenty minutes, I kept the Manta on a northwesterly course that brought us to inside a mile of the Amery Ice Shelf. To simulate the feeling of operating in a tight enclosure, Jonas insisted I keep the sub within six feet of the frozen surface while maintaining a velocity in excess of twenty knots, a harrowing endeavor culminating in no less than half a dozen wing scrapes and Valkyrie collisions.

"Jonas, it's my first time out. Give me a chance to get a feel for her."

"This *is* your chance, Zach. From here you graduate straight to a subglacial river squeezed beneath the Antarctic ice sheet. If you can't handle this, how are you going to deal with that claustrophobic nightmare?"

Jonas checked our target's position on sonar. "That's close enough. Slow to three knots and power up the Valkyries.

"Now dive to fifty feet and put us in a slow, steep ascent. Allow the lasers to open a hole in the ice directly above us. The moment you see the night sky, cut your engines and the Manta will float topside."

I followed his instructions, opening a gap in the ice large enough to accommodate the sub. We surfaced, bobbing beneath a star-filled sky awash with a pink swoosh of southern light. A quarter mile to the west, we could see the surface ship's stern lights, our night-vision binoculars revealing an A-frame towering above her aft deck, a Canadian registry, and the name *Tortuga* written across her backside.

Mac searched the ship's name on the *McFarland's* computer, finding three dozen matches but only one vessel her size flying a Canadian flag. "She was built by the U.S. Navy, decommissioned in 2002, then purchased and refitted by a private Toronto firm owned by a subsidiary of the Bank of Liechtenstein."

I turned to Jonas. "The bank's a private institution, a tax haven for billionaires. I realize this will sound like more conspiracy theory, but hundreds of billions of dollars have passed through the Bank of Liechtenstein to fund MJ-12 projects. I think we'd better submerge. There's a GeoEye-1 satellite over Antarctica, equipped with an imaging payload that can locate any surface object on the planet."

I descended the Manta to ninety feet and leveled off just above the sea floor.

A blip appeared on sonar as we headed for the *Tortuga*'s keel.

Jonas donned headphones. "Lots of noise up ahead. Sounds like it's coming from the ice shelf. Come to course two-seven-seven, we'll take a look."

* * *

With the early arrival of its support ship, the *Tethys* had launched fourteen hours ahead of schedule. Jonas and I arrived at the Amery Ice Shelf moments before the tail section of the thirty-seven-foot submarine disappeared from view, following its laser-spewing bow on a thirty-degree down angle into the base of the Loose Tooth Rift and a newly formed underwater cavern.

Jonas stared at the hole, dumbfounded. "That was impressive. You say Skunkworks built that beast?"

"With your tax dollars." Banking the Manta into an awkward turn, I raced east toward open water.

"Zach, where are you going?"

"Back to the *McFarland*. I need to pick up Angus, load the Manta with supplies, and get through that passage before the *Tethys* gets too far ahead of us."

"It's a suicide mission. You'd be lucky to make it a mile before getting lost down there."

"I'm not just going to let my son die."

"Agreed. But how will getting you to Vostok save your son?

Explain that part to me, and I'll take you there myself."

A text message flashed on both our monitors: **MOVE!**

My eyes darted to the sonar where dozens of blips were converging upon us. "Jesus, what is that?"

"Whales. And we're in their path. Shift controls back to my console—"

A forty-five-foot humpback whale shot past us out of the ether, its thrusting gray fluke barely missing the sub.

Two more bulls followed, and suddenly there were whales everywhere. They were not just humpbacks. I saw minkes and fins, and a pygmy sperm whale struck our portside wing, spinning us about.

Jonas attempted to accelerate out of the roll, only to have the Manta sideswiped by another fleeing dark gray body.

It was a cetacean stampede, and we were swept up in it.

Jonas ignited the Valkyries, attempting to fend off the swarm. "Zach, start pinging. Find that monster before it finds us."

"What monster? You mean the *Liopleurodon*? "

"What the hell else would be causing these whales to panic? Ain't no Megs in these waters."

Manning the sonar, I attempted to switch from passive to active, only nothing was working. The monitor blinked off and on. The radio turned to static in my headphones.

I tossed them aside. "The *Tortuga*'s jamming our electronics."

Having managed to point our bow east, Jonas accelerated, maneuvering ahead of the panic-stricken behemoths before banking hard to port, momentarily freeing us from the frenzy of moving goliaths.

Then I saw the cause of the cetacean disturbance, and fear suddenly took on a whole new meaning.

34

In Loch Ness, I had confronted a legendary beast. In Vostok, I had been attacked by giant crocs and Miocene whales. Years later in Monterey, I had watched a captive megalodon feed and thought I had seen the definition of true terror.

Nothing could have prepared me for the monster racing at us out of that olive-green sea.

Its jawline alone had to be thirty feet long, its mouth filled with ten- to twelve-inch dagger-like teeth, the largest of which jutted outside of its mouth. *Big?* It seemed as long as a city block, propelled by thirty-foot flippers—all wrapped around a lead-gray-and-white hide that partially blended into the backdrop of ice.

Most frightening, it seemed to be hyperactive, its movements on overdrive. Its head turned on a swivel as its crocodilian jaws snapped at the fleeing whales, its mind unable to single out the most vulnerable member of the herd until it saw our twin lasers blazing in the darkness like two vermillion eyes.

"Oh, geez. Jonas, hard to port!"

Jonas tried to get us out of its way, but the creature was far quicker and cut us off. My eyes bugged out as the left side of the pliosaur's mouth suddenly bloomed into view, its jaws agape.

The back of my head slammed against the seat as the Manta leaped forward, Jonas attempting to escape by passing between those hideous rows of curved teeth like a car trying to beat a train across railroad tracks.

I squeezed my eyes shut—

—and we were through, only the creature was right behind us, snapping at our tail.

We were dead.

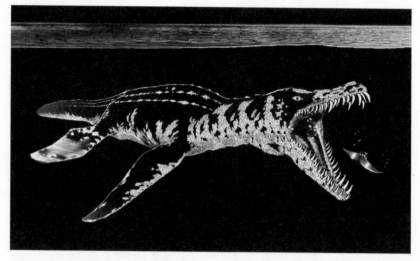

And then it was gone.

I took a moment to catch my breath before I relocated it, the dark blotches of its back and tail blending in with the sea. It was up ahead chasing another Manta, this one far quicker than ours.

"David?" Jonas switched his headphones to the radio setting. "Mac, contact the *Tonga*. Have them put me through to my kid. Damn this static!" He slammed his fist against the dome above his head, then accelerated after the monster, now chasing his son's submersible.

"Zach, there's a communication panel by your right foot. Pop it open."

"Got it."

"You'll see a series of toggle switches set in the OFF position. Is there one with a blinking blue light?"

"Yes."

"That'll be David's sub. Flip it on. Hopefully he's turned on his inter-sub comm link.

"David?"

"Dad? What took you so long? I've been hailing you since the Lio went after those whale pods."

"I didn't know you were in the water. Thanks for saving our arses."

"Consider us even. But, Dad, seriously—stay back. I've been playing cat-and-mouse with this pregnant bitch for weeks. This time she won't escape."

Escape? The crazy kid was trying to capture *it!*

Our sonar array flickered back on as we continued to distance ourselves from the *Tortuga*. The monitor revealed the presence of two surface ships that were entering the bay from the north, and David was leading the *Liopleurodon* right for them.

* * *

The two Dubai ships had converged upon the bay's entrance the moment the creature had entered the shallows. Deck hands aboard the *Tonga* hustled to lower an immense trawl net over the tanker's starboard side, while their counterparts on the *Dubai-Land* retrieved it from below, attaching cables to one side of the net's loop. When everything was ready, the trawler gradually separated from the tanker, stretching the trap in place.

From the bridge of the *Dubai-Land*, Fiesal bin Rashidi, first cousin to the crown prince of Dubai, ordered the two ships under his command to shut down their engines.

Now it was up to the American daredevil.

* * *

David Taylor was out in front of the creature, making his way toward the net. He knew the pregnant behemoth was nearing exhaustion. Every time she seemed ready to quit the chase, the twenty-one-year-old pilot would slow down and bank hard from side to side, succeeding in keeping the tiring pliosaur interested, while taking some of the fight out of her.

Our sub surfaced south of the tanker. We watched on sonar as David led the *Liopleurodon* east toward the two motionless vessels.

Jonas was tense, counting down the distance. "Two hundred

yards... one fifty... a hundred yards. Come on, kid, you're moving way too slow to jump that net. Throttle up!"

* * *

Sweat poured down David Taylor's face. Cruising at only eighteen knots, he knew the Manta could not generate enough lift to leap out of the sea to clear the net. Yet he also had to keep the creature close. He knew she was tiring, knew that if she sensed the net, she'd turn on a dime and flee.

So he took a chance.

Throttling back, he dropped his speed to thirteen knots, allowing the *Liopleurodon* to move in close enough for her nostrils to inhale his sub's jet-pump propulsor bubbles.

Reinvigorated, the creature opened its jaws to devour its prey as David slammed both feet to the floor and pulled back on his joystick, easing up on his starboard engine a few precious seconds before he reached the surface.

Instead of attempting to clear the net, David launched the Manta sideways out of the sea. The submersible cleared the steel cables running from the trawler to the left side of the net—

—And smashed nose-first into the *Dubai-Land*'s portside bow.

Unaware that its prey was gone, the *Liopleurodon* swam into the trawl net, stopping only after its fore-flippers struck the unseen object. It attempted to turn and run, but the crew manning the *Tonga*'s starboard winch was already tightening the noose upon the unnerved colossus, whose reflexive maneuver only succeeded in gathering its lower torso into the closing net.

And that's when all hell broke loose.

Before the hunters stationed behind their deck-mounted harpoon guns could aim their drug-filled steel lances below, the enraged pliosaur twisted its one hundred tons of fury beneath the starboard keel of the tanker.

Having been refitted as a mobile aquarium, the *Tonga* lacked the ballast of an ocean-bound tanker filled with crude. The unstable ship was pulled hard to starboard, flinging its harpooners and winch crew seven stories into the bay. Anything not bolted down—equipment, crates, and humans—was hurtled across the tanker's plunging deck.

Aboard the *Dubai-Land*, the winch that had been holding the net open was bent sideways, making it impossible for the trawler's crew to release control of the captured pliosaur over to the *Tonga*. Instead of being hauled out of the water, the *Liopleurodon* was left to twist and turn in the net, caught in a tug-of-war between both ships.

Jonas tried to reach his son by our sub-comm link, but David didn't reply. Accelerating to thirty knots, he raced for the tanker. "Zachary, start pinging. Find me David's Manta."

I switched my headphones to sonar, my ears assaulted by a cacophony of sound.

A minute later we arrived on the scene.

Jonas slowed our approach, in order to sort through the chaos. On our right was the *Tonga*, its towering superstructure surreally swaying east to west and back again like a giant steel buoy. On our left was the trawler—at least what was left of it. The vessel had been flipped completely over, its barnacle-encrusted keel now an island of survival for its crew, who were hanging on for dear life, the inverted boat dropping and rising beneath them.

Ahead of us was the center of the maelstrom.

One hundred sixty million years ago, *Liopleurodon* had ruled the ocean as a carnivorous marine reptile, all except for the subspecies that had evolved gills to inhabit the Panthalassa Sea. Caught in the net, the creature before us couldn't swim. And if it couldn't swim, it couldn't breathe.

By swaying the two ships, the monster managed to channel just enough water into its mouth to keep from drowning. It had flipped the *Dubai-Land*, but the steel cables connecting the trawler to the net had remained in place, keeping the trap sealed.

"Zach, where's David's sub?"

"There… by the trawler's bow. Those crewmen are using it as a flotation device."

The water was a frigid thirty-three degrees Fahrenheit. The paralyzing temperatures had already claimed at least a dozen lives. I was about to radio Mac to send the hopper-dredge when we heard the unmistakable *snap* of steel.

It was the last cable connecting the trawler to the net.

The *Liopleurodon* felt its bonds loosen. With renewed vigor, the trapped beast began to worm itself free.

"Zach, it's getting free!"

"Kill it."

"How?"

"Use the Valkyries. Aim for its neck."

Jonas dove the sub to avoid a swirl of lifeless bodies, moving us steadily toward the opening net, the lasers heating up. The inverted trawler appeared on our left, along with David's Manta. The disabled vessel bobbed upright along the surface, surrounded by seven pairs of kicking legs.

Jonas would not allow the creature to escape.

"Its head is free. Here it comes!"

The monster lurched forward, catching its left hind flipper in the net.

That was all Jonas needed.

I ducked as the Manta's bow forcibly struck the *Liopleurodon* just above its chest cavity, the twin lasers burning matching holes three feet deep into the creature's flesh. Blood spurted across our cockpit glass as the insane beast flung us to and fro until we were tossed free.

Mortally wounded, the animal propelled itself away in obvious pain.

* * *

The hopper-dredge arrived ten minutes later. Jonas maneuvered the sub into its berth, impatiently waiting for the chamber to drain and pressurize before he could open the cockpit and make his way up five flights of stairs to board a waiting lifeboat.

Waiting inside the craft were Mac and the ship's physician.

I watched from the starboard rail as Jonas used a reach pole to pop open David's hatch. The physician climbed inside the cockpit to work on him.

After a few minutes Jonas climbed in.

The captain of the hopper-dredge approached and handed me his radio.

"Mac? How is he?"

"The impact broke his neck. David's dead."

35

When a loved one dies, we grieve. And through that process we are offered words of comfort. *"They are out of pain. They are in a better place—the soul immortal, an eternal spark of perfection. One day we'll be reunited in the ever-after."*

There are no words of comfort for a parent who loses a child. Children are simply not supposed to die before their parents. It's unnatural. It defies universal law. The loss of a child is a loss of innocence, a promised future stolen. Hopes and dreams shattered.

A child's passing affects a community. But from the parent, it takes a piece of the heart, and in its place it leaves a hole that can never be healed. A hole infected with depression and often filled with anger. Anger aimed at God. Anger that targets a spouse or a physician, a stranger at fault, a path crossed by evil... or oneself.

When you play with fire, you risk getting burned. Skydiving, surfing big waves, cliff diving, drugs... That's the problem with addictions: you never know when you've crossed the line until you cross it. Adrenaline junkies know the risks. They shrug them off. *"Hey, everybody dies. You could die crossing the street. At least I have a choice in how I go."*

That choice, that philosophy, that line of reasoning changes when you have children. And when your child dies participating in an activity that you taught him to do...

* * *

Part of Jonas was in shock, the other part of him detached so he could function. He made sure his son's remains and the remains of the other crewmen were placed in body bags and stored in a freezer. He spoke to the captain of the *Tonga* and saw to the survivors of the trawler. And when he was done, he went into his stateroom to speak by Skype to his wife, Terry.

I gave him an hour and forty minutes before knocking on his door.

Mac answered, red-eyed and more than a little inebriated. "Doctor E.T.?"

"Mac, I need to speak with Jonas."

"Not now. Maybe tomorrow."

"Tomorrow's too late. I need to speak with him *now*."

"Yeah, well, that ain't going to happen. Oh, and the mission you had planned? Forget about it."

"Mac, I'm geared up. The Manta's being prepped—"

"No more Mantas. No more missions. Boss's orders."

"Then let the boss tell me himself." I pushed past my fellow Scot and entered the cabin.

Jonas was propped up in bed, a half-empty bottle of whiskey on his night table. He looked up at me with sullen eyes and shook his head. "He was such a good kid. As a father, you want your son to be better than you. He was better. A lot better."

His words made my eyes burn. "Jonas, back in the Manta, you asked me how returning to Vostok could save my son. The answer is complicated but—"

"The answer is no. As my soon-to-be ex-wife so aptly pointed out, my choices have led to enough loss of life."

"As have mine. And I need that sub to rectify things."

Mac grabbed me by the biceps. "You heard the man."

"Let him go, Mac." Jonas stood, staggering close enough for me to smell the alcohol on his breath. "All right, Dr. Wallace, I'm listening. Tell me how returning to Vostok gets your son outta whatever trouble he's in."

"There's more than just an alien ship down there. Inside is a portal, a junction that allows one to access the higher dimensions. Jonas, I can go back in time to a different point in my life and prevent these events from ever happening."

"A time machine? That's what this is all about?"

"Not exactly. How did the entity explain it? Every choice we make creates an infinite number of alternate universes. David, for instance, could have leapt the sub over the net or gone under it, or swerved around the tanker. The possibilities are endless, and each choice leads to a parallel existence. Consciousness is the variable that differentiates a potential outcome from reality. I died multiple times in Lake Vostok, but after each death the entity kept bringing me back, until I followed the path where I acquired the knowledge of zero-point energy it intended me to have. The portal allowed me to explore multiple existences until I found the one that led to my survival."

Jonas fought to dissect the information. "Say you go back and jump into another parallel universe... how can you be sure it's one where David survives, where your son's not kidnapped?"

"The extraterrestrial that communicated with me definitely has an agenda, but it's one that I sincerely believe is intended to help humanity. I'll ask it to allow me to go back to a multiverse where I can change the events that took place in Washington, D.C. Before the congressional hearing takes place, I'll use the media to expose MJ-12's false flag event, preempting it while saving hundreds of lives. That will force the Colonel to cancel the attack, prevent the kidnapping, and remove me from today's events."

Jonas stared at me, red-eyed. "There's no guarantee your absence today will change a thing. David may still die."

"I won't stop jumping multiverses until I find one where I can warn you."

Mac remained skeptical. "Were you able to warn yourself when you kept dying and reviving in Lake Vostok?"

"No. But the entity can read my mind. It will know what I seek. One thing I do know: if Colonel Vacendak gets to the portal first, it gives the military access to a device that can alter our species' evolution in the cosmos. And that makes us a threat to these E.T.s. Humanity's already in timeout for detonating nuclear weapons; there's no way MJ-12 will be allowed to access the higher dimensions. Our species will be annihilated before that happens."

Jonas turned to Mac. "Have Mr. Reed prepare one of the Mantas for launch. Get Dr. Wallace everything he needs, and pack my ECW gear as well. I'm going with him."

Mac looked shocked. "Jonas, you don't honestly believe this nonsense?"

"I've been drinking, so I'm not sure what I believe. All I know is that Zach was given information seven years ago that could have altered our planet's future for the good. Maybe this was just a trial run to see if humanity was ready. Regardless, if there's even a remote chance of altering what happened today and saving David, then I'm willing to take it."

The two men embraced.

"Mac, see to it that my son is taken to Davis Base and shipped to Monterey for the funeral. If his mother calls again, tell her—"

"Tell her nothing," I said. "Mac, whether you believe this or not, no one can know. The people on board that research vessel, if they suspect I'm alive and chasing down their sub, they'll go after your loved ones just like they went after mine."

Jonas sat down to think. "Zach's right. We need to fly both of our families somewhere safe until we return."

"Terry's in shock, Jonas. She won't go anywhere until after the funeral, and there will be no convincing her otherwise."

"Contact bin Rashidi, tell him I need to speak with the crown prince. I'll ask him to arrange a special ceremony at the Dubai aquarium, honoring David and all those who died today. You call Terry. Tell her David's body was flown to the United Arab Emirates along with the other dead crewmen. Tell her I'm already en route. Then have your wife arrange a private jet to fly both our families to the Middle East as soon as possible. I'll ask the crown prince to safeguard them and delay the ceremony until you and I arrive.

"If this works"—Jonas looked hard at me—"there won't be a funeral."

357

"And if it doesn't... ? Never mind. C'mon, Zach, let's get you what you need."

* * *

Angus and I loaded the Manta with climbing equipment, flashlights, and extreme weather gear for two, while Mac stocked the sub with food and water. He wanted to add a few guns, only I stopped him. Violence had already gotten our species into enough trouble with our extraterrestrial visitors. The last thing we needed was to end up in a shootout, fighting over an advanced technology we lacked the morality to use.

Jonas had sobered up by his third cup of coffee. After a final trip to the toilet, he climbed into the port cockpit, lowered the acrylic glass over our heads, and signaled to Cyel Reed to flood the chamber.

Mac's voice came over the radio. "Jonas, can you hear me okay on this frequency?"

"Yes. Are you in place?"

"We're en route. What's your ETA?"

"Twenty minutes, using a biologic pattern."

"Roger that. Angus and I will be ready."

The keel doors opened, releasing the Manta into a sun-lit emerald sea. "Jonas, what about the *Liopleurodon*? Should I go active on sonar?"

"It's probably dead. If you start pinging, that research ship will know we're down here." Jonas kept the sub close to the sea floor, our movements and speed intended to mimic those of a giant manta ray.

We were less than two miles from MJ-12's surface ship when our sonar monitors began to flicker.

"We're being jammed. Zach, how close are we to that hole?"

"Six thousand feet. And the *Tortuga*'s sitting over it like a mother hen."

"Then what we need is a fox. Mac, you ready to ruffle a few feathers?... Mac, can you hear me?"

The radio spat back static, followed by an unnerving quiet that ended with a *crunch* as the sub's belly settled upon the silt-covered sea floor.

"Sonuva bitch, our engines just powered off." Jonas fought the suddenly rigid controls. "Your pals aren't playing around this time. Everything's down—including our life-support system."

* * *

The supertanker *Tonga* pushed its way south through Prydz Bay at a steady eight knots, her starboard flank hugging the eastern face of the Amery Ice Shelf.

Mac stood on her bridge next to my father, both men's binoculars focused on the surface ship less than three nautical miles away. The *Tortuga*'s bow was pointed at the Loose Tooth Rift, her starboard flank exposed.

"Captain, any response from the Manta?"

"Nothing but static, Mr. Mackreides."

"Shut down your engines. Full reverse. Mr. Al Nahyan, you may begin transmitting the message."

The radio man spoke with an urgent British accent. "Mayday, mayday. This is the United Arab Emirates research tanker *Tonga*. Our rudder is badly damaged. We cannot navigate. We strongly advise you to move your ship or risk a collision."

Mac stared at the steel vessel growing larger in his binoculars. "Angus, I believe it was Robert Burns who once said, 'No man can tether time or tide. Time is short and the tide is out.'"

Angus grinned. "Those tha' cannae be counseled cannae be helped."

"Who said that?"

"My father, before he'd beat my arse with a hickory switch. Jist a wee love tap, he'd say."

"What say we give MJ-12 a wee love tap?"

* * *

We were powerless, our sub lying on the floor of Prydz Bay, weighed down by our two lasers. Silt had buried all but the Valkyries and the top of our cockpit dome. The *Tortuga*'s keel was just visible in the distance, anchored in 320 feet of water.

We felt the rumble of the steel beast before we saw it, its 300,000 tons displacing the surface while vacuuming up the bottom, its presence causing the ice sheet to reverberate.

Then I saw the 1,100-foot supertanker's bow converge upon the *Tortuga*'s starboard flank, and for the second time that morning I prepared to meet my Maker.

* * *

The process of slowing a supertanker must be initiated miles in advance using a braking pattern called a slalom, which veers the ship back and forth from starboard to port while her engines run full astern. Mac had either seriously miscalculated Newton's Law of Conservation of Momentum, or he simply didn't give a damn.

The prow of the supertanker struck the exposed flank of the *Tortuga* like a steadily moving train plowing through a double-decker aluminum bus, crushing the starboard infrastructure while its submerged bulb-shaped bow scooped up the vessel's disfigured hull and carried it away with hardly a drop in speed or forward momentum.

Passageways crumpled. Water blasted through shredded steel plates. Internal pipes and cables ruptured. From Angus and Mac's perspective, it must have appeared as though the supertanker had bitten off a chunk of the *Tortuga*'s ribs. From our perspective, it looked like a megalodon had snatched an orca in its jaws and was carrying it off to be consumed.

And then an unseen force swept us off the bottom into the eye of a hurricane.

I squeezed my eyes shut and held on as the vortex created by the two passing ships inhaled us, spinning us end over end toward the supertanker's propeller shafts, the blades churning in reverse.

Jonas was a rock. Knowing the *Tonga*'s impact would shut down power to the *Tortuga*'s sonar array, he focused only on his command console. The moment the lights powered on he jammed the controls hard to port and pulled us away from the spinning blades into a steep dive.

Moments later a submerged wall of ice materialized into view. Jonas quickly honed in on the Loose Tooth Rift's jagged chasm, which harbored the cavernous opening created nearly six hours earlier by the *Tethys*.

The borehole was now a clogged artery of white ice. Powering up the Valkyries, Jonas pressed the Manta's nose to the frozen gauntlet, which quickly liquefied and inhaled us into its dark, widening orifice.

We were on our way.

36

"How puzzling all these changes are!
I'm never sure what I'm going to be, from one minute to another."
—Lewis Carroll

The sub's lights illuminated a near-vertical shaft of ice so crystal-clear that Jonas struggled to discern the boundaries of the funnel. After the Manta's fifth collision with the borehole's walls, he shut down the exterior lights and relied strictly on the cockpit's night-vision glass, which generated a view that reminded me of a miniature medical camera plunging down an olive-green esophagus.

After descending nearly six hundred feet, the passage leveled out, depositing us in a shallow sea of meltwater that separated the bottom of the ice sheet above our heads from the floor of Prydz Bay. Squeezed between these two titanic forces, the water pressure within this narrow, seemingly endless cavity registered an eye-popping 12,656 psi, the weight above us muffling everything but the sound of our breathing.

Visibility was limited to an olive-green patch that extended ten to twelve feet in every direction. For several minutes we maintained a snail's pace through this vast, dark, liquid space, until the overwhelming sensation of claustrophobia sent Jonas fumbling for the lights. He flipped the switch, and our beams illuminated a hidden chamber of breathtaking beauty.

For millions of years the ice sheet had surfed this watery conveyor belt as it inched its way across East Antarctica before slaloming along the Amery Basin into Prydz Bay. Perpetually melting and refreezing, the bottom of the glacier appeared a rich azure-blue, its sculpted patterns and textures creating a three-dimensional mosaic so mesmerizing I was tempted to ask Jonas to direct a light at the ceiling, just so I could absorb its incredible details.

Complementing this chapel of art was a boundary of fresh water so pure and clear it actually magnified our twin beacons of light, extending visibility for miles. As for what resided below, for now it was dark silt. But that would change.

Jonas was still too overwhelmed by grief to allow himself to be dazzled. "Zach, this subterranean waterway seems to run forever. How do we know which direction to go?"

"We need to follow the Amery Ice Shelf inland about 340 miles, where it will meet the Lambert Glacial Basin. A subglacial river with a northern outflow should merge with this meltwater. We follow it southeast into Lake Vostok."

"Not exactly navigating by the stars, is it?" Jonas typed a search command over his computer's keyboard. The GPS finder zoomed in on East Antarctica, honing in on the Loose Tooth Rift. "Here we are. Here's where the ice shelf meets that glacial basin. That's a huge expanse. How the hell are we supposed to find a river amid an ocean of meltwater?"

"I don't know, Jonas. Maybe we'll be able to hear it on sonar."

"So that's 340 miles to the north and at least another five hundred to the southeast. At our best speed, it'll take us eleven hours just to hit the river, assuming this meltwater remains stagnant. Traveling another five hundred miles into a head-current—that alone could take twenty-four to thirty-six more hours.

"When I was an undergrad at Penn State, my roommate and I would drive down to Fort Lauderdale over Christmas break. We'd take two-hour shifts, twenty hours straight. We were so wiped out by the time we arrived that we'd have to sleep all day. And we were nineteen."

"Is there any way you can program the autopilot to at least get us to the river?"

"The GPS navigator isn't functioning with that ice sheet over our heads. What I can do is program the autopilot to remain on a solitary heading. It'll use the Manta's sonar to navigate around perceived obstacles, but one of us should still stay awake to monitor our surroundings. I'll take the first shift while you sleep."

I reclined my seat, removed my shoes, and covered up with a wool blanket. I was exhausted, having barely slept since arriving in Antarctica. Lying back, I looked up through the thick cockpit glass, gazing at the bottom of the ice sheet.

Jonas accelerated to thirty knots, turning the glacier's artwork into a blue blur.

Within minutes I was asleep.

* * *

I awoke as Avi Socha.

I was in a cave close to the ocean. I could hear the echo of the sea and feel the pounding surf through the rock upon which I sat. The night howled at my back, glistening with stars. Berudim shone brightly in the northern sky, a cloud-covered world orbited by a solitary moon one-ninth the mass of Charon.

I was anxious to begin; the alignment of Berudim with Charon was a powerful cosmic antenna that facilitated the best reception with the upper worlds. Closing my eyes, I recited my mantra, tapping into the universal consciousness.

ANA BEKOACH... GEDULAT YEMINECHA... TATIR ZERURA ...

My consciousness was moving through the void, passing over a dark sea.

KABEL RINAT... AMECHA SAGVENU... TAHARENU NORA ...

The sea moved inland, becoming a twisting river that separated a rift valley.

NA GIBOR... DORSHEY YICHUDCHA... KEBAVAT SHOMREM ...

Mountains rose along either bank as the river emptied into a vast lake, its waters dark and forboding...

BARCHEM TEHAREM... RACHAMEY ZIDEKATCHA... TAMID GOMLEM ...

On the western bank appeared an alien dwelling that was somehow familiar...

HASIN KADOSH... BEROV TUVECHA... NAHEL ADOTECHA ...

My consciousness hovered over the center portion of the dwelling until it was drawn through a glass partition.

YAHID GE'EA... LEAMECHA PENNE... ZOCHREY KDUSHATECHA ...

I was inside a dark chamber, the only light coming from the floor-to-ceiling windows, which offered a view of the lake and the snow-covered peaks of the mountains rising above the far eastern bank. An extraterrestrial being was seated before the glass, its demeanor melancholy as it stared outside at the weather.

SHAVATENU KABEL... USHEMA ZAKATENU... YODE TA'ALUMOT... *I had moved to hover over the life-form when my consciousness was suddenly drawn into its aura by a magnetic force, inhaling me into a vortex of physicality. And I could hear!*

"Zachary, this woman is here tae speak with you. Are ye sober?"

I stood, my temper flaring. "Of course, I'm sober. Hi, I'm Zachary Wallace."

* * *

"C'mon, Zach, wake up!"

I floated in a pool of warmth and serenity, my consciousness gazing down upon the Manta, adrift in the crystal-clear water. Through the cockpit glass I witnessed Jonas straddling my vacant body, pushing against my chest until—

—Gravity gained a foothold, dragging me back into my flesh-bound prison.

Registering the blood rushing into my face, I opened my eyes.

365

"Sorry. Did I oversleep?"

"Oversleep? Jesus … " Jonas climbed off me, falling back into his seat. "According to the bio-sensors built into your harness, you all but died." He pointed to a flashing screen showing my steadily rising vitals. "At one point your heart rate dropped below ten beats a minute, and your blood pressure hit goose-eggs. What the hell happened?"

I adjusted my seat, sitting up. "I don't know. I mean, I know what happened, only it wasn't me doing it. I was just sort of along for the ride."

"Try speaking in coherent sentences."

"I had an out-of-body experience, and instead of sticking around, my consciousness was in another time and place. It had slipped inside another being's body. And then I was back in *my* body, in my father's resort. Seven years ago."

Jonas just sat there and stared at me like a guy who realizes—too late—that he's hitched his mule to the wrong wagon.

"Something big is happening here, J.T. Get us going and I'll try to explain."

Jonas shook his head, then buckled his harness and powered up the engines, reengaging the autopilot. "I'm listening."

"There's a big piece of the puzzle still missing, but I'm beginning to grasp what's going on. At first I thought this entity had selected me to disseminate its zero-point energy technology to mankind because, well—"

"Because you're smart."

"More like intuitive, but, yeah. Then I started having these really lifelike dreams, like this one and the one on the plane. In these dreams I'm living on another planet during another time period."

"Past or present?"

"To be honest I'm not sure, but I'm leaning toward the past. The planet—it's called Charon and it's in big trouble. Something devastating is going to happen and this guy, the one I share my consciousness with, is trying to figure out a way to save his people. By reentering the E.T.'s ship and accessing the portal, I think I might be able to help him."

My analysis did not sit well with Jonas. He stared at the portside wing, his mind grappling with this new information. Glancing at his bio-sensors, I watched as his blood pressure climbed.

"Jonas, you okay?"

"You said you were back at your father's resort seven years ago. You realize that none of this would be happening if you hadn't come to me back then, asking me to invest in your company? Your son would be safe, and David would be alive."

"We don't know that."

"Yeah, we do. Because if David hadn't died, I sure as hell wouldn't be sitting in this sub with you. So why do I get the distinct feeling that these extraterrestrials are manipulating events in order to make sure you get back to Lake Vostok to save their sorry asses!"

Jonas was livid, but I understood where he was coming from. David Taylor had been an experienced pilot. Out of all the possible multiverses that could have been realized from his recent encounter with the *Liopleurodon*, my guess was that only a few would have actually resulted in his death.

Was Jonas right? Was I being maneuvered into a specific reality that served the E.T.s?

It made me wonder how many cause-and-effect dominoes had to tumble into place just for me to be en route to Vostok. Big Oil conspiring to subvert new energy systems, MJ-12 burning my assembly plant to the ground, William and Brandy's kidnapping, Susan's murder... Was I living out this specific multiverse of eventualities through free will, or was I following a course of the entity's choosing?

"Jonas ... " I turned to console him, only to realize he had fallen asleep.

* * *

The farther we traveled inland, the deeper our underwater passage descended, reflecting the thickening ice sheet overhead. Donning a headset, I passed the hours switching back and forth from the white noise of sonar to a classic rock CD.

We had closed to within fourteen nautical miles of the Amery Ice Shelf's intersection with the Lambert Glacial Basin when I heard a faint rush of water over sonar. Disengaging the autopilot, I altered our course and honed in on the sound, which was originating from the southeast.

The horizon of water sandwiched between the bottom of the ice sheet and East Antarctica's ancient geology was changing rapidly, the dark silt below yielding to patches of brown sea grass, the width of the passage narrowing quickly, forcing me to reduce our speed. Once placid waters became a minefield of eddies, each invisible swirl of current threatening to drive the Manta into the ice sheet.

Jonas awoke on our second collision, the submersible pilot disturbed to find our passage reduced to a ten- to twelve-foot-wide divide. "Where are we?"

"We're nearing the glacial basin, the very beginning of the ice shelf. The subglacial river's close. You can hear it on sonar."

Jonas took over command. Guided by sonar, he directed us farther to the south.

We felt the river before we saw it, the current pelting us with watermelon-size ice cubes too clear to see and too numerous to dodge. Fifteen million years ago, the waterway had been as wide as the Amazon, twisting across East Antarctica to empty into the enormous delta now occupied by the ice shelf. We only realized the extent of the river's boundaries when Jonas dived the sub to escape the current and found that the bottom had dropped nearly one hundred feet.

Hazards were everywhere. The riverbed was littered with vortex-channeling boulders and petrified tree trunks as wide as redwoods. Chunks of ice gouged out of the bottom of the ice sheet soared past us like miniature comets.

"Activate the sonar, Zach."

I pinged, sending sound waves reflecting off objects both stationary and propelled by the current. It was impossible, similar to driving a racecar down a crowded speedway—the wrong way.

Then a different blip appeared on sonar, and I knew this one was going to be trouble.

37

"I am the captain of my soul."
—William Ernest Henley

Jonas read the incoming data as it crawled across his sonar screen. "Range: twelve kilometers and closing. Still too far out to gauge its size, but it's way too quiet to be that other sub. Maybe it's an alien vessel, come to collect you and save me the trip."

"Jonas, I think it might be a life-form."

"A life-form? Come on. What kind of life-form could survive down here?"

"Vostok's rich in geothermal vents. There's a thriving food chain that dates back to the Miocene. How close do we need to be to get a size reading?"

"On a biologic? Less than six kilometers. What are you afraid of, Zachary? Don't tell me a Meg—"

"It's not a megalodon." I tapped my index finger repeatedly on the sonar REFRESH button until new data scrolled across the monitor.

RANGE TO TARGET: 5.78 KILOMETERS.

TARGET SPEED: 8.3 KNOTS.

TARGET SIZE: 18.89 METERS

TARGET COURSE: **INTERCEPT**!

Jonas swore. "The damn thing's over sixty feet long, and it's headed straight for us. Speak to me, Wallace. What's out there?"

"There's a species of Miocene sperm whale inhabiting Vostok. Ever hear of *Livyatan melvillei*?"

"That whale with the big teeth and the lower jaw of an orca? Damn it, Zachary. Why didn't you mention this to me before?"

"I didn't think they could follow the river this far from Vostok. Once we were in the lake, I figured you'd be able to outmaneuver them in the Manta."

"Not with these lasers strapped to our wings—Geez! There it is."

A dark mass appeared in our starboard headlight's periphery some two hundred yards ahead. Jonas was about to make an evasive maneuver when we both realized something was wrong. The whale's movements seemed erratic, the tip of the creature's box-shaped head scraping the bottom of the ice sheet. As we halved the distance, we could see the fluke hanging motionless below the leviathan's body.

It wasn't swimming; it was dead. The current was propelling its carcass along.

Jonas banked into a tight turn and brought us up beside the whale. Along its right flank was a fresh wound scorched ashen-gray, a twelve-foot-wide crater of blubber corresponding to the approximate dimensions of the bow of Colonel Vacendak's submarine.

* * *

The next twenty-seven hours were maddening—the equivalent of flying from Los Angeles to Sydney, Australia, and back again, in heavy turbulence, while being forced to remain seated. Under its best behavior, the subglacial river ran deep over stretches of flat bottom. Under the worst conditions, it was a twisting vortex with rapids that caught the Manta's wings and threatened to flip us head-over-tail—which happened twice, the last time sending us tumbling like a pinwheel a half-mile back from whence we'd come.

Then there were gaps where the river simply stopped flowing, walled off by a dam of ice. The first time this happened left us both disoriented and unnerved, and too mentally exhausted to reason. A twenty-minute yelling match ensued, after which we decided to shut down the engines and get some much-needed sleep.

The thought of having another out-of-body experience didn't bother me as much as it did Jonas. The last thing he wanted was to awaken beneath the Antarctic ice sheet next to my cold, lifeless corpse. Not that a part of him didn't want to strangle me, but I was no good to him dead. And so he kept vigil until he was convinced I had entered R.E.M. sleep.

Now I lay me down to sleep; I pray the Lord my soul to keep. If I should die before I wake, I pray the Lord my soul to take.

* * *

Brandy woke me.

I was sneaking in a nap, sequestered in my study in our home in Solihull, a quaint town in England's West Midlands. The window was partially frosted, our garden blanketed by last night's snow. The air inside my office was tinged with the scent of a basting turkey and the dying embers from my fireplace.

Life was good. I had retired seven months earlier, having served the last nine years as the Dean of Solihull College. With pensions coming from Cambridge and S.C., along with royalties generated from three patents, we were well-off financially and able to assist our three children and their families.

The boys had arrived last night: William, his wife, Jackie, and their two girls from London, and Andrew, his wife, Rachel, and the baby from Drumnadrochit. Claire and her fiancé were due in, their plane arriving from Boston later this evening. I heard the boys playing ping-pong in the basement and the grandkids playing with their Christmas presents in the den.

Brandy's dark hair was pulled back in a tight bun, revealing a few gray roots, her apron tied around her torso. Feeling slightly guilty over having fallen asleep while she cooked, I feigned innocence. That's when I noticed that my wife's blue eyes were red-rimmed and frightened.

"Zach, something terrible has happened."

My chest tightened. "What's wrong? Is Claire all right?"

"It's not the kids." She searched my desk for the remote and turned on the television.

The *news was on every station, the story coming from the States. Reporters talked over fluctuating images: lava as wide as a river, swallowing a neighborhood; collapsing bridges and billowing chocolate-brown smoke; highways backed up in traffic as far as the eye could see.*

While I slept, hell had opened its gates beneath Midwestern America.

Brandy paused from channel-surfing at a newscast featuring an animated aerial view over a national park.

" *...to recap if you're just joining us, at approximately 4:47 a.m. Wyoming time, the Yellowstone Caldera, an underground magma chamber fifty-five miles long, erupted beneath Yellowstone National Park. Categorized as a supervolcano, the Yellowstone Caldera has erupted three times in the past 2.1 million years, the last major eruption occurring 640,000 years ago to form the crater beneath the park. Experts say this morning's blast was two thousand times more powerful than the 1980 Mount St. Helens eruption.*

"Dawn Marie Hurtienne is a volcano expert working with the U.S. Geological Survey. She joins us now from Wyoming. Dr. Hurtienne, this is Melody Matney. Thank you for taking time to speak with us. We understand you are in the process of evacuating your family. Was there any warning this eruption might occur?"

"Scientists began warning Washington about this event as far back as 2004, when the ground above the caldera began rising at a rate of 2.8 inches a year. Yellowstone trails had to be shut down when ground temperatures exceeded 240 degrees Fahrenheit. Yet they never took our warnings seriously."

"Was there anything that could have been done to prevent it?"

"We proposed several potential solutions to deal with the caldera threat, including the construction of a deep-well venting system. Congress vetoed the deal three years ago, claiming the $23 billion price tag was far too excessive for a tourist attraction. When we protested, news pundits on one politically slanted network accused members of the U.S. Geological Survey of using scare tactics to fund our department."

"Obviously, a blast of this magnitude striking so early in the morning represents a worst-case scenario. We're getting death estimates ranging from eight to ten thousand—"

"Ms. Matney, I don't think you comprehend the magnitude of this event. It's not the initial blast or the lava flow we have to fear; it's the ash cloud. As it rises into the stratosphere it will span the entire globe, blanketing the atmosphere and blotting out the sun's rays. Photosynthesis will cease, which means crops will fail, leading to mass starvation. The Earth's temperatures will plummet, initiating another ice age. What we're looking at is the opening act of a planet-wide cataclysm—an extinction event."

The announcer couldn't find her voice, forcing her colleague to take over the interview.

"Dr. Hurtienne, this is Tyler Bohlman. How long will this theoretical ice age last?"

"I can assure you, Mr. Bohlman, the ice age is not theoretical. Sixty-five million years ago an asteroid struck the Gulf of Mexico, wiping out the dinosaurs. It wasn't the impact that caused the mass extinction, but rather the ash cloud that caused a radical change in climate. As for how long the ice age will last, the answer is anywhere from a thousand to a hundred thousand years."

* * *

"Huh!" My eyes snapped open, my heart pounding in my chest. For a distressing moment I felt lost.

Jonas was snoring softly in his command chair, his congested breaths nearly concealing the faint sound of rushing water. Locating my headphones, I listened in on the sonar.

The sound was coming from the riverbed below the Manta, along the base of the ice sheet now walling us in. Deciding not to wake Jonas, I restarted the engines and dove the sub to the bottom.

The subglacial waterway hadn't ceased; its outflow had been dammed by ice extending from the bottom of the glacier to within seven to ten feet of the riverbed. Reduced to a narrow bottleneck, the current was rushing beneath the ice sheet at a swift twenty-three knots.

It would be a tight squeeze, but the Manta could slip through. The danger lay in the fact that the extended bottom of the glacier was essentially river water that had frozen, rendering it unstable.

Traversing the passage could cause the ceiling to collapse on the sub and trap us for all eternity.

The *Tethys* had most likely forged its own tunnel through the glacier, its superheated bow plates eliminating any risk. I thought about searching for their borehole, but we were already six hours behind.

Gritting my teeth, I guided the sub through the horizontal channel.

It took full throttle just to enter the restricted passage. The ungodly current rocked the sub, slamming the cockpit repeatedly against the ceiling of ice and grinding its undercarriage into the gravel riverbed.

Jonas woke up. Taking command of the pitching submersible, he powered up the Valkyries and ignited the lasers, creating a vacuum effect that accelerated the Manta smoothly through the widening crawl space.

"Guess I should have used the lasers to begin with, huh?"

He shot me a pissed-off look. "Next time wake me."

"I was afraid you might not risk it."

"Obviously you have me confused with someone who has something to live for."

"Be careful what you say. I had another dream."

"Which planet were you visiting this time? Uranus?"

"The dream took place on Earth, about twenty years from now. Brandy and I were still married, with three kids and a slew of grandkids. Not sure what year it was, but it was Christmas, give or take a day—the day the Yellowstone Caldera erupted."

Jonas looked at me, incredulous. "Was this real or just one of those multiverse things?"

"There's no way to tell; it hasn't happened yet. Obviously. But I don't think it's a coincidence that it parallels the event that must have destroyed Charon."

"Zach, scientists have known about the Yellowstone Caldera for decades. You think a dream is going to convince the authorities to take the threat any more seriously?"

"No, but I do think the dream serves a purpose. I just haven't figured out what that is yet. What's our ETA to Vostok?"

"How the hell should I know? We're still over two hundred miles away. Who knows if we'll even get out from under this giant ice cube?"

As if the glacier heard him, the passage suddenly reopened, depositing us back in the main river.

For the next thirteen hours, we forged our way to the southwest, averaging eighteen knots. We stretched and ate and relieved our bowels and bladder, and we watched movies over the computer and alternated piloting duties with restless catnaps. Finally, the waterway twisted to the north, the riverbed dropping away several hundred feet as the ice sheet receded overhead, creating a six-foot space of air into which we surfaced.

Lake Vostok. The northern basin.

We had arrived.

38

"The rule is jam tomorrow and jam yesterday—but never jam today."
—Lewis Carroll

Migrating from the ocean, a salmon will fight its way upstream to return to the river where it was born so it can spawn and die, completing its circle of life.

My circle had begun seven years ago when an alien entity had redirected my life, sending me down a multiverse not of my choosing. Now I had returned, hoping for a do-over at the point where my consciousness had jumped the tracks into a radically different reality, which had somehow become my destiny.

Multiverses.

Ten dimensions of existence.

The theory that started it all originated in 1997 when a physicist by the name of Juan Maldacena introduced a model of the universe in which gravity arose from thin microscopic vibrating strings residing in nine dimensions of space, plus one of time. Quantum theory became a mathematical Rosetta Stone, filling in key gaps within Einstein's theory of gravity. More unnerving were Maldacena's implications—that the nine upper dimensions were the true reality, while our physical lower dimension of time was the equivalent of a hologram.

In 2013, two physicists from Japan's Ibaraki University made huge strides in proving Maldacena's theory when they discovered that the internal energy and properties of a black hole precisely matched the internal energy of our physical universe—that is, if there were no gravity.

Was our physical universe simply one big holographic projection?

377

Was time an illusion and gravity its shepherd?

Seeking to rise above "the hologram" and rediscover my life, I had returned to Lake Vostok, arriving nine hours after Colonel Vacendak and his MJ-12 maniacs.

* * *

Having entered the northern basin, I instructed Jonas to take us deep and go active on sonar, warning him that the lake's bull sperm whale population was extremely aggressive when it came to safeguarding their pods. My concerns seemed unfounded, as we made it all the way to the plateau without a single sonar contact.

It took Jonas twenty minutes to locate the river we needed to follow inland. Reducing our speed to five knots, we entered the *Livyatan melvillei* nursery.

"My God... how could he do this?"

The Tethys had shown no mercy. The tributary flowed red with blood, the shallows clogged with the butchered remains of the Miocene whales. Beached cetaceans lined the snow-covered banks, bleeding out from laser burns that had effortlessly sheered blubber from bone. The dead were too numerous to count; those few still dying slapped the surface with their flukes as a warning, and the survivors clicked the waterway in search of their missing calves.

The scene sickened us. Once more, man's ego had blinded him to recognizing that there was a universal consciousness in play; every negative action causing a ripple that would one day come home to roost.

The E.T.s were here as mentors, reaching out to those who demonstrated purity of heart. As such, I knew the Colonel and his fear-mongers would not be granted access into the alien vessel. And that would lead them to desperate measures.

"Jonas, we have to hurry before there's no vessel left to access."

* * *

378

Thirty minutes later we were moving through the partially frozen waters of Lake Vostok's bay. Jonas used the ice floes as sonar camouflage as we progressively made our way toward the shoreline—like everything else about the island— was undergoing beyond which we would find the extraterrestrial vessel.

Aided by night-vision binoculars, I located the Tethys. The nuclear submarine was anchored offshore, only the shoreline, like everything else about the island, was undergoing a rapid transformation.

Teams of men dressed in ECW gear and wearing chemical tanks strapped to their backs were using flamethrowers to melt the ice and snow, exposing sections of what appeared to be a metallic, saucer-shaped vessel, whose diameter rivaled that of an aircraft carrier. While most of the crew focused on clearing fifteen million years of packed snow from the floating alien landscape, a dozen men had forged a path to the base of the mountain, their wall of flame focused on the summit. The intense heat caused great swaths of ice to fall away from a four-story dorsal-shaped mast, partially concealed behind swirling curtains of steam and fog.

Jonas stared slack-jawed through his binoculars, the sight of the E.T.'s vessel no doubt changing his attitude about our mission and energizing his hope to alter his son's fate. "It's real. Everything you told me is real. But how the hell are we going to get you inside that thing without being seen?"

"Dive the sub. There may be an entrance near the saucer's belly."

Jonas banked the Manta into a deep descent, giving the Tethys a wide berth as he approached the submerged alien hull. The superstructure materialized out of our olive-green night vision, its disk-shaped keel plunging ninety-six feet below the surface and its dark mass hovering above us like an enormous thundercloud.

Jonas powered on an exterior light in the Manta's prow. Aiming the beacon, he illuminated a smooth expanse of dull-gray metal, its surface devoid of ice, rust, or barnacles.

As we passed beneath the vessel's teardrop center, a blue ring of light sixty or seventy feet across materialized overhead, its luminescence bathing us in its aura even as it held us within its grip. A moment later a dark pupil opened in the center of the circle, its widening orifice slowly drawing us in.

The Manta levitated into the vortex until we were enveloped by a darkness so dense that even our exterior light couldn't penetrate it. We registered the hull resealing beneath us and the pressure differential changing as water was vented from the docking chamber, leaving our submersible to settle on an unseen surface.

For several long minutes we simply sat there in the dark and waited. Then white recessed lighting flickered on like a swarm of fireflies, illuminating an auditorium-sized chamber. Our sub was situated in the center of a circular ring that resembled one of my Vostok energy generators, only this one was twelve feet high and large enough in circumference to corral a Miocene sperm whale.

The device looked like it hadn't been operated since Antarctica was free of ice.

Jonas was busy running an analysis of our surroundings. Determining the air fit to breathe, he popped open the Manta's cockpit and stood up on his leather bucket seat, groaning in pain from having been stuck in such a cramped space for more than thirty-six hours.

I followed suit, my leg muscles burning as I stretched. Attempting to increase the circulation in my knees, I performed a slow squat and recovery—shocked to find myself levitating away from the cockpit!

"Zach?"

"We're in some kind of anti-gravity well. Try it."

Jonas jumped—only way too hard—and shot straight toward the dark recess above our heads.

"J.T.?" Hovering in mid-air a foot above my seat, I stared up at the void. "Jonas, are you okay? Can you hear me? Jonas!"

Nothing.

Damn.

Placing my right foot on my headrest, I launched my weightless body into the air like Superman, the sensation of flying causing me to grin from ear to ear despite concern for my colleague. Within seconds I was high above the Manta, looking down at the triple-ringed generator, the interior rollers of which were either rotating very slowly or at a speed so fast their velocity rendered them an optical illusion.

Looking up, I realized a polished metal ceiling loomed less than twenty feet overhead and there was no way for me to slow down. Covering my head, I braced for an impact that was going to hurt—only to feel a bizarre, titillating sensation from my hands down through my skull, neck, upper torso, and legs as the atoms of my body *passed through* the surface.

Opening my eyes, I found myself on the opposite side of the permeable barrier, standing in a dimly lit circular chamber on a polished metal floor, my body once more weighed down by gravity. The circular walls and twelve-foot-high ceiling were made of the same metallic substance that seemed to radiate its own blue-white light.

Ten feet to my left was Jonas. He was on his hands and knees, a dark figure standing over him.

The surface of the circular floor beneath us brightened, revealing Colonel Vacendak—

—The barrel of his Beretta 9mm pistol pressed firmly against the back of Jonas's skull.

"Nice to see you again, Dr. Wallace. You're looking well for a dead man." The Colonel nodded to two armed men, who stepped from out of the shadows to guard Jonas.

The Colonel approached me, one hand reaching out to grip my right arm above the elbow, the other poking the gun barrel against my temple. "You look surprised to see me. Did you think we lacked the knowledge to access this ship? MAJESTIC uses a neutrino light detector to track E.T. vessels as they enter our dimension. Then we bring 'em down and reverse-engineer them. Been doing it since your father started making young girls cry.

"You didn't really think his ploy would fool us, did you? We practically invented disinformation and misdirection tactics." He leaned in. "If I had a dollar for every time one of our guys kidnapped some dumb hick farmer and put him through an alien abduction… Of course, I'm sure a few of them actually enjoyed the anal probes."

Without warning, he struck me on the top of my skull with the butt-end of the Beretta's magazine.

I dropped to one knee, warm blood pooling around the wound.

Then I lost it.

With a primal yell, I drove my right shoulder into the Colonel's gut as if he was a blitzing linebacker, slamming the older man flat on his back. The guards stayed with Jonas, allowing me a few seconds to pummel Vacendak's face into a bloody pulp before one of them dragged me off him.

Furious, the Colonel regained his feet and aimed the gun's barrel between my eyes, his body trembling. For a moment I was convinced my life was over—but I've been *there* before.

Spinning around to face Jonas, the Colonel fired.

The force of the gun blast startled me, the sound echoing in my ears. I saw a puff of smoke leave the barrel as it burped a slowly spinning lead projectile through gelid air, which appeared to ripple outward from the Beretta.

The bullet made it a third of the way to Jonas's brain before it stopped. In fact, everything stopped except for yours truly and Joe Tkalec, who now stood beside me, observing the frozen scene.

"Joe, is he going to die?"

"Yes. But he served a greater good. He brought you here."

382

"To the portal?"

"To a state of universal consciousness known as Da'at; a place of infinite light, energy, and perfection, where all ten dimensions are united as one. Physical beings who are giving, like your friend, are able to draw from its energy. Those who receive for themselves alone cannot access it. One who has awakened Da'at is able to perform the miraculous. Are you ready to perform the miraculous, Zachary?"

"What miracle, Alien Joe? What are you asking me to do?"

"I cannot say without jeopardizing your free will. However, if you choose to bring your consciousness into Da'at, then the multiverse you entered seven years ago and everything hence forward shall become the reality."

"Whoa, hold on. You're asking me to sacrifice William and Brandy, now Jonas and his son, plus all the people that these bastards killed in D.C.? For what? For some alien race on a distant planet that died long ago? Why are you placing that burden on me? I mean, come on, isn't that God's will?"

"God has given you the will to choose."

"Okay, so what happens if I choose not to go to this Da'at place? What happens then?"

"Then you'll return to seven years ago to the ice tunnel, and whatever reality has manifested as a result of your decision. Of course, this time, instead of entering this vessel, you'll simply come to a dead end."

"In my last lucid dream, I was much older. Brandy and I were still together; William was a man. And the Yellowstone Caldera erupted… Was that real?"

"It was one reality among a multiverse of possibilities."

"You know what I'm asking! Will it really happen, or did it occur as a result of my decision to enter Da'at?"

"Entering Da'at resolves nothing. It simply returns your soul to a past life."

"You mean Avi Socha?"

"He is known on his world as a soul searcher. Once you enter Da'at, your consciousness will awaken to his reality. You will retain no memory of ever having been Zachary Wallace."

"Then how do I get back to this life?"

"There's no guarantee you will. The soul is immortal, of course, but the only certainty once you enter Da'at is that you will live and die as Avi Socha, and the course of action you take, or refuse to take, may determine the future of your species."

The blood drained from my face.

There are times when life shits on your head, when reality unravels with a diagnosis of cancer or paralysis or the loss of a loved one. That's the moment you realize your contentment was all an illusion, that you never had any control, that the money and notoriety and long hours and better job titles and great sex and the whole rat race chasing after the pursuit of happiness was all bullshit. Because if and when you do find yourself alone in that foxhole or on that surgical table, in a sinking boat or a hospice bed or trapped on a dying planet, and it's just you and your fear—that's the moment you realize the only thing you have left, the only thing of substance that life can't strip away from you, is your faith in a higher power.

For me, Dr. Zachary Wallace, lord of the skeptics, I had to believe because the alternative—going back seven years to the ice tunnel—was a death sentence.

Sometimes, better the devil you haven't met...

"Okay, Alien Joe, I'm ready. Send me back."

I felt myself sinking feet-first through the floor, my body atomizing as my consciousness was inhaled into the center of the whirling electrogravitic rings.

Part Three
Before the Beginning...

39

*"There were many dark moments when my faith in humanity
was sorely tested, but I would not and could not give myself up to despair.
That way lays defeat and death."*

—Nelson Mandela, *Long Walk to Freedom: Autobiography of Nelson Mandela*

I awoke on an alien world as another person.

Avi Socha—mated to three, father of ten.

Avi Socha—born into servitude, subcitizen of the Kohenim Tribe.

Avi Socha—discredited scientist and soul-seeker, now a prisoner of the state.

Avi Socha—a forgotten man on the verge of death.

Nearly one solar year had passed since I'd been arrested in a seaside cave by the Council's secret police. My neighbor had turned me in, hoping to acquire "loyalty credits" for the lottery, a contest in which a thousand subcitizens would be chosen to board a transport vessel that was to safely orbit our doomed world, Charon, when the Miketz struck.

The lottery turned out to be another Council lie designed to stave off civil unrest.

Weak from hunger, I remained in my sleep sack until the midday sun beat down upon me. It shone through from octagonal openings in the two-story-high ceiling of my quarantine. Using my soiled tunic as a tent, I curled beneath the fabric to shield my light-sensitive eyes.

The prison cells were occupied by the dead and dying, but our jailers were gone. They had abandoned the facility three weeks earlier, when a massive earthquake had rocked the continent, spawning a planet-wide exodus thirty-nine days ahead of the anticipated doomsday event. Once the cartel and their military capos had gone, the republic's infrastructure collapsed, chasing the vendors who had serviced the elite into the mountains—my jailers among them.

Hundreds of ships now orbited the planet, linking together to form clusters, their pods occupied by past and present Council members and their families. The rest of us were forced to remain behind, waiting for a volcanic eruption that would wipe out all traces of life.

Left alone to die, I was surviving on the rainwater that poured in from the ceiling and a solitary green leaf a day, taken from what little remained of my four-plant garden.

Being locked away in exile is a perception-altering experience. Initially there is pain. Pain comes in a variety of forms, from the physical agony brought about by incessant hunger, to the mental anguish of being confined to a small cell, to the emotional torture of being deprived of seeing your loved ones.

The first few weeks were by far the hardest, the darkness accompanied by nightmares, birthed by the screams coming from the other prisoners. I adapted by stuffing my earholes with torn fabric from my tunic. My stomach gradually adapted to starvation by shrinking, my mind to the tediousness of endless time by creating a routine.

Yet even that was not enough to slow the onset of madness.

Being held in solitary confinement brings waves of insanity, time melding into lucid dreams and waking delusions. The first episode happened one scorching day. As the heat baked me alive in my cell and the noonday sun reflected off my stone floor to blind me, I sank into a panting, heart-pounding delirium, muttering a long-forgotten mantra as I welcomed death.

It came with a blissful release of pain as my consciousness rose out of my body to the ceiling, my mind's eye looking down upon a tortured being lying in a hammock. I had become so emaciated that at first I didn't recognize myself.

My skin hung loose from my skeleton; my black eyes were sunken and red. Having left my body, my consciousness floated joyfully out an open vent to the prison courtyard.

At the time of my first passing, the facility was being abandoned by the guards. There was chaos and fear and uncertainty, the violet horizon laced with vertical rocket plumes from ships racing into orbit ahead of the mobs.

Moving over the prison walls into the city, I witnessed a crime spree evolve into a bloodbath, as decades of military rule gave way to the inevitable "whatever it takes to survive" mentality. Looting, murder, rape, intoxication—I could feel my species' life force sink deeper into the mire as they turned on one another, trading morality for survival.

And then a force of energy summoned me, its white light intoxicating. I floated toward it and was enveloped in the love of my birth parents, both of whom had been put to death by the last regime eight solar years ago. Bathing in their aura, I wished only to join them; however, they told me it wasn't my time. They said the upper worlds had tasked my soul with a mission—to lead my people off of our dying world.

Before I could inquire how I was expected to do this, I found my spirit moving over water, heading for a desolate coastal region known as the southern rift valley. Meteors had impacted the terrain eons ago, leaving the geology pockmarked with enormous craters. Some had formed lakes. Others remained dry beds. One of these had been outfitted with camouflaged netting, concealing a rebel camp.

As my spirit toured the facility, I recognized physicists and engineers whom I had known from my adolescent years at the academy. As members of the twelve tribes who suffered as a subservient class under the Council's autocratic rule, these scientists and their skilled laborers had been working together in secrecy to design and construct a fleet of saucer-shaped starships. Unlike the conventional transports now in orbit over Charon, these vessels were powered by an electrogravitic propulsion system, a generator that produced an anti-gravity vortex that would theoretically make interdimensional travel possible. The technology had threatened the Council's carbon-based hold on the economy and had therefore been banned, and now the planet's twelve tribes—Charon's lowest rung society—were on the brink of using it to flee our star system in search of a habitable world suitable for colonization.

It would have made for a delicious irony had the propulsion system actually worked.

* * *

With a sudden wave of pain, I found myself back in my cell, once more imprisoned in a dying body.

Pain is part of the physical condition; suffering is a choice we make.

389

Having been given a task, I decided that I would no longer suffer my fate. I would use it as a means to save my people.

First, I needed to be free.

Even lacking guards, escape was out of the question. The cell door was bolted from the outside, the open ceiling slats too high to reach. Physically, I barely possessed the strength to stand. Even if I could replicate my out-of-body experience, it offered no means of communicating my dilemma to others. And while I still maintained the ability to communicate with my past lives, there was nothing they could do to release me unless …

I had been raised and educated on the scientific, philosophical, and spiritual belief that life is interconnected through a single consciousness that pervades all existence. This universal mind is present everywhere at the same time. One must simply know it, believe in it, and apply it through meditative practice, and miracles can happen.

The miracle I would seed was a visual message, a map that began in the rebel camp and led to my prison. At the culmination of this dream, the dreamer would witness a functioning electrogravitic propulsion system whirling away in my cell.

My targeted viewers would be the scientists working on a means to escape Charon, half a continent away.

* * *

Solitude and starvation made for intense meditation sessions that bordered on delirium.

For weeks, I teetered on the brink of death until one late afternoon when my cell door was wrenched open on its rusted hinges.

The rebel leader was tall and lanky, his youth and dark complexion revealing his lineage to be one of the eastern tribes. Three other males accompanied him, one of whom performed a quick physical examination on me before feeding me intravenously.

I felt the warmth spreading through my blood vessels, easing my pain. Through heavy eyes I gazed up at the octagonal holes in the ceiling, watching with amusement as they started to spin.

* * *

I must have slept for some time, because it was dark when I awoke. We were in the main cabin of an aerial transport, the leader immersed in reading my prophecies, which he had recovered from my cell, recorded in a series of word gusts on a transmitter scroll.

He acknowledged that I was awake. "You are Avi Socha ben Amram."

"And you are Zaphenath Paneah. I remember you from our days in the science academy."

"And I remember your theories on soul searching that got you expelled."
He motioned to the scroll. "May I?"

I nodded, finding the strength to sit up for the first time in a month.

He selected a recording I had made before weakness had replaced my anger.

Epithet to an Extinct Race

Beneath violet skies and silent screams,
and shadowed faces
fleeing burning streams;
whose shorelines danced with lifeless limbs
and hallowed halls
and hope turned grim.

Scorched by greed.
Death laughs.

Lies and smiles
and justice without trials,
wrapped in bundles of hope
and no one can cope
except we did.

Who asked you to thicken
our air until it was rendered unbreathable,
to poison our food, to safeguard the inconceivable?

We did.

In the end of times,
when an uprising was needed,
we ignored the call.
The victim was its own executioner;
the seed destroyed the soil;
our hatred taught a child.
The caldera was left to boil.
In an epithet to an extinct race,
only ignorance shall reign forever.

For several silent moments he reflected upon my words. Then he walked over and sat on the floor before me, a gesture of humility. "The Miketz shall arrive in less than a month. Its eruption shall destroy all life remaining on this planet. A team of scientists from the twelve tribes have been laboring in secrecy for many years on a means to escape not just the Miketz but our star system altogether. For weeks now they have shared the harsh reality of their failure with a dream that appears to point to you as the one who holds the key to their success. You are responsible for this?"

"I am."

"Translate the vision. Tell me what you think you know."

"I know your scientists have created a propulsion system capable of travelling faster than light. I also know there is a flaw in the design that affects the electromagnetic field. As a result, the anti-gravity vortex isn't strong enough to provide inertial shielding. Without it, your ships won't be able to survive transdimensional flight. Like the Council's fleet, you will be stuck in this star system until your supplies run out and you perish."

"And you possess a solution to this challenge?"

"Not yet. But with your help I will seek an audience with one of my

soul's future incarnations, who lives in an advanced society powered by these devices. What he knows I shall know."

"Avi, I think imprisonment has affected your mind. How can one communicate with an individual who hasn't even been born yet?"

"The soul is immortal. It belongs in the Upper Worlds, where time does not exist. In order to earn its way into the higher realms of existence, it must live out many lives in the physical world. Each incarnation of the flesh is judged, each judgment influencing the next incarnation. Inflict pain upon another in this life, and in the next you might suffer a disease. Treat others with love, and in the next life you may have bliss. Commit atrocities like the members of Council, and you might live out your next life as a slug. Each incarnation bears its own consciousness even though they share the same soul. By tapping into the soul's energy stream, I am able to locate these incarnations and communicate with them using the universal consciousness. Because time has no bearing in the Upper Realms every inevitability has already happened, including the lives of every incarnate that will ever accompany each soul. As long as the future caretaker of my soul will one day exist, I can find the means to communicate with him."

The leader shook his head, unsure. "Avi, I sent a transport to collect your family. Your senior wife, Lehanna, claims you soul searched for a future incarnate before you were arrested. She says you failed and that there are no future Charonian incarnates out there to connect with. This suggests our mission will also fail."

"Things happen for a reason, Zaphenath. Even the Miketz serves a purpose, one we cannot see. Prison gave me time to reflect. Among the thousands of probabilities that will end in the death of our people, I believe I have found the means to set one alternate reality into motion, one that could alter our species' fate. And the implications of our actions are incredible."

40

"You don't have to have a great faith or anything. The whole thing is so simple—as though it's too marvelous to be true. I don't and never did imagine God as one thing. But now I can see God as a power source, or as an energy."

—John Lennon

At my request, our transport was diverted to Charon's City of the Sciences, the place where I had been assigned to live and train two years after my birth.

Every child born on Charon since the time of the Great Uprising was required to be submitted for G.A.T.—Genetic Aptitude Testing—within two solar years of conception. DNA and brain chemicals determined where each offspring would be raised and educated. Only the children of the Council were exempted, a ruling which virtually assured our militaristic rulers to be among the least educated populace inhabiting the planet.

We landed in the Biological District, where the regent's top exobiologist, Dr. Kabir Parker, had been summoned to his lab for our meeting. I had studied under Kabir until I'd had a near-death experience during my pre-pubescent years. Upon recovering from the drowning incident, my psyche had changed, my logical mind evolving into one that was more intuitive. When my studies faltered, my G.A.T. was retested, the results sending my education into a free fall.

There is no place in an autocratic society for a free thinker, especially one who claims he can communicate with the dead.

* * *

Zaphenath Paneah and I listened while Kabir lectured us on how life first evolved on Charon. "It began over 400 million solar orbits ago with chemiosmosis, a process in which the chemical adenosine triphosphate was broken down and re-formed to release energy. Biological evidence indicates the first living organisms on Charon were not self-replicating molecules, but a byproduct of a chemical combination that contained the instructions for

394

processing energy and replicating. Incredibly, the enzymes required for this specific metabolism were not found on our planet; they were delivered by meteorites. Ribose, adenine, and cytosine were the key ingredients lined inside these space rocks, which most likely metabolized into bacteria after coalescing in hot, acidic pools of liquid that contained phosphorus chemicals."

"Kabir, in order to save our people, we need to seed the ingredients of Charon's life matrix on another world. Just for argument's sake, let's say you could package this biological soup aboard a conventional rocket and crashland it. Which planet or moon in our solar system represents the best candidate for life to take hold and develop as it has on Charon?"

"At present? The answer is none."

"I realize that. But what about in the future or distant future?"

Communicating with his control console via thought wave, the exobiologist powered on a holographic map of our star system revealing our sun, orbited by four inner worlds and four outer, the divide separated by an asteroid belt.

"The two innermost planets, Nekudim and Akudim, are far too close to the sun for life to ever evolve. The outlying gas giants beyond Charon aren't suitable either. That leaves Berudim."

The hologram zoomed in on the third planet from the sun. Charon's neighbor was a hostile world, its surface obscured behind a dense layer of gray atmospheric clouds. "If we're speaking strictly in terms of a planetary lifetime, then Berudim would be my choice. Although its atmosphere is presently toxic to life as we know it, our probes indicate that the cloud cover obscuring the planet's surface contains massive layers of moisture and that it is in fact raining on Berudim. Water, as you know, is a necessary ingredient for life on Charon. Berudim's atmosphere is in flux, and probability models suggest a breathable air in approximately ten to fifteen million years. What I also like about Berudim is that it's twice the size of Charon, with a much larger magnetosphere to protect it from the solar wind."

Zaphenath Paneah turned to me. "The magnetosphere is an issue the Council has hidden from the masses since the revolution. It has been steadily eroding for centuries. Another fifty to seventy years and we'll have no atmosphere. No atmosphere means no air and no greenhouse effect to maintain temperature stability. With or without the Miketz, Charon is destined to become a cold, desolate world."

Kabir never liked being interrupted while he was in mid-gust. "Listen to me, Avi Socha. We can engage in hypotheticals between now and doomsday, but there's a difference between seeding the ingredients of life on Berudim and expecting it to one day become an intelligent race of beings. Evolution has its own catalysts—asteroid strikes, ice ages, runaway genetic mutations. Duplicating an abiotic process to produce RNA or RNA precursors that result in a species suitable to communicate with is a one in a million shot."

"One in a million is better than no chance at all," Zaphenath Paneah said. "Kabir, how many probes are available to launch to Berudim?"

Kabir used his thought waves to review the institute's inventory of space drones. "Seventy-two vessels still remain under the institute's control. As fate would have it, the journey can be completed in six days, because the two planets are rapidly approaching their maximum perihelic opposition, the closest they've been since life first took hold on Charon. Before you go congratulating yourself, Avi Socha, you should know that this isn't just a coincidence. Berudim is actually the cause of the Miketz. The third planet's gravitational pull on Charon is what is increasing the pressure in the calderas. Sometime before the maximum perihelic orbit is achieved, Charon's magma pockets will erupt, unless we take the necessary course of action."

Kabir's tone caused the back of my skull to tingle. "What does that mean? Zaphenath, what is he referring to?"

The rebel leader was not happy with his scientist's lack of discretion. "It's a course of action that has been proposed. When the Council discovered that Berudim's gravitational pull was causing the calderic pressure increases, they instructed the Science Institute to develop a means of destroying it. Our scientists succeeded where theirs failed."

Zaphenath Paneah focused his thought waves on the hologram of Berudim until three drones were positioned around the planet. "The device is called a scalar weapon. Unlike conventional electromagnetic waves that propagate outward in ripples through our physical dimension, scalar waves travel through space longitudinally in the higher dimensions. When fired simultaneously from drones orbiting Berudim, the scalar waves shall cause every molecule on the planet to broil at a temperature hotter than the sun, vaporizing everything into plasma. Berudim's atmosphere will expand until it explodes, the entire event lasting less than a second."

He nodded, causing three electric-blue beams to ignite on the holographic simulation, yielding a massive white explosion that expelled rings of plasma across the vastness of space.

By the time my eyes adjusted, the third planet from the sun was gone.

41

"The distinction between past, present, and future is only a stubbornly persistent illusion."

—Albert Einstein

Whether to destroy an uninhabited planet in order to save your own might seem like an easy decision for the rebel leaders representing the twelve tribes, but there were complex variables in play. If Berudim was destroyed and Charon spared, the Council would return to enslave the people. As for using the scalar weapon on the Council's orbiting ships, if fired from Charon the anti-gravity burst could potentially set off the calderas.

Then there was Charon's decaying magnetosphere. Destroying Berudim only represented a temporary solution, for at some point during the next decade the atmosphere would collapse. At least my plan offered us a chance to begin over in a new world, without being dominated by an oppressive regime.

But some didn't want to crawl out from the shadow of oppression. They had been servants for so long that the thought of being free actually frightened them. Even if transdimensional travel could be achieved in the coming weeks, there were too many unknown variables for tribal leaders to even consider a mass exodus.

How long would our people have to venture across the cosmic desert before a suitable planet could be found?

What if this new world was ruled by a hostile force far worse than the Council?

Under the Council's rule the tribes had been housed and fed, trained and employed. Yes, there were inequities derived from power and pain inflicted upon our people, but sometimes the safer option is the devil you know.

While voting arrangements were being organized among the eastern tribes' outlying communities, Kabir and his biologists were hard at work preparing containers of "primordial soup." At the same time, rebel forces raided the Space Institute, with teams of engineers assigned to prepare as many drone rockets as possible for launch. Slightly larger than the interior dimensions of my cell, these two-stage capsules were programmed to pierce Berudim's atmosphere at an angle and velocity that would ensure they would survive the journey until impact, bursting their chemical payloads on Berudim… Or so we hoped.

As Kabir explained it, the success of the mission came down to sheer luck, which relied heavily on a numbers game. Unlike Charon, Berudim's surface was mostly water. Because the atmosphere obscured our view of any landmasses, we needed to launch as many rockets as possible, spreading them out. Each probe carried a twenty-six-percent probability of impacting land. An ocean burst would dilute the biological soup, rendering it useless.

The good news was that the results of the mission would be known to me immediately. If life evolved on Berudim in the distant future because of our efforts then, theoretically, I should have a new incarnate to communicate with right after the drones' impact. If we failed, then a void would remain in the universal consciousness.

Seventy-two drone rockets were readied for the mission, with three larger drones and two back-ups armed with scalar weapons.

Now it was up to the people. Would they be ruled by faith or fear, hope or uncertainty? I realized that two worlds' fates hung in the balance, Charon's and every species that might potentially existed on Berudim.

Eleven days before the Miketz calderas were predicted to erupt, the twelve tribal leaders cast votes that represented the will of their people. By a count of seven to five, a decision was rendered in favor of destroying Berudim. Though I argued with anyone who would listen, the five drones containing the scalar weapons were launched, beginning a six-day journey to vaporize our approaching neighbor.

A day later the plagues struck, and suddenly no one wanted to stay on Charon.

Scientists theorized that the unpredicted events were caused by a bad combination of seismic activity and the effects of Berudim's gravitational forces on Charon's iron and sulfur core, causing it to slow its rotation.

The tribes didn't care what was causing the upheaval—only that it was happening. First the lakes and streams that provided our drinking water became tainted with red clay. This sent the amphibious wildlife—frogs and other creatures—evacuating the water to invade our homes. Our livestock drank the water and quickly fell sick. Fleas and lice, seeking new hosts, targeted our people, inflicting their skin with boils and rashes.

On the second day a small caldera erupted in the eastern province. Darkness covered our planet as the ash cloud spread across the atmosphere, the poor air quality causing severe breathing problems among our youngest children as well as the elderly.

By the morning of the third day a new vote was taken among the tribes. It was decided that my option would take precedence over the scalar weapons, granting me one day after the drones' impact to make contact with a being from our future. If I failed to receive instructions regarding a zero-point energy system, then Berudim would be destroyed.

Midday arrived with a worsening darkness, and seventy-two rockets launched from antiquated launch silos. Each drone carried a sphere-shaped titanium probe filled with containers of chemicals that represented the primordial building blocks of Charonian life.

Two rockets exploded in the clogged atmosphere. A third struck a Council ship orbiting Charon and was destroyed.

Two more vessels veered off course.

Six days later the remaining sixty-seven rockets jettisoned their payloads into the Berudim atmosphere and abruptly disappeared off our sensory screens.

* * *

Zaphenath Paneah escorted me across the paved crater floor to a vessel so immense that it rivaled the Council Assembly Hall. Saucer-shaped with a triangular mast, this particular ship had been assigned to my tribe, assuming I could turn the useless disk of polished metal into an anti-gravitational device able to travel the cosmos beyond the speed of light.

The rebel leader prompted an entrance that led into the bowels of the ship. "The central chamber is located directly over the propulsion system. It has been prepared as you requested. We've cleared the crater of all personnel; it's just your thoughts and whoever or whatever is listening. Good luck, Avi Socha."

I nodded and entered the transport.

* * *

The chamber was circular, located just above the ship's gravitational well and massive electrogravitic generator rings. Surrounded by darkness, I situated myself before the glow of a crimson candle. Closing my eyes, I began reciting the forty-two-word mantra that dated back to the time of creation, its energy helping me to access the universal consciousness.

"ANA   BEKOACH...   GEDULAT   YEMINECHA... TATIR ZERURA ... "

In my mind's eye my consciousness was moving through the void, passing over a dark sea.

"KABEL   RINAT...   AMECHA   SAGVENU... TAHARENU NORA ... "

The sea moved inland, becoming a twisting river that separated a rift valley.

"NA GIBOR...   DORSHEY YICHUDCHA...   KEBAVAT SHOMREM ... "

Snow-covered mountains rose along either bank as the river emptied into a vast lake, its waters dark and forboding.

"BARCHEM   TEHAREM...   RACHAMEY ZIDEKATCHA... TAMID GOMLEM ... "

Looking down, I saw immense water creatures moving just below the surface, their backs sprouting streams of vaporized air.

"HASIN KADOSH...   BEROV TUVECHA...   NAHEL ADOTECHA ... "

Sensing intelligence, my consciousness followed these immense creatures inland to a bay. Lying in the water was a transport ship identical to the saucer in which my physicality remained back on Charon.

"YAHID   GE'EA...   LEAMECHA   PENNE... ZOCHREY KDUSHATECHA ... "

I was inside the vessel, entering a dark chamber illuminated by the light coming from a violet candle.

'SHAVATENU   KABEL...   USHEMA   ZAKATENU...

YODE TA'ALUMOT … "

As I completed the last verse of the mantra, I saw a figure seated on the floor on the opposite side of the candle. The alien was a biped, clothed in a strange body garment. Its skull was narrow, adorned with brown fur that stopped at its jawline. On each side of its head were two fleshy protusions that appeared to accentuate the being's hearing holes.

I wondered if the creature could see, for its eyes were small and partially concealed behind skin flaps. Its flesh was thick, especially around the nose and mouth. Most bizarre—each paw possessed five thick digits.

Was the being intelligent?

Endeavoring to find out, I communicated my thoughts. "I am called Avi Socha."

* * *

I opened my eyes, disoriented from having passed through the center of the whirling electrogravitic rings. For some reason I was back inside the chamber above the generator, the darkness pierced by the light coming from a violet candle.

Seated on the floor opposite the flickering light was an extraterrestrial, one of the Grays described to me by Colonel Vacendak. Its head was elongated and hairless and perched precariously atop a spindly neck. Its eyes were big and black and had no exterior lids. Nor did it have ears, just holes. Its hands were thin and double-jointed, possessing three long fingers and an opposable fourth digit. The E.T.'s torso was clothed in a white tunic. I had no idea whether it was male or female… or both.

I jumped as its inner voice communicated to me. *"I am called Avi Socha."*

"I am Zachary Wallace," I said aloud.

My spoken words appeared to startle it. *"You cannot*

communicate telepathically?"

"No. But I can hear your thoughts."

I felt the being's emotions darken, as if my response had disappointed it.

"Is there a more intelligent species on Berudim that I might communicate with? Perhaps one more like me?"

"I don't know. Where is Berudim?"

The E.T. mentally projected an image of an alien planet above the candle, its atmosphere consumed in dense gray clouds.

"Where is Berudim in relation to Charon? Is it in our galaxy?"

The E.T. grew excited. *"You know of Charon?"*

"I've been having lucid dreams, out-of-body experiences. I think my consciousness was somehow sharing yours."

"Our consciousnesses remain independent while our physical forms harbor the same soul. This is how we can communicate, through the universal mind. Show me your world, Zachary Wallace."

I imagined Earth as seen from space.

"So much water… Show me more."

I zoomed in on the United Kingdom, hovering over London. Gave him a quick tour of the city, then Cambridge University where I had taught long ago.

The image brought back memories of Brandy and William.

"So much sadness. Were we wrong to seed life on Berudim?"

"Wait, are you telling me Earth is Berudim? But that image—"

"—is how Berudim appears to us in my time."

"Avi Socha, show me Berudim in relation to Charon!"

The hologram returned to the gray world, pulling back to reveal a smaller blue world, the fourth planet from the sun.

Multiple thoughts raced through my consciousness as I processed the information. If Berudim was Earth, then Charon had to be Mars—ancient Mars. If Avi Socha's species had seeded ancient Earth with life, then I was communicating with a being that had lived 3.8 billion years ago.

The suddenness of the history lesson was overwhelming to both of us as I realized the E.T. was tuned in to my thoughts.

"Charon is called Mars; Berudim is called Earth. You are a human. Life has evolved differently on Earth, but your RNA was harvested from our genetic matrix. Despite our appearances we are one."

"Avi Socha, what happened to your planet? In our time Mars is a dead world lacking oceans and an atmosphere."

"Charon's ruling clans engaged in technologies that weakened our atmosphere, while they ignored the threat of our calderas. The magma pockets became unstable as our two planets' orbits coincided in a doomsday event prophesied as the Miketz. We seeded Berudim in the hope that intelligent life would evolve, allowing my consciousness to communicate with an incarnate who could provide us with the secret to generating a quantum vacuum flux field. We need it to leave the solar system, to relocate our people to another suitable world."

And suddenly everything made sense.

I had been chosen to be the gatekeeper of zero-point energy not because I was intuitive or smart, but because my soul had inhabited this being's body billions of years ago. The information imparted to me by the alien Joe Tkalec would save Avi Socha's species, the forebearer species that had seeded life on Earth.

Joe was right. In a sense, I really was saving my species.

"Avi Socha, I have been given the knowledge you seek. Do you have the ability to extract it from my memory?"

"I already have, my brother. Take care of our soul."

And he was gone.

42

My consciousness passed through the center of the whirling electrogravitic rings. When I opened my eyes, I found myself back inside the chamber, which had again been created to resemble Joe Tkalec's home library. I was seated in my familiar padded rocking chair adjacent to a wall of books. Alien Joe was in my mentor's easy chair, a leatherbound copy of Lewis Carroll's *Alice in Wonderland* open on his lap.

Adjusting the book's page to the light from his flickering red candle, the E.T. read aloud:

"'The time has come,' the Walrus said,

'to talk of many things:

Of shoes—and ships—and sealing wax—

Of cabbages—and kings—

And why the sea is boiling hot—

And whether pigs have wings.'

"You have questions. Ask."

"Was it all real?"

"It was simply one potential multiverse. Your participation has made it real."

"And if I hadn't participated?"

"That would be another multiverse."

"You know what I mean. Did life on Earth begin from a primordial soup delivered by an extraterrestrial species?"

"If it did, wouldn't that make the E.T.s a homogenous

species? Or, at the very least, a parent species? And like all good parents, they seek only what's best for their children."

"Who are you?"

"What does your gut tell you?"

"At the very least, my guardian angel. *Guardian*, because you've kept me alive through some harrowing times. *Angel*, because the person who I suspect you to be died long ago."

"And who was that?" he asked.

"You're Avi Socha. At least you're his consciousness. That's how we're able to communicate, through the shared energy of our soul."

My mentor smiled. As I watched, his appearance changed, morphing into the Gray I had conversed with earlier.

"No, Zachary. The being you conversed with during the zero-point energy transfer was the consciousness of Avi Socha as it existed 3.75411 billion years ago. I speak with you now as an Avatar, a servant of the Light, the effect of the cause."

"What happened to you after you returned to Charon?"

"The information you transferred to me gave our ships the ability to escape the caldera eruption. From there we left the solar system but were denied interdimensional travel for another four generations until every last child of the Miketz had passed on, including myself. Only then were the tribes of Charon of a high enough morality to be allowed to access the Upper Worlds. This was our punishment for allowing our enemies to die."

"Wow. That seems pretty harsh. How can a people who were tortured to death be expected to save their abusers?"

"Zachary, stop thinking like a physical being and think like our Creator. If you desire mercy, you need to show mercy. There is neither hatred nor judgment in the Upper Worlds, no greed or violence—just love. And this is why humanity should never fear their E.T. brethren, because we could never have been permitted access to traverse the universe through the higher dimensions without exemplifying this morality, a morality that refuses to consider vengeance upon a hostile military regime that downs our vessels and kills our kind.

"There is a plan in effect, Zachary Wallace, and all multiverses lead to it. The question is how much pain and suffering we must endure from incarnation to reincarnation before we realize the simple truth of existence—that we are all children of the Light, the sparks from one unified soul, communicating through one universal consciousness."

"I get it, Avi. But looking back at *my* last seven years, how am I—my tribes, my people—expected to collapse the paradigm of the rich and powerful, a shadow nation that shows no mercy, a group that controls the media and the message and hides the truth about E.T.s and zero-point energy and other technologies that can save our planet? What happens when our caldera erupts?"

"There are things we cannot see, Zachary, because our perspective is so small. The Miketz appeared to us as a curse, a time of chaos that would lead to our extinction. Instead, it turned out to be the cause that led to the birth of your world and the salvation and evolution of ours. Both our oppressors prospered by understanding that without a threat there is no need for a cure, or a cause. Those who choose an existence in darkness will suffer their choices before they are permitted to access the Upper Worlds. Each of us has a role to play, including the villain. In some cases the bad guy is a magma pocket that forces a species to evolve... or die.

"But make no mistake, our choices lead to our destiny, and the soul chooses its next life before a new life is born. Our soul chose us because it knew that we would not sell out our people for a few pieces of gold. Use the last seven years to guide you. If you decide to introduce zero-point energy to your world, then a new multiverse of possibilities will unfold for humanity. The enemies of true freedom are everywhere. Your first vanguard shall always be the masses. The public needs to be part of the solution if the technology—and its caretaker—are to survive the launch."

407

EPILOGUE

"Huh!"

I opened my eyes to my heart pounding rapidly in my chest. The chamber was dark, the only light coming from floor-to-ceiling windows offering a breathtaking view of Loch Ness and the snow-covered peaks of the Monadhliath Mountains rising above the far eastern bank.

Am I really back?

Excited as a kid on Christmas morning, I flipped open my laptop to verify the date, only to be confronted by an article in the *Science Journal*... today's *Science Journal!*

Life on Earth—Death on Mars: New Evidence

Scientists agree that life on Earth began approximately 3.8 billion years ago, but exactly *how* it began has long remained an unanswered question. Biologists theorize asteroids—space rocks containing water molecules that created the precipitation that filled the oceans—bombarded our still-evolving planet. But Dr. Sankar Chatterjee, a professor of geosciences at Texas Tech University, believes that in addition to bringing water, these asteroids contained the chemical constituents of life that ultimately gave rise to living cells.

My eyes quickly scanned the rest of the article.

About the same time that Earth's primordial soup was spawning life, death was occurring on Mars with the eruption of Olympus Mons. The largest volcano in the solar system, it towered sixteen miles above the surface of the Red Planet—three times higher than Mount Everest—and is roughly the size of the state of Arizona. Olympus Mons contains six collapsed craters known as calderas. These magma chambers are stacked atop one another to form a depression that is fifty-three miles wide at the summit. The worst of the lot are resurgent calderas—geological time-bombs responsible for massive eruptions and extinction events.

In the United States there are three resurgent calderas less than 1.5 million years old—the Long Valley Caldera in California, the Valles Caldera in New Mexico, and the Yellowstone Caldera in Wyoming. The last caldera eruption on Earth occurred 74,000 years ago on the Indonesian Island of Sumatra. The Toba caldera complex generated nearly three thousand times more pyroclastic material than Mount St. Helens and

410

unleashed an ash cloud that encompassed Earth's atmosphere, which led to a decade of volcanic winter that wiped out nearly every hominid on the planet.

I closed the story.

I was back. I was really back, back at Loch Ness! My family was safe and intact, True was alive, and David Taylor was just a middle school kid hitting puberty. Vostok hadn't happened yet, but Ming and Ben would be arriving any minute to make their pitch.

Screw them!

Avi Socha had allowed me to retain the knowledge of my past multiverses, and in this reality I'd be ready.

Creating an encrypted file on my laptop, I typed furiously, describing every detail I could about the zero-point energy generator and the Yellowstone Caldera.

That gave me pause.

A cataclysmic eruption had transpired on ancient Mars, ending an autocratic rule while pushing a civilization to venture into space. Yet, only by vanquishing their egos were the descendants of Avi Socha allowed access into the higher dimensions and taught how to traverse the cosmos and mingle with other races.

For thousands of years, advanced species of extraterrestrials had kept an eye on us. That relationship changed once we had discovered how to split the atom. Like an adolescent with a new gun, we had become a threat to ourselves and others.

Much had changed since Hiroshima, Nagasaki, and Roswell.

Forty percent of the wealth on our planet was now controlled by one percent of the population. Two billion people lived in poverty; another two billion were starving. Meanwhile, we were polluting our oceans and atmosphere, our forced addiction to fossil fuels causing the earth to warm, the ice to melt.

Could zero-point energy save us?

Would the shadow government allow it?

If not, was the Yellowstone Caldera the catalyst that would advance our species... or end it?

I made myself a quick reminder to meet with Jonas Taylor and convince him to incorporate airbags into his Manta sub blueprints. I thought about providing him with details about his main attraction's pending escape and death, but preventing the monster's demise didn't seem like a good thing.

Finally, I made a quick list of people not to trust: Ming, Ben, Colonel Vacendak, Susan McWhite.

Susan...

Was she really a Nordic, or was she just a member of the JASON Society who had learned how to thought-communicate? Either way, she was the Colonel's pet and needed to be avoided.

I saved the file just as Brandy abruptly entered the restaurant—alone.

"Zachary, you could have told me ye were expecting guests. A sexy Asian woman and her entourage are waiting outside the restaurant. I'm leaving with William tae visit my—"

Brandy was startled as I swept her up in my arms, planting kiss after kiss. "You're the only sexy woman I want. I'm sorry for everything that's happened. You and William come first, but you're absolutely right; I need to do more to help the Highlanders. I have an idea for an invention, something that can spawn a new industry right here in the Great Glen."

"Whit kind of invention?"

"I can't say, but—"

The restaurant door opened and Ming entered. "Excuse me, Dr. Wallace? I'm sorry to interrupt you and your wife, but my associates and I have traveled a long way to meet with you. My name is Dr. Ming Liao and—"

"I'm not interested."

Brandy grinned as Ming's cheeks flushed red. "I haven't even told you why we're here."

"I don't care. Now you and your companions have two minutes to get out of my hotel before I have my brother-in-law feed you to the croc—er, to Nessie."

"I thought you killed Nessie?" Ben Hintzmann said as he entered the restaurant.

"I did, but it had babies. In fact, I spotted one of them in Urquhart Bay just before you arrived. Big one, too. The kind that eats deer."

Before I could say another word, Brandy's lips were pressed against mine.

Ming was far from through. "Whatever this new invention is, you'll need start-up money. Sorry, I couldn't help overhearing."

Brandy pulled back. "Perhaps ye should listen."

"Nah. I know a guy; he'll be rich real soon."

Ming Liao began again, "Dr. Wallace—"

Brandy turned to Ming with fire in her eyes. "Ye heard my man. Fuck off!"

The restaurant door opened again, and Dr. Stewart entered, followed by Susan McWhite. The memory of Colonel Vacendak putting a bullet in her brain flashed across my mind's eye, causing the blood to drain from my face.

Different multiverse, different probabilities. Play it cool, Wallace.

The twenty-seven-year-old grad student was dressed conservatively, but nothing could conceal that figure. Her eyes seemed to look straight through me.

Dr. Stewart stepped forward, offering me his hand. "Chris Stewart. I'm a friend of your father."

"That's your problem, *friend*. Now, if you'll excuse me, my beautiful wife and I were just on our way to visit her ailing father—"

"After I screw yer brains out."

"Correct." I squeezed my wife's hand.

Flustered, Ming looked to her three colleagues, then left.

Ben was about to say something, but Dr. Stewart was already herding him out, leaving only Susan standing by the door.

"I'm a big fan of your work, Dr. Wallace. What's your new invention?"

"It's a Nessie dildo so women like you can go—"

"Zach!" Brandy clamped my mouth shut with her hand. Then, with a Cheshire Cat smile, she sauntered over to Susan. "I want tae apologize for my husband's rude behavior. He's a bit awnry today. Now if you'll excuse us, we're aboot tae commit a few health code violations."

Guiding her out of the restaurant, she bolted the door while I dialed a number on my cell phone.

"Whit are ye doing, Zachary?"

"Calling True. I want to make sure he doesn't rent these people a room."

Pushing me down onto the table, my wife pulled off my pants and hitched up her skirt. "Call 'im after we're through. It feels like years since we've been together."

* * *

Rain punished the closed green umbrellas outside of Fiddler's pub. Seated at the bar, Susan watched Ming and Dr. Stewart attempt to pitch Angus Wallace on their venture.

For whatever reason, the old Scot was having none of it.

She drained her third whisky, pondering what it must be like to have biological parents, or any parent that cared. Created in Groom Lake's genetics lab from a human egg and donor sperm from a dead E.T., Susan McWhite had led a sheltered life with other hybrids. She had not left her subterranean quarters by herself until she was eighteen, after she had completed her required assimilation fieldwork and extensive Kama Sutra training—something the Colonel "tested" her on frequently—everything designed to prepare her for her first assignment. Only then had she begun her course work at UNLV.

She ordered another malt liquor, still shaken over the image she had lifted from Zachary Wallace's memory.

Her cell phone vibrated. It was the Colonel.

She answered, "I'm listening."

"Has he accessed the portal in another incarnation?"

"No."

"You're certain?"

She glanced up as two bouncers rushed over to Angus's table. "I'm certain."

"Then we'll need to get him to Vostok."

"That won't be easy. He refused to meet with Dr. Liao, and his father just punched Dr. Stewart in the mouth."

"He has a wife and kid. It couldn't be easier."

"No."

"Excuse me?"

"If you take that route, I'll expose you."

"Are you challenging my authority?"

"Consider it more of a threat."

The line went dead.

She crushed the phone beneath the heel of her boot, then looked up as True MacDonald returned from the men's room.

The big Highlander sat down next to her. "So, lass, have ye thought aboot my offer?"

"I accept, on one condition: I want to swim in the loch."

"Like the wacky Polar Bear ladies? Sure. They meet every Sunday afternoon after church."

"No. I want to go now."

"Now? It's dark outside, and the water's damn near freezing."

"A two-minute swim to cool my blood, big fella, then I'll rock your world."

"There exists a shadowy Government with its own Air Force, its own Navy, its own fundraising mechanism, and the ability to pursue its own ideas of the national interest, free from all checks and balances, and free from the law itself."

—Senator Daniel Inouye, Iran-Contra hearings